FOR THE LOVE OF A POET

Marilyn Z. Tomlins

Published by Raven Crest Books

ISBN-13: 978-0-9926700-7-8
ISBN-10: 0-99-267007-1

DEDICATION

For Louise

AUTHOR'S NOTE

You will recognise some of the names in this novel. For example the names Trotsky … Gorky … Krupskaya … Yaroslavsky … Yagoda … Tukhachevsky … Mussolini … Hitler and of course Lenin and Stalin. It would have been impossible to have written this novel without having brought real people into it.

Tanya and Beretzkoy and their friends did not exist as such, but as the poet (Beretzkoy) says in this novel, no one's story is solely his or her own.

There was no village named Zernoye Selo. As such.

-0-

I wish to pay homage to the Irish poet and journalist, James Adam Whiston, who sadly left us on 19/6/2012, and I say thank you to him for granting me permission to use his poem Nocturn in this novel. (Part One, Chapter Three)

-0-

The young girl on the cover is named Marilyn McDermott.

Thank you, Marilyn, for allowing me to use this photo of you on the cover of my novel.

... to think you can change your life by changing
its outward conditions is just like thinking, as I did as a boy, that by
sitting on a stick and taking hold of it at both ends
I could lift myself up ...

Tolstoy, January 15, 1891

PROLOGUE

April 2000 : Moscow (Gerald Lombard/Biographer)

On Wednesdays she went to Moscow. That was where I found her. She was walking around Red Square. She went to Moscow to speak to strangers; gravitating towards those she heard speaking English or French. She was fluent in both.

It was easier to speak to strangers than to people she knew: her neighbours, the woman in the bakery, her doctor, the old man who walked past her *dacha* each morning. He told her one day he was taking his dog for a walk, but she never saw a dog.

The strangers always listened to what she had to say. She said, she thought, they listened because they pitied her. Perhaps they thought she was a beggar. Even on the hottest days she wore a grey gabardine coat and fur-lined boots. Half of the heel of one of the boots was walked away. Age, woman's greatest enemy, had robbed her of the beauty which once was hers.

"Perhaps the strangers listen to me because they like the sound of the name Zernoye Selo," she told me.

Zernoye Selo: Village of Corn.

It was there, 150 kilometres from Moscow where she had once lived.

On the official map of the Soviet Union, a small black dot indicated the village named for the corn-growing *kolkhoz*[1] on its periphery. Such a map hung in my bedroom when I was a young lad with communist leanings. The poor imbecile, my father, the wealthy stockbroker, used to call me, disgusted at what he considered his only child's naivety.

She told me about the village.

"It was the Vozdh'[2]s idea that we, the poets, should live there. It was easier for his OGPU[3] to keep their eye on us if we all lived in the same village. All the dangerous wild animals locked in one cage. But the cunning bastard - forgive me for using such a crude word please, Mister - wanted us to believe he had only our happiness in mind, so he chose Zernoye Selo, pretty little Zernoye Selo.

---

[1] **Collective farm.**

[2] **Russian for leader and as the Soviet people called Stalin.**

[3] **The Soviet State Security Organisation (1923/1934).**

1

Comrades, every day you will eat fresh bread and not even to speak of the cream cakes you will be eating, and you will have the motorway and the train which will get you to Moscow in no time, no time at all, he told us. And Mister, some of us cried when that bastard died!"

She was not a poet, but she was to become one of the villagers and they called anyone who lived by the written word - journalist, translator, interpreter, novelist, playwright, printer, and indeed a writer of poetry - a poet. She used to be a copyreader at *Pravda*[4]. This was before she went to live in Zernoye Selo.

-0-

My publisher told me I would find her on Red Square on any Wednesday of any month.

"A blizzard won't keep her away," he said.

As he also told me about the gabardine coat and the fur-lined boots, I had no problem picking her out from among the motley crowd of ice cream peddlers, ticket touts, postcard sellers and beggars who hung about the square.

"Are you the woman named Tatyana Nikolayevna Brodovskaya," I asked her.

She was quick to reply.

"My friends called me Tanya, my father called me Tanoshka. He was French. To my mother I was never Tanoshka, always Tanya. To the poet too I was Tanya. He was not one for sweetie pie names. It's sweetie pie you say in the West don't you?"

I invited her for a drink.

"That would be a really wonderful thing, but young man your Russian is not good. In fact, it is atrocious, so do take some time off from making money and learn to speak my language correctly."

She said this without rancour. She was smiling and I noticed what beautiful teeth she had. They were small white pebbles which reminded me of corn not yet fully ripe.

I took her to my hotel, to the bar. The waiter jumped like a grasshopper in order to get behind her. He did not want her to see him shake his head and point at her. Beggars aren't allowed in here, said his face.

"The lady and I will have some champagne. *Moët et Chandon*. A bottle please. Something to eat too," I told him.

I watched the old woman lift the flute to her lips. Her calloused hands were trembling. Champagne trickled down her chin and pooled in the crease of wrinkled skin between her two sagging breasts.

"I presume you knew I came here on Wednesdays or you would not have recognised me looking as I do," she said.

---

[4] **Official Communist Party newspaper.**

"Once a beautiful woman, always a beautiful woman," I told her.

We drank to Lily: I proposed the toast.

"Ah, so you know the story?" she asked.

I shook my head.

"Only how others have told it, so, I would like you to tell it to me, to tell me how it was with you and the poet."

I thought her eyes were glistening with tears.

"Ah, the poet! Boris Petrovich Beretzkoy! The poet ... yes ... my poet ...," she said.

Later, she would write to my editor. He took my ugly old hands in his and we drank to Lily and to what has gone and will never return. How gallant you English men are! Real gentlemen. And they say the French are the gallant ones.

"I am writing a book about Boris Petrovich Beretzkoy," I confessed.

She put her flute down and looked me straight in the eye.

"I thought as much, Mister." She paused. "Relax! I will speak of him. I will speak of him."

She was smiling.

-0-

PART ONE

CHAPTER ONE

The English gentleman has come to stay. He has come for two months.

I can see him through my kitchen window. He is sitting cross-legged on my garden bench. It is summer and he is wearing green shorts and a yellow short-sleeved shirt. How oddly foreigners dress! He is going to take me to a restaurant later so I do hope he will change into some proper trousers and he will put on his elegant yellow tie: he likes the colour yellow. He has a notebook balanced on his naked hairy knees.

"Tanya, shall we start now?" he calls out.

"Why not!" I call back.

"I'm waiting," he says and picks up a sharpened pencil.

Happily, I will walk down my lane of memories.

-0-

CHAPTER TWO

It is February, 1931.

It is Wednesday, mid-morning, and Vasily, my husband, has been gone for three months. I am at my desk in *Pravda's* editorial room. It is snowing as it did on the day the Chekists[5] had come for my poor dear Vasily.

Our editorial room is on the second floor. It is a small circular room and it has only one window. My desk is in front of the window. Some of my colleagues think I am privileged having this desk. I tell them not to talk nonsense. The window overlooks the courtyard where our rubbish bins are kept. There is therefore no beautiful view to feast my eyes on.

This morning, in offices all over the building, we are putting to bed tomorrow's issue. I am editing a report on collectivisation.[6] To be exact: on the *wreckers of collectivisation.* The word 'wrecker' is much in use these days. Anyone who does not agree with Stalin is a wrecker: Trotsky and all Trotskyites, and our Kulaks. Vasily, also, was called a wrecker, and, I suppose, I, too, am regarded by some people as one: here in the Soviet Union we are responsible for the words and deeds of our spouse.

The report I am editing is ninety pages long. It is a Party[7] report. I knew it would be when I saw our supervisor sprint across the editorial floor. Our supervisor's name is Yury Fiodorovich Makarov, and he has a small dark cubicle of an office which leads from our editorial room. He moves fast only when the Party has sent over a report. Comrade Yury has a wooden leg. The real leg, his left one, he lost during our civil war. Now, his family and friends speak of him having been *awarded* the wooden leg. The wooden leg as well as the medal which is always pinned to the lapel of his jacket. Wherever he goes in Moscow people ask him about the wooden leg and when they hear a bullet from the rifle of a White[8] had robbed him of his left leg, they call him a great Soviet hero.

---

[5] **A member of the Cheka, the first of a succession of Soviet State security organisations, founded by Lenin in 1917.**

[6] **Stalin's enforced policy to consolidate individually-owned land into giant collective farms.**

[7] **The Communist Party, the only political party authorised in the Soviet Union.**

[8] **Pro-tsarist fighters during the civil war which had followed the Bolshevik revolution of 1917.**

His story, and I have heard it often enough, is that, despite the pain he felt after he was shot, his left leg dangling from his thigh like he was a broken puppet, he had reloaded his rifle, and shot the bastard White right between his repulsive tsar-adoring eyes.

On a warm day when it is not necessary for him to wear a jacket, he pins the medal to the collar of his shirt: part with it, he will not.

I also know, because he has told me often, wide rubber bands tied around his waist hold his wooden leg in place.

The medal weighs ten grams; the wooden leg, ten kilograms.

"Quite a fucking weight to carry, but I had to do it, make fucking war against fucking Nicholas' fucking Whites," he always says.

He never asks to be excused for such language.

He now stands at my desk. His weight rests on his good leg. The foot of the wooden one points outwards as if he is a Bolshoi ballet dancer about to perform a *grande pirouette à la seconde*.

"Comrade Emilyan Yaroslavsky has decided the report is to be tomorrow's front page lead," he says.

Emilyan Mikhailovich Yaroslavsky is our editor.

The headline is going to be: *Glory to Collectivisation, Glory to the Proletariat, Glory to our Leader!*

Comrade Victor Deni, our cartoonist, is working on a set of cartoons to accompany the article. Yury has seen one of the cartoons. It shows a huge tractor crushing half a dozen Kulaks[9]. On the tractor sits Stalin. Deni thinks the caption should read, *Safe as long as he steers Russia.*

He - Iosef Vissaryonovich Dhughasvily - Stalin.

-0-

I hear a clock strike noon. There are clocks all over our building. In our country, no time should be wasted: *World Revolution should not be delayed!*

I turn and look down into the courtyard. A black cat with white paws sits on one of the rubbish bins. He rounds his back and tries to catch a snowflake with one of those paws.

The door to Yury's office flings open. I fear he has come with another Party report, but he is not sprinting. He is walking with a slow lopsided gait. It means he has come to make an announcement which is unimportant.

I return to the report.

Old Russia was an agrarian country as we all know ... Seventy-five per cent of the employed population was engaged in agriculture ... Agriculture ...

Yury stops at Comrade Konstantin Alexandrovich Kasygin's desk. Konstantin is also a copyreader. I do not like him. Like Yury he has a medal

---

[9]**Land-owning farmers.**

pinned to the lapel of his jacket. It is the medal of *Best Student of the State Institute of Red Journalists* for the year 1928.

It is not because of the medal I dislike him. I do so because he grabbed Vasily's desk before Vasily's blood had even dried on the floor of our editorial room. Yes, blood was spilled the day the Chekists came for my husband.

Yury says something to Konstantin and they laugh. Both are in their thirties and being, as they are always saying, *from the loins of tsar-haters*, they get on well.

I am not really listening, so all I hear is someone is coming to see Comrade Yaroslavsky.

"… at three …"

"Do you know why?" asks Konstantin.

I continue editing the report.

A large-scale collective farm is more profitable … the reorganisation of small peasant households into large-scale farms is an inevitable historical process…

"Yes, Beretzkoy is going to do a feature for us about Tolstoy. He's coming to discuss it with Comrade Yaroslavsky," says Yury.

Beretzkoy …

I push the report aside.

"Beretzkoy? Did you say Beretzkoy?" I ask Yury.

"I did," he replies.

He is leaning against Konstantin's desk, the desk I still think of as Vasily's.

"The poet – you know," says Konstantin.

He turns and stares at me with tiny blue eyes.

I look straight into those eyes.

"There is no need for you to tell me who Beretzkoy is!"

Konstantin turns towards Yury.

"Lofty as always, isn't she?"

Yury nods. He starts walking back to his office. He is walking even slower. There are times when he finds his wooden leg very heavy. When this happens, he tells us, he can hardly lift the leg, not even to speak of walking. He halts for a moment and, with a quiver that rolls over him like an ocean wave over a dead seagull, he walks on. The wooden leg he is pulling behind him. I watch. He bangs the door of his office behind him.

I should continue with the report.

I pick up my pencil and start to read the next paragraph.

The Soviet Government will provide extensive financial … In 1925 the country … collectivisation will be promoted by the rapid development of industry … Without a …

I point the sharpened end of my pencil at the next word – *doubt* – but my mind wanders away from collectivisation. I think of what Yury came to tell us. The poet Beretzkoy is coming to *Pravda*. Boris Petrovich Beretzkoy. I have been obsessed with this man for years. My parents say I have a crush on him. I have been telling them it is not a crush. It is reverence. Reverence not only for the man but so too for his talent: his poetry. If anyone asks me whether I have a wish, I will say, *if only I can meet the poet Beretzkoy.*

As Emilyan Yaroslavksy's office is off a hallway behind our editorial room, we always see his guests, because to reach his office, they have to walk through here, and, often, after their meeting with him, they come and speak to us. They always want to know what will be in the next day's *Pravda*. I will, therefore, see Beretzkoy, and, maybe – just maybe – my wish will come true and I will be introduced to him.

For the first time since the Chekists took Vasily, I am smiling.

-0-

I think of Vasily every day. I married him eleven months after I joined *Pravda*. He too was a copyreader. Our getting married was my idea. The Chekists put him on their list[10]. I believed that, because of who I was – the daughter of a man who was in exile with Lenin - I could, no, I *would* be able to save him. I told my parents I had proposed to him – I really did ask him to marry me – and my father sat me down because he said we would have to speak about it. He said he wanted to tell me about Voltaire and what the latter wrote in *Candide*. I thought it was not a time to talk French literature or philosophy, but he told me to try to keep silent for just once in my life.

"My darling Tanoshka, Voltaire wrote, *pour vivre heureux: vivons cachés*," he said.

To live happily: live hidden.

In the past, living hidden was not his way. It had, though, become his way. And now he wanted me to make it mine too.

My father, Nicholas Jean Tissier, French, young and Communist, had left his comfortable home and hearth in Paris to join the exiled Lenin in London and in April 1917 he was with Vladymir Ilyich – never did my parents call Lenin anything but Vladymir Ilyich - on the sealed train when it pulled into Saint-Petersburg's Finland Station. In Russia – Soviet Union as it was to become soon afterwards – he had changed his name to Nikolai – Nikolai Nikolayevich Tisinski - and he had fallen in love with my mother, the girl who was teaching him Russian: Tatyana Alexandrovna Bubnovskaya. She was the daughter of two Bolshevik revolutionaries whom Tsar Nicholas II had executed. Together my father and mother then fought for *the cause* – transforming our country into a socialist paradise. My father had done so at Lenin's side in the Kremlin - he had become the Kremlin's emissary to the French sector of the Komintern/[11] - and my mother had joined forces with Krupskaya, Lenin's wife, in caring for our *Bezprizorni*.[12] But Lenin had died and Stalin had taken over after having ended

---

[10] **The expression used when the OGPU began to show an interest in someone.**

[11] **International Association of Workers and/or Communist Parties.**

[12] **Homeless children who flooded the cities and towns after the 1917 Revolution.**

the triumvirate rule which had followed Lenin's death, and my parents, never having liked or trusted *the man of steel*, had thought of Voltaire's words, and had decided it was wiser to live hidden. Immediately, my father had given up his position in the Kremlin and took up the minor post of assistant to the assistant interpreter-translator at the French language studies department of the People's Commissariat of Education, and my mother had retired.

Marrying a man who was on the Chekists' list was drawing attention to myself.

"You are our only child, we cannot lose you," my father told me.

-0-

I hear footsteps on our stairs. Footsteps and voices. One voice I recognise. It is that of Nina Mikhailovna Ivanova. A septuagenarian, she is our receptionist and she is the one who brings Comrade Yaroslavsky's guests upstairs. Like Yury, she also did her duty for our country during the civil war, and like him, she was rewarded. Her reward was not a medal – and fortunately for her not a wooden leg. It was her position as *Pravda's* receptionist: hers until she draws her last breath. She is beginning to feel her years but every day she tells us she is still up to the job. So, if someone drops a pencil on the floor, she will pick it up and sharpen it before she hands it back. When Yury asks her to pin a note on the notice board, she will make copies to pin up all over the building. And she never walks at a normal speed, but always fast-fast-fast. She even walks fast when she brings one of Comrade Yaroslavsky's guests upstairs, no matter how illustrious, old or frail the comrade may be. Today, I will offer to help her sharpen every pencil in Moscow and to help her make copies of every notice Yury has ever written in his capacity as our supervisor, but, today, she must not hurry the poet through our editorial room. Today, she must walk him through slowly. I want to have a good look at him: feast my eyes and fill my heart with the look of him.

The footsteps and voices are now behind the door which leads from the staircase to our editorial room. I drop my pencil. The door flings open. Nina is in her bottle-green dress, her uniform, as she calls it, but we all know the green dress is the only one she has. But who has wardrobes full of clothes here in this country of ours?

Behind Nina is the poet: I recognise him from the photographs I have of him. There are strands of grey in his black hair. A curl hangs over his forehead. His eyes are dark, almost black. His eyebrows are thick and greying, like his hair. He is wearing a brown corduroy suit. My mother will say the suit has seen better days: the elbows are patched and the corduroy is unravelling at the seams.

Konstantin clears his throat. I turn to look at him. He rolls his eyes: he is telling me to get back to work. I roll my eyes at him too. He shakes his head and mouths something in my direction. I contemplate shaking my head at him in turn, but I will let him be the victor this day.

-0-

I am still untouched. This is how my mother will call my virginity should she know Vasily Sergeyevich Brodov and I were never lovers. We were colleagues and friends - best friends - but on the few nights we were together after we had been to ZAGS[13] to make our *marriage* official, and before the Chekists had come for him, he slept on a mattress on the floor of the small room which was his home in a communal apartment and where I still live, and I had slept on his bed. We might have gone to bed together had the Chekists not come for him. Who knows? He was an attractive man with his sand-coloured curls and green eyes, and these are the things young girls look for in a lover. And was I not a young girl?

Vasily and I were on the dance floor in a tavern when I heard from him the Chekists have put him on their list. *Three men have started to follow me.* This, was what he said to me. I said he was imagining it. He was not: I saw them. When we left the tavern they were outside on the pavement. They were easily recognisable because they wore the Chekists' trademark attire: long black leather coats. We boarded a tram and they got on too, and, while silence descended over the frightened passengers, the three sat down behind us. When I descended at the stop closest to my parents' building, they stayed on the tram with Vasily. The next morning, standing at his desk, I asked him to marry me.

"My father was with Lenin in London and he was with Lenin on the sealed train and my father was with Lenin in the Smolny[14] and his name stands for something, and as his son-in-law Stalin won't be able to touch you," I said.

"Tanya, my dear little Tanya, I cannot drag you into this," he replied.

I told him my proposal stood.

"It's here should you change your mind."

He did not change his mind. Forty-eight hours later it was changed for him. The Moscow Housing Committee summoned him to discuss his housing problem.

"You don't have a housing problem," I told him.

"No, but there is no doubt now I do have a Chekist problem," he replied.

Two days later, we went to ZAGS and signed the required documents to make us man and wife: until death do us part.

For all I know, death has already parted us.

-0-

No one ever stays long in Comrade Yaroslavsky's office. He is inclined to say to his guests something like, *although I would love to listen to you, I will have to end our*

---

[13] **The civil registry office where all births, deaths and marriages had to be recorded.**

[14] **A school for young girls from the Russian aristocracy, the building had become Bolshevik headquarters during the 1917 Revolution.**

little chat. Sometimes, he will flick his head towards the wall on his right and wait until the visiting comrade looks that way, and then he will say, *Comrade Stalin has asked to see me.* On the wall hang portraits of Marx, Engels, Lenin and Stalin. Stalin hangs between Engels and Lenin and it is by far the largest portrait. It is also the only one in colour. I have seen it. Stalin's skin is pink; Stalin's hair and moustache are biscuit-brown; Stalin's uniform is pinkish-brown and Stalin's eyes are fuchsia. Vasily told me of the day the portrait was carried up from our printing presses, transformed from black and white into colour. Many came to watch and Comrade Yaroslavsky stepped from his office, in jacket but without tie - ties are bourgeois and are not to be worn - to escort the portrait to its place on the wall. Later, our chief printer was named *Best Worker of the Year.* He was told Stalin would be sending him a congratulatory telegram, and he had danced with joy, his hands folded over his chest and his legs kicking into the air. The telegram never materialised.

How I wish Comrade Yaroslavsky will again use the *meeting-with-Comrade-Stalin* excuse so the poet will not stay long with him but will come to chat with us here in the editorial room.

Wishing is a waste of time my mother always says.

-0-

Nina is first to step back into our editorial room. She looks like an apple in her green dress, an apple which is over-ripe because she has turned a little red in the face: she is blushing. A few paces behind her, follows the poet. She speaks to him over her shoulder and she points to the office they have just left. He nods. She points to Yury's office. He nods again. The door to Yury's office opens and Yury appears in the doorway and beckons the two to enter. Unlike Comrade Yaroslavsky, our supervisor is a talker - he has many civil war stories to tell - and his guests undoubtedly stay long: some of them even have to start backing out gradually while he is still talking. He always tells of how he had, with his last breath - which of course turned out not to have been his last breath at all - lifted his rifle to aim at a spot just above the tsarist pig's snout and how he had watched life escape the tsarist pig's snake-like eyes.

I count the minutes and I keep my eyes on the door of Yury's office. I have finished my edit of the Party report and I have even already started to type it out for our printers. Fortunately, I am a fluent typist and my eyes do not need to be on the keys of my Cyrillic-keyboard typewriter, a gift to *Pravda* with another few dozen such typewriters, from some foreign millionaire philanthropist.

The door opens.

Out steps Nina and behind her the poet, then Yury. The latter is trying not to pull his wooden leg behind him: he is doing well. He puts each foot down firmly on the wooden floor like a man with two good legs. He touches the poet's arm and points to the door and the stairs. The poet ignores the hand on his arm and walks over to the nearest desk in our editorial room.

It is Andrey Antonovich Shalamov's desk.

Andrey is about to retire. He is a dull man. His only topic of conversation is honey: he keeps bees. He and his wife live in a communal apartment shared with another two couples and their numerous children and grandchildren. He keeps the bees on the roof of their building.

The poet shakes Andrey's hand and Andrey begins talking. I cannot hear what he is saying but he must be talking about bees. Or honey.

Yury turns and pulls his wooden leg back to his office. He has heard all Andrey's bee and honey stories. So have we all. Nina, though, stays to listen to what he has to say. She likes Andrey – he is always bringing her little pots of honey in which dead bees float, their wings spread out as if they are making a last effort to fly away.

The poet's eyes are small and slightly slanted. My mother will say there must be Levantine blood in him from two or three generations back and such blood will make him a determined man. Determined to have what is best and prettiest. I can hear her say, "Mark my words Tanya, such a man is best not to fall in love with".

The poet shakes Andrey's hand and says goodbye. Without stopping my typing, I watch him walk to the next desk: once again he stops and talks for a while.

Will he stop at each desk?

Will he stop at mine?

He stops at Konstantin's desk. The two shake hands. My desk is next. I continue typing, but now, bashfully, my eyes are on the keyboard.

"*Tovarishch?*"[15]

He is at my desk. He has spoken to me.

I look up and into his eyes. They are the colour of the sky on a winter night. They are smiling. The rebel strands of hair still lie over his forehead. He flicks them back with a swift flip of his head. He is no longer a young man: this, too, my admiring eyes can see. There are lines, fine lines, but lines all the same, at the corners of his mouth. Again, I hear my mother's voice. "Tanya, he is too old for you, you are asking to be a young widow." And my father will ask whether they brought me up to see me in widow's weeds, weeping over a coffin.

"Yes?" I reply to his greeting.

Da.

My parents have taught me, drilled into me, to always add *tovarishch* when I address an older person, yet, I have omitted to do so.

He holds a hand out to me. His skin is cold. Cold and soft. It is not the hand of a man who works the earth or lays bricks. It is the hand of an artist. His nails are short, clean, shiny, the edges cut straight.

"Are you a journalist too?" he asks.

---

[15] **Comrade.**

16

Do I not look like one?

"Copyreader," I mumble. "I only correct what others have written."

"Why do you say only?"

"Should it not be only when one is only correcting what others have written?"

"Don't tell me you do not realise that without people like you there will be even more inaccuracies in the truth?"

Truth.[16]

Comrade Yaroslavsky will not tolerate such a pun.

Fortunately, Nina is not with us - she has remained at Konstantin's desk - or she might quite possibly denounce me at our next workers' meeting for having participated in an anti-Soviet conversation.

"I didn't realise, no," I lie.

He smiles.

"I think you did. I can see it in your eyes."

I smile too. Shyly.

"Green eyes. Beautiful green eyes. Where did you get them?"

"My mother."

"May I?"

He points at the sheet of paper in my typewriter. I know I have made some errors typing. The keys of my typewriter jam. *Don't bash that keyboard so hard, it's not your property,* Konstantin shouts at me almost every day. Any day now I will lose my temper and shout a big word back at him, and I will do so in French, my father's mother tongue: *Merde!* And what would I care if he can understand French?

The poet bends over me to read what I have been typing. His breath is warm against my face.

"Do you agree with this?"

His breath has the metallic smell of Soviet toothpaste.

"You shouldn't ask me such a question," I reply.

"No, I shouldn't. My apologies."

Yury walks back into the editorial office and joins Nina at Konstantin's desk. He glares at me. He starts shifting his weight from one leg to the other, resting on the real leg a little longer. He is in pain and wants to sit down.

"I think you have to go," I whisper to Beretzkoy.

I have started to think of him as Beretzkoy, and not, the poet. Always, he has been - *the poet.*

Yury clears his throat. Once only, but loudly.

"Is that what the clearing of the throat means?" whispers Beretzkoy.

"Always."

"I'm getting you into trouble."

---

[16] **Pravda in Russian.**

"That's alright."

He looks around the room. Our editorial room is not pleasing to the eye. It is a brown room: The brown of *papirosi*[17]. The walls are brown; the ceiling is brown; our desks and chairs are brown; our notebooks are brown, and even the thousands of past editions of *Pravda* piled onto the shelves covering almost half of one brown wall, are brown, and even the bits of string, which hold these bundles together, are brown, and so is the ink with which the dates of the editions have been written on the side of each bundle. Even the sheet of paper in my typewriter is light brown and we use brown ribbons, and how our typesetters manage to read what we type, because we are not often issued with fresh ribbons, I do not know.

He looks back at me.

"Are you really happy working in such a dull room?"

"My work is interesting," I tell him.

He points to the sheet of paper in my typewriter.

"This?"

"It's a Party report."

"Oh!" he laughs, his dark eyes glistening mischievously, "I will have to get *Pravda* tomorrow!"

Yury clears his throat yet again.

"I think I ought to go or you will be in real trouble. But it was pleasant talking to you," says Beretzkoy, straightening up.

I do not want him to go.

"If I knew you were coming here today I would have brought one of your books and you could have autographed it for me," I tell him.

"You have one of my books? A young thing like you?" he asks.

"I like to read. I love to read poems," I mumble, embarrassed at being called a *young thing*.

"I'll tell you what. I'll autograph one of my books and post it to you."

What to say but 'thank you'? *Thank you very much indeed: you have made me the happiest woman on earth talking to me.*

He holds his right hand out to me.

"*Do svidaniya*[18]," I say.

"Not yet," he says.

He takes my right hand and turns it over like gypsy women do when they grab our hands on the street to foretell our future, but he is not a teller of the future. He slips his right hand underneath mine and puts his left over both our hands and this way he holds me, locked, secure, for a few moments.

---

[17] **A Soviet cigarette.**

[18] **Goodbye.**

I watch him walk away. He does not turn to look my way.

-0-

I tell my parents I have met Beretzkoy. I do not say *the poet*. I say Beretzkoy.
  "I trust you didn't make a fool of yourself," says my mother.
  "He was at my desk for only a moment," I protest.
  "That would have been long enough," says my father.
  "Young girls can be so silly," adds my mother.

CHAPTER THREE

A week has passed.

It is evening.

I knock on the door of an apartment where an illegal literary evening is being held. It is the apartment of Marina and Aleksander. Marina Alexandrova Darmolatova and I were at school together, we were in the same class, and she had loved Aleksander Aleksandrovich Zenkov already then. They are married now and expecting their first child and cursing because a communal apartment, as they say, is no place to bring up a future Tolstoy.

Nervously, I look down the hallway waiting for the door to open. Since Vasily's arrest my fear of the Chekists is great and one of them may be lurking at the end of the corridor.

The door opens.

In front of me, holding it ajar, stands Beretzkoy. He wears a pair of brown corduroy trousers - the trouser part of the suit he had worn to *Pravda?* - and a black turtle-neck sweater.

"*Zdravstvuyte.*"

We spoke in unison this greeting of people who still do not know each other sufficiently well for the casual *privet*.

I am wearing my only overcoat. It is made of some kind of fur, certainly a fake fur like the *shapkas* of the Chekists who came for Vasily. I smell of damp and candle grease. My feet are encased in a pair of well-worn boots. This is my only pair of boots. Ours is a country of *only*: only and *if only*. *If* Lenin had not died; *only* Stalin can give us such a terrible life; *if only* I had a more elegant coat; *if only* I had a less shabby pair of boots.

"When I heard we were waiting for a Tatyana Nikolayevna Brodovskaya of *Pravda*, I wondered whether it could possibly be you or whether there might be two of you," he tells me.

"There is only one."

"This is what I hoped and I see I have not hoped in vain."

"How do you know my name?" I ask.

"Nina. I asked her. But you'd better step inside."

Marina is a teacher. Aleksander is an electrician. The lobby of the apartment is small and it is almost as cold - several degrees below freezing - as it was a moment ago out on the snowy street. A painting of a beautiful blue mountain hangs on a wall. It looks warm and sunny on the mountain.

He helps me out of my coat.

"I could have brought the book I promised you. I didn't forget I did. I'll post it to you tomorrow."

He points to a stool in the corner of the lobby for me to sit down so he can help me get out of my boots.

"My, these are drenched!" he murmurs.

He puts my boots down on a square of cardboard placed in the lobby especially for this and I slip into high-heels, also my only pair of shoes with heels. They are black with a strap around my ankle. He is wearing maroon-coloured leather bedroom slippers. I, in heels, and he, in slippers, make us the same height. He notices and I can see it does not please him: he straightens up, trying to make himself taller.

In the living room, Marina kisses me on both cheeks in the French manner: once my father showed her this was how the French greeted one another. Aleksander greets me with a true Russian bear hug. He is a big man and I disappear in his arms.

Someone brings Beretzkoy and me tumblers of vodka.

We sit down: Beretzkoy perches on the arm of my chair.

"*Tovarishch*, may I call you Tatyana Nikolayevna?"

"Please do."

"Please do, Boris Petrovich," he says.

"Please do, Boris Petrovich," I repeat, dutifully.

"I would not have thought you would remember me," he says.

"I would not have thought *you* would remember *me*," I reply.

He smiles. "I remembered."

He has good teeth: white, equal in size.

"Nina didn't tell me you asked her my name."

"I asked her not to and she promised she won't."

"I didn't know there were still people who kept their promises."

"I do," he says. "I keep mine."

He wants me to remember he keeps his promises. I tell him I will.

Twenty of us sit in the kitchen - this includes the couple Marina and Aleksander shares the apartment with - and we eat *zakuski* [19] and drink strong Georgian Teliani wine and we listen to Beretzkoy read us some of his poems. He plays with the words. Some he hurls into the air like a child would a ball, over others he hesitates, his voice deepening to a rich baritone.

Broken stems, falling rain, vapour clouds;
Shining stars, veiled night, blackly still;
Pattering noise, falling rain, silver streams;
Splashing drops, shimmering pools, rippling mere;
Glistening reeds, falling rain, trickling down;
Moisture flows and water runs, and deepening

---

[19] **Hors d'oeuvres.**

Shadows smudged in blue dark hold the murky lights;
A deep unknown in a tiny world,
A little sphere of watered runs and moonlit swirls
'Neath the leaning, swaying stalks wet bent ...

He does not look at me. Not even once. It is as if I do not exist.

All too soon the chimes of an old clock come from somewhere in the apartment. Midnight has struck and it seems it is time to go. Aleksander hands out cups of strong black coffee and more tumblers of vodka. We are supposed to drink each in one fast, toxic hit. I do not accept the vodka.

In the lobby, getting back into our overcoats and boots, Marina asks us to be as quiet as we can possibly be when going down the stairs: the neighbours must not to be disturbed. I ignore Beretzkoy while I slip back into my overcoat and wet boots. Going down the stairs, I still ignore him: it is pay-back time. Reaching the bottom step, I feel a hand brushing against the back of my neck. The hand is icy. I turn. It is Beretzkoy. He is now dressed in a grey double-breasted greatcoat and his black hair is hidden under a *shapka*.

"I'll give anything to walk you home," he says.

-0-

Home.

On my first night in the small room Beretzkoy has just called my home, Vasily kissed me goodnight, but not on my lips, on my forehead. "Remember my dear wonderful friend as soon as I'm off the Chekists' list, you can have your freedom back," he said.

It was on a Friday, late in the month of December, when they had come for him. Four men walked into our editorial room. They looked ordinary, dressed in ill-fitting suits and shabby overcoats and worse-for-wear *shapkas* of fake fur. They looked as if they were minor Party couriers who brought a Party report for us to run; I did not pay them much attention. They went to speak to Yury but they returned to the editorial room without him. They were walking fast just as Nina always does and I smiled because I was wondering whether their jobs - whatever their jobs were - were also a reward for civil war bravery. I quickly stopped smiling because they stopped at Vasily's desk. "Brodov, come with us, please", one of them said, he being the shortest of the four. I relaxed momentarily: I had my idea of what a Chekist arrest would be like and the word *please* did not come into it. I should have known better than to trust this civility. The short man drew a gun from underneath his overcoat and brought it down hard on to the top of Vasily's head. I jumped up. "*Nyet!*" I shouted. "Sit!" another of the men shouted back at me. He, too, was holding a gun and he was pointing it at me. Vasily turned and smiled gently at me. It was a smile I understood as his way of reassuring me nothing serious was going to happen. He had a hole as large as a fist in the top of his skull: blood gushed from it like water from a tap. Despite being told to sit down and the gun still pointing at me,

23

I stayed on my feet, trying to work up the courage to go to Vasily. He had slumped forward, sending his stationery and inkpot to the floor. One of the Chekists - by then I had no doubt who they were - had not moved away quickly enough and his boots were streaked with ink. *"You lice!"* he hissed. Vasily slid from his chair to the floor. He twitched like a chicken that has had its head chopped off.

I stumbled back into my chair and I watched the Chekists push Vasily's hands into handcuffs and swing a chain around his ankles. They had pulled off his boots and these stood upright on his desk. Grabbing the chain, they pulled him, by then motionless and silent, from the editorial room. *Clank clank clank.* The noise was deafening. My colleagues did not move, did not blink an eye even and, once we could no longer hear the clanking of the chain, the typewriters started up again. Yury came and dropped sheets of paper on my desk. "For tomorrow and you better get on with it because the typesetters are waiting," he barked. Go fuck yourself I wanted to tell him, but, frightened, I did as I was told, and the typesetters did not complain about the sheets smudged with tears. At the end of my shift I went to get Vasily's boots and cradling them in my arms as if they were my two new-borns, I walked from the editorial room without a word to my colleagues.

Later, alone in Vasily's room I grabbed a bottle of vodka which Vasily had still bought and I drank myself to sleep. It was the first time in my life I had done such a thing. In the morning, my head splitting, I went to tell my parents the Chekists have taken Vasily.

"I'm going to find him!" I said. "I will not allow Stalin to murder him!"

My father did not remind me of what Voltaire had said and for that I was grateful.

-0-

We are in the third year of collectivisation, and economise is the watchword, so, most nights Moscow's streets are in darkness in order to save electricity. It is a long walk to Vasily's room, but tonight I do not mind it is. I look up at Beretzkoy and he is smiling. Perhaps he also does not mind that the walk to Vasily's room will be long.

We walk slowly. Not only are all the city's lights dark but the *dvorniks*[20] have been out with their twig brooms and as they had swept the snow into the gutters, the pavements have been left covered in ice.

We talk. We talk about everything and anything: about *Pravda*, my colleagues, Emilyan Yaroslavsky, of *Izvestiya*[21] and whether it is a more honest paper than

---

[20] **Women, often old, who swept Moscow's pavements and cleaned it of snow.**

[21] **The official newspaper of the Soviet government.**

Pravda and we agree neither tells us the truth. We also speak of the ugly prefabricated concrete buildings - *Stalin's marvels* - we pass: rows of small windows, all dark too, under flat roofs.

We speak of the snow, the flakes white like moths, of the slippery pavements, of the *dvorniks* and of how hard their lives must be working outdoors in the middle of the night when we are indoors, warm and asleep.

We do not speak of ourselves. He is a married man, I know. It is his second marriage. They have two sons. But I am a married woman too and although my husband has been taken away, he may well return.

We also do not touch. We do not even brush against each other although we keep on slipping on the ice.

Vasily's building is also a *Stalin marvel*. It is four storeys high and has, like the others, dozens of small square windows. These windows too are dark. It must be one in the morning.

Beretzkoy looks up at the building.

"The Muscovites are asleep."

"I too would have been asleep by now."

"Instead, you have been walking the city's streets with a stranger."

"I don't usually walk the streets with strangers."

The white moth-snowflakes are clinging to his eyebrows. His eyebrows are too thick I think and should be trimmed. My French father trims his with comb and scissors and he tells me all the men of Paris do so.

Vasily's communal apartment is on the fourth floor.

"I'll be off now," says Beretzkoy.

I unlock the street door, a gateway made of thin strips of wood, painted black.

"I'll say goodnight then," I say.

I hold on to the door because should it bang the supervisor will wake up and how will I explain to her I have brought a man home, my husband only just gone.

Beretzkoy says there is something he has to tell me.

"I am married and I have two sons and we live in Zernoye Selo."

His wife's name is Nadezdha Konstantinovna. He does not tell me this: I know it.

"You are married too," he adds.

"Nina told you this as well?"

He nods.

"Did she tell you my husband has been arrested?"

He nods again.

"He was a colleague," I say.

"I know."

"Nina?"

"Yes. Nina. I asked because I wanted to know."

"I am still living in his room."

"I thought you would be."

There is a freight train he can take back to his village. The train leaves Moscow at three in the morning.

"You will have to hurry," I tell him.

"I may be speaking out of turn, but I do not want to go."

"As you wish," I say.

I step across the threshold into the lobby. I do not look back but I can feel the warmth of his body, so he must be close behind me.

"No," I hear him say. He is speaking almost into my right ear. "I'll go. I ought to go."

I turn round.

"Do you often attend literary evenings?" he wants to know.

His body is almost touching mine.

The lobby is dark: there is no bulb in the overhead socket. The chair where the supervisor always sits has been knocked over.

"Yes, I often attend such evenings."

"Strange we have not met at one before."

"Perhaps we have," I reply.

"No," he says, "we have not. If we had, we would not now be having this conversation."

He takes my right hand in his.

"I will go for that train now."

"Thank you for walking me home."

He slides my gloves over my fingers.

"The other day at *Pravda* I wanted to kiss your hands."

I hold my hands out to him and he kisses first my left and then my right. His lips are cold against my skin.

"If you had done that the other day at *Pravda* … I would not have minded," I tell him.

-0-

I watch him walk away. I remain standing in the doorway, one of my feet against the door. I stand there and I watch until the footprints he leaves in the settled snow are filled with downy flakes of fresh snow. I want him to turn and come back. As at *Pravda*, he continues walking.

I cannot fall asleep. I lie awake. I try not to think of Beretzkoy, but to think of Vasily.

-0-

As I told my parents I would, I did indeed try to find Vasily. I looked everywhere for him. I began by calling in at whatever administrative office I thought there might be someone who would know where he was taken: this is information the Chekists would never supply.

All of the offices had small side doors over which hung signs which instructed *Enquire Within*. I knocked on them all. When a door opened - not all did - I demurely asked whether I might be allowed a word with the comrade director. A few of the comrade directors received me and listened to what I said, but after having heard me out, they reprimanded me for wasting their time and told me to go before they became angry. I even called at the Lubyanka - OGPU headquarters and our main political prison. I did not expect the Lubyanka to have a small side door as I knew the Chekists would want to intimidate people like me by forcing us to approach the building from the front: from Dzerzhinsky Square. I was right. There were khaki-uniformed guards at the gate and *black ravens*[22] were parked in the front courtyard. Smoke rose from a chimney at one end of the building, in a room directly underneath where the Chekists were burning forbidden books. Inside the building, in a large lobby with a marble floor,[23] a pot-bellied man in a grey uniform, the uniform of the OGPU, sat behind a desk at the foot of a curved gilded staircase. He made me wait for several minutes before he looked up and asked me what I wanted. He told me to write the name and last known address of the missing person with a piece of white chalk on a dark-green slippery slate he handed me. "Go wait your turn," he said. I walked to a concrete bench he pointed to. The bench was chained to a pillar still partially covered in tapestry. Six people were already sitting there, waiting. I joined them to wait my turn as the odious pot-bellied man had ordered me to do. I waited for half an hour, then I needed to get out, get the hell out of that place. I had decided I made a dreadful mistake coming to the Lubyanka. That no one in their right mind would ever willingly enter that building. Yet, I had done so. You do such *stupid* things, my mother would have said had she known. Another half an hour ticked by and with my panic uncontrollably increasing, I made up my mind to leave. Fortunately, an opportunity arrived to do so: the pot-bellied man in the grey uniform left his desk. Quickly, I turned to a woman sitting beside me. "Do you know where the toilet is?" I asked. She was young and pretty, but her red, swollen eyes bore witness to the fact she had been crying. "I feel sick," I whispered. "Like you are going to vomit?" she wanted to know. "Yes, yes, please, quick, where is the toilet?" Those red eyes flashed thunder. "Toilet? I'll tell you where the toilet is. It's here, right here! This entire country is a shit house!" I jumped to my feet, not only to get away from the Chekists but also from her. She was endangering my life by delaying my escape and my sympathy for her had evaporated. I held my hands over my mouth, pretended to retch violently and ran from the building. The pot-bellied man was nowhere in sight. Outside, the *black ravens*

---

[22] **Police transport vans.**

[23] **The building was once the headquarters of a building society.**

were still parked where they were earlier, the smoke was still rising from the chimney and the guards were still at the gate. I ran past them with my heart thumping. I did not look in their direction, I just ran. A few metres from the gate a tram pulled up at a shelter. I sprinted to catch it. The comrade controller touched his cap in salute. "Looks like you were lucky this time, my pretty," he said." You don't know how lucky," I told him.

I still did not give up looking for Vasily.

I asked my parents for the names of all those in situations of power or influence whom they had met in their years of fighting for *the cause*. Reluctantly, they gave me names. I checked the names in *Pravda's* archives and called on those who were still alive. I knocked on their doors just as I had knocked on the little side doors. Most refused to receive me. Those who did politely heard me out and promised they would see what they could do for me. *Don't however contact me again, I will contact you*, they said. Only one ever did and it was to tell me, in a letter, I should not grieve as grief was for the old and not for the young. *The ocean is large and filled with fish*, he ended his letter. Not that such a response discouraged me. I would appeal to the highest one of all: Krupskaya, Lenin's widow. She and my mother, in those years of fighting for *the cause*, had become friends. I wrote to her. *You may not remember me but one day you came to my parents' apartment in the Kremlin and you picked me up so that I could sit on your lap. You then braided my hair and you called me a 'real little doll' and you asked me not to grow up too quickly because the world of grownups was not a happy place.*

Krupskaya did not reply and I did not hold her silence against her. As I knew, as we all knew, she had her own problems because of our *man of steel*.

Her silence did persuade me though to stop looking for Vasily, to accept he was gone, gone at least for the moment and there was nothing I could do about it.

Stalin will not last forever, no one does, said my parents when I told them I would not be knocking on any little side doors for a while.

"You," I said accusingly, "you have not won *the cause*. It is still to be fought! All you have done is replacing one despot with another: Tsar with Stalin!"

"Tanoshka, what a thing to say, what an accusation to utter," my father replied, his tone exceptionally weary.

-0-

Again, a week passes. It is morning and all is quiet in our editorial room. Yury comes sprinting from his office. The Party has sent over another report. It is headed: *The Meaning of Cultural Transformation in a Socialist Society*. It is eight pages long. It does not take me long to edit. I start typing it out for our typesetters. Nina, in her bottle-green dress, rushes into the editorial room. There is a telephone call for me. I have to take it in the operator's cubicle on the ground floor.

"It is Boris Petrovich Beretzkoy and it has something to do with a book he is sending over," she whispers.

She had to whisper because we are not allowed personal telephone calls.

I fly down the stairs.

"You will have to speak very loudly to be heard, and don't blame me if you get into trouble because of this," says Anna Mikhailovna Anakhova our telephone operator, a young woman with yellow hair. She hands me the receiver. "Try not to shout though please because you will get *me* into trouble too."

"I will try not to," I promise.

"*Zdravtsvuyte*," he says. "I am in Moscow, can we meet?"

"Yes. We can."

Anna does not hide the fact she is listening: she has her earphones on. Nina, too, standing in the doorway, is listening, even if she can only hear one side of the conversation.

"At what time does your shift end?" asks Beretzkoy.

Anna's eyebrows shoot up.

"At six."

"Will it be in order for me to wait for you outside the building on the pavement?"

"*Pravda's* building?"

"No, where you live."

"It will be in order."

"In that case, I will say, see you this evening."

"This evening."

Anna pulls at a cable on her switchboard and the connection is cut. On the board in front of her a red light starts to flash.

"Another call. Sorry!" she says.

Nina walks back with me to our editorial room.

"Rest assured, what Anna hears she keeps to herself," she tells me.

-0-

He stands leaning against Vasily's building. It is snowing again. The collar of his greatcoat is turned up and the earflaps of his *shapka* cover most of his face: protection against the snow - snowflakes cling to his thick eyebrows - or protection against prying eyes?

"*Zdravtsvuyte*."

"*Zdravtsvuyte*."

Still the greeting of those who do not know each other well.

We shake hands.

"I didn't know whether I should call you," he says.

"But you did."

We climb the stairs to the fourth floor: elevators are things we see on photos in foreign magazines.

"I was going to ask you to come ice fishing with me," he says.

He is behind me.

"Tonight?" I ask.

"Some night."

"I would have come ice fishing with you tonight, Boris Petrovich."

"Call me Beretzkoy. Everyone calls me Beretzkoy."

"Not Boris?"

"No."

I can feel his breath against the back of my neck.

"Not Borya?"

"No. She calls me Borya."

She.

My mother once warned me about falling in love with a married man. *Tanya, there will always be a 'she' between you and your love.*

"Call me Tanya," I say.

"So you ice-fish, Tanya?"

"Actually, I've never done so."

But for you I will try. For you I will do anything.

I ask him whether he is hungry. We are in Vasily's room. A child cries from behind the paper-thin wall that separates us from the apartment's other tenants.

"I have two of those," he says. "Mind you, they are big boys now. They no longer cry."

I light Vasily's old wood-burning stove and I heat Vasily's samovar to make tea and I open a tin of pressed meat which was sent to us - to the Soviet Union - by an American philanthropic organisation. The meat is called *spam*, apparently.

"Tell me about yourself? Tell me what I don't already know about you?" he asks sitting on the bed, the bed I never shared with Vasily.

"There is nothing to know about me. I'm not interesting," I reply.

"So, I want to know all the uninteresting things."

"I was a Pioneer[24]. I was a Komsomolka[25]. I was a good little communist girl. I was a good scholar. I was a good student. I went to Moscow University. I am the wife of a wrecker. I am a wrecker. Should the Chekists let my husband … Vasily … go, I will have him back, and I will stay with him as long as he wants me to."

"What about what you would want?"

"That is what I would want."

"I understand."

---

[24] **The All-Union Pioneer Organisation was founded by Lenin in 1918 for Communist children aged from 10 to 15 years. It was modelled on the British Scouts.**

[25] **The Russian Communist Union of Youth was founded by Lenin in 1918 for young Communists from the age of 15 to 28.**

"No, you do not."

"I did ask you to tell me, did I not?"

I nod.

"Vasily was not a lover ... not my lover. And he won't become so should he come back. He will need care ..."

"... and you will be his carer."

I nod again.

"He was my best friend."

He comes to stand beside me.

"Now you know about me, now it is your turn. What about you?" I ask.

"Fair enough. Here goes. I'll tell you what and who I am."

He sits down on the bed again. His legs are slightly apart and he folds his hands in his lap.

He was born in Leningrad. His father was a schoolteacher and his mother a pianist who also taught music. He has only one sibling: a brother. The brother is a surgeon in Kiev. They do not get on because the brother loves Stalin.

"I wanted to be a pianist like my mother and so I studied music at the Moscow Conservatory, but ... I had ten wooden fingers whenever I sat down in front of a piano. I started to write. Write poetry. My first sexual experience was with a German girl I met at the Conservatory. She was a cellist. One day she told me her parents had decided to leave Russia. They were going to America. I told her the devil lived in America. They left all the same and all I wanted to do was die. I met another girl and with her I went to ZAGS. The marriage did not last. She met someone else and I met someone else. The someone else is the woman I am married to now: Nadezdha Konstantinovna. She was married to a choreographer: I will not name him. He was everyone's darling and she was so overcome with guilt at betraying such a wonderful man she decided to tell him about me. He threw her out and we went to ZAGS. My sons are named Paul and Grigory. I love them very much. Paul Borisovich was born within a few days of the ninth month of our visit to ZAGS. Then Nadezdha Konstantinovna fell pregnant again. It was the time of our first great famine. It was not a time for the beginning of a life. On the contrary, lives were ending all around us. I asked her to terminate the pregnancy, but she refused. She said the child she was carrying was conceived in an act of love and would be received with love. Grigory Borisovich was a beautiful baby. I forgot I had not wanted him. Or rather, that I had not wanted another child, not then. She, however, would not forget. She is not one who forgets, ever forgets. When it was once more possible for me to love her ... love her physically, she lay with her face to the wall. *Not now, not now,* she said. The next night she said *no* and the night after that she said nothing at all. She had gone to sleep in the children's room. She never returned to my bed. I wanted to end the marriage but I stayed. I felt that, because I had caused her pain, I had to compensate her for that pain. I told myself I would have to continue to love her and prove to her I love her. Love her and our sons. Both our sons. I also hoped if I did not insist on her lying with me, she would return to me soon enough. But she didn't. She turned cold. The famine ended and our financial situation improved because I was no longer an unknown because a volume of my poetry had been published. One day, I said to myself, to hell with this, I will no longer beg this woman for affection. I went in search of affection elsewhere. You can say I went in search of someone who did have affection to offer me and to whom I could offer affection. We lived in Moscow at the time and I took the train to Leningrad. I stayed there for ten days and on my return she did not ask me where I'd been. I waited a while and then I set off again and on my return she again did not ask me where I'd been. Our marriage was over. I realised our marriage was over, but I was still fond of her. Tanya, rumour would have you believe I am unreliable. It is said that I break hearts. I do not break hearts. I am not unreliable. I want you to know you can trust me."

He gets up from the bed and pours two glasses of tea. I am sitting at Vasily's writing desk. He hands me a glass and sits down on a chair opposite me.

"I have to go, but first I want to ask you something."

"Do."

"Would you like me to return?"

"If you should wish to return, Boris Petrovich, I will be here."

"I want to."

Dawn has come. A candle flickers from the writing desk. He blows out the flame and I walk him to the door. He does not look at me. I stand there until I can no longer hear his footsteps on the stairs.

I cannot believe that once again he did not turn to look back at me.

-0-

"Another call for you!" whispers Nina in my ear. "Him …"

Two days have passed. Two days of silence is a lifetime when one is in love.

"I am in Moscow," says he. "By what time will you be free?"

"By seven."

Anna and Nina are smiling. Again, they are listening to the conversation.

"Can we meet?"

"Yes, of course."

-0-

He is there waiting on the pavement outside Vasily's building. He sees me and he smiles.

"*Privet.*"

"*Privet.*"

The greeting of those who know each other well.

Vasily's room is clean and relatively spartan. My clothes, the few bits and pieces I have, hang in the only cupboard in the room. I have washed the morning's tea glass. It seems forlornly abandoned on the kitchen drainer.

"Will you like ... tea ... a glass of tea, perhaps?" I ask Beretzkoy.

"Not right now, Tanya. Later maybe."

He helps me with my old coat, slips it off my shoulders. His hands rest at the nape of my neck for a moment. I can feel my stomach muscles tighten: my fingers pick irritatingly at the folds of my dress.

"Tanya ..."

"Yes, Beretzkoy?"

I step back and away from him, sitting down on the end of the bed. He sits down beside me. It is quiet in the apartment. Something inside me longs for a noise: a crying baby, or the shuffling of feet. Any noise to break the silence.

I look towards the stove.

"Beretzkoy, would you ... ? I will put the samovar on."

I turn towards him.

"Tanya, my Tanya, don't go. Stay here with me?" he whispers.

He starts to pull his overcoat off his shoulders using just one hand. The other, lightly fisted, is resting on his knee. His posture looks uncomfortable and I put one arm around his shoulders to help him with the coat, to show him it is alright, what he desires I do also. The coat falls to the floor. I automatically go down on my knees to pick it up.

"No don't ..."

He is on the floor beside me, his eyes are fixed on mine, his hands rolling my dress up over my hips, my shoulders, my head.

I know I am not voluptuous like the women photographed in the foreign magazines I sometimes have an opportunity to see, but Beretzkoy's hands, warm and soft as they explore my body, make me feel beautiful suddenly. I pull his face to mine and I boldly kiss him full on his lips, my mouth open. He begins loosening his own clothes and finally I am able to forget my own feelings of reserve. I lose track of time and notice only vaguely the roughness of the wooden floor beneath my knees. He lifts me up, his fingers digging deeply into my thighs and suddenly I feel a moment of intense pain and pleasure filling my entire being.

When I am truly his, he carries me lightly over to the bed. We fall down on to it. We pull the blankets over us because it is cold in the room. For a while, who can say how long, we lie very still, but our bodies soon become melded together again.

-0-

CHAPTER FOUR

Beretzkoy is still asleep. I sit on the bed. I have brought him a glass of tea and slices of buttered bread. I balance the tray on my lap. He lies facing me. He needs to shave. His mouth is slightly open and he is making little noises, almost cries; a bad dream perhaps? He was silent and still during the night. Russian men, I have been told by Nina, are great snorers. I won't marry one who snores I told my mother once. *'And how would you know that he does or does not before you marry him?'* she asked. I had not thought of that.

I touch Beretzkoy's cheek. He opens his eyes. He looks at me, his eyes showing a moment's confusion.

"You've forgotten where you were," I say.

"Not true."

"I've made tea and buttered some bread. It's all I have in the room. I do not know if you usually eat something early morning."

I think I am blushing: I have spent a night with the man and I do not know whether he eats something with his morning glass of tea.

"I don't, but I will now."

He sits up, the blanket slipping to his waist. He is naked and I try not to look at his navel, which seems to stare at me like a peering eye. I am in my nightgown, but underneath it, I am not naked. On waking, my nakedness had shamed me and I hastily slipped into layers of underwear. He rubs his eyes and he yawns and pats the space beside him on the bed.

"I'm on the ten o'clock shift. I can't be late as Yury will make me come in on my day off," I say rapidly.

He drinks his tea and I start to dress. I do not look at him, but I can feel his eyes on me. I let my dress slip over my head. Earlier, putting on my underwear, I was in two minds whether I should also put on a dress. I decided not to. Why? I do not know. I think I did not want him to think of me as a prude. Or immature. My virginity had already embarrassed me. Me - the married woman.

"About your day off," he says.

I pull at my dress. Smooth it out around my stomach.

"I always have Thursdays off."

"I will come each Thursday."

"Each?"

"If that is in order with you."

"Yes, it is."

I sit down on the bed to put on my boots.

I wonder how many Thursdays there are in a lifetime.

"If you have any regrets, about last night, you only have to say so," he says.

I take the tray from him.

"I have no regrets."

I find it hard to look at him somehow.

"I will be here on Thursday. I will not be able to stay the night. This is how it will be for the future, at least for the immediate future. Later ... later, we can work out something else."

There is an early morning train from Zernoye Selo to Moscow on Thursdays and a midnight train back to the village.

"Fine. Good," I say.

"Do you have an extra key you could give me? I should not be seen hanging around outside."

"Of course ... of course ... you can't."

I fetch Vasily's key from a drawer and I put it down on the bed.

"I'll get here at about ten in the morning and I will only leave at eleven or so at night. I will bring something for us to eat."

"To eat? Couldn't we just go to a tavern?"

"No. We won't be able to go out. There are other things too we won't be able to do anymore. I won't be able to call you at *Pravda* and we won't be able to attend the same literary evenings and the next time I come to *Pravda* we will have to pretend we do not know each other and should we ever walk into each other, I will ignore you and you will have to ignore me."

"*Ladno.*"[26]

I drop my eyes again and fiddle with the buttons on my dress.

"I'm putting you in a cage," he says.

"I am a willing prisoner, I suppose."

I smile, trying to make light of the bitter truth.

"No! First hear me out. You must understand our Thursdays will always be the same. There will be no spontaneity. No surprises. It may appear to you we are two actors on a stage repeating carefully rehearsed lines."

He throws the blanket back and swings his legs off the crumpled bed. During the night I had not really looked at his body. Now, knowing it a little, I do. His body is firm and his skin seems very pale.

"Beretzkoy, I must be off or Yury will be on to me," I say quickly because I know what will happen should I stay.

Despite his nakedness he walks with me to the door. He has hair on his chest, but this I already knew because during the night I laid my face on his chest to hide my shame at my inexperience.

At the door he grabs the lapels of my coat, pulls me in and holds me tightly, the way a child holds on to its mother.

"Tanya, when you want out, you will tell me?"

---

[26] **Ok.**

"I will tell you, Beretzkoy."

"I will see you next Thursday then. At eleven ... just after eleven."

He had told me there would be no spontaneity and no surprises in our relationship. Already, I realise this will be so. I presume when one goes into a relationship with a married man, spontaneity is a word one bans from one's vocabulary.

Instead, one timetables one's life like one would a train journey. First, one has to find out on what days the train runs which will bring him to you, and at what time he will walk in and what the two of you will do once he has arrived because no time ought to be lost. And one will have to find out at what time there will be a train to take him back home again, home to his wife and his children. Because eventually, home he will go. This was what I heard a friend of my mother's tell her one day and I had then made up my mind I would not ever be as stupid as to fall in love with a married man.

Nevertheless, now I wonder how many Thursdays there are in a year.

-0-

CHAPTER FIVE

I count the days.

Friday, the first day without him, is day one.

For two months, Beretzkoy and I have been lovers and for two months this is what I have been doing.

"What is this counting of days," asks Nina.

One Monday I had, without thinking, called it day four. *I don't know what you are talking about*, had been my reply.

What can I say about our Thursdays? Perhaps that they are indeed one like the other. But they are different too, different from the other days of the week. I rise early and by ten I am dressed and waiting, but never at the door. I once overheard my father call the wife of a neighbour lecherous. What an ugly word: *lecherous*. Not that I knew its meaning: I had to look it up in a dictionary. Lecherous: *derives from the French verb lechier (to lick) which derives from the 12th century French word lecheor … general meaning is indulging in something … food … sex.*

It is at Vasily's writing desk I sit, waiting. I keep an eye on the clock on the wall. It is a cuckoo clock: a small Swiss chalet with a tiled roof, a door and two windows with red paper flowers in window boxes. Where Vasily found it, I did not have a chance to ask him. I have not had a chance to ask him many other things as well. Each hour, on the hour, a small door in the tiled roof swings open and a little yellow bird appears and coo-coos the correct number for the hour. It is somehow comforting.

When Beretzkoy finally arrives, I want to jump up and into his arms, but the word *lecherous* makes me shiver and I stay where I am.

He and I talk a lot. Always: first, we talk. We speak of the week which has passed. I hide nothing from him. Frankly, there is nothing to hide. I get up in the morning, I take the tram to *Pravda*, I edit the Party's propaganda and at the end of my shift I take the tram back to Vasily's room and after my evening meal of bread and tea I go to bed. One evening a week, I visit my parents. "How are you," my mother asks and my father wants to know, "What you've been up to, Mademoiselle?" "Working hard," I reply. Beretzkoy hides things from me. He must do so because he never mentions his wife and sons. He tells me what he has been writing. At present he is writing a short story which might become a novella. It is a love story. He reads what he has written. "Does it sound right?" he asks.

We do not make love each Thursday. I am after all a woman and there are certain bodily cycles which prevent love-making. When we do make love he holds me so tightly, I cry out with pain. Afterwards, he covers my body with kisses of apology. "A man forgets his strength when he feels what I am feeling right now," he says. I wait for him to put a name to what he is feeling, to describe what he is feeling, but he falls silent and I remain silent too. I do not ask this man whether he loves me. I do not tell him I love him. He must be the one to speak of love, to speak of it before I do. He will, I know. I will wait. Patiently.

At noon we sit down at the writing desk to eat our lunch. Beretzkoy cooks what he has brought with him. I do not know how to cook. He finds it amusing that I, like a Parisian bourgeoise, have never learnt to cook. My mother has always refused to teach me to do so. You are going to become a writer and not a maker of pies, was what she said. I even asked my father, the Frenchman, to teach me to cook, but he, too, told me they were not giving me the best possible education so I could slave in a kitchen.

Our meals are not lavish because collectivisation is starting to cause shortages: fruit and vegetables are rare and meat has become a luxury. We eat what he has been able to buy from *babyshkas*[27] who stand alongside the railway track. Our trains do not go at a high speed and such illegal trading is therefore possible. Drop the kopek in the outstretched old hand and grab the bunch of onions or bag of potatoes and you have a bowl of soup, and damnation to Stalin, the lame-armed devil in the Kremlin.

Some Thursdays he brings us a bottle of wine, also bought *nalevo*[28].

In the afternoon, he writes.

I tell him I will go for a walk so he can have peace and quiet. "Don't go," he says, "it is so pleasant having you beside me." At four we have tea and whatever has been left over from lunch. Night falls. We throw a blanket on the floor in front of the stove. Here we lie until it is time for him to run for the midnight train. He never wants to leave. I say neither go nor stay. If he is going to stay for the night, then it must be his decision.

-0-

The days lengthen and grow warmer. The snows begin to melt. Awful grey mud appears wherever one steps. Children, their little fingers red with cold because they no longer want to wear gloves and muffs, throw watery snow balls at passers-by. One morning the twittering of birds awakens me. They spent the winter sheltering between the beams of the roof.

It is Thursday again. Beretzkoy stands at the open window watching children play hop-scotch on the pavement down below. Excited laughter fills the room.

"We are going out tonight," he says.

---

[27] **An old woman or a grandmother.**

[28] **On the black market.**

"We are going out? Is it wise?" I ask, bewildered.

"No, it is not, but it is summer and in the summer no one is wise."

Darkness comes.

"Now?" I ask.

He is taking me to meet his two closest and dearest friends: Dan and Yelena Olminsky.

Daniel Mironovich, the poet, is, along with Beretzkoy, our country's finest poet. Yelena Fyodorovna is an authority on foreign literature: she lectures at Moscow University. They are outspoken critics of Stalin and both have paid the price of internal exile for their indiscretion. For Dan it was a second term of exile. Tsar Nicholas punished him similarly, but then it was for his anti-Tsarist sentiments. Because of their political views they are not friends of Nadezdha Konstantinova: she, my lover's wife, loves Stalin, therefore, the anti-Stalinist Olminskys are the devil incarnate.

At the door, I can feel cramps of anxiety shooting across my abdomen.

"I don't think I will be able to meet Dan and Yelena after all," I say.

Beretzkoy looks at me.

"Don't be silly now Tanya, you are just nervous."

Yes, I am nervous. I know so little and my limited knowledge will show up in the company of intellectuals like Dan and Yelena. It is already showing up when Beretzkoy is with me. I have been spending my mid-shift breaks in libraries reading up on world history, geography, science, art. I want to be able to say, "Oh yes this is the fish that swims backwards" when Beretzkoy likens Stalin to a Chaetodon, and when he speaks of the Siege of Ladysmith, I want to know he is talking about the war the Boers fought against the mighty British Empire.

Dan and Yelena live not far from where I live. Their apartment, also in one of *Stalin's marvels*, is on the ground floor. It is not a communal apartment which is, in our land of equality, due to Yelena's position at Moscow University. Their name is on the blue door. Olminsky-Olminskaya, written on a piece of cardboard. It dangles from the doorknob. It is not our custom to put our names on a door, it makes it too easy for the Chekists to find us, but I know such daring behaviour is typical of these two.

"*Devushka!*"[29]

Dan has opened the door. Like Marina on the night of the clandestine literary evening, he kisses me on both cheeks in the French manner. I can only see his face. The rest of him, despite the warmness of the evening, is draped in black: a black overcoat reaches to his ankles, a black woollen bonnet, hand-knitted as the large uneven stitches bear witness, perches on his head, and his feet are in black fur-lined boots.

The room behind him is small and cluttered. I am reminded of the reading room in *Pravda's* archives room. Books lie everywhere: on the floor, the sofa, on

---

[29] **Young girl.**

arm chairs. Books are even piled ceiling-high on top of the cupboards. In the middle of this maze of books stands a small creature: Yelena. She too is dressed for winter in a long red woollen dress and red cape.

She holds a bowl of knobbly gherkins out towards me.

"You won't be able to stop eating these."

She bought the gherkins in the morning from an old woman who sets up a stall on the pavement outside.

"In the winter she sells herring. I love herring," says Dan.

He smacks his cracked old man's lips.

"We're Jews, of course we love herring!" says Yelena.

She sweeps books off the sofa and two arm chairs, and puts the bowl down on a low table. A mask of grey dust covers the table. I can write my name in the dust.

Dan uncorks a bottle of wine.

"French. Bordeaux. Some French marxist imbecile gave it to me."

Blue eyes smile at me.

"More than ten years ago that was. Dan's kept it," explains Yelena.

She rolls her eyes. They are blue like those of her husband.

Dan looks at me.

"Are you an infidel?"

"I ..."

"If she is, good for her, but if she is not, let her be," reprimands Yelena. She turns to me, "Religion doesn't go very far with Dan and me."

Dan puts down his glass. He is still looking at me.

"We are misfits, the two of us, my dear Yelena and I, and always we have been. To Nicholas we were Jews and intellectuals and now to the Ossetian[30] we are intellectuals and Jews. So, do we fit in anywhere? No. We are misfits."

The red curtain in front of the window behind us is tied in a large knot. The window is wide open. Neighbours are sitting on chairs on the pavement now. They are drinking vodka and they are screaming with laughter. Dan shakes his head.

"No respect. No respect for others."

They tell me their histories: in the Soviet Union we have to know who we befriend.

Both were born in Kiev. They were born in adjoining houses in the Podol district of the city, were the Jews lived, and many do still live. Dan was born three months before Yelena, yet he looks years older with his wispy grey hair, grey complexion and sunken cheeks. He was *Bar Mitzvahed* and the two of them had signed the *ketubah*[31] before their marriage.

---

[30] **Some Russians said that Stalin was not Georgian as he claimed, but from Ossetia and Russians looked down on Ossetians.**

[31] **Marriage contract.**

"We were obliged to do so. We knew we wouldn't need it because we were together forever," says Dan.

Yelena carries plates, knives and forks in from the kitchen. She has prepared filled gooseneck. She calls it *gefilte helzel*. There is a neck for each of us. These are filled with mashed potatoes and fried onions.

"Took three hours to cook," Dan tells us as if he wants us to understand this is a veritable feast they are laying on for us.

"We observe *kashruth*," says she. "Out of habit. But ... well, we are infidels. Our parents sat *shiva* for us, these two lost Jewish souls, when they realised that God has ceased to exist for us."

We drink liqueur. It is dark red, made from plums. It is very sweet. We drink too much of it. Like teenagers we start to giggle. Soon, we are laughing as loud as those sitting outside on the pavement.

Still laughing, Yelena and I go into the kitchen. She pours water from a lukewarm samovar into a bowl. I hand her the dirty plates and cutlery to wash.

"Don't dry," she says. "I never dry... waste of time to dry. I am glad he has found you. He is a good man. Despite ... whatever ... you know ... whatever some say, take it from me: he is a good man. As for that wife of his ..."

She did not change the tone of her voice and therefore at first I was not sure she was talking about Beretzkoy. I wonder whether I should ask her what Nadezdha Konstantinovna is like, but, no, I decide I should not do so. She and I have only just met as it is.

The time comes to go. Dan has been shooting glances at the clock and yawning. It is eleven o'clock. The pavement is deserted now. I nearly trip over an empty vodka bottle. An old wicker chair and some more empty vodka bottles lie in the gutter. Dan and Yelena lean from their window. They wave.

"I won't go back home tonight," says Beretzkoy.

He is waving to Dan and Yelena. He did not turn his head to look at me when he spoke those words.

We walk along the Moskva River. We are holding hands. We turn and see Saint Basil's Cathedral looming in the distance behind us, moonlight on its onion domes: the domes are yellowed by the light of that distant moon.

"I'm going to go in for a swim," says Beretzkoy.

He scrambles down the river bank. The water is dark. He kicks off his shoes. I watch from the pavement. He calls out for me to join him. I shake my head.

"No, the water must be icy!"

He starts to pull off his clothes: jacket, socks, trousers, shirt. The moonlight illuminates half of his body, turning it as yellow as the domes of Saint Basil and he looks like some strange creature from another planet. He turns to face me, lifts his arms above his head and falls backwards into the water. For a moment his head bobs on the water. Next, all I see are ripples on the water's surface. Quickly, his head reappears.

"Come on in!" he calls out.

Why not?

I run down the bank. At the water's edge, I quickly undress.

As I saw him do, I turn my back to the water and fall into it.

"Not cold as you expected, is it!" he calls out.

"Speak for yourself!" I reply, gasping for breath.

I try to keep my head above water so as not to wet my hair, but like a stone, I start to sink. Hitting the bottom, I am unable to turn onto my stomach. I start to kick and I see clearly in my mind's eye my last moment on earth has arrived. Beretzkoy appears beside me, grabs me around my waist and paddles up to the surface, pulling me after him as if I am a rag doll. My head above the water, a dead fish floats past my face. It is on its back, its scaly stomach, pearly-white.

"I didn't know you could swim, if I can call what you've been doing, swimming," says Beretzkoy. He grins and a drop of luminous saliva drips from his upper lip into his mouth. "If you put your head under the water you won't feel the cold. Come I'll hold you. You won't drown."

I shake my head.

"I'm getting out."

I start wading to the river bank.

"Oh don't go, Tanya," he begs.

Again, he grabs me around the waist and pushes me down into the water, but he does not let go of me. When I resurface, again gasping, he fills my lungs with his breath. Both his arms are around me and his feet tread water to get us to the muddy bank. The current plays with us, sweeping us along, making it hard for him to keep us afloat, and washes us like driftwood onto the mud of the bank. Beretzkoy is rolling underneath me, his body white as porcelain against the brown of the mud. I shake the water from my hair and try to roll off him, but he holds me to him, locks me into a firm grip. Feeling his readiness I move on top of him. I am overcome with love for this man. My hair drips water down onto his face as I arch myself forwards and backwards. When it is over and our thoughts return to the real world, we laugh at one another's muddy body.

"Like survivors of a mud slide," jokes Beretzkoy.

-0-

Our night is not over yet. Hair wet, shivering with cold, we stop at a tavern.

Beretzkoy orders champagne. The waiter brings us a bottle of *Moët et Chandon* and he struggles with the cork, trying to loosen it with one of his short, thick, dirty-nailed thumbs. *Hold your glasses ready*, he warns. The cork flies out, it hits the ceiling, and the patrons, red-faced and bleary-eyed from too many tumblers of vodka, clap and cheer. *What's the occasion?* one of them calls out. We do not reply. The champagne is warm. "No one asks for stuff like this," the waiter apologises. He brings us a pewter cup filled with cubes of ice. The ice gives the champagne a metallic taste. We finish the bottle.

It starts to rain. We are sitting at a table at the window. Rain water starts to seep through the warped wood of the window frame. Our faces, reflected in the pane, become long and thin.

"I'll make you a lion's face," I tell Beretzkoy.

The tavern is silent because the patrons have lost interest in us.

"Yes, go ahead, become a lioness."

I open my mouth wide and I silently mime what I think is the roar of a lion. He laughs.

"A lioness, I ask you! You're no lioness! That's a *Munch* face you pulled," he says. "*The Scream.*"

"No," I protest. "I am a lion! I am King of the jungle!"

I throw my arms up in the air: never have I heard of Munch and The Scream.

"No," he says, "You can't be. Stalin is King of the jungle."

-0-

When the rain stops, he helps me into my jacket.

My head is spinning and I stumble walking from the tavern.

"I think I am drunk, Beretzkoy," I say.

I mean *drunk with happiness,* but I do not dare say it.

He puts an arm around me.

-0-

It is morning and he does not leave but stands at the window looking into the room. I am dressing to go to work.

"Do you not have a feeling of isolation when you are here alone?" he asks.

"Right now, I am not alone. You are here."

"Am I all you want, Tanya?" he asks.

I do not reply.

"What do girls your age do, Tanya?"

Again, I ignore his question.

"Would you not like to go dancing?" he insists.

"I used to go dancing with Vasily on Thursdays. Then, after the Chekists took him, I went over to my parents every Thursday. Now my mother wants to know about my Thursdays, she wants to know why I do not come over anymore."

"Nadezdha Konstantinova does not ask me about my Thursdays," he says.

The little birds from the overhead beams are chirping noisily in the sunshine.

"Should she ask, Beretzkoy, what will you say?"

"She won't ask."

"But say, she asks?"

"Then I will tell her about you … about us."

-0-

CHAPTER SIX

It is now autumn and an influenza pandemic is raging. It began in Eastern Siberia and, like a summer fire on the Steppe it has spread westwards to Moscow. It marks its passage with fresh graves. Yury gives me a Party report to edit. The Party is telling us what we should and should not do. We should cover our mouths when we cough and we should not drop soiled handkerchiefs onto the pavements. We should not leave our districts unless we have to. We should also not bring the sick to the hospitals: aspirin will do fine as treatment. *Take your dead to the mortuaries.* The report does not say how we are supposed to: the Soviet Union has long since run out of hearses. *No hearses, I ask you*, my father keeps on saying. In fact, the Soviet Union has run out of everything, but no one will admit it.

"Don't come next Thursday. Don't come until the pandemic has ended," I tell Beretzkoy one Thursday.

The Party also sends daily reports of where the influenza has hit. No one in Zernoye Selo has as yet gone down with it but it is rife in Moscow.

"I'm of solid stock. I won't get ill. You'll see me next Thursday," Beretzkoy assures me.

Thursday comes. The cuckoo steps from his little chalet and announces the hour: it is noon. Beretzkoy has not come. All night I lie awake, worrying he is ill.

-0-

It is a new day. I am at my desk. Nina is standing in front of me. "There is a call for you. Hurry!"

I run down the stairs and grab the receiver from Anna.

It is Beretzkoy.

"I'm slightly off colour," he says.

His sons are ill, but not seriously. Nadezdha Konstantinova, too, has the flu.

"Keep warm. Rest. And stay in bed," I beg him.

Anna nods. She does not try to pretend she is not listening to the conversation.

"I'll keep in touch. I'll call again," he promises.

He walked to his village post office to make the call. There is a telephone in the Beretzkoy *dacha* but their connection is of the kind which allows a subscriber to receive calls only, as most of our connections are.

A week passes.

The door to Yuri's office flies open. He stomps to my desk and I know he

47

has another Party report for me to edit. It consists of four pages. About the pandemic. Unusually honest, the Party includes a chart giving the number of victims, district by district. No names: numbers of dead, gender and ages only. Four children have died in Zernoye Selo. So too an adult. The adult is a member of Profpro, our writers' union, the Union of Proletarian Writers of which we, we who live by the written word and of which Beretzkoy, Dan and Yelena, and I, are members: under our constitution membership to a labour union is not compulsory, but as we know what happens to those who do not run with the pack, we run with it. Another Profpro member is seriously ill and a patient in Kremlin Hospital: care at the hospital is a perk of union membership.

I go to Yury's office and ask him if he may know the name of the member who has died in Zernoye Selo. He says he does not. I stop at Konstantin's desk, the desk I still think of Vasily's, to ask him. He is also editing a Party report. I glance at it. My eye catches the name Beretzkoy. He is the Profpro member who is seriously ill in Kremlin Hospital.

Konstantin ignores me.

Back sitting at my desk, Nina walks up to me. She clears her throat.

"You know, that one who calls you? He's ill. He's in hospital."

"I know."

More, I am unable to get out.

Nina brings me a glass of tea.

"I've put lots of sugar in this, so it will calm you down."

She hands me another lump to dip into the tea.

"Get on with your work, Tanya Nikolaeyvna!" shouts Yury from the door of his office.

I hate him!

Like an automaton in a show of puppets I type out the report for our typesetters. My fingers thump on the keyboard and my brain feels numb.

I scuttle away as soon as my shift ends.

The Olminskys live three blocks from *Pravda* and I run all the way to their apartment. They have not heard of Beretzkoy's illness. Dan immediately sets off for the hospital. After an hour he returns.

"He's fine, Beretzkoy's fine. He doesn't want you to worry."

"Get some food in you," Yelena tells me.

She is going to heat some left-over soup.

"Yelena, I don't know where I stand with Beretzkoy," I tell her.

She and I are in the kitchen. Dan has gone to the bedroom to take off his long black coat and boots.

Yelena puts down the spoon with which she has been stirring the soup.

"What are you talking about, Tanya?"

"We never speak of love ... Beretzkoy and I ..."

She is wearing glasses today and these slip down to the tip of her nose.

"Dear child, men don't," she says.

"So how is a woman to know?"

"His eyes will tell you what you want to know."

"It would be nice to be told... to hear him tell me he loves me."

She takes her glasses off and she holds them over the boiling pot of soup so the steam rising from it can clean the lenses.

Dan walks back into the kitchen.

"You young ones do always want to hear this magic word 'love', do you not, Tanya?"

He has overheard our conversation.

He loves me, he loves me not, was a game young girls played when I was still a teenager. We pulled the petals from a flower and we said, *he loves me, he loves me not*, and, whichever one it was when we reached the last petal, was the answer. I understand life better now to indulge in such a stupid game of chance.

"Come on," urges Yelena. "Get something into you. It will make you feel better." She points to a chair at the kitchen table. "Come on! Sit!"

She pushes a slice of buttered bread across the table towards me.

"Oh, this word *love*," murmurs Dan.

"Yes," says Yelena. "It is just that - a word. It is made of breath and spit. Even if Beretzkoy goes on his knees six times a day to tell you how much he loves you, the word's worth, - its power, its strength, - can still only be measured in the breath and spit he had spent saying it. We can all say 'I love you', but what counts, my dear Tanya, is what is written in the eyes. Not what is said with the tongue. Read his eyes, Tanya. Read his eyes!"

If only I could see Beretzkoy. I want to read his eyes.

"Eat your soup, young girl!" orders Dan, firmly.

-0-

The pandemic calms and we think it will soon be over. Be behind us.

Yury comes running with another Party report. We have been warned we are not to speak of a pandemic - it was only a run of bad colds. The warning goes onto *Pravda's* front page. I am told I must make it clear to the typesetters the warning is to be underlined.

As suddenly as it has started, the run of bad colds ends.

Dan comes to *Pravda* with a letter for me from Beretzkoy. "I will be out of here in a couple of days," he writes. The doctors are keeping him in hospital because he has an unsteady heartbeat. He signs his letter, "Yours, Beretzkoy."

"Was that who I think it was, that old Yid rascal Olminsky?" asks Yury.

The old Yid rascal, Olminsky, returns a day later.

Beretzkoy has sent me a second letter. I read it on the tram going back to Vasily's room.

'My very dearest Tatyana Nikolayevna, what I wanted to say to you in yesterday's letter is: I love you. Yours this day and every day and forever. Boris Petrovich Beretzkoy.'

I start to cry silently. Uncontrollably.

An old woman sitting beside me looks at me with tenderness.

"Dearie, is something wrong?" she asks, examining me with red watery eyes.

"No, nothing." My eyes and nose are streaming.

"Tears of happiness then?"

I nod.

"How wonderful to see tears of happiness."

-0-

I can see Beretzkoy from afar. He is in his greatcoat and *shapka*. He is leaning against the building and, as he is not looking my way, I creep up on him.

"Boo!" I say.

I tap him on his back.

He swings around.

"*Privet*. How is your heart?" I ask.

He rests his grey hand on his chest.

"There is nothing wrong with my heart. In fact, it is exactly where it was the last time I saw you and right now it is banging away crazily at the sight of you."

"I want to feel it beating."

"Here? On the street?" he asks.

"Here, on the street," I confirm.

I put my hand under his, resting it on his chest.

"Every beat is for you. Remember this," he tells me.

I cannot feel his heartbeat through his overcoat, but I imagine to myself, I can.

We walk slowly into the building.

I know he will stay the night.

-0-

Morning comes. I am awake and up early. I must get to work.

Beretzkoy comes to stand with me at the door even though he has not yet dressed and is covering his nakedness with the blanket from the bed.

"Tanya, why have you not said anything about my letter?" he asks.

"I did, Beretzkoy," I reply. "I asked about your heart."

"Do you not know what I am talking about?"

"I know."

I cannot look at him.

"Did I speak out of turn in my letter?" he asks.

"No, Beretzkoy, you did not speak out of turn. What you have written was something I've been waiting to hear for a long time."

"Why should that be?"

He has taken my hand.

"Because I love you, Boris Beretzkoy."

Finally, I meet his gaze.

"So, I didn't speak out of turn?"

"No, you did not."

"I so feared you did not feel as I do."

He is smiling.

-0-

In the winter things start to go wrong for Russia. In December, we hear rumours of hundreds of thousands, some say millions, dying because of collectivisation. There is widespread hunger in the countryside. No, not hunger. *Famine.*

I am on my way to work. I see some people had spent the night sleeping at the tram shelter. I think it is a family: father, mother, two teenage children and a toddler. They are lying on the ground on old *Pravdas.*

"*Tovarisch?*"

I touch the man's arm. He does not wake up. The woman sits up. She brushes snow from her face. The toddler lies in a cardboard box. I think the child is a girl; she is awake, her eyes are blue, the blue of cornflowers. They look at me.

"Her name is Tatyana, she's four months old," says the woman.

"My name's Tatyana too," I say.

The woman is on her feet now. She has no teeth. Her breath stinks. She stinks. Her head is bare. She is almost bald. There are many bald men and women, even children, in Moscow. "This is what famine does, our hair will fall out, our teeth will rot and fall out," says my father.

"Hey you, young girl, do you have a kopek?" asks the woman.

"Sorry," I tell the woman, "I do not carry money on me, but come with me to my room which is just here across the street. I have some bread there which I will give you."

Afterwards, I walk to *Pravda* - I do not want to pass the tram stop again. I am a full hour late in getting to work.

"Make sure you get here on time. Put more water in the glass," reprimands Yury.

Konstantin is nodding in agreement.

-0-

It is a new day. I am again walking towards the tram shelter. I am walking fast, because I must not be late again. It did not snow during the night, but the roof of the tram shelter is covered in a layer of ice and more shards of ice which look as if they would be as sharp as an axe, hang from the roof.

Behind the shelter, a group of people, men and women dressed in heavy overcoats and *shapkas* - commuters waiting for a tram to take them to work - are talking excitedly. They appear to be talking about something lying on the ground: a cardboard box. I quicken my pace. I know what is in the cardboard box: it is the toddler Tatyana. Her cornflower eyes are wide open. They are turned to the grey sky and clearly life has gone from them. She looks like a doll: blue eyes, yellow hair, pale skin. I want to touch her, pick her up. Kiss her. A wail comes from behind me. It is the child's mother. A distance away lies the man. He is naked. Snow conceals the intimate part of his body: someone has tried to restore his dignity. His eyes, like those of his daughter's, stare lifelessly at the grey sky. The two teenage boys sit beside their father's body. They are eating, each is stuffing scraps of bread into his mouth. They seem unaware of what is going on around them in their eagerness to consume this most pathetic repast. A van drives up and the woman falls silent. Two men in white protective clothing get out and walk up to the man on the ground.

"This the one?" one of them asks us.

He touches the man's cheek, tries to pinch his taut skin, but cannot. The man's skin is the colour of parchment.

"A goner. No doubt about that," says the second man.

He and his colleague try to lift the dead man. They cannot.

"A dead weight," smirks one of the commuters.

The woman starts to wail again. She is howling with a primitive yowl like a wolf welcoming the night. I touch her arm but she jerks it away. The two men are still trying to lift her husband. They swear and spit onto the snow: the body has frozen to the ground. There is going to be only one way to free it. They will have to rip the flesh and leave flesh sticking to the ice. With a violent wrench they do so, without flinching, without remorse, without sorrow, without offering the widow their condolences. *All part of a day's job.* They hurl the body into the back of their van. The woman jumps into the vehicle, but immediately she jumps off again. The two men have moved towards her daughter's body and this she is not going to allow. She throws herself over the cardboard box, her arms flailing to keep the two men back.

"*Nyet! Nyet!*"

She hits out at the two, her hands red and swollen as though the skin may split.

"Does anyone know this woman?" one of the men asks.

They are angry now.

I step forward.

"I do. They're homeless. They've been sleeping here in the tram shelter."

The woman looks at me; there is recognition in her eyes.

I walk towards her. A pulse of nausea rises in my throat because of the smell of her.

"Please. Your baby is cold out here. Let them take her."

I manage to pull her awkward frame to its feet. She offers no resistance.

The two men give the box several hard tugs and the ice releases it. The teenagers have finished eating the bread and they are standing beside their mother and me. She is sobbing quietly now and they start to cry too, their thin bodies trembling. The men carry the box over to the van and hurl it into the vehicle. Within moments they are back inside it and drive off. The woman and her sons try to run after it and I automatically run after them. I want to tell the woman she and her sons can come home with me. When my breath becomes short, I stop running: what is the use? The woman and her sons keep on going, running into the distance. Finally, I lose sight of them.

I walk to *Pravda*. I cry all the way.

Yury stands at my desk.

"Late again!"

"I've just seen death."

"Wipe your face. There is a first time for everything," he snaps.

I wipe my face.

-0-

It is January and things begin to go wrong for us too now.

My father is called to the office of the comrade director of the French Language Studies department of the People's Commissariat of Education. He is told he has been retired.

"You know how it is. In tough times teaching Russians French is not a priority," says the comrade director.

"We will get by," says my mother.

In February, Beretzkoy echoes my mother's words.

Gozuzdom, our state publishing house, told him they will not be issuing books for a while. He had the publication of a new volume of verse scheduled for the spring, but publication has been cancelled.

"Only postponed surely," I say.

"No. Cancelled."

Gozuzdom has though commissioned him to translate Goethe's *The Sorrows of Young Werther* for our schools.

Gozuzdom also cancels a volume of Dan's poetry. He is given Shakespeare's *Hamlet* to translate, also for our schools.

Yelena keeps her employment at Moscow University.

"At least you are secure too at *Pravda*," she tells me.

Am I?

Before February ends Nina comes to stand at my desk. Comrade Yaroslavsky has been dismissed she tells me. Our new editor is Lev Zakharovich Mekhlis. He is already in Comrade Yaroslavsky's office. An electrician comes to connect a second telephone line for him. The phone rings and we think our fire alarm is sounding. The electrician comes back and works on reducing the noise.

Comrade Mekhlis does not come to our editorial room to introduce himself. He does not have to: we know who he is. He comes to us from the Central Committee where he has been head of the press section. He is not one who ever speaks for himself: always he speaks in the name of Stalin. Therefore, the *Vozdh* is now our *de facto* editor.

"There will be disappearances," prophesises Nina.

Here, in my country, we speak of disappearances and not of dismissal. Retirement like in my father's case is rare.

Yury disappears also. It is Wednesday and it is already close to noon and there is no sign of him.

"He's down with the flu probably," suggests Konstantin.

"The run of bad colds has ended," I reply.

A stranger walks in and goes into Yury's office. He closes the door. A few minutes later the door flings open again. The stranger holds up several sheets of paper.

"Comrade Brodovskaya!"

The stranger's voice is authoritative. I rush to his side. He is waving a Party report at me.

"Edit it! Now!" he barks.

"Comrade … comrade? What did you say your name was?" I ask.

"Moscow," he replies.

He walks back to Yury's office.

Nina walks up the stairs.

"Yes, his name is Moscow," she whispers to me. "He was born abroad and his parents were nostalgic for the good old country. He's replacing Yury."

Moscow Ivanovich Syrtov does not have a wooden leg but he does have a medal pinned to the lapel of his jacket just like the missing Yury.

"What has happened to Yury?" I ask Nina.

"I do not know. And frankly, Tanya, do we care?"

Yury's disappearance is followed by those of some of my other colleagues. None ever says goodbye and their replacements never say hello.

"They're not professional journalists, just propagandists sent over by the Central Committee," says Konstantin, scorn in his voice.

"Look who's talking," retorts Nina.

Next, Konstantin disappears. We think one of our new colleagues must have denounced him as anti-Soviet for what he had said about them.

"Had nothing to say for himself at first and then he said too much," says Nina.

A woman replaces Konstantin. She is tall and thin and wears her long grey hair braided in a circle around her head and she has not just one medal pinned to the bodice of her faded red dress, but four: when she walks, she rattles as if she has chains tied around her body. Moscow tells us from now on she will write our daily *Cevodnya v Nomere*[32] editorial, something Comrade Yarovslavsky used to do. She sits down at Vasily's desk - I still cannot stop thinking of the desk as Vasily's. Immediately, she starts writing tomorrow's editorial.

---

[32] **In Today's Issue.**

"Her name is Vera Shittskaya," says Anna. "Her enemies call her 'Vera Shit'."

"Nina will love that," I say.

Nina has not turned up for work.

"She's ill," says Anna.

A week goes by. Nina is still off ill. A sandy-haired youth with a face covered in festering acne comes up the stairs. He stops at the door.

"Attention!" he shouts.

He has come to pin up a notice from Comrade Mekhlis. *No person-to-person telephone calls will be tolerated anymore.*

"Nina's gone," says Anna. "This young man's name is Vladymir and he is replacing her."

"Where has she gone?" I ask Anna.

"Who knows."

Vladymir does not tell us his surname.

"Call me Comrade Vladymir," he says.

"I cannot take this anymore," I say to my parents.

"I so wish you'd meet a nice young man and settle down and have his babies," says my mother.

"She's still a baby herself," says my father. "Plenty of time for her to fall in love."

I do not tell them a man is already the core of my existence.

-0-

CHAPTER SEVEN

On the last Friday of each month a *Pravda's* workers' meeting is held. My parents told me that during those years of fighting *the cause* with Lenin, they decided workers should be consulted on how their work places should be run. This is what workers' meetings used to be *before* Stalin and what they are still supposed to be. But they are now only opportunities for colleagues to denounce one another. Our supervisor always chairs our workers' meetings and this Friday is Moscow's first. He has decided to bring in a band so we can dance afterwards.

It is six o'clock. The meeting begins. Moscow stands at the door of our canteen and hands out glasses of tea. This is new: Yury never did this.

"Welcome! Welcome Comrades!" Moscow calls out.

I hate workers' meetings. I always stand at the rear of our canteen. The canteen is on the first floor, right under our editorial room. I stand by the window breathing the cold air that filters through the cracked frame. Two boys are rifling through the rubbish bins in the courtyard below. Ragamuffins. *Bezprizorni* no doubt, yet officially there are none left in our country. Comrade Mekhlis walks in. He is wearing a suit and white open-necked shirt: nothing as bourgeois as a neck-tie for our comrade. A dozen dignitaries accompany him. Two are still in their overcoats. The others, among them Vladymir, are in flannel trousers and *rybashkas*[33]. Are the two in overcoats, Chekists? Will they take note this evening of the denunciations and accusations that are sure to be made? If only Vladymir Ilych had not died my father always says.

Moscow reads a progress report. He mentions the *Vozdh's* name and we cheer. I do so as enthusiastically as my colleagues. One thing one learns in our glorious proletariat state is how to be a hypocrite, and hypocrites clap their hands and cheer when the Great One's name is mentioned. Moscow is wearing brown corduroy trousers and a black turtle-necked sweater: I wish I am far away, concealed in the arms of someone else I know who also likes to wear brown corduroy trousers and a black turtle-necked sweater.

Moscow asks whether there is anything we would like to report or comment on. Down in the courtyard one of the ragamuffins knocks a bin over. I look out. The boys, frightened, are scuttling across the courtyard like sewer rats. They clutch some old editions of *Pravda* under their arms: are they really going to read those?

" … Comrade Brodovskaya …"

---

[33] **A shirt that hangs over a man's trousers as worn by peasants.**

Even if one is not paying attention to what is being said, one hears one's name when spoken. Mediums and clairvoyants say our spiritual guides whisper in our ears to warn us of imminent danger.

It was Vladymir speaking.

"... Comrade Brodovskaya has not even manifested the least regret for this incident ..."

He stands at a lectern. Comrade Mekhlis and Moscow stand to each side of him. He is picking with the nail of his forefinger at a swollen pimple on his forehead.

Like a frightened schoolgirl, I raise an arm.

"... I ..."

Mekhlis shoots me a glance and it silences me instantly.

Vladymir continues. He is accusing me of bourgeois behaviour.

"... I ... please?"

My arm is above my head.

I did not, he was explaining, congratulate him or his wife on the birth of their child.

"It was the birth of a Soviet citizen. What do you have to say in defence of yourself?" asks Moscow.

I was not aware Vladymir's wife had given birth to a child. The only personal details I know about him is he has the most virulent acne.

"I do apologise. Of course, it was so ... so ... it was disgraceful the way I had not congratulated him and his wife ... I do so now. My heartiest congratulations Comrade Vladymir on this extraordinary achievement," I say.

I tried my best not to have sounded sarcastic.

"Thank you. Thank you, Comrade," gushes Vladymir.

The pimple is oozing puss. He dabs at the bloody liquid.

Moscow steps forward. He is sweating: beads of sweat cling to his upper lip.

"If you wish to remain at *Pravda*, Comrade Brodovskaya, your colleagues would expect you to mend your ways. I will grant you a month's probation during which you will have to prove you are worthy of remaining one of us. Each day Comrade Vladymir will report to me on your behaviour. It will be decided at the termination of this month of probation whether you are to be pardoned, demoted or dismissed."

My probation is to commence immediately.

I decide not to stay for the dancing.

"I don't feel like it," I say to one of my new colleagues.

"I'd force myself if I were you," he replies.

"Oh, I force myself. Most of the time I am forcing myself to do whatever I have to do here at *Pravda*," I tell him angrily.

I can see the venom in my tone surprises him.

Now, report me, you bastard, I whisper, walking away from him.

-0-

Two weeks pass.

Moscow calls me to his office. My probation period is over. They've shortened it to two weeks.

"I've made my decision," he says.

Vladymir, my probation officer, decided I was beyond saving.

"Can't I please have a second chance? Please?" I beg.

He shakes his head. Dandruff flakes fall onto the shoulders of his jacket.

"We will be accommodating, Comrade Brodovskaya," he says.

He does not fire me. He hands me a letter. I am authorised to leave *Pravda* on indeterminate leave in order to further my studies. He hands me a second letter. The letter is addressed to the comrade rector of Moscow University. He is recommending I be granted admission to the next study session of the Russian-French-Russian interpreter-translator course.

I do not walk from his office. I back out as if he is a tsar and I am his pathetic minion. In this country of mine to be without a job is classified as vagrancy and vagrancy is against the law and carries a prison sentence. He is therefore saving me from being locked up in a cell in the Lubyanka. He may even be saving my life. So, my heart sings, *Thank you. Thank you so very much, Comrade Moscow.*

I bid my colleagues, those whose names I know, goodbye. Their handshakes are limp, disinterested. Their eyes are blank. Turning blank eyes onto the world is one way of protecting ourselves. I hand Moscow's letter to the man it has been addressed to. I am told he will be in touch. Soon.

I do not tell my parents I have been dismissed from *Pravda*. I do tell Beretzkoy, the only person to whom I am unafraid of telling the truth.

"Who wants to work for *Pravda* anyway," he says.

"I do," I murmur.

I do not hear from the comrade rector of Moscow University.

It is Beretzkoy who comes to my rescue.

"I will teach you how to interpret and translate," he tells me.

I borrow Honoré de Balzac's *Le Père Goriot* from my father and I have my first lesson. Beretzkoy, fluent in English, French and German, tells me a writer or, for that matter, a public speaker is inclined to use the same words and phrases and, all I will have to do, will be to memorise such words and phrases.

-0-

A month has passed. I am working as interpreter and translator at the French Embassy. Beretzkoy put in a word on my behalf with the head of the embassy's cultural sector - I will call him Pierre – and now, after our Commissariat of Labour has granted its permission, I am officially a Russian-French-Russian interpreter and translator.

Nothing wrong with interpreting and translating. My father was one too after all and he is an honourable man.

-0-

CHAPTER EIGHT

There are six apartments, all communal ones, here on the fourth floor of Vasily's building.

The door of one of the apartments stands open most of every day, even on a winter day. One of the apartment's tenants - an old woman - says closed doors remind her of prison: she has done time, but as punishment for what, she does not say.

The old woman's name is Tatyana like mine and like the toddler from the tram shelter.

I am returning home from the French Embassy. Music, a doleful tune being played on a balalaika, drifts from the apartment where Tatyana lives. She stands just inside the door. She mouths something and points down the corridor towards the door of the apartment where I live. I look that way. Two broad-shouldered men lean against its door. They are not wearing long black leather overcoats, so they will not be Chekists, but who knows? Was I not fooled before on the day the Chekists had come for Vasily?

The two are chain-smoking and are standing in a circle of ash, pungent swirling smoke and cigarette ends. Obviously they have been waiting for some time.

"Who are you?" the taller of the two asks.

His face is red and his nose bulbous. He blows stale cigarette smoke into my face.

"My name is Tatyana Nikolayevna Brodovskaya and I live here."

"For the moment you do, Brodovskaya," the other replies.

They are bailiffs they tell me and the taller of the two hands me a letter.

"Read!" he barks.

The letter is from the Moscow Housing Committee. I am informed that the room in the communal apartment previously allotted to the detainee Vasily Sergeyevich Brodov has been re-allocated. The name of the new tenant is given. It is not mine.

"Come in," I say.

I show the two the ZAGS certificate Vasily and I signed which makes me his wife.

"I am therefore allowed to remain living here, Comrades."

They shake their heads in unison like marionettes in a *guignol*[34] show.

---

[34] **An amusing French puppet show, usually for children.**

"Kykla[35], your piece of paper changes nothing! You have two hours to get out or we throw you out. Which is it to be?" says the taller one, who appears to be senior in rank to his colleague.

He yanks the eviction letter from my hand and shoves it under my nose.

"Read it again, Kykla!" he snarls.

I do as I am told.

"Can I speak to someone - to have the eviction order cancelled?" I ask, looking from him to his colleague.

"If you don't move, Kykla, we throw you out. Simple as that!" says the taller one.

A head appears around the doorway. It is one of Vasily's neighbours.

"I can help you move? I have a wheelbarrow and a baby carriage and two strapping young sons. We'll get you out of here in no time," he says.

The walls of a Stalin marvel are paper-thin.

"I don't have any money to pay you," I tell the man.

"My sons sleep on the floor. We need a mattress."

I turn to look at the mattress on the bed behind me.

"Will it do? It's a spring mattress."

He rolls his eyes. I had just offered him a small treasure: in our country we sleep on mattresses made of sawdust and horse's mane. How Vasily had got hold of a spring mattress, I do not know.

"We need a stove too."

I point to Vasily's.

"Take this one. It's old but it works."

The neighbour whistles loudly through his fingers and two lads come running pushing a wheelbarrow and a baby carriage.

At midnight I am knocking on my parents' door. They, like Dan and Yelena, are among the rare privileged to have an apartment all to themselves.

My father, in pyjamas, opens the door. He is shivering. Is he cold or is he scared? Midnight is the Chekists' favourite hour for visiting. *Get a man when he's half-asleep and he will confess to anything.* The first rule in the Chekists' handbook.

I throw myself into his arms.

"*Merde*, Tanoshka, *qu'est qui se passe?*"

When my father is taken by surprise he speaks French.

My belongings lie scattered on the floor behind me: Vasily's neighbour and his two sons fled with the wheelbarrow and the baby carriage. I have left most of Vasily's belongings behind in the apartment and they probably want to get to those before someone else does.

My mother appears behind my father. She, too, is shivering. She is wearing a thin nightdress, but this is not the reason she is shaking. Her eyes reveal fear.

I start to cry.

---

[35] **Doll in Russian.**

This is the night I will have to tell my parents what I have been up to since December 1931.

Tell them I was dismissed from *Pravda*.

Tell them about my new job.

Tell them about Beretzkoy.

-0-

"Mamoskha ... Papa ... I ... Beretzkoy ... I ..."

How to tell them?

My mother is making tea. My father leans against the kitchen door. He has thrown a jacket over his shoulders. My mother is also wearing a jacket over her nightdress.

"The poet ...," I begin. "The one I've always ... admired. I met him. And now I know him rather well. We have become friends. Are friends. I was sacked from *Pravda* and I didn't know how to tell you. But I am now with the French Embassy. Father, I'm working as an interpreter and translator. I like the work. I think I was dismissed, because of Beretzkoy."

My mother's glasses are lying on the table. She picks them up gently and puts them on as if she needs to see me more clearly.

"Because of the poet Beretzkoy?" she asks. "What has he got to do with you?"

"He's the poet. The one I mentioned. We are together. Him and me. *I love him.* We are in love. Lovers."

My voice cracks and falls away.

"*Mais merde alors!*" exclaims my father.

He was sitting at the kitchen table, but now he is on his feet.

Steam rises from the samovar. My parents have had this samovar as long as I can remember. A Russian's samovar is like a family member: we sit down and weep when ours start to leak and we know its life has ended, and we never throw it away, no, we store buttons or pencils in it.

"I'm so sorry I'm telling you about Beretzkoy only now," I manage to say.

"At least you are doing so ... now," says my father.

He again sits down at the kitchen table.

I decide I must tell them everything.

I tell them about the day Beretzkoy came to *Pravda* and I tell them what he told me about his marriage and he would, most probably, never be free to marry me, but I love him all the same and I will never stop loving him.

"I am so sorry. I must be such a disappointment to you. I never meant for this to happen ... never ..."

I stop. They had listened without interrupting me.

"We better get to meet him," says my mother slowly but determinately.

"I see him only on Thursdays," I say.

"*Mon Dieu!*" says my father. "She sees him only on Thursdays! Does he make an appointment with you, or what?"

He looks as if he is going to vomit and I feel a whore.

-0-

I wait for Beretzkoy outside Vasily's building. It is Thursday again now and because I am not allowed to telephone him, he does not know I have been evicted. We leave for my parents' apartment immediately. My mother opens to our knock. My father, hearing our voices, steps from the bedroom.

"I felt I should come over immediately," says Beretzkoy.

"No," says my mother, stepping aside for us to enter, "you should have come over a long time ago."

We go to the kitchen. My mother fills the samovar. She rips open our biscuit tin. Biscuits scatter to the floor. They crumble.

"Tatyana, help your mother pick those up!" orders my father.

Tatyana and not Tanoshka. I can see it is going to be a morning of frank talk. Of angry talk.

My mother pours the tea. It splashes around the glasses, unsettlingly.

"Tanya is still so young. How could you, an older man and one who should know better, have allowed this child to fall in love with you?"

It was my father speaking. He is trembling and it hurts deep inside my chest to see him like this - so upset.

"How could I not have allowed it? I love her too?" Beretzkoy replies.

"No matter! You should have known better. You should not have done this to her."

"But I did. And what is more, I cannot say I regret I have done so."

"*Mon Dieu* man, you should have known better!" shouts my father, spittle flying from his lips.

"We do not always do what we should," Beretzkoy replies calmly like a man admitting he had done wrong.

My mother runs from the kitchen. She is silently crying. I follow her, but I do not run, I walk. My mother is sitting on the sofa in the living room. I stand facing her. We listen to my father's attack and Beretzkoy's defence. My mother is still silent: eyes wide and sad. She has stopped crying.

"No harm should come to Tanya." says my father firmly.

Again not Tanoshka.

"I will not harm her. I love her, Nikolai Nikolayevich."

"You have to know we will intervene should we think your relationship is becoming dangerous."

"You have my permission to do so. I give you my permission to do so."

Beretzkoy promises my father they will never have reason to intervene.

The two join us in the living room.

My mother hugs my father.

Begrudgingly, resignedly, my parents seem to have accepted a set of

64

circumstances they are entirely unable to change.

"Thank you," I say to them.

-0-

CHAPTER NINE

"I want to ask you to move to the village. I want you to come and live in Zernoye Selo. I want you near me, Tanya," says Beretzkoy.

For two months I have been living with my parents and, now, Beretzkoy has found me a place in his village. It is a small *dacha* and it is not in great condition but it is vacant and it belongs to Profpro which means I, as a member, am entitled to it. There are a few advantages to being a Profpro member. We have access to Kremlin Hospital, we can undergo health cures at our union's sanatoriums and we can holiday at any of its many guest houses. Living in a *dacha* in Zernoye Selo is another perk, and a considerable honour. A member can either buy a *dacha* with an interest-free loan from the State, thus owing the *dacha* but not the land it stands on[36], or rent one. Beretzkoy bought his. I will rent mine.

"I will pay the rent," he says.

"No," I say. "If there is a sobriquet I do not want, it is that of kept woman."

He shakes his head.

"You will not be a kept woman."

Gozuzdom has commissioned him to compile an encyclopaedia of Russian literature and he is allowed an editorial assistant. I will be the assistant.

-0-

My parents do not want me to move to Zernoye Selo. Their liberalism does not stretch to the point they will allow their daughter to live in a *state of indecency* with a man.

Dan and Yelena tell me I should not listen to my parents.

"But we are never alone," Beretzkoy complains to me.

"I am sorry, but I can't very well ask my parents to go for a walk so that you and I can - you know," I reply, unable to keep the flush from rising to my pale skin.

He puts a key in my hand.

"Which door will this unlock?" I ask.

"The apartment of someone I know."

"Who is he?"

---

[36] **Land in the Soviet Union belonged to the collective proletariat, in other words to the people.**

"She," he says.

It is the apartment of Galina Mikhailovna Usipovskaya. I know her. Or rather I know about her. She is an actress and a playwright. Once she and Beretzkoy were lovers.

"I don't want to go to there," I say quickly.

She is not in Moscow and she said we could use her apartment if we need a place. Why does this sound so disgusting I ask myself: *if we need a place.* A place? A place for what? To do what?

The apartment is not in a *Stalin marvel,* but in a tsarist-era building. The façade is of intricate brickwork, the lobby of green marble and an elevator takes us up to the apartment. We call an elevator, this rare thing, a *bourgeois accoutrement,* and this is my first ride in one. Its walls are covered with brown velvet and the ceiling is a mirror. The mirror turns us into dwarfs. The apartment is in black and white. Its walls are covered in shiny white brocade. The sofa and armchairs in the room are black. The carpet is black and white. The place looks like a giant chessboard. In the bedroom the colours are reversed: the walls are black and the carpet is white. The eiderdown on the bed is white also. The sheets are black. I have never seen black sheets. I do not even know such things exist.

"Silk," explains Beretzkoy.

"How do you know?"

"We are not going to have an argument are we?" he asks.

I take the eiderdown off the bed. The sheets are slippery and cold like ice. When I lift the top sheet in order to lie down, the sheet glides from my hands to the floor. We do not retrieve it.

-0-

Now, afterwards, I explore the apartment with Beretzkoy walking behind me as if he has never been here before.

The walls of the short, narrow passage which leads from the living room to the kitchen are covered in black-framed charcoal sketches. There is one of Anna Pavlovna as the *Sugar Plum Fairy* in Tchaikovsky's *Nutcracker,* another of Vaslav Nijinski in *Giselle* and another of Mathilda Kschessinskaya, once Nicholas II's lover, in Fokine's *The Dying Swan.* All of the many others show Galina. Galina in white fur coat and *shapka* as Anna Karenina; Galina in frock coat, men's boots and braided tri-cornered hat as Catherine the Great; Galina in nightdress as the consumptive *Dame aux Camelias;* Galina in a wedding dress as Natasha and Pierre Bezukhov's bride in Tolstoy's *War and Peace,* and Galina covered in jewels and her nose in the air as Russia's last tsarina – Alexandra - in a play which, as Beretzkoy tells me over my shoulder, Galina wrote herself.

Suddenly, there is a loud knock on the apartment's door.

I look at Beretzkoy. He smiles.

The door opens slowly.

"Anyone here?" a voice calls out.

Galina stands in the doorway. She is beautiful. She is what my father calls *petite:* small-boned, fine featured. She is dressed in red: dress and shoes. Her hair, nails and lips are red also.

"Tanya?" she asks, ignoring Beretzkoy.

"I am so sorry. I ... no, we ... we are in your home."

I am embarrassed.

"Oh quiet with you!" she snaps, playfully.

She throws her head back and gives a raucous laugh.

"I did ... well ... I did not want to come," I stammer.

"I know what you are thinking, but don't blame him. Letting you have my apartment was my idea," she tells me.

"I'll go make the bed," I mumble.

She motions for me to stay where I am.

"So you are the one he has been hiding from us all this time. Well. Well. I say! The old goat!"

Her voice is like that of a teenage boy: deeper than a woman's, but not as deep as a man's.

Beretzkoy hugs her and she plants a kiss on his chin which leaves behind the rouged outline of her lips and which she wipes away for him with the back of her tiny, very white hand.

The front door opens yet again and a young man, oiled black hair combed over his face to hide a premature widow's peak, walks in.

"Grishka. My major-domo," explains Galina.

The major-domo is smiling.

"If it suits you my lovely one, then, I will be the major-domo."

Galina ignores him and points at Beretzkoy.

"Tanya, I suppose you know this man was once close to me?"

"Yes."

"Now listen. I know you are going to hear I am still in love with him. You are going to be told I am forever going on about how much I love him. Yes, I adore this man, but this is what I want you to know. To me, to Galina Mikhailovna, love is carnal, whereas adoration, is congeniality of spirit, and this is how it is between us today. I adore him. Understand?"

I nod.

"Now, we can become friends. Good friends!" she says.

She is in a play, Victor Hugo's *Notre-Dame de Paris*. She is *Esmerelda*. She hands me a complimentary ticket.

"Now, do make sure you come over. You will love the play!"

I only smile.

-0-

I decide I will go to the play. I will go alone. I clutch the ticket in my hand nervously, feeling the dampness of my palms penetrate its surface, smudging its printed lettering. I sit in the darkness in awe of this unfamiliar and strange place: our life - my parents and mine - has been one without refinement; it has been a life of struggle, of revolution.

Galina spots me in the audience and greets me with a discreet motion of her right hand. During interval Grishka brings me a note. It is from Galina. I am invited to come to her dressing room at the end of the play.

The final curtain descends and Grishka comes to fetch me and he takes me by the elbow and guides me past old ladies standing at a large table ironing costumes, oblivious to the young men with naked sweating torsos who are dismantling stage props around them. In Galina's dressing-room he uncorks a bottle of *Moët et Chandon*, and Galina sweeps in just as he starts to fill two crystal flutes.

"Tanya! Oh, I am glad you came. Liked the play? Say, Grishka, where are the reinforcements?"

Grischka is growing a moustache but it is still in the stubbly stage where it only looks as if he has not shaved for a few days: growing beards has become fashionable because our great socialist utopia has run out of blades and razors.

Galina collapses on a red velvet sofa and Grishka helps her to take off her shoes. He kisses her naked feet, licks their pearl-white skin, slips one of her big toes into his mouth and sucks it.

"Galina, Beretzkoy has asked me to move to Zernoye Selo," I say quickly.

"Ah-ha!" she laughs. "And what are you still doing here?"

"What if he stops loving me?"

Grishka has begun to wipe make-up from Galina's face with a wet cloth. She pushes his hands away.

"Oh, later Grishkin my darling! Do you not want me to remain beautiful?"

She turns to me.

"My dear Tanya, nothing lasts. Everything ends. But who in our dark days speaks of always when speaking of love? What a child you still are! My dear little dove, love is for the here and the now. Yes, it can end: wham! Yes it ends. Wham! Yes, it hurts: boohoo you sob. You think you're going to die. You wonder who will come to your funeral. You wonder whether you should leave that old so-and-so witch your purple cloak. Yes, then you die! But alas, you are born again. And yes, oh yes, love ends. Another pair of eyes is prettier than yours or another pair of arms will hold him tighter than yours. Another pair of tits is bigger, rounder, softer ..."

Grishka coughs.

"Stop my sweetheart!" he groans. "You're not Anna Karenina!"

She throws one of her shoes at him.

I watch them: they do not look like two people so in love with one another they would die without the other, yet they look so happy. And there, a moment ago, I was going on about love having to be forever. I was behaving like a silly teenage girl with no perspective.

-0-

April 2001: Moscow (Gerald Lombard/Biographer)

After Tanya had agreed to speak to me, I sent an e-mail from Moscow to my editor in London. I wrote: *She'll talk. I can't believe my good fortune."* Can she be trusted?" he asked me later over a beer in a pub in Covent Garden. "I believe she can," I told him. "Remember, we want the dirt on her," he said.

A typical tabloid prerequisite.

-0-

She is no longer alive. *I've got cancer,* she wrote me after her diagnosis. *I don't mind dying. I don't mind the nothingness that awaits me. I would like to be around when your book is published but I fear it is unlikely. The doctors have given me four months. Apparently, I've been ill for some time. It was nice talking to you. It was nice talking about him. For a while I felt he was here again …*

-0-

And so I continue my investigations and research.

I hear in the beginning there was the pretty girl with the round face framed with ash-white curls and the blue-green eyes whose name was Tanya. I hear there was Yelena whose eyes cried even when she smiled. I hear there was Galina, always vivacious: *une femme comme il faut.* I hear there was Dan who was the love of Yelena's life and I hear of Beretzkoy whom Galina had once loved and who was the love of Tanya's life. And I hear of Nadezdha Konstantinovna whom Beretzkoy had once loved and of how the love had died but he could not let her go all the same. I hear of the others. Her friends. Neighbours. Her parents.

I hear the story.

The story began in the spring of 1932 when what was supposed to have been a secret was not a secret.

The secret which was not a secret was the poet Boris Petrovich Beretzkoy, who lived on Lena Street in the village of Zernoye Selo with his wife Nadezhda Konstantinovna and their two blond-haired boys who flushed with pride when they wore the triangular red neckties of the Pioneers, was going to bring another woman to the village. The woman was going to move into the vacant *dacha* on Ob Street. The villagers wondered whether his wife knew about this woman. Some said of course she knew. Other said no, she could not have known or she would have stopped the affair.

71

I am told, Nadezdha Konstantinova met Beretzkoy in Moscow. In central Moscow there was a theatre, it was small and could seat only forty people. Some nights she sat on its stage behind an old piano and sang folk songs. Her voice was not great, but because she was the wife of one of Russia's favourite choreographers her name filled the theatre. One night, walking from the stage, her voice hoarse from trying to reach the higher notes, Beretzkoy put a hand on her arm, *I've heard nightingales sing but I've never heard a human being sing like a nightingale,* he told her. There and then she fell out of love with the choreographer and in love with the poet. Over a glass of tea in a tavern he told her he was married but the marriage was over: *she met someone else and I met someone else and it was no good continuing.* Loving him already at that moment she did not ask him where that someone else was. His dark eyes told her he no longer cared to know where that someone else was and therefore neither should she.

For a month he picked her up at the small theatre every night, then, she told him, *I cannot live a lie.* She had decided to tell the choreographer she had fallen in love with someone else. The choreographer threw her out, but first, he hit her in the face and pulled her to the ground by her long blonde hair and told her he never wanted to set eyes on her again. He called her a whore. Her clothes were strewn across the pavement and the street.

Freed from their respective marriages, the poet and Nadezdha went to ZAGS.

Nadezdha bore two sons.

The first, Paul, was born within a few days of the ninth month of their marriage and not long afterwards the second, Grigory, was conceived but there was little delight in the knowledge there would be another mouth to feed. The First Great Famine was raging. People were eating the meat off the carcasses of horses which had died of a mysterious disease, so it was certainly not a time to bring another human being into the world. *We will pull through: I'll get us through,* he said, while he doubted he would be able to do so. Food, the people screamed for, not poetry. So there was no income in what he was doing. She could not help out either: the door of the small theatre in central Moscow had been closed to her from the day the choreographer had thrown her out. *Nobody would want to listen to an adulterous slut sing,* the theatre director had said to her. What her new husband said to her on learning she was again expecting a child was *Please terminate the pregnancy ... we can try again when the famine has ended.* She had refused. *This child has been conceived in love and it will be born and raised with love,* was what she told him. *See,* he said, *it is still only an 'it' to you, so terminate the pregnancy.* Never again would she allow him to touch her. *Not now, not now* she told him, turning from him, always. He rapidly found others to give him what she no longer would. This was obvious to her. The lightness of his step, the sheen of his skin, the assuagement in his eyes, but also the guilt when he asked her whether there was anything he could do for her on walking in from having spent a night away from home, told her. Only the names of those women - his whores - she did not know, and did not want to know.

The name of the woman from *Pravda* who came to live in the *dacha* on Ob Street she did however learn. *I need an assistant for the encyclopaedia project* was what he told her.

Ob Street was a stone's throw from Lena Street: no more than a five-minute walk.

On a clear day one could even see the *dachas* of Ob Street from the *dachas* of Lena Street.

-0-

PART TWO

CHAPTER ONE

It is June. Summer.

I am on the Moscow-Kiev train. I am on my way to Zernoye Selo. My mother is with me.

"We must show your neighbours you are part of a family," she says.

She straightens her straw hat.

My mother and I sit facing each other. We are in a *zhestky*[37] carriage. The bunks are hard: *zhestky* is hard-bunk class. Beretzkoy wanted us to go *miagky*: soft-bunk class. Why waste the money I told him.

An old man sits beside my mother. He coughs into a stained cloth. Tuberculosis is rife in our country. A woman in a dirty frock with a baby on her lap sits beside me. The baby smells dreadful. My mother tries to draw the woman's attention to her child's nappy-cloth, but the woman continues to stare out the window. What is there to see? Certainly, no beauty. Stalin's henchmen have been this way before us, collectivising the land. All there is for the eye are dry, unploughed, abandoned land, uprooted trees, cattle carcasses bleached white in the sun and deserted *izbas*, their roofs ripped off by the wind, thistle growing from the holes in the walls where there had once been windows and doors. Those who lived in the *dachas* - our Kulaks - are in prison or in forced-labour camps. Those are the lucky Kulaks; the unlucky ones are dead. Or are they perhaps the lucky ones?

We pull into Zernoye Selo's station. It is noon. People come running. Some will board the train and head for Kiev hoping for a better life there. Others carry bags and boxes: they have come to sell produce from their little private gardens: potatoes, fresh red earth still clinging to them; bunches of leeks, carrots and onions; a few wrinkled and over-ripe apricots.

The station's waiting-room has the pungent odour of dirty bodies: half a dozen people sit half-asleep on a bunk. A pool of yellow liquid soils the floor and guessing instantly what the liquid is, we tip-toe around it to avoid soiling our boots.

My mother is always drawing comparisons between what Lenin promised us and what Stalin is giving us, and I feel I need to explain something to her.

"The station looks bad but it is to be pulled down and will be reconstructed soon, so don't think it will always be like this, because I can tell you, it won't."

"Yes, give Stalin time and he will demolish the entire country," she replies.

---

[37] **The equivalent of First and Second Class rail travel.**

Beretzkoy is in Leningrad for a literary conference, but I have the *dacha's* keys. We, my mother and I, are going to walk to it. Beretzkoy has drawn a map for us indicating the shortest route.

A man with a horse-drawn buggy tries to talk us into allowing him to take us to our destination. He wants ten kopeks: a fortune.

"We have a map," says my mother, unsmilingly.

Beretzkoy pinned a note to his map. *My love, I hope you will never say you should not have walked this walk.*

The village has two principal streets: Pushkin and Constitution. Pushkin runs north and south; Constitution, west and east. The two, neither of them long or wide, or paved, form a crucifix.

We pass haphazard clusters of timber and stone buildings. We are each carrying two heavy suitcases, and with the sun right overhead, it is becoming increasingly hot.

The two streets cross on Marx Square. The obligatory statue of Lenin adorns a large plinth in the centre of the square. Our late leader is chiselled into a block of sandstone. He wears a cloth cap and holds a scythe in his right hand. His left points upwards; so it does on all statues of him. He looks stern; so he always does on all his statues.

Bars protect the windows of a building facing us from across the square. Bars? OGPU headquarters without doubt. A Hammer and Sickle flutters from one of the windows. Yes, without doubt, OGPU headquarters.

We pass a tavern hearing merry voices and laughter drifting from within. Red Banner Tavern is the name. It is a dilapidated two-storey building within a garden of tangling shrubs and withered trees. The top floor is a bathhouse and sauna: windowpanes have been painted over and from one of the windows protrudes a metal pipe. It is spewing stinking black smoke.

The streets now all bear the names of rivers. It is here in this part of the village where Profpro's members live. The rivers are all Russian: Angara, Amur, Dnieper, Don, Lena, Ob and Volga. My *dacha* on Ob is at the most western end of the street. It is numbered, One. We approach it from the eastern end. The *dachas* now look alike: half-timbered cottages with slated roofs the colour of sunburnt orange-peel. Mine is partially hidden behind a wall of ill-matched poles and planks. The gate can lock and it is locked. I retrieve the key from underneath a stone by the flaking gatepost.

"Oh, you ought to be secure here," says my mother, her voice tinted with cynicism.

She points at the walls and instantly a dog starts to bark from an overgrown garden next door.

"Ah! Even more security!"

There is a wasteland beyond my *dacha:* more thistles growing wild. A wind sweeps up and rattles some pieces of scrap iron lying about.

Number One Ob Street is small. Its smallness strikes me the moment I unlock the front door. It consists of only two rooms - no, three rooms - a living room, bedroom and kitchen, which here in Russia counts as a room, because it is in our kitchens where we do most of our living. We not only cook our food in the kitchen, but it is also where we eat it and where we receive our friends and where, in the winter, we sleep to benefit from the heat of the stove. Two short narrow passages connect the three rooms and one of the passages continues to give on to a glazed veranda. Beretzkoy has already told me the veranda will be his study.

My mother wants to know where the bathroom is. It is out in the back garden, ten paces from the back door. Brown water spurts from a rusted wall-mounted tap onto stained tiles in front of a rickety door. The door opens into a latrine. My poor mother pulls back and quickly covers her nose and mouth with both hands. The latrine is a wooden commode into which a large bucket has been fitted.

"Archaic!" she shrieks.

I think she is going to start vomiting. If not, it seems certain she will cry.

Stone steps lead from beside the back door up along the *dacha's* façade to a loft. Mother does not want me to go and see what is in there but I tell her not to be silly. This is going to be my home and it is better to know all about the place before it is too late to return with her to Moscow. The loft, ominously dank and distinctly shabby, stands empty.

Beretzkoy has furnished the *dacha* for me. Or rather, he has bought a few items of furniture locally.

"Meagre and tasteless," states my mother.

In the living room stand a red velvet sofa, two matching armchairs and an oblong glass coffee table with metal legs. In the veranda stand a desk and two upright wicker chairs. The bed in the bedroom is a double and has seen better days. Around the kitchen table stand eight chairs: *I will have to make friends fast!* The wood-burning stove is new: it is still partly wrapped in newsprint.

Workers today are …

It is Pravda.

I do not read on.

A cupboard is filled with homemade preserves in glass jars with screw tops: herring, sardines, gherkins, onions, tomatoes, cucumbers. A bottle of vodka and two bottles of wine stand on the table. A letter lies on the table too.

My dearest Tanya, when something is important it should not only be said but it should also be written. I love you. Please stay here with me always.

I show it to my mother, hoping these sentiments will weaken her stance of opposition.

"Nice of him," she concedes, shrugging her shoulders." But, then, Tanya, he is a poet and words come easily to poets."

We start cleaning up. Cockroaches scuttle from the kitchen cupboard. We argue over what to do about it. We hear the distinct scratching and scraping of rats in the loft. We ignore the missing floorboards, cracked walls and peeling paintwork around us and we hang curtains we have brought from Moscow. By happy coincidence they are red – the only colour we could find - and match the sofa. In the garden we pull out weeds and collect the dead leaves into great mounds. I climb up the gnarled branches of a pear tree and start pruning it.

"I hope you know what you're doing," calls my mother from down below.

"Don't have the faintest idea!" I call back.

"I thought as much," she says.

I see a weak smile linger on her lips.

"Now, we will show your neighbours you have a mother," she says when there is nothing left to clean.

She bakes a cake, a *vatrushka*[38], for each of my neighbours, and I walk to Constitution Street and I buy several bunches of wild sweet peas to offer them as well. Beretzkoy told me at Numbers Five and Six live the respective widows of an engineer and a physicist. At Numbers Three and Two live two retired schoolteachers and their wives. Because the two retired schoolteachers had written school text books they are members of Profpro and the late husbands of the two widows wrote industrial manuals and had therefore also been members of our union. No one lives at Number Four. The poet who lived there hanged himself.

We start our visit to my neighbours with the widow Natalya Petrovna Primakovskaya. Grey curls frame her wrinkled face. She pours tea and plunges a knife into the cake we have just offered her.

"No! No! It's for you!" cries my mother.

"You're telling me you're a Jew?" she asks, astonished.

I manage to stifle a little laugh at this random remark and notice my mother has too.

"No," I reply as loudly as I can without shouting. "the cake's for you. *For you.*"

"Oh, I'm sorry," she says "I'm a little deaf."

Alexandra Mikhailovna Nininskaya, the widow from Number Six, is buxom and her hair is the colour of a peach.

"You're from Moscow? I know Stalin well," she says.

"So do I - know Stalin well," replies my mother.

A quivering smile plays on the Widow Alexandra's lips.

"Oh well," she murmurs.

She puts the cake we hand her in a tin.

"I know you wouldn't want some of this now," she says.

Retired schoolteacher Ivan Ivanovich Gromyko and his wife Anna Davidovna live at Number Three. Ivan's eyes squint a little. He opens them wide when he listens to us as if he is questioning the verity of what we are saying. Anna wears heavy-rimmed glasses with thick lenses. Each time she speaks she pokes the bridge of the frame further up her long nose.

---

[38] **A Russian cheese cake.**

The Kravchinskys - Leonid Mikailovich and Alisa Fiodorovna - live at Number Two, the *dacha* next door. The barking dog is theirs. Leonid is wearing grey flannels and a grey cardigan. He has a paunch which the cardigan fails to cover. Alisa is a round person. She has a small, round body, and small round blue eyes above small round ruddy cheeks.

"Come and visit me whenever you feel like it," I tell her.

I have said the same to the others.

-0-

I walk my mother to the station. She has been with me for five days and now she is going back to Moscow where my father is waiting.

"Tanya, if it doesn't go right here, you come back home. I know you are determined this will work. Determination is not though always all that is needed," she tells me.

Alone, I carry one of the kitchen chairs into my front garden. It is almost dark. I climb onto the chair. I want to see what the village looks like after dark. Are any lights on anywhere? I see some *dachas*, but only their tiled roofs and smoking chimneys. Recalling the map Beretzkoy drew for me I realise the *dachas* must be on Lena Street.

No one told me one can see Lena from Ob.

-0-

CHAPTER TWO

A man of a certain age in white shorts and white *rybashka* tied at his waist with a red satin sash stands in the street outside my *dacha*. He has been banging on the gate to draw my attention.

"Kolya. Nikolai Nikolayevich Rozanov," he introduces himself.

He lifts his straw hat. The hat is tied under his chin with a white ribbon. He is wearing Greek sandals. His heels are cracked and the cracks are filled with what looks like paint - red, blue, yellow, orange paint.

"I paint. I am an artist," he explains. He must have seen I was looking at his feet.

Beretzkoy told me about Kolya. So have Dan, Yelena and Galina, and I therefore know he is a member of Profpro and his *dacha* is beside that of the Beretzkoys'.

He has brought me a bouquet of startling beautiful sunflowers. They are made of paper.

"For you. I only wish they are real but real ones will die. These will last forever," he tells me.

He hails from Leningrad - St Petersburg as it was at the time of his birth - and spent six years in the Peter-and-Paul Fortress accused of plotting to assassinate Tsar Aleksander II. His co-accused was Aleksander Ilyich Ulyanov, Lenin's brother.

We move through the *dacha* into my tiny kitchen.

I offer Kolya tea. He asks whether I will mind very much if he tells me he prefers coffee.

"So does my father, and I must admit I also like a strong black coffee ever so often," I confess.

"To paint is to engrave the mind. That's how I started to paint. I used to be a butcher, then in Peter-and-Paul I told myself should I ever leave the place I will paint, I will paint every beautiful thing I see, I will engrave my mind with their beauty so I will never be deprived of beauty again," he tells me.

"Is it not rather the soul one engraves?" I ask him.

"Soul?" He laughs with more than a hint of cynicism. "A Russian does not have a soul! We have minds. And I am quoting Stalin. He said, 'We have no souls and no hearts. We have minds. And he who has a mind does not need a soul or heart.'"

He invites me to his *dacha*.

"You live beside the Beretzkoys, so I cannot come to your place."

"Come after nightfall and walk from the north. It will be a bit of a roundabout way, but you won't have to pass Number Fourteen."

"Number Fourteen?" I query.

"The Beretzkoy *dacha*."

-0-

I go to Kolya's place.

It is not a *dacha* but an *izba*. He tells me the *izba* was once Number Fourteen's garden shed. Thus, each spring small green shoots appear between its log-pile walls.

"I used to cut the shoots away, but one year I missed one and it grew into a passionflower," he tells me.

He has cooked *kasha*[39] for us. He has a bottle of white wine. He struggles to uncork it. He does so by pushing the cork into the bottle with one of his thick thumbs. The wine is not chilled. He fills two glasses.

"When the passionflower was in full bloom I painted it," he continues with his story.

"May I see the painting?"

"A rat ate it. Then, my cat ate the rat, and the cat died. I was surprised. I would not have believed I was that bad an artist."

"Allow me to judge," I ask him.

The walls of his d*acha* are bare.

"Where are the paintings?" I ask.

"Stalin obliges me to hide them."

Enthusiastically, he pulls a portmanteau from underneath his bed. The canvases are rolled up and tied with string and neatly stacked in the portmanteau. Slowly, pensively, he straightens each canvas, lays it down on the bed. He places small glass jars on each corner of a canvas to prevent it from rolling up again.

I look down on to the bed and I am transported into a summer afternoon, to a winter morning, to a field in which a child is playing with a red ball, to a bed on which lies an old woman. She is crying.

He takes a small framed painting from his wardrobe. It is of a young girl in a sleeveless lilac dress. She stands barefoot in a field of white and yellow spring daisies. He holds the painting out to me.

"It's beautiful," I say.

"She was beautiful, yes."

Quickly, he grabs the painting, puts it back in the wardrobe, and bangs the door.

-0-

---

[39] **Porridge.**

Leaving, I stand for a moment in Kolya's small, tangled garden. Which way shall I walk to return to my *dacha*? Walk north as I had come? Walk south and pass the Beretzkoy *dacha*?

I walk south.

The Beretzkoys' *dacha* is a big place of two brown timbered storeys. There is a white-framed bay window on the left side on each floor, the white-painted roof slanting to the ground on the house's right side. A few steps lead up to the front door, painted brown and tucked under the slanting roof. A lamp shaded by an oval glass shade hangs above the door, and beside and behind the house tall fir trees grow, their branches rigid, like sentinels, in the airless night.

I turn my eyes away and I cut across the wasteland to get home.

According to the Widow Alexandra the wasteland is haunted. She says a coffin falls from one of the trees on full moon nights.

The moon is full this night, but I see no coffin, no phantom, no ghost.

All that haunts me this night is how serene Number Fourteen Lena Street looks.

What right do I have to upset its serenity?

-0-

CHAPTER THREE

This is the day Beretzkoy will come over to Ob Street for the first time.

I am up early.

I straighten family photographs my mother and I hung over the cracks in the living room walls. I have bought cushions and these I move from one end of the sofa to another not sure where they look best. I swipe mosquito blood from the mirror in the bedroom: rain the night before drew large brown mosquitoes from their hiding places and I have been squashing them with a fly swatter.

Beretzkoy knocks on the gate.

"Who says welcome to whom?" he asks.

The Kravschinskys' dog starts to bark.

Concealed within my modest *dacha* Beretzkoy pulls me into his arms and I feel myself crumble with love for him.

Our life on this street, named for a river, in the village named for corn, begins as married life ought to and I am overwhelmed.

-0-

We agree we have to speak of money. My mother will say this is how married life begins and not the way we have just willingly surrendered to a moment ago in the bedroom.

We are going to be poor. We are going to struggle to keep the wolf from the door. I fetch what money I have. What I have are in notes and coins and I keep these in a tin, the tin in which Vasily kept his pencils and which I retrieved from the wastepaper basket because Vera Shits one day threw it away.

I lay the notes and the coins out on the kitchen table in a circle. The circle is small.

Beretzkoy tells me what he has and what his contribution can be towards the upkeep of Number One Ob Street.

"My circle will be hardly bigger than yours, Tanya."

"You are not responsible for me," I tell him.

"Oh, I am. I've brought you here to the village because I love you and because I love you I want to be responsible for you. I want to look after you."

"You *are* looking after me. Sitting here with me is looking after me. Loving me is looking after me."

He again draws me to him and he holds me so tightly I can barely pull in a breath.

The day comes to an end far too quickly.

"Walk with me to the gate," he says.

I do not step out on to the street.

"Editorial assistants do not see their bosses off at the end of the working day," I tell him.

Both of us burst into laughter.

-0-

March 2002 : Moscow (Gerald Lombard/Biographer)

From those I speak to I hear there was not much to Zernoye Selo. Not a street was paved and only the village's two principal streets - Pushkin and Constitution - were lit at night and only dimly as if someone was holding a public wake for a dead Soviet hero.

Constitution cut through Pushkin - or I suppose you can say Pushkin cut through Constitution - and the two streets formed a crucifix. The village's shops, not one of them grander than a shack, and with dusty window panes behind which lay cracked empty bottles, dented empty cans and fly-blown empty boxes, were on those two streets. In the shops, in rocking chairs, the shopkeepers sat snoring. They did not care to be awakened. *Can't you see, Comrade, the shelves are bare, so why do you come and disturb my rest?*

The shelves were bare, yes. It was the time of collectivisation and the Second Great Famine had begun. It was then that *the girl from Pravda* went to live in the village of Zernoye Selo.

I hear only three of the village's buildings looked as if they could withstand a storm. One was on Marx Square. It was a three-storey oblong building of grey stone: OGPU headquarters. The second was a dental clinic which Stalin had ordered built back in 1927, and the third was the House of Endeavour, a guest house belonging to Profpro and where its members were allowed to holiday.

The clinic was a two-storey timbered building on Land Development Street. It was painted dark blue and it stood within a rock garden that gleamed in the snow. There was a sundial in the garden and two benches stood nearby. *Tolko Patsienty* read a sign tied to one of the benches. *Patients Only*. One such patient was Stalin because he no longer allowed Kremlin Hospital's dentists to treat him, claiming they were no good.

The House of Endeavour was also a timbered building. It stood on Freedom of Speech Street and its patio overlooked the street. A bronze bust of Stalin stood on the patio. *Lenin gets the square, but Stalin only made it to the patio*, they tell me.

Unlike Lenin on his statue, Stalin on his, smiled. The smile curled his moustache upwards, making his eyes crease up into angled slits. He looked like a kind man. Little children, when they passed the patio, called him grandpa and their grandmothers used to ask: *Who needs God when we've got Stalin?*

In the north-west of the village was Moscow Street, so named because it was the road to Moscow. There stood the jail and the mortuary. "It is not a coincidence they are beside one another," I am told.

In front of the mortuary grew a poplar tree. Into the trunk had been carved the words, *Dorogoy Yvan, do skoroy vstryechee.*[40] Who this Yvan was, no one can tell me.

There was a dispensary in the village but not a hospital. The dispensary was behind the mortuary and to reach it one had to walk up a lane which ran between the jail and the mortuary. The dispensary used to be the school building, but the Commissariat of Education had opened a school on the *kolkhoz* outside the village. The mothers had not liked the new school because it was far for the little ones to walk. They also had not liked the fact the school was in what were, in tsarist days, the village's church: would bad spirits not linger there? The *kolkhoz's* chairman had ordered the church's onion dome to be pulled down. It had been quite a palaver. The villagers could not get the dome down so the chairman had to write to the Kremlin to ask what he was to do. Someone in the Kremlin had promised to send a technician down who would know just how to make the dome crumble and tumble, but the man had failed to turn up. The villagers had to find a way to pull it down themselves. Using rope and standing on ladders, they had succeeded in getting half of it down; the other half would however not budge. "It was as if God had said this far and no further," they tell me. Eventually, storks had made a nest in the half which had stayed up. The other half was turned into a paddling pool for the children. Each year as soon as the warmer weather arrived, the women filled it with water. One of the children who learnt to swim in the pool later represented the Soviet Union in the Olympics. He won a bronze. *Pravda* wrote about him, said he had grown up on the *kolkhoz,* Corn State Farm Number 24 – CSFN24 - near to the poets' village of Zernoye Selo. *CSFN24.* This was the abbreviation the OGPU used on their reports of denunciation.

They tell me about the corn.

On a summer's day it was corn as far as the eye could see. Hidden where the eye could not see was a barbed wire fence: the corn was protected from the hands of the starving. Or, as the chairman of the kolkhoz said: *the hands of the gluttons.*

During the Second Great Famine armed *kolkhozniks* patrolled the fence in a beaten old truck. "The *kolkhozniks* had it good," I am told. "They were collectivisation's privileged." Each *kolkhoznik* had his own few square metres of land around his *izba* and there he grew potatoes, onions, leeks, pumpkins and he might even have kept a cow, pig or goat, and a few chickens. Each Tuesday they took their produce into the village to sell: milk, still warm and laced with the odour of the animal's udders; potatoes with fresh earth clinging to them; onions the size of pumpkins; pumpkins the size of a tractor. They also sold moonshine vodka on those Tuesdays. It was much cheaper than the legal brand. It was also much stronger. At the dispensary the doctor used to put patients into a state of unconsciousness with a couple of tumblers of it. The dentists at the clinic did

---

[40] **Dear Yvan, see you soon.**

the same.

I am told of how the *kolkhozniks* laid their produce out on the floor of Stalin Hall. The hall was part of the Park of Culture and Rest. The chairman of the *kolkhoz* was Sava Alexeyevich Soloviev and everyone called him Sas. He used to stand at the door of Stalin Hall to see that those who came to buy were villagers because he had refused to allow outsiders - non-villagers - to buy the *kolkhozniks'* produce. Some days the chairman of the Village Soviet, Viktor Georgiyevich Gogorov, called Vitya, would stand beside him. Vitya was obscenely fat and wore a red sash across his enormous chest. Half a dozen medals were pinned to the sash. The emblem on one of the medals was a cob of corn. Sas had a similar medal. The story was that for three consecutive years the *kolkhoz* corn production had been greater than every other corn farm in the world, even greater than the largest corn farm in America, and the two's contribution to such a wondrous feat had been recognised by the Kremlin.

"They were two good men, Sas and Vitya," I am told.

There was Alyosha the thatcher who used to go about the village in a cart loaded with bricks, slates, straw and buckets filled with tar steaming like a boiling samovar. There was Gosha the baker who used to pinch the bottoms of all the young girls. If they did not shout at him and called him a dirty old bastard, he wrote their names down in a ledger and they were given the freshest loaf the next time they stepped into his shop. There was Petya who was one of the nurses at the dispensary. Once he had been a boxer but on his marriage to Alla he had given up the boxing. She had insisted he did so. She had told him that she did not want a husband with a flat nose. Seemingly Alla stopped Petya's boxing when it was too late as he already had a flat nose. He used to go round the village after his shift at the dispensary to help out where there was sickness. No task was too menial for him. He emptied bedpans as willingly as he massaged limbs misshapen with arthritis. There was Rodya and Roma. They were waiters at the House of Endeavour and lovers despite that both were males. Both could speak French and spoke French to the girl from *Pravda*, because her father was French and she knew the language. There was Slava who played the piano at the Red Banner. Slava was a heavy drinker but the drunker he became, the more agile were his fingers on the piano keys. He could not sing, though; not to save his life. Had a dreadful voice which sounded like water gurgling in a blocked drain. There was Zoya who lived with Gosha the baker. She was a midwife. There was Yulya who drove Stalin's *nachtwacht*. This was what the villagers called the truck which came at midnight on Friday to fetch the full latrine buckets and to leave empty ones. There was Sveta the telephone operator. She sat behind her switchboard from 9 a.m. to 4 p.m. seven days a week. If she liked someone, she pulled a woollen bonnet over her ears to show she was not interested in overhearing conversations. If she did not like someone, she stuck her pencil behind her right ear, crossed her arms and looked that person straight in the face while they shouted into the mouthpiece because always they had to shout, the lines never clear and often crossed; they could often hear someone in Moscow shouting to someone in Alma-Ata. There was Nellya who sold *Pravda* and *Izvestiya* and ice cream from a stall on Marx Square. All these people were known by their nicknames. Their given names were for OGPU denunciation reports only.

-0-

And there were the poets.

They lived in the south-western corner of the village, on the streets named after rivers.

There was Stanislav Petrovich Rogov. He wrote poetry. He lived in the largest *dacha* in the village. The *dacha* was a perk of his position: vice-chairman of Profpro. The *dacha* was on Lena Street. He and his wife Alexandra Alexandrovna had seven children. *Seven pairs of hands to build socialism*, he used to say. Two of the children they had adopted.

There was Beretzkoy, of course. He was a polite man. A good father. His wife, Nadezdha Konstantinovna, was a recluse. Once she had been a singer but few had been able to picture the silent and morose woman they knew, standing on a stage, singing.

Finally, there was the girl from *Pravda*.

"What did you think of her?" I ask.

"The waiters Rodya and Roma thought she was gorgeous. Slava from the Red Banner sometimes said that what she was doing - being the lover of a married man, and one who was the father of two children - was wrong, yet, he could not get it into his heart to dislike her. Gosha liked her too. He always gave her the freshest loaf of bread and he never slapped her on the bottom," they tell me.

The only one, as they also tell me, who hated Tanya, was the poet Rogov. *He could not stand the sight of her.*

-0-

PART THREE

CHAPTER ONE

It is August. I have been living in Zernoye Selo for two months. Beretzkoy and I, being unable to speak of our married life, speak of our communal life. We spend it behind these walls of ill-matched poles and planks enclosing my *dacha* because we cannot step out together, cannot be seen together. I am his employee. He is my employer.

Some days I wonder whether my neighbours know what my real role in Beretzkoy's life is.

I ask Kolya.

"My dear little friend, they were not born yesterday, so, yes, they are sure to know."

"Well, not that I care," I tell him. "I am happy."

Kolya comes to my *dacha* every afternoon. His *izba* being so small, I have told him he can use my decrepit loft as an atelier and he is fixing it up. He is replacing missing floorboards and filling the cracks in the walls with a grey mixture of mud and small stones which he has to bake in his oven until it is a rock-hard substance. He has set a trap for the rats; at night I can hear a sound like a gun being fired above my ceiling which is followed by squeals. First, the squeals are piercingly loud, but they grow weaker until there is again only the silence of the night. Kolya made the macabre-looking trap himself using the soles of an old pair of sandals, a metal bed spring and an old rusty knife.

I write to my parents to tell them I am happy. *Beretzkoy comes in at about nine and he stays until nightfall. He lunches with me every day but he never stays the night. I've become so domesticated; you wouldn't believe it! I clean the dacha even when it does not need cleaning. I've even started to cook; Alisa from next door is teaching me. At night, after Beretzkoy has gone back to his own home, I light a smoker[41] and by its light I type out the work he has done during the day. Or I do translations for the French Embassy; fortunately, they're sending me quite a bit to do because the money is most welcome but not all that important because I am very happy and I know Beretzkoy is happy too.*

I also write letters to the Olminskys and Galina. Galina adores my domesticity. The Olminskys and my parents are appalled by it. *Tanya, your letters are full of thyme and tarragon and not a word of Tolstoy,* my mother reprimands. *Don't vegetate dear girl,* writes Dan. *Keep your mind occupied because there is nothing uglier in a woman than an empty head,* writes Yelena.

Kolya brings a box of crayons - blue, yellow, orange, pink, green, brown - the

---

[41] **A wick and kerosene burner used during electricity cuts.**

tips sharpened.

"I'll sketch you in front of the stove and we'll send the sketch to your parents."

He tells me where and how to stand.

"Smile!" he orders as a photographer does before he takes a photograph.

I smile. I smile because I am remembering what Galina said about the congeniality of spirit existing between her and Beretzkoy, and I feel this is so with Beretzkoy and me as well. Our relationship is also intensely physical. We hold each other and in these moments only the two of us exist. Yet, I must admit I can never completely banish from my heart and my mind there are other people in his life. I know he can also not banish it from his because he leaves short notes which I can only describe as apologetic on the kitchen table for me to find after he has returned to Lena Street. In one he wrote, *I feel total harmony when I am with you. When I leave you at nightfall, I leave the harmony at Ob Street.* One afternoon I found a longer letter, tucked into my apron pocket. *If I were to write down my one aim in my life this aim is to remain joined to you … and I hope it is your aim too. Tell me it is, because only then will there be order in this chaos which has become my daily routine. If I have brought chaos to your life, please forgive me. Believe me, when I set eyes on you for the first time, what I wished for you was happiness, only happiness - the kind of happiness one experiences only once in a lifetime and which one never wants to experience again because it will mean the first time had not been perfect: it had been transient. What I feel for you is different. It will never change or diminish. No, my dearest Tanya, I will love you always.*

I post Kolya's sketch to my parents. They hate it. My father calls me a *paysanne.* A peasant. What I wish to say to my father is: *Father, if turning into a paysanne is loving Beretzkoy and him loving me, then I am happy to be a paysanne.*

They send the sketch back to me.

-0-

CHAPTER TWO

The way it was once forbidden to speak of an influenza pandemic it is now forbidden to say there is famine in our land, yet with summer drawing to a close, it is obvious there is, because long lines form in front of the village's shops. There has never been much to buy, but now there is almost nothing, only a few sticks of celery, a few potatoes and a few anaemic tomatoes from the *kolkhozniks'* little gardens.

Pravda writes *force majeur* is to blame for the shortages. This conveniently expunges anyone or anything from taking the blame. But, as the paper tells us, Stalin will give us food. I still buy *Pravda* occasionally. I buy it from Nellya who sells newspapers on Marx Square and always I hand over my five kopeks with a smile. I smile because I no longer have to edit the paper's lies. Nellya used to sell ice cream too, a kopek per scoop, but not now because the *kolkhoznik* from whom she used to buy the necessary milk is keeping it for his family.

"It is each man for himself now," she says sombrely.

What *Pravda* does not write is what we see around us. People, skeletal and dressed in rags, getting off trains from Moscow, dragging heavy suitcases, even portmanteaux, up Constitution Street. They come to barter their possessions - crystal vases, gilded clocks, silver candelabra, paintings, gold pocket watches and bejewelled hat pins - all frivolities from tsarist days, in exchange for food. They lay the things out on Marx Square and the chairman of the Village Soviet, Viktor Georgiyevich Gogorov, who we call Vitya, turns a blind eye to such overt law-breaking, just as the chairman of the *kolkhoz*, Sava Alexeyevich Soloviev, who we call Sas, does each Tuesday when the *kolkhozniks* come to sell us their produce.

We go and have a look at the Muscovites' little treasures, but this is all we do - we look because we have no money to buy any of it.

"Who needs silver candelabra anyway when one does not even have a candle to light? Who needs a diamond hat pin to adorn a crumpled velvet hat or a pocket watch made of gold when all one wants is the clock's arms to stop turning, for time to stand still, because one fears what tomorrow might bring?" asks Alisa from next door.

At the end of the day when the shadow of Lenin's statue is long, the Muscovites put their precious things back into their suitcases and portmanteaux and scramble back onto the trains. They go further south. South, there may not be hardship. Maybe there is famine only in Moscow they say to themselves as they sit down on the *zhestky* bunks. But no. There is famine everywhere.

They will find out.

-0-

Rationing commences. A town crier brings us the news. All of us, excited like children, run outside to see what is going on when we hear the shouting. The crier is an old man. He comes walking towards my *dacha*, leaning on a stick.

"No life left in the poor bastard but a voice like a thunder clap," observes Leonid.

The Village Soviet will start issuing ration cards in the morning from their headquarters on Pushkin Street. We can collect ours from six o'clock until four in the afternoon and it will be a card per household. The shops have been closed and will remain closed.

"Be orderly! Fall in line on Pushkin Street and wait patiently for your turn to collect your card! Disorderliness will not be tolerated!" shouts the crier.

There is a rush for Pushkin Street, to the dilapidated stone *dacha* from where the Village Soviet governs us. I wait to collect my card. I am not being gallant letting those whose need is greater, go first, before me. No, I am cautious: Nadezdha Konstantinova will be going for the Beretzkoys' card immediately, and I do not, I cannot possibly, run into her. I have not seen my lover's wife in the flesh yet, but I picture her in my mind. I see a woman with a matronly figure, her hair no longer the yellow of a sunflower but the colour of sandstone. There are lines around her mouth. Lines of bitterness, no doubt.

-0-

"What are the names of your mother's sisters?" asks the woman behind the desk.

I am standing at a desk in the Village Soviet building. As we no longer carry identity documents (the first tsarist indignity Lenin said he would abolish and did) we have to prove we are who we say we are.

"My mother is an only child," I reply.

"Are you certain?" she asks, brushing yellow hair from her face.

"Yes, I'm certain."

"What are the names of the husbands of your grandmother's sisters?"

"I don't know. I'm sorry. I don't know."

"Can you find out?"

"No. I'm sorry, I cannot. Who can I possibly ask?"

"Can you give me the names of your maternal uncles?"

"I do not have maternal uncles."

"How come?"

"I've already said that my mother is an only child, that's how come."

"Don't try to get uppity with me," she says, another yellow curl falling over her forehead.

"I'm sorry, I did not mean to. I have no maternal uncles."

"What was the cause of your maternal grandmother's death, if she is dead of course?"

"Her name was Tatyana Sergeyevich Bubnovskaya and she was a member of

FOR THE LOVE OF A POET

the social revolutionary movement."

"What did she die of?"

"She was hanged. Nicholas's henchmen hanged her."

There are no more questions.

The ration card is a small sheet of yellow paper. It bears my name and address. I fold it carefully and pop it into my bra for the walk home. At home I will lock it away. It is my salvation - our salvation - because whatever it will allow me, I will share with Beretzkoy.

Force Majeur will not get us.

-0-

CHAPTER THREE

Pavel. The town crier's name is Pavel.

He shouts out that a consignment of goods has arrived from Moscow. We are to go to Stalin Hall. I go with the women of Ob Street. Leonid and Ivan walk with us to the end of the street, carrying their wives' big bags: they expect these to be full on our return. The Widow Natalya's bag is small. She says she makes do with little. The Widow Alexandra's bag is also big. She says she has always been a healthy eater. My bag is big too. Beretzkoy told me in a famine one buys whatever there is to buy because what one does not need one can always sell or barter.

There is a crowd outside the hall. Sas stands at the door. Vitya stands in the middle of the hall on a wooden crate. He is shouting into a megaphone.

"Fall in line!"

We fall in line behind a crate like the one Vitya stands on.

Moscow has sent us umbrellas and cooking woks. There are hundreds of both. The umbrellas have been manufactured in the Italian city of Milan. All are red.

"They must be Communist, the people of Milan, to be thinking of us so," says the Widow Alexandra.

"Where is Milan?" asks the Widow Natalya.

An umbrella costs ten kopeks.

The woks are Chinese and someone lining up with us says China has sent them to us in exchange for arms - rifles and bullets - because there is a war going on in China.

A wok is eight kopeks cheaper than an umbrella. I need neither but I buy six of each.

"I see you are already an old hand at famine survival," says Alisa.

She buys eight of each.

The other three women buy three of each and laden as we are we are glad to see Leonid and Yvan are waiting for us at the top of Ob Street to help us carry our purchases home.

-0-

Each day we wait for Pavel's voice. When we hear it, we run outside. We take turns to hand him something to eat and drink. Some days it is just a slice of bread and a glass of cold tea, but we do always give him something.

"I should pray to God that the famine never ends," he says on accepting our alms. He smiles a wonderfully toothless smile.

"You'll serve ten years if you carry on talking like this. Five years for the praying and five for uttering the word famine," warns Yvan.

"I'm serving my time now," he replies, and he walks slowly away.

Sometimes what he comes to tell us makes us laugh. Like a few days ago he came to say we should shear our dogs and bring the hair to the Village Soviet. Someone in the Kremlin has decided as Russia has millions of dogs walking around covered in good wool, we should rob them of it. A Dog Wool Trust has been founded.

"From now on, no knitting needles. We've run out of knitting needles," shouts Pavel this morning.

"Who needs knitting needles when there is no wool," the Widow Alexandra says mockingly.

"There will be wool now we've got the Dog Wool Trust!" he tells her.

The country has also run out of soap.

"Forget about fucking soap. We can wash without soaping ourselves like Americans. Tell us about the meat situation," orders Yvan angrily.

"I've not been told a thing about meat," replies Pavel.

He returns in the afternoon. I do not even bother to run out. I listen from the kitchen window.

"Stationery! Coal! Kerosene! Fabric! Footwear! Milk! Eggs! Flour! Sugar! Aspirin! Chloroform! Ether! Morphine! There is no more of these!" he shouts.

Leonid and Alisa are in their back garden. Leonid is handing Alisa clothes from a bucket to hang on their clothes line.

"Come on Pavel, surprise us, tell us something we don't know!" he calls out.

Their dog starts to bark frenziedly.

-0-

CHAPTER FOUR

It is autumn again and the Village Soviet seems to be up to something. For days bulldozers have been clearing a wasteland beyond the railway station. Rumours are rife about what it plans to do once the land has been cleared. Some say the Kremlin is clearing the land to erect a forced labour camp.

"Aren't there enough of these already," muses Leonid.

The bulldozers arrived on a flat-top train. The train arrived in the middle of one night and it was shunted onto one of the side tracks south to Kiev, and the following morning Vitya and a delegation of Village Soviet officials went to look the bulldozers over.

"What do you think they thought they were getting: dead horses we can cook?" asks the Widow Natalya.

Those who are to operate the bulldozers arrived in the village next, not though on a flat-top train, but as *miagky* passengers on the Moscow-Kiev train.

They wore workers' blue dungarees and knee-high sheepskin boots. They could not get the bulldozers off the train and just as Vitya was going to put a telephone call through to the Kremlin to ask how on earth one gets such big machines off a train, did they work out what to do: lower the flap at the end of the train and drive the bulldozers off. The railway workers stood cheering as the first bulldozer rolled away. Some villagers also stood by and they too cheered in celebration of this fine example of Soviet brilliance.

Only Vitya did not cheer.

"Enough! We have wasted too much time as it is; so get on with it," he ordered.

Wasting time when what should have been done? Vitya is not saying and the railway workers say they are as much in the dark as we are. Even the men who came from Moscow are not saying, and all efforts the villagers have been making to loosen their tongues with the *kolkhozniks'* moonshine vodka the Red Banner has started to serve because no real vodka is arriving anymore from Moscow, have proved fruitless.

-0-

"Tanya! Tanya!"

The Widow Alexandra is outside.

It is October, early morning and it is snowing. Beretzkoy has already arrived and he is working on the veranda. The widow is still in her nightdress. She has a blanket wrapped around her shoulders. Something is lying in the road outside the dead poet's *dacha*. She wants me to accompany her to see what it is.

Kolya, working in the loft, rushes down the stone steps taking three at a time and risking slipping and breaking his neck. He wants to know what is going on. Beretzkoy has already joined us.

The *something* is a man. An old man. He lies in the foetal position. He wears a threadbare pair of trousers and a thin and frayed jacket. His naked feet are uncovered. His hands are black, the colour of rotten liver. He cannot be alive. Yvan touches his face. His body does not react.

"Dead," Yvan confirms.

From the dead man's jacket pocket protrudes a piece of paper.

"Let's see what it is," suggests Leonid.

It is a Party card. The card was issued in Moscow in 1927. The first name on the card - we presume it is the old man's Party card - is also Leonid. A dark stain obliterates his patronymic and family name. So too the date of his birth and the number of the card.

I run to fetch a blanket and we cover the body and Leonid and Yvan set off for the Village Soviet office to report our discovery. We wait with the body; only the Widow Alexandra disappears into her *dacha* to change from her nightclothes.

A cart turns into Ob Street. It is an ordinary handcart, one like Alyosha the thatcher has. Two men are pulling it and two are pushing it. Leonid and Ivan walk beside it.

"Our first," says one of the four.

He looks younger than his colleagues. They are wrinkled and grey-haired. His skin is smooth and his hair is black. He smiles. It is a smile which reveals satisfaction. He must have looked forward to this moment for a while.

"We collect for the Village Soviet," says another of the men.

"What? Old clothes?" asks the Widow Alexandra, sarcastically.

The young man sniggers.

"We collect the dead, but I can see there is still enough life in you to be cheeky."

He had spoken into the Widow Alexandra's face.

The old man's body has frozen into the ground just as had happened that day at the tram shelter in Moscow. The men fetch two hewing chisels from their cart and start digging a ditch all around the body in order to stand in it to pull the body free. Two men grip the dead man's shoulders and start to pump it like one does a flat bicycle tyre, while the other two take hold of his feet, pulling hard to free them. After a few seconds of pushing, pulling and pumping, the ice releases its captive with a sound of cloth ripping.

"The old devil's still quite heavy," says Yvan. He watches as the four pull the old dead man to their cart.

On the ice stands a pair of boots.

"Good quality by the look of them. Wonder where he got hold of these," says the Widow Alexandra.

The youngest of the four body collectors lets go of the leg he is holding and rushes over to take possession of the boots.

"Why waste them eh, Grandma!" he sniggers.

Unfortunately, for him, the ice is also holding the boots captive.

"Shit!" he curses. "We'll have to cut these free!"

His colleagues let the old man's body fall to the ground and patiently they stand beside it waiting for the young man to return.

"Fucking thieving bastard!" murmurs Leonid.

The boots freed, the four body collectors hurl the old man's body on to the cart and then begin to push and pull the cart back up Ob Street. Leonid and Yvan say they are going to follow to see where they are taking the body. The Widow Alexandra says we should throw soil over the spot where the old man had lain. We are unable to do so: all around us the earth is frozen solid.

"It shouldn't be like this. A life shouldn't end like this," says the Widow Natalya bitterly, shaking her head.

She makes the sign of the cross. *Two fingers. Right shoulder. Left shoulder.*

Leonid and Yvan return. They tell us the four men took the body to the mortuary. There, they handed it over to two old women who came rushing from the building. Each carried a shovel, a length of sackcloth and some rope. Working fast, they lifted the body from the cart, wrapped it in the sackcloth and tied it up like a package which has to go a long way. They then carried their package to the furthest corner of the mortuary's yard and there they left it.

"Feet east, head west," says Leonid.

"Lying that way the two old grandmothers said he would be able to see the sun rise," says Yvan.

"They're not to bury him?" I ask.

"Not yet. But in the spring yes. They will bury him then … bury him and those of us who are not going to make it …"

"The bulldozers!" cries the Widow Natalya, jubilantly slapping her thighs. "They are digging graves for us! That's what they're doing!"

-0-

Pavel comes to tell us about the cart. We are to call for the cart when someone dies. No one is to be buried in the village's cemetery anymore.

"The Village Soviet will see to the burial in its own time!" says Pavel.

We call the cart the Chariot of Death.

-0-

CHAPTER FIVE

The trains coming from Moscow now bring us beggars. Old men with their civil war medals pinned to their tattered overcoats, old women leaning on sticks, young couples holding hands, their sunken eyes still smiling at each other. Entire families come: husbands, wives, grandfathers, grandmothers, grandchildren. Vitya drops his head into his hands. He does not know how he is going to accommodate all these people, not to mention feed them. Burying them, he will be able to manage. The bulldozers have cleared a vast area of land beyond the station.

We know why these people are fleeing Moscow. The Muscovites have started to die of hunger.

I receive a letter from my mother: *We heard that the shop on Economic Street had received flour so your father rushed out to get some for us but he had hardly left before he was back and vomiting into the bath. Right outside our front door your father tripped over something which he thought was a bundle of rags but when he tried to push the rags out of the way, he saw it was a body. It was the corpse of a young child – six or seven years of age. At that moment Grisha – you remember Grisha from across the landing? – appeared and pulled the rags off the little mite; your father had to turn away because he could not bear to watch. He knew that the child was a boy and that he was just skin and bone. Children dying on the streets of Moscow once more! What a tragic shame for Russia! Years ago, when we discussed with Vladymir Ilyich what it was going to be like in Russia when Nicholas was gone, we did not envisage this. How can we be living through this again?*

My father writes saying he hopes our scientists will invent an injection with which we could wake the dead so we can wake Vladymir Ilyich.

Yelena writes of the death of one of their neighbours. *Pyotr lived right next door. He lay dead for days before the supervisor broke the door down.*

Galina writes only two things in Moscow are in plentiful supply: *golod* and *kholod*.

Hunger and cold.

This is true here in the village as well. Moscow is no longer sending us food or fuel and all the *kolkhozniks* come to sell at Stalin Hall on Tuesday - all they have now - is their moonshine vodka.

"At least there is oblivion at the bottom of a bottle of vodka," says Kolya.

-0-

107

CHAPTER SIX

So how do we avoid the Chariot of Death coming for us?

"My young man is willing to help you out," says the Widow Alexandra.

She has taken in a lodger. He has moved into her loft. Beretzkoy and I have not met him yet.

"Tanya, if there is anything - and there must be something - you cannot do without, just ask my young man to get it for you," she says.

The young man has contacts.

Maksim Mikhaylovich Zorin comes to introduce himself. He is a technician at the dental clinic. He is also a trader in *nalevo* goods: a black marketeer.

"I'm not a dentist. I don't have the education. I make teeth," he tells us.

"I write poetry," replies Beretzkoy.

"I used to be with *Pravda* but now I am with Beretzkoy," I say.

Why I do not feel the need to hide from this young man that Beretzkoy is my lover, I cannot say.

His hair is yellowy blonde and yellowy down sprouts on his forearms, and his youthful eyes are clear blue like the sky on the first day of summer.

"I want to tell you about myself so you do not judge me too harshly," he says.

He has brought a bottle of wine along.

"Not to open immediately. Keep it. It's a gift."

It is a French Medoc, dark red: black market, no doubt.

It is mid-morning. The heat from the stove warms the kitchen. On the stove stands a pot of soup. Potato soup. Every day we eat potato soup. Only potato soup. Some old men have started to come round with sacks of potatoes. They do not want to tell us where they hail from and we do not ask because they are black marketeers too and we want them to know we will not denounce them to the OGPU.

"Will you join us, Maksim?" I ask pointing at the pot of soup.

He has a dimple in each cheek and a slight cleft in his chin and he is wearing a sheepskin overcoat and matching *shapka*. He takes off both.

"I want to go to America," he says.

We sit at the small kitchen table and I ladle the steaming broth into mugs.

"Did you say America?" asks Beretzkoy.

"Yes. America. It's Hemingway. You know. The writer. Ernest Hemingway. I am going to look him up. Visit him."

"Hemingway...?" Beretzkoy and I ask, simultaneously.

Maksim pauses to loudly slurp up several mouthfuls of soup.

"I am ... I was a *bezprizornik*," he says.

He puts his spoon down.

"One night the men and women who used to go around collecting the waifs there were they ... where we ... lay sleeping on the streets, in order to take us into care, came across me. I was sleeping in a disused tram depot. My memories of my life start from that night. I suffer from partial memory loss having no recollection of the years which had preceded that night. I was taken to an orphanage. I was asked my name and age. I knew neither so they gave me the surname Zorin. It was Zorin because at the orphanage a letter was attributed to each day of the month and the letter for the day on which I was *processed* - that was the official name for it - was Z. Maksim was the name of the man who processed me and Mikhaylovich was the patronymic of a member of the orphanage's staff. A place and date of birth were next decided for me. Moscow became my place of birth because that was where they found me, and the date of my birth became the date of that day, and they decided I looked ten or eleven years old and they asked me to choose and I chose ten because I thought they would give a younger child larger helpings of food. I was accordingly born on February 24 in Moscow."

He slurps up another spoonful of soup.

"Similarly, when the time came for me to start earning a living, a profession was chosen for me. I were to become a dental technician because our country needed dental technicians and I have healthy teeth and healthy teeth, they said, instilled envy in patients and envy eliminated the fear we all have of dentists. I was taken by train to Tajikistan to learn how to make teeth from the local gold and silver. Then, once I knew how to make false teeth, they sent me here to the village's dental clinic. But they do not know that I will not always be here. I am going to push off. I am going to America. I must meet Ernest Hemingway. I am going to defect."

"Defect?" asks Beretzkoy.

Maksim nods.

"How will you do so?" I ask.

"I have a plan. One of my patients is a high-ranking official at the Commissariat of Health and he has promised to include me in a future dental delegation to America. Of course he does not know why I want to go to America, just as he does not know I will not return."

"Do you speak English?" Beretzkoy asks.

Maksim nods yet again.

"I am teaching myself English and I already have quite a large vocabulary from reading Ernest. Have you read Ernest?"

We say we have not read Ernest.

"I read him for the first time in Tajikistan. One of my instructors was an American Communist who came to teach English here in our country and he'd translated Ernest's *Old Man And The Sea* into Russian, and so I learnt of Ernest. It is for Ernest I am trading. To have money to go to America to meet him. My supplier is a Kremlin official. For your own protection I will not tell you his name but I can tell you he is close to Stalin. I can give you any cut of boar and swine. I take it you eat swine, you are not Jews? It is Ukrainian - the best. If you prefer chicken or rabbit or hare or pork liver sausages, I can get you those too. I can get you oranges and apples too, and cooking oil. It will be olive first pressing. Some French cheeses too, and eggs, flour, sugar, tea, coffee, potatoes, rice, aspirin, paraffin, wool, knitting needles, soap and toothpaste. The aspirin tablets are in cartons of a hundred. We can talk about the price some other time but I will not cheat you. Ask my widow. Ask Alexandra. I am an honest man."

I ask the Widow Alexandra.

"Believe me, you will not be taking food from the mouths of our children. It's all Kremlin food. So either you are going to eat it or it goes to the table of that lame-armed bandit and his cronies."

"We will buy from Maksim," I tell Beretzkoy.

-0-

CHAPTER SEVEN

A letter from Gozuzdom for Beretzkoy arrives at Ob Street. It pleases me he is giving my address as his address.

The encyclopaedia project has been shelved.

Please do not take this personally. We have suspended all our projects. Please take note we are to discontinue reimbursing your assistant's wages.

"We will have to cut down," he says.

We half the number of logs which go into the stove. We half the number of smokers we light. We use half the amount of kerosene to light them. Where four potatoes have gone into our pot of soup, only two do so now. I write to my parents and tell them Beretzkoy and I are alright. *Please don't worry*, I write. I write on both sides of a sheet of paper and I make my script tiny in order to save on paper.

"You've lost weight," says Kolya.

"I was fat!" I laugh.

I put my arms around Beretzkoy. I feel bones where there was flesh only a month ago.

"It's tough at Number Fourteen," he says.

"I should return to Moscow so you do not have to worry about me," I suggest.

"You will do nothing of the kind."

But he must go to Moscow. He is going to ask Gozuzdom - beg them - to reconsider the cancellation of the encyclopaedia project. Of course, they refuse to do so.

"What now?" I ask.

"We'll be just fine," he replies.

Gozuzdom has not sent Beretzkoy back to Zernoye Selo empty-handed. They asked him to translate several of Kleist's short stories. Also Daniel Defoe's *Robinson Crusoe*. I find it amusing that this book is recommended reading here now: it is a story of survival and we should take special note, we are told.

And so it comes to this. We have been buying a few things from Maksim, but now we will not be able to continue to do so, because now, we have no money.

"Tanya, have this," says Maksim.

He has brought me a basket of small red apples.

"Open an account for us and put the apples on the account," I say.

"It's a gift."

"Then I can't accept it."

"Don't be silly," he says.

"I owe you, Maksim," I tell him.

"I am going to Moscow now," I tell Beretzkoy.

I do not tell him why because he knows. A new decree now divides our country into first and second class zones and only those who are working are allowed to live in a first class zone and the cancellation of the encyclopaedia project means I am unemployed. There are thirty first class zones and Zernoye Selo falls into one of them. The OGPU can therefore arrest me. I also will not be able to hide because the hated tsarist compulsory internal passport has been reinstated and should I apply for one, the OGPU will undoubtedly put me on their list - and grab me.

-0-

The city of Moscow is under snow. There is a disquieting blankness on the faces of those I pass on the street. They are huddled in threadbare overcoats and the heads of some are bare: they must have bartered their *shapkas* for food.

I walk along Moscow River to my parents' apartment. The river is a block of ice. A young boy on skates guides a young girl, also on skates, across the ice. Is it a smile I see on their faces? Or is it a grimace?

My mother pales at seeing me.

"You've come back. It's not ...?"

"... over? No, it's not."

Her face drops. Is she disappointed? She turns her gaze from me.

"I need work. I've come to ask the French Embassy if they can't send me more translations. And I might just go to Gozuzdom too to ask it for translations," I tell her.

"Voltaire!" mutters my father from his chair. He seems somehow to have shrunk.

The Gozuzdom receptionist points to a door marked *Translations*.

"See if anyone's there," she tells me.

There is. It's a young bearded but balding comrade.

"What can you do?" he asks me.

"I am fluent in French. I've done both French to Russian and Russian to French translations for the French Embassy. I would like you to give me some translations to do."

"What's your name?" he asks.

I tell him and I say I used to be with *Pravda* but then I was sent to assist the poet Boris Petrovich Beretzkoy in compiling an encyclopaedia of Russian literature.

"Comrade Brodovskaya, do you think anyone feels like reading decadent French novels right now?" he asks sarcastically.

"Please. I really need work."

"So do I," he smirks.

"You work here," I tell him.

"I won't be if I do as you ask."

I apologise for wasting his time.

I walk to the French Embassy to see Pierre.

"I was just going to write to you," he says.

They need someone to chaperone a group of French students. They arrived in Moscow earlier in the morning and are staying at a Komsomol hostel. If I accept the job I will have to start as soon as possible. I will have to stay in the same accommodation as the students and I will eat with them. They will be in Moscow for three weeks.

"I can start today?" I ask eagerly.

"Tomorrow will do," he says.

I write to Beretzkoy. I tell him I will be away for a while. I will write when I can and I will be back, also when I can, I tell him. I seal the letter and I slip it into a larger envelope. I post it to Kolya's address. I know he will be discreet when he hands the letter over to Beretzkoy.

An official from the Commissariat of Education briefs me on where I am to take the students and what they are allowed to see.

I tell the cultural attaché what the comrade's told me.

"*Ca, c'est de la merde!*" he shouts, spraying saliva over me.

The students - there are ten - are all male. We come to an agreement. I will show them whatever I wish, this includes the forbidden places, but they will not tell the authorities.

I eat well with the students. Each day their embassy delivers a food parcel to us. The parcels are huge.

"Come on," urges Claude, one of the students, a handsome youth with black hair and black eyes. "What's left is yours!"

I make food parcels of the non-perishable items and these I post to my parents and to Kolya. I write him a note asking him to share with the Beretzkoys.

The Embassy also pays me well and in American dollars.

-0-

The three weeks pass and here I am laughingly running along the station platform for the Moscow train. The Yankee dollars are heavy in my bag. It is a wonderful heaviness.

I bought a *miagky* ticket.

-0-

CHAPTER EIGHT

The old man we found in front of the dead poet's *dacha* is going to be buried. The mortuary's back yard is full now and before the Chariot of Death can drop off more, the older corpses must be removed.

"Come and look," Pavel shouts.

"Vitya thinks if we see how we end up we will not be the wreckers he clearly thinks we are. But I will not go," announces Kolya.

Beretzkoy also refuses to go.

I decide to go with my neighbours.

We set off at noon. Rain sweeps down on us. Soon we are drenched.

"The dead go straight to heaven if they are laid to rest when it rains," says the Widow Natalya.

"Ooi!" says the Widow Alexandra. "What a stupid thing to say!"

"If it rains when a departed one is laid to rest they will go straight to heaven," insists the Widow Natalya.

A small crowd waits on the road in front of the mortuary and we scuttle forward to join them. A truck draws up and four men in white dungarees and rubber boots jump from it. They carry the bodies to the truck. Some of the bodies are naked and all are perfectly preserved because of the cold, snow and ice of the past winter.

"Living dead," murmurs the Widow Natalya.

"Oh woman, you and your stupid beliefs!" reprimands the Widow Alexandra.

We count the bodies. There are sixty-seven. The presence of breasts and penises reveal which are male and female. Our curiosity is obscene.

"It's about half and half I would say," says Ivan. "Poor bastards!"

Three of the men scramble into the truck's cabin and the fourth jumps onto the mudguard at the back. Off they go, driving towards the station. We follow. We walk fast to keep up. More people join us at the station. Some are carrying suitcases and must have arrived on the morning's Moscow train. Do they know what is going on here?

The bulldozers have dug eight long pits. Leonid and Yvan start to argue over whether the sixty-seven will all fit into one pit.

"I've seen a hundred go into a grave the size of this," says Yvan.

"Where?" I ask.

"Civil War. I thought I was never to see something like that again."

He shifts uneasily from foot to foot.

The truck stops at the first pit. Two of the men clamber on to the truck and start throwing the bodies down to the other two to catch. The bodies are packed head to foot and foot to head into the grave. A snow-plough drives up from the direction of the station. Its driver is also wearing white dungarees and boots. Within minutes both earth and rain pelt down upon the rows of bodies. Have these men been briefed on how to fill a mass grave without making too much of a mess? Has the snow-plough's driver been told the earth must be flattened over the bodies? He is drawing a giant figure of eight with the wheels of the cart, a final flourish to complete his well-honed duties.

"Eight," says the Widow Natalya. "The number of destiny and karma. As you have sown, so shall you reap."

The Widow Alexandra does not react. Unless crying is a reaction, because tears are streaming over her cheeks.

Suddenly, I conjure up an image of Vasily, I wonder if he lies in such a mass grave, beneath a figure of eight. Or maybe, just maybe, he is still alive somewhere? I feel a cramp rising in my stomach; sweat forming on my brow.

"This field ought to be able to take five hundred," says Leonid pensively.

"There are more than five hundred of us. So where will they take the rest of us?" asks the Widow Alexandra, still crying.

"Speak for yourself. I'm not going anywhere," replies Leonid determinately.

"I feel sick," I tell them, clenching my fists.

"Poor child," says the Widow Natalya.

Reaching Ob Street, I sink to my knees in the dirt beside the road. I start to vomit.

"A woman vomits when she's pregnant," says Alisa.

"I would not know," I reply.

-0-

CHAPTER NINE

My American dollars are spent.

"Oh, they did go swiftly. But don't worry, I will sell something," I tell Beretzkoy.

"I will," he says.

He brings a briefcase filled with antique parchment maps to Ob Street. The lettering on the maps is gilded. He has spoken of these maps before. They belonged to his father.

"Not these, Beretzkoy," I say.

"We need food. Number Fourteen needs food."

"The Muscovites will snap these up. I would take them off your hands myself, Beretzkoy, but I do not have the money," says Kolya.

I set off for the railway station and when I get there I lay the maps out on a blanket. The Moscow-Kiev train steams in.

"Comrade, where did you nick these?" asks a man in a fox-fur *shapka* and an elegant long overcoat.

"They were my granddad's."

"How much?" he asks, his eyes glittering with interest.

"Give me what you think they will be worth to you. They're antiques. My granddad cherished these. It breaks my heart to have to part with them but one has to eat."

"Kykla, how far do you think will you get in the world if you can't even price an old map?"

Again, I am a *kykla*.

He offers me five roubles.

"Ten."

He drops ten one rouble coins into my hand.

"I am interested in old things, or rather my clients from the embassies are. If I were to speak about myself I'd say I like young things. Is there a price for you too?"

His fingers are fat like worms and the nails of his pinkies are long. I wonder whether his clients would have been interested in the old man we found in front of the dead poet's *dacha*?

I buy a carp, some gherkins and onions with the money.

"Its eyes are dull," says Beretzkoy of the carp.

"Its flesh is viscous," adds Kolya.

"And so what?"

"And it is not fresh, my dear Tanya," says Beretzkoy.

119

I cover the carp in all sorts of herbs - the herbs come from the Kravchinskys garden - and I grill it out in my garden over a twig fire. I hand the fish's head over the fence to Leonid.

"For your dog."

"The eyes are dull, but so are ours," he says.

"It's for the dog," I repeat.

"Who says? Alisa will cook us a nice soup."

-0-

CHAPTER TEN

Every morning I am consumed by waves of nausea. Often I vomit. I close the latrine door so Beretzkoy and Kolya do not hear me vomiting.

"You are pale," says Alisa.

"I'm fine."

"You sure?"

"Of course. And tonight I'm going with Kolya to the concert at Stalin Hall."

An Estonian orchestra has come to the village to entertain us.

Kolya and I set off.

"What's the matter? You look very pale," he says, worriedly.

Stalin Hall is packed and the air is sour and hot. After only a few minutes my head starts to spin.

"I have to go home. Sorry," I tell Kolya.

"It's that rotten carp!" he says.

We are sitting in the middle of a row and no one is pleased at having to make way for me to get by.

Turning into Ob Street, I see Maksim. He is walking towards me, happily savouring a cigarette.

"I'm on my way to Stalin Hall," he says.

He wears a black karakul jacket and *shapka*.

"The concert has started," I tell him.

"Did you walk out? Is it that bad?"

I shake my head. My mouth is filled with saliva and I rock unsteadily on my heels.

"Maksim," I stutter. "You are ... disappearing in a mist."

The acrid smoke from his cigarette has reached my nose and I feel as though I cannot breathe.

"Tanya?" he asks.

I stumble forward and projectile vomit all over his lovely black karakul jacket.

"It's nothing, nothing at all. Don't worry," he assures me, his face saying something altogether different.

"I'm sorry. Sorry," I mumble. I look down and I see my own coat is also soiled.

"Come let me see you home," says Maksim.

He asks for the front door key.

"Bathroom," he orders. "Let's get you cleaned up."

He steers me through the kitchen to the bathroom in the back garden and gently wipes my face and hands with my washcloth.

"Go! Change! Make yourself decent."

He waits for me in the kitchen. The samovar is boiling. His *shapka* and coat hang over the top of the kitchen door. The front of the coat has been wiped down and is dripping wet.

"Carp. We had carp," I tell him. My words sound muffled to my own ears.

"When was this?"

"Two days ago."

"No, it can't be the carp. It would have had made you sick within six hours."

"Because of me you've missed the concert," I say, apologetically.

"I can live with that."

He pushes a glass of tea across the table.

"Drink. It will do you good but tomorrow morning you must consult the doctor about the vomiting."

In the night I start to bleed. In the back of my mind I allow myself to feel relieved. I thought I was pregnant, but I am not pregnant: at least no more. The flow is unusually heavy and my stomach cramps relentlessly. I pull my legs up to my chin and I lie very still hoping such immobility will stop the blood from flowing.

I do not go to the doctor.

I do not tell Beretzkoy what happened.

I do not vomit again.

-0-

CHAPTER ELEVEN

Our *golod* and *kholod* worsen.

"Things must get worse before they can get better. This is Stalin's Law," says the Widow Alexandra.

Pravda reminds us no one is to blame for what is going on in the country and repeats it is *force majeur*.

The bulldozers return and dig more mass graves beyond the station and Vitya decides the famine's victims will no longer be taken to the mortuary's back yard but will be buried straight away.

"At least Stalin is bettering something about our lives. He is getting us into our graves faster," jokes Kolya.

Such brisk trade is being done at the station that Vitya makes us hand over a kopek before we can lay out our goods. In other words, he is renting our pitches to us.

"The Village Soviet can do with the money," he says.

"Capitalist!" mocks Leonid.

Kolya is selling his possessions too now, and so does the Widow Alexandra. Kolya does not mind handing a kopek over to Vitya but the Widow Alexandra does and calls Vitya a thief right to his face.

She sells such pretty things: rings and earrings, their stones shining brightly in the sunshine; porcelain teapots, leather-bound books to which the lovely aroma of a library still clings.

"Stalin's now robbing us of our memories too," she tells me.

A Muscovite walks off with a diamond pin of hers.

The Muscovite who bought Beretzkoy's father's antique maps stops at my blanket each time he is in the village and each time he buys something from me.

"He has taken a fancy to you," says Kolya and winks.

He says Maksim fancies me too and winks again.

"I've noticed how he waits for Beretzkoy to leave and then he walks over," he says.

I do not tell Kolya a man cannot possibly fancy a woman who has vomited all over him.

-0-

The New Year starts. It is 1933.

"Good!" says Kolya.

Soon, the passionflower, the one which grows between the logs of his living room wall, is in bloom again.

"It is spring, my love," says Beretzkoy.

"It ought to go better with us now, yes?" I ask hopefully.

"Of course," he says.

We receive a letter from Dan. He writes: *Once the Ossetian said that the Russian man was different from the Western man because he has guts whereas the Westerner has only a gut, but now the Russian man also has only a gut because here in Moscow the people have turned to cannibalism. The Ossetian denies of course that we've started to eat our deceased neighbours, but why would the nalevo traders be buying up bodies from the mortuaries if it's not to sell them as meat?*

In Zernoye Selo we are hungry and cold too, but we are not yet cannibals. No. Sas has slaughtered all the *kolkhoz* horses and these are keeping us alive. And as much as I hate to admit it, there are villagers who have started to eat dogs.

Leonid and Alisa keep their dog indoors now.

-0-

Someone bangs on my gate. I run to see who it is.

"Here, take it! It's for you!"

A man in civilian clothes holds a parcel out to me. My name's written on it in big determined letters.

Kolya is with me. Beretzkoy is in Moscow begging Profpro for more translations.

The parcel is not heavy. I untie the string wrapped around it and tear the paper away.

"Men's clothing," says Kolya.

A pair of flannels, a *rybashka*, an overcoat and a boot - yes, not a pair of boots, but just one boot - lie on my kitchen table. All are threadbare and filthy, stained with something dark brown or black.

"Who would be playing such a sick joke on me? Who would be sending me old, filthy clothes?" I ask Kolya.

"It's not a joke, Tanya."

"What then?"

He picks up the *rybashka* and puts his nose to it.

"Blood. Sweat and blood."

"Blood? Whose blood?"

"Tanya Tanya," he tuts. "Whose blood do you think?"

"Vasily's?"

He nods.

"This is the Leather Coats[42] way of telling us it is all over. I'm sorry. So sorry. But yes, he will not return. "

---

[42] **The Chekists.**

I feel a well of sadness building up in the pit of my stomach, like a bitter pill that must be swallowed. I have been hoping I will still find Vasily. That I - Beretzkoy and I - will be able to look after him here in Zernoye Selo.

Kolya reads my thoughts and puts his hand on top of mine. His skin is dappled and as thin as paper.

"Tanya, my girl, it is hopeless to hope," he says.

-0-

Someone bangs on the gate again. Beretzkoy is back from Moscow. Kolya is up in the loft. The man who brought me the parcel stands outside on Ob Street. He hands me a letter. It is from OGPU headquarters, the dreaded Lubyanka, from which I ran so fast once. The letter bears the date October 24, 1931. It is April now. April 1933. I cannot decipher the signature of loops within loops.

The official with the undecipherable signature had written to me: *The criminal Brodov is dead.*

Vasily died on June 18, 1931.

This means he died six months after the Chekists dragged him from his desk at *Pravda.* That was a little more than two years ago. He died of septicaemia caused by acute appendicitis.

"It does not say where he died and where he lies buried," I say.

For a while Beretzkoy holds me. I feel shaken and numb at the same time.

In the afternoon, we - Beretzkoy, Kolya, my neighbours and I - bury the clothes in my front garden. Leonid gives me a sprig of bay leaf.

"Push it into the earth. You will see how well it will grow. Your Vasily's soul will be in it. The soul, you know, never dies. The soul goes on."

-0-

The man returns. I recognise the knock: one loud rap. I take my time opening up. He has brought me another letter.

"Do you really not know where the parcel has come from and where these letters are coming from?" he asks.

"I know now."

"I'm sorry."

"For what?"

"That I am the one who has to be the messenger."

"That's a wrong reason, but thank you all the same."

"I have a wife and a child. Either, I am the messenger, or my wife is the recipient," he says.

Yes, there is logic in such thinking.

The letter comes from the ZAGS office in Moscow where Vasily and I registered our marriage. It is dated October 25, 1931. It was written the day after the previous letter. An appointment was made for me with the Comrade Chief

Registrar for 10 a.m. on November 2, 1931. But, as the letter continues, I was to sign the accompanying document to revert to my maiden name of Tisinski. *We know that you would be glad to receive this information as you would not wish to continue to bear the name of a criminal.*

Again, I cannot decipher the signature, but the letter is no longer valid surely as it was written seventeen months ago.

"I will continue to use the surname Brodovskaya," I tell everyone.

I paint the name on my gate: T. N. Brodovskaya.

"You're so defiant," says Beretzkoy, grinning widely.

"But not wise," says Kolya.

"Sometimes it is wiser to be defiant than to be wise," Beretzkoy tells Kolya.

I find a note from Beretzkoy on my kitchen table. Night has fallen and he has made his way back to Lena Street.

Tanya, there are times in life when we have to defend those who have been defeated. So my love, keep the name Brodovskaya. I admire you. And I love you.

Defiant …

Defier …

Defiance …

Never Defile the Defeated …

But Deflorate the Defamer …"

I will stop using the name Brodovskaya only after I have been to ZAGS with Beretzkoy.

But I have a good idea this is something which will never happen.

-0-

January 2003 : Moscow (Gerald Lombard/Biographer)

Back in Moscow, I have to plead to be told how it was in Zernoye Selo during the Second Great Famine.

"You do not want to write about this. People who have never experienced a famine would not understand," they tell me.

I tell them people who have never experienced a famine should be told what famine is like.

"We had to survive. We had to learn to cheat death," they say and their cheeks colour with unease.

And when they do start to speak, they cannot stop.

I hear of the Chariot of Death. Of the old man who was found on the street where the girl from *Pravda* lived. Of what had gone on in the back yard of the mortuary and I hear about the mass graves. That at first there were eight which could hold sixty bodies each but another eight had to be dug as trucks began to bring bodies from all over, even as far away as Leningrad. The new graves were larger and deeper and could hold a hundred bodies each. They too were filled.

"But we didn't go that way. We survived," they say.

They turn their faces away to tell me how. It was by eating what they never would have imagined they would have been able to eat. To swallow and keep it down. It started, this eating of repulsive things, when a mysterious sickness began killing off the horses on the *kolkhoz*. The first horse to die they buried but when the second died Sas was away in Moscow and the *kolkhozniks*, although unanimous they might be making a mistake, cut the horse up and shared out the morsels and for a week the smell of grilled meat hung over the village. On Sas's return he heard what the *kolkhozniks* had done and as not one of them had suffered any ill effects, no horse was buried again.

When the mysterious sickness was over, other meat had to be found because the taste of meat was on the people's tongues, and their hunger therefore so much greater. They considered eating rodents but the thought was too revolting. Then one of the *kolkhozniks* wanted to know what was wrong with eating a dog or a cat and they held a hand vote and those 'for' had to raise their right hand and *all* the right hands shot simultaneously up in the air.

We didn't eat our own. We ate the strays, is what they say.

They killed them gently. They twisted their necks with one swift movement. Then they fleeced them. The Dog Wool Trust had sent the *kolkhoz* a spinning wheel and a demand for so many yards of wool per month. Once fleeced, the dogs were cut up and became stew.

"There was a big pot of stew to be had from a dog or a cat. And there were many strays. But more terrible things went on in Moscow. There the people ate human flesh to survive. We in the village did not do that. We buried our dead," they tell me.

They quote Dostoevsky.

Someone condemned to die thinking an hour before death that if he had to live on a steep pinnacle or on a rock or a cliff edge so narrow that there was room only to stand, and around him there were abysses, the ocean and everlasting darkness, eternal solitude, eternal tempests – if he had to remain standing in only a few square inches of space for a thousand years or all eternity, it would be better to live than to die. Only to live, to live, to live, no matter how …

But, they cannot understand why I would want to write of such things.

"Write about the solidarity which had existed in our village. Write that hardship draws people together. Past quarrels are forgiven and forgotten and wrong-doing is tolerated.

"Write that the famine made us accept those things which we could not do anything about. Which is what the poet's wife did. Write about how she accepted what she couldn't do anything about.

"Why write about what we ate?"

-0-

They tell me how Nadezdha Konstantinovna found out her suspicions about the girl from *Pravda* were correct.

It was the poet, the one who was Profpro's vice-chairman, and who lived in the largest *dacha* in the village - Stanislav Petrovich Rogov - who had confirmed to her what she had suspected from the time her husband had first spoken to her of the girl from *Pravda*. *You have not heard this from m*e, Rogov told Nadezdha Konstantinovna, and she replied, *As you say, I have not heard this from you.*

Everyone called Rogov by the name Dushenka Koba. It was the poet Dan Olminsky who had given him the sobriquet. He did so because not only did both the names Dushenka and Koba[43] have an affiliation with literature, but they were also synonymous with Stalin. And Rogov loved Stalin. The sobriquet therefore fitted.

The Rogovs and the Beretzkoys were friends. First, the two men had become friends and then the two wives - Dushenka Koba's wife's name was Alexandra Alexandrovna - had become friends. The two couples had moved to the village at around the same time: the Dushenka Kobas into a large three-storey stone *dacha* on Lena Street and the Beretzkoys into the smaller two-storey *dacha* across

---

[43] **Koba was a nickname Stalin chose for himself in his youth; it was the name of a Georgian folk hero in the 1883 novel The Patricide by Alexander Kazbegi (1848/1893).Dushenka was the title of a Russian folk tale written by Ippolit Fyodorovich Bogdanovich (1743/1803) in the form of a long epic poem. Stalin claimed that The Patricide and Dushenka were his two favourite literary works.**

the street. Their children - the Beretzkoys' two sons and the Rogovs' five girls and two boys - were also best friends.

Dushenka Koba was a stout man with darting black eyes which glared at the world angrily from behind pince-nez glasses. He was bald and as the villagers said – but behind his back only - he had a pig's arse for a head. He was aware of what they said so that he felt compelled to explain his baldness on first meeting someone. He said he lost his hair because of an ointment his mother rubbed into his skull to cure a severe bout of eczema. The ointment, a folk-remedy, was made of cow dung and the entrails of a rat, and though it cured his eczema, it also robbed him of his hair. It had happened to him at the age of six. "Not that I mind in any case, because this way I have no problem recognizing myself when I look into the mirror," I am told he always said. Not entirely true because once he had worn a wig.

His wife was a woman of little education. It was even said in the village that she was illiterate. Not that it mattered because she was a good wife agreeing with everything her husband said and performing her marital duties as often as he pointed to the bedroom door.

It was in the month of March in 1933, when everyone thought the famine was at its worst, that Dushenka Koba enlightened Nadezdha Konstantinovna to the true reason for the girl from *Pravda's* presence in the village. Afterwards he told some of the other poets he had not done so intentionally. The wrong words had slipped out and once he had started, he had to finish. *She insisted on me telling her. She said she had to know.*

It was his habit to call in on Nadezdha whenever he was at home in the village. Both he and his wife knew what was afoot in Ob Street and he used to say he thought Nadezdha was lonely and needed support.

On that March afternoon he had again called on her. He found her in her kitchen where she was cooking potato soup. They spoke of the famine because in a famine each and every conversation began and ended with talk of food.

This was how the conversation went, I am told.

Nadezdha Konstantinovna: "Borya used to bring a lot of food home but not anymore."

Dushenka Koba: "Must have been the French stuff."

Nadezdha Konstantinovna. "French stuff? What French stuff?"

Dushenka Koba: "That was how she was paid. With food."

Nadezdha Konstantinova: "Who? What are you talking about?"

Then, he told her.

"Afterwards, when he used to speak of that afternoon he always said as he had already said too much, he had to tell her the rest there was to tell. All the rest," they tell me.

That night as the poet walked in Nadezdha Konstantinovna confronted him.

"She told him he should tell his strumpet she was grateful for her help in keeping their sons alive as he was obviously incapable of doing so himself."

He told her he had never lied to her and her reply was he had not lied to her, quite correct. Not with words, he did not, but with his silences he had. *You never asked, you never asked because you never wanted to know*, he said to her, and she replied, *I never wanted to know because I didn't care enough for you to have wanted to know.*

The poet then asked his wife whether she wanted him to leave and her answer was she did not wish that to happen. *I will tell you why, my poor Borya*, she told him. *I will tell you why I will not ask you to leave and why I have not, in the past, asked you to leave. It is because I know what pain leaving causes to those who are being left, but perhaps you have chosen to forget that once, I was the one who had left. Yes, I am sure you had forgotten that, but I have not forgotten because every day I remember the pain my leaving inflicted on the one I left behind, and, this my poor Borya, this is why I do not ask you to leave. I do not want to be the cause of such pain again, the pain my sons will feel should you go because I have shown you the door. As for me, I feel no pain. So stay, my poor Borya, and enjoy your whoring.*

Having said what she wanted to say, she rose, saying she was going to bed, and he replied that the hell she was. *You are going to listen to me*, he said. He told her of the sterility of his existence in the period which followed the birth of their second child and to the day he walked into the *Pravda* editorial room. On that day his desire to live was restored because the girl he met that day gave him a new goal in life. *I was given a reason to exist and to protect that existence and not to take my life for granted or to allow others to take my life for granted. All these things I lost during that period of sterility, but now that I've found them again, I will not allow anyone to rob me of them.*

They tell me the poet added that the girl from *Pravda* also returned to him the courage to confront and defy, which, in turn, returned to him the courage to think and to take decisions, and therefore, to create.

"It was his justification for his impropriety," they tell me.

"Did she accept his justification?" I ask them.

"No," they say, "Nadezdha did not. She told him, *It is just lust. It has always been lust with you*, and he replied, *It is not lust I am talking about. It is love.*"

They tell me it was on that night that the poet left his wife. Left her in his head, as he had left her in his heart a long, long time ago already.

"You will write this in your book about the poet," they tell me.

I tell them I will.

-0-

PART FOUR

CHAPTER ONE

There are better times ahead, or so *Pravda* and *Izvestiya* tell us.

It is summer again and the days are long. The sun caresses our faces and our limbs become tanned. My garden is beautifully green and alive. A tiny yellow bird with a green head wakes me every morning. He comes to sing his good-morning-get-up-lady-a-new-day-has-come at my window.

Stalin announces a new Five-Year Plan and the OGPU is dissolved; the NKVD replaces it. A new decree proclaims that the last of our Kulaks have moved from their unproductive farms to our productive state farms. Collectivisation is something of the past.

Does this mean the Second Great Famine is also behind us?

We do not know and we cannot ask, because how can one ask whether something which has never existed, has ended?

Pravda reports a New Era has begun. I can imagine what excitement there must be among my former colleagues as they write or edit the wonderful news.

The New Era begins well for us here in Zernoye Selo. Pavel comes to tell us our shops have reopened. The two widows rush to Constitution Street to see what there is to buy. They come back with long faces.

"Still nothing on the shelves," says the Widow Alexandra.

"Perhaps there will be tomorrow," I comfort her.

The Chariot of Death makes a final voyage through the village. Two men push it down Ob Street.

We run out to watch.

"Who have you come for?" asks Beretzkoy.

"No one this time. We're taking it to the *kolkhoz*. They'll be chopping it up for fire wood. Wouldn't mind a couple of planks myself!" laughs one of them.

Vitya must still decide on the future of all that good land where the famine's victims lie buried. Keep the land as a cemetery and plant a cross here and there to appease people like the Widow Natalya? Or extend the *kolkhoz*? Grow corn on the graves? Bring in some cattle, perhaps? Sheep? Pigs? Who knows? Why not do it all? Why waste the land? The bones of those who lie buried there certainly will not sprout peas and beans.

Since the Village Soviet is planning for the future, so we decide will we. I throw the windows of Number One Ob Street wide open. My neighbours do the same with theirs. I carry my mattress outside and my neighbours carry theirs outside. We sing as we beat the winter's dust out of the pitiful things. Leonid gives me some tomato seeds to sow. Beretzkoy receives a letter from Gozuzdom. They have resumed publication and the encyclopaedia project has been revived. I am back working as his assistant. I am also translating Flaubert's *Madame Bovary* for the French Embassy.

We have survived the famine.

Our hearts are singing.

But what about those who have not survived the famine?

"Don't feel bad about it. We live. We die. We all will get our turn," says Kolya.

-0-

CHAPTER TWO

I know nothing about bringing up a child, but I am thinking of babies. My past vomiting may have been a pregnancy and I think back to that night I bled so badly. I will never know if I lost a child that night, but the pain I suffered, makes me think I did. And now I wonder what it would be like being the mother of a child. Of Beretzkoy's child.

"You are pensive," he says.

I grab him by the hand.

"The encyclopaedia can wait for a while. Let's go sit in the garden."

"No. I have to work," he says, freeing himself.

It is Tuesday. I could go to the Park of Culture and Rest. Sas and Vitya now invite musicians to make music for us on Tuesdays and there is dancing in the hall. As Leonid and Yvan like to dance but Alisa and Anna say they are too old and will only look ridiculous being swung around, my two neighbours have been going dancing with me.

Or I could go for a walk. There is a large wood beside our Park of Culture and Rest. Beretzkoy calls the wood, the Wood of Somnambulism. Its beauty, the pines and firs, the daisies and wild strawberries springing up everywhere as soon as the winter's ice and snow have melted, and the tranquillity such beauty provides, he equates with walking in one's dreams.

I do not go to dance and I do not go walking in the Wood of Somnambulism. I want to speak to Beretzkoy about us having a child and it will be today.

I lay out a picnic lunch on a blanket outside in my garden. We have started to buy from Maksim again so we are going to have a small feast: fish mousse, smoked herring, sticks of rhubarb, pumpkin cakes and a dill purée.

I fetch Beretzkoy.

"Oh Tanya! You can be such a child at times!" he says exasperated.

We sit down on pillows on the grass. Around our heads, in the warm sunshine, little insects buzz, no doubt waiting for an opportunity to share in our food.

"So come on, Tanya, out with it. What's mulling in that pretty head of yours?" Beretzkoy wants to know.

"What do you take me for?" I ask with mock anger.

"A very beautiful woman with a plan in her head."

"Me?" I ask.

"You," he confirms.

I shake my head.

"Eat," I tell him.

I will speak of a child later.

-0-

It is late afternoon and he rolls down his sleeves to put on his jacket. He is getting ready to return to Lena Street. I walk with him to the gate.

"Beretzkoy, what would you say if you and I were to have a child?"

The words jumped from my throat as if they were some of those little insects of the afternoon which I had accidentally swallowed.

"A child?" he asks, bewildered.

"A child."

"Are you serious?"

I nod.

"Tanya, are we not complete as we are? I think we are."

He is frowning.

"I'm happy," I tell him.

"So why do you want a child?"

"I didn't say I wanted one. I just thought ... but it's not important ..."

"Well, *you* are all I want, but you may feel ..."

"No. No. No. I don't want a child. Forget it! You are also all I want. I was just wondering. Forget it! It is of no importance."

I will not speak of a child again.

-0-

CHAPTER THREE

"I need to tell you something."

We are in the kitchen. Beretzkoy is sitting at the table and I stand by the sink with my hands in the soapy water. My back is to him. He is playing with a spoon, tapping it against the table. The noise irritates me.

"I'm writing a novel."

I swing round.

"A novel! I didn't know that!"

He gives a little laugh.

"I've always wanted to write a novel. It's ...well ... it's something I've had on my mind for a long time ... for years. In fact, I've started several but I've always abandoned them. Never finished them. Something ... something always intervened."

"She did?" I ask.

She. I do not often refer to Nadezdha Konstantinovna, but when I have to she becomes *she*.

Beretzkoy shakes his head.

"No. A dreadful sickness befell me. A sickness called 'cold feet'."

"Cold feet?"

"Fear. I stop because I start thinking what the book would do to others."

"Your wife and your sons?"

"And you too. Now, you too. Most of all you, because I could not bear you to suffer because of me."

"Does she know about it? Did you tell her about it?"

"She knows ..."

"You told her but not me!" I interrupt him.

He is still holding the spoon. I take it from him and I turn my back to him and I hold the spoon under the tap and I let the water run over it.

"For how long have you been working on this book, Beretzkoy?" I ask. I do not turn round.

"From the time it looked as if the famine was ending."

I turn round.

"May I read it?"

"I would like you to, yes. Yes please, Tanya, please read it. Read it tonight and tomorrow morning you can tell me what you think of it. I will get it, and then I must be off home."

He fetches a green folder from the veranda.

I walk with him to the gate.

"I am not in search of flattery, Tanya. I prefer truth to flattery," he tells me.

I watch him walk towards the wasteland. He always takes the short cut back home.

-0-

The Kravchinsky's dog welcomes the night with loud barking. This is something he started to do during the famine when he was held captive indoors so he would not be slaughtered and stewed.

"Quiet!" shouts Alisa from somewhere inside their *dacha.*

Even our dog fears what tomorrow will bring, she said to me a few days ago.

The dog yelps and I can hear him shuffle into his kennel.

I sit down on the bed. I open the green folder. *Doctor Rudi Zinn.* This is the novel's title. Neither Rudi nor Zinn is a Russian name. I wonder how Beretzkoy thought of the name, how and why he chose it.

The child could not understand why his father who was a doctor and had healed so many people could not also heal his mother who everyone said was so ill that she had fallen asleep forever.

I read on. I read what is written on each and every of the pages. I read the pages again. And yet again. I press the pages to my chest. My embrace is so strong it is as if Beretzkoy himself is in my arms.

-0-

I am waiting at the gate. Beretzkoy is walking up the street.

"I want to hear about the cold feet," I call out to him.

He smiles.

"It strikes when I am writing something which I know Stalin will not approve of. And it strikes, as I've said yesterday, because I fear what he will do to those I love."

"Don't fall ill with it again, Beretzkoy."

"Do I take it that you like *Doctor Rudi Zinn?*"

"Beretzkoy ... Beretzkoy ... I love the book ... I love you ..."

He puts an arm around my waist and pulls me in tightly. His stubbled chin scrapes painfully against my cheek.

"It is bound to strike again, Tanya, because of you," he whispers into my neck.

"I'll protect you. Don't you worry. I'll protect you."

I breathe in the smell of his skin.

Realising we are in the street, I motion for him we ought to step inside. I close the gate behind us. My eyes catch the T. N. Brodovskaya I had written on it.

Had I saved Vasily?

No!

So what makes me think I can save Beretzkoy?

-0-

I clear one of the shelves of one of our bookcases. It will be for Beretzkoy's manuscript.

"I don't want you to have even a peep. Let me get on with the novel and then in a while you can read it again," he tells me.

I am also not to tell anyone about the novel.

"Is she allowed to speak of the novel to people?" I ask.

"No."

"So you've been working on it at home."

"Yes."

"I never asked you what you do when you are home."

"I do ordinary things, Tanya. The things one does without planning. I read. I write. Some evenings, I cook. I do crossword puzzles with the boys. I am teaching them French. I sleep. I get up in the mornings. I shave. I make myself a glass of tea. Ordinary things."

"At least I know she knows about the novel."

"Yes, she knows about the novel and she knows about you too."

"She knows about me?" I ask, bewildered.

"Yes, she knows about you. Someone mentioned your name to her. Whether it was done intentionally or unintentionally, I do not know, and it does not matter because I am glad she knows about us."

The Kravschinsky's dog starts to bark. Someone must have walked by on the street because he barks when someone does.

"Damn thing!" I say. "That dog is always barking!"

Beretzkoy closes his eyes as if deep in thought.

"Tanya, listen to me. That woman means nothing to me anymore. I have separated myself from her both emotionally and physically. It is you I love. But … but I cannot leave, because I can neither emotionally nor physically separate myself from my sons. And so I remain living where I live. I understand how frustrating our situation must be for you. You have the right to complain, the right to ask me to leave her. To leave them. But I need to ask you something. Please do not allow Nadezdha Konstantinova to become an issue? Please?"

I nod.

I am not going to ask him who it was who told Nadezdha about me. Knowing who this person was, is not important. What is important is when she told him she knew about me, he had an opportunity to leave her, and he chose not to. That hurts.

-0-

139

CHAPTER FOUR

Winter returns. The fountain on Marx Square freezes.

"Such an early freeze means the winter will be very cold," says Alisa.

I finish my translation of *Madame Bovary* and Beretzkoy finishes the first tome of the encyclopaedia. The Soviet Union becomes a member of the League of Nations. *Ah, now we are robbers!* So writes my father: Lenin once called the League of Nations, a robbers' den.

The winter ends.

April starts.

There is again a knock on my gate.

I am reminded of how the news of Vasily's death reached me.

I run out to see who the visitor is. A young man stands outside in the cascading snow. It is April, but it is still snowing.

"*Zdravstvuyte!* May I please speak to you for a moment? Please? Inside please?" he asks.

I can tell the young man is a foreigner. His Russian is grammatically correct but he rolls the letter R. My father does so too which means the young man is French. He is jumping from foot to foot like an impatient man on a station platform. He is wearing a pair of *valenkys*[44] and they are falling apart, so I can see his toes. They are blue with cold.

"I am not allowed to let you in. There is a law in our country that forbids us contact with foreigners," I tell him.

"I know. That's why I said please three times. Now I ask again – please may I come in?"

He is not wearing gloves and his fingers are as blue as his toes.

"Who are you? Did the French Embassy send you?" I ask.

He nods. I stand aside for him to pass.

"The French Embassy did not send me," he confesses, quickly, turning to look at me.

"You're in now," I say.

I can feel the hairs rising on the back of my neck, but, I like the look of this young stranger.

"I've come to see the poet. I won't stay long. The last thing I want is to get you into trouble," he says.

Beretzkoy joins us in the living room.

---

[44] **Top boots made either of leather or wool.**

"My name ... here ..."

The young Frenchman hands Beretzkoy his passport. His name is Jerome Bernard. He was born in Paris and the passport was issued there two months ago. His Soviet visa is valid for fourteen days. He is a footwear manufacturer, he explains. Seeing the state of his own shoes, this is somewhat ironic.

He works for a company called *Bernard et Fils*. He must be one of the Bernards and his father the other.

He is smiling. Like Maksim he has good teeth. And like Maksim, the French footwear manufacturer is attractive, but he is dark: dark skin, black hair, black eyes.

"You are wearing *valenkys*," says Beretzkoy, and he points to the young Frenchman's shoes.

"And?"

"You are a footwear manufacturer. Don't you have anything better to put on your feet?"

"Your pavements and this cold are hard on footwear. These were perfect when I arrived here in your country."

He shakes his head.

"*Non, non, non*," he mutters, "I cannot let there be a lie between us. I am not a footwear manufacturer. I am a student."

"What are you studying?" I ask.

"Art ... the Old Masters ... and so on."

"You can't stay. I'm sorry," I say, quickly.

"I understand," he says.

Beretzkoy looks at me.

"First, we will offer him a glass of tea. Then, he can go. Do you agree, Tanya?"

We move through to the kitchen.

I heat the samovar.

"Why did you come to the village, Jerome? May I call you Jerome?" asks Beretzkoy.

"To meet you, Monsieur, and of course you, Madame."

"Oh, do drop the monsieur and madame and tell us more about you. At least let us know who you are before they shoot us!" says Beretzkoy, laughingly, revealing he likes the young man too.

Bernard grew up listening to his communist father speak of the Soviet Union as Utopia and of our people as people of courage, honour, justice and virtue. He began to study Russian, and his teacher, a Russian refugee, introduced him to the work of Akhmatova, Mayakovsky and Dan Olminsky. Next, the teacher gave him a small volume of Beretzkoy's poetry.

"Of all of them, you were the one who moved me most," he tells Beretzkoy.

He has been struggling for three years to obtain a Soviet visa and received one only because a friend, a fertilizer manufacturer, helped him to obtain a passport in the name of Jerome Bernard and then to obtain a Soviet visa identifying him as a footwear manufacturer accompanying a trade delegation. The delegation was headed by his friend. They have just spent a week in Moscow and the others are now on their way by train to Kiev. He descended at our station and his friend will be covering for him saying he stayed behind in Moscow because of a bad case of influenza.

"My name - my real name is Valjean Bernet. Valjean after Jean Valjean from *Les Misérables*. I chose the profession of footwear manufacturer because my father is a cobbler. In my childhood, during school holidays, I used to help him in his workshop, so I can hold my own in a conversation about shoes."

"So what *is* your profession?" I ask.

"Well ... I am a student ... sort of. I am here to learn about the Soviet Union. So yes, I am a student because I want to learn. I have a few days before I have to be back at your railway station to rejoin the delegation. May I stay here with you?"

Beretzkoy turns to me.

"Tanya, it is for you to say."

I shake my head.

"Oh come on, Tanya! He can sleep here in the living room on the sofa," says Beretzkoy.

The Frenchman stays.

Beretzkoy opens a bottle of ruby-red *nalivka*[45].

"It's Stalin's favourite pre-dinner drink," he explains to our guest.

"Monsieur Student, that was your first lesson," I say.

-0-

We give our guest a new name. We call him *Morne*. He has been here with us for two days and he is *morne*[46] because he is beginning to realise what life in our country is like, and we are *morne* too because we are realising in what ignorance and isolation we live. We know now we really know nothing about what is going on in the rest of the world and we do not even know what is going on in our own country.

Morne tells us Trotsky, living in self-exile in France[47], is saying Lenin ordered Nicholas II, his wife and their five children to be put to death.

We argue profusely on many subjects such as this.

"Lenin would never have done such a thing," I say.

Nicholas's death was fully explained to us in 1925, some years after the

---

[45] A liqueur wine made from vodka, cherries and sugar.

[46] French word for 'gloomy'.

[47] Trotsky would later set off for Norway and from there to Mexico.

family's disappearance. *The Red Gazette* [48]told us that on the night between July 16 and 17, 1917, the Ural Provincial Soviet, the ruling body in the town of Ekaterinburg where Nicholas and his family were being held captive, had hastily decided to shoot the family because the White Army was approaching.

"You are wrong Tanya. Lenin instructed Sverdlov[49] in this matter. He told him Nicholas and his family must be executed to make the world understand there is no place for a tsar in Russia. Sverdlov then authorised the Ural Provincial Soviet to liquidate the family," insists Morne.

"But this is barbaric and not like Lenin at all! Like Stalin yes! Lenin was not like that," I say. I want so much to believe in what I'm saying.

"Not all of Nicholas' five children succumbed to the hail of bullets though. Two survived. Nicholas' son Alexis Nikolayevich and the youngest child, Anastasia Nikolayevna, too survived. Alexis is hiding somewhere in Poland and Anastasia lives in Germany and calls herself Anna Tchaikovsky. Tchaikovsky, you know, like the composer."[50]

"It is something Stalin could have authorised, yes. It's much more *his* style," says Beretzkoy.

"He had Lenin killed as it is," says Morne.

"He had Lenin killed!" I gasp. "Stalin killed Lenin!"

"He ordered Yagoda[51] to poison Lenin, yes, of this there is much evidence."

We shake our heads in disbelief.

Morne speaks of collectivisation.

"It is because of the millions who died during collectivisation - Stalin's collectivisation - that your country won't be able to defend itself when Hitler attacks."

"Millions died?" asks Beretzkoy.

"At least four million of your compatriots died during and because of collectivisation, yes, and another ten million, perhaps more, were dragged from their homes and forced onto your collective farms."

"You said Hitler will attack us. Do you think there's going to be a war?" I ask.

---

[48] **Krasnaïa Gazeta of Léningrad.**

[49] **Yakov Sverdlov was Chairman of the Central Executive Committee.**

[50] **This would later be revealed as incorrect information, as the Tsar's five children died with him and his wife, Tsarina Alexandra.**

[51] **Genrikh Grigoryevich Yagoda, called Yagodka - the little berry (yagoda is Russian for berry) -because he was so short, headed the Kremlin's toxicological department at that time. Stalin later made him first Deputy Head of the OGPU in charge of GULAG, and then Head of the NKVD after the removal of Vyacheslav Rudolfovich Menzhinsky.**

"Oh yes, there is going to be a war, a European war, perhaps even a global war. Just as in 1914. Many politicians are saying that Hitler[52] still needs a few years to reconstruct his armed forces, but he'll be ready soon enough, certainly before 1940. Then, everything will change."

"But Stalin says Hitler is an insignificant man. Just a while ago he dismissed him as nothing but a symptom of capitalist weakness," argues Beretzkoy.

"Well, it's being said in the West that Stalin will try to keep Russia out of the war. He will offer Hitler some kind of treaty, a friendship treaty, but mark my words, Herr Hitler will eventually turn his guns on you too."

"We are still on our knees after the First Great War ...," reflects Beretzkoy.

"Wait!" Morne interrupts him. "I wouldn't be so quick to condemn Hitler. Don't misunderstand me. I am not a Nazi - far from it! - but you have much to gain from this war because just as the Kaiser saved Russia from Tsar Nicholas, so Hitler will save you from that monster Stalin."

-0-

---

[52] **Adolf Hitler had been Chancellor of the Third Reich since January 1933.**

CHAPTER FIVE

I want to tell everyone what Morne is telling us, but this I cannot do because no one should know he is here at the *dacha*. Kolya of course knows because we could hardly hide Morne from him. I think Leonid suspects a man is staying here because a few evenings ago he came for a chat and Morne had to dash to the bedroom, but had left his *valenkys* in the living room. "Yours?" Leonid wanted to know and a smile spread over his face. Maksim, too, I think, suspects I have a man here; at least I do at night. He too walked in unexpectedly - Russians do not wait for an invitation to visit - and Morne again had to make a dash for the bedroom, his *valenkys* once more remaining behind in the living room. "Tell Beretzkoy I can let him have a new pair," Maksim said with a laugh in his voice.

"Here lies a man who should have kept his boots on will be the epitaph on my tombstone," Morne said after Maksim left.

-0-

We fear Morne, cooped up as he is, is going to become bored and he would want to return to Moscow earlier. This is something we do not want to happen. We not only want to continue to listen to his revelations, but we really like him and like having him around.

"I have an idea," says Beretzkoy. "The three of us are going to go ice fishing."

There is a lake some eighty kilometres from the village as the crow flies - Lake Legyshka.[53] Each spring, overnight, as if by magic, thousands of frogs appear on its banks where they remain until the autumn, announcing their imminent departure with a night of mournful, interminable croaking.

We are going to take a bus to the lake. It leaves early-morning from the bus depot opposite the railway station. Morne and I will set off from Ob Street before daybreak because the darkness will protect Morne. All the same, should anyone approach us on our way to the depot, I will explain he is mute, a cousin from Kiev and mute since birth. Beretzkoy will take the same bus but we will ignore him. At the lake the three of us are to rent a cabin. We will stay for two nights. We will take food with us and a great deal of warm clothing. The temperature at the lake will be many degrees below zero. Beretzkoy will bring his

---

[53] **Lake of Frogs.**

147

fishing rod.

Morne and I choose seats in the rear of the bus. Beretzkoy arrives and sits down in a single seat directly behind the driver. Besides the three of us there are only another two passengers, a woman and her young son. The woman ignores us. The boy fixes a pair of inquisitive eyes on Morne. Is the child able to detect something is afoot?

Our driver takes the Moscow-Minsk highway. I have not yet been on the highway. It is tarred but pot-holed and slippery. It stopped snowing for our walk to the depot, but the snow has started up again. Quickly, most of the window panes of the bus are covered and ice crystals form delicate figurines on the bus' windscreen. The bus skids, its brakes squealing hopelessly like an animal being slaughtered. The cutlery and tin cups I have brought along rattle in the canvas bag above our heads. Morne has some blankets and pillows in his bag which he pushed underneath our bunk.

A few miles from the village, the highway straightens out. We drive through tiny hamlets with only two or three ramshackle *izbas* each. Smoke rises cheerlessly from their chimneys. Villagers run desperately alongside the bus, their faces pleading. They are holding up things they want us to buy: pairs of *valenkys;* painted leather belts; knitted bonnets, scarves and gloves and a headless chicken, blood still dripping from its long thin neck to which feathers cling. A young man holds up a baby's cradle.

"It has not always been like this," I say to Morne, apologetically.

He takes my hand and presses it.

"I know how it is, Tanya."

We turn onto a narrow, winding, gravel road. The driver starts to swear in a deep-throated growl because the snow is coming down in densely packed sheets and the road ahead has disappeared behind a blanket of grey swirling fog. The boy, frightened, begins to cry. His unsympathetic mother tells him to be quiet. The road narrows until we reach a steep winding track. We have entered an iced gorge.

"Shut him up, woman!" shouts the driver, but not taking his eyes of the road ahead of his bus.

She slaps him against the side of his little blond head and he howls louder.

Ahead, a beam of sunlight breaks through the snow-filled clouds. The driver slams his booted foot against the brake.

"This is as far as I can take you," he states.

Far below us lies the lake: large, white, as if a washerwoman has spread out a huge sheet for it to bleach in the sun. We will have to follow a winding path down to it on foot.

"Do you want me to pick you up? If so I want to see your money now. Twenty kopeks each," the driver tells us.

Beretzkoy hands over his twenty kopeks and Morne hands over forty for the two of us. Having known we would be asked for advance payment, we had prepared the money.

"I won't forget to come for you," says the driver, grimly. I wonder if his intention is to reassure us as his remark seems to have the opposite effect.

The woman and her child remain on the bus. Perhaps they are the driver's wife and son. The boy sticks his tongue out at us as they drive by.

"A universally understood gesture," laughs Morne.

The path down to the lake is as slippery as the highway. Beretzkoy and Morne walk ahead of me in case I fall.

"Don't worry about me," I say. "I will slide right down to the lake on my behind and will get there long before the two of you."

Beretzkoy is carrying our fishing gear. It consists of a rod, pickaxe, a kerosene lamp and a very small wooden box in which are a corkscrew, a pocket knife and a soup ladle. We are going to need the pickaxe to break the ice, the corkscrew to drill a hole in the ice, the ladle for scraping away the chunks of ice, the lamp for fishing at night, the knife if we need to cut anything, and I will be able to sit on the box instead of directly on the iced lake, when we are fishing. Morne and I carry the two suitcases. Slowly, as we descend, small black ants start to appear on the ice below. Soon, legs, arms and heads sprout from them. The ants are men in sheepskin coats and *shapkas*: our fellow anglers.

The cabins, small dome-roofed wooden structures, cling to a slope on our side of the lake. There are twenty cabins. A heavy-hipped *babyshka* unlocks ours. She does not leave the key with us.

"No one ever returns a key to me and keys cost money. Leave your door open. This is not the Kremlin. No one here steals," she tells us nonchalantly.

"I'll go down to the lake to buy bait," offers Beretzkoy.

Morne goes with him.

Logs are piled reassuringly up in a corner of the cabin.

I set about lighting the stove.

-0-

At dusk, the time of day when the fish surface in search of food, and the best time of the day for fishing, we set off for the lake. Beretzkoy and Morne share the burden of carrying our fishing gear. Reaching the lake, we stomp about in circles. We are looking for a spot where the ice is not too thick. After a while, Beretzkoy says we can start to dig our hole. He bought worms for our bait. We are to fish for pike and they like worms whereas carp like peanuts. The worms are in the box which is double-bottomed and lined with felt which is the best insulator that there is because the worms must not freeze. All of this Beretzkoy told us yesterday.

We start to dig our hole. Anglers are sitting all around us, hunched over their holes. Some of them have lit twig fires. A smell of cabbage fills the air: it is not correct behaviour to eat fish while fishing. So, the anglers will be having cabbage soup.

Half-full bottles of vodka stand upright on the ice.

After a while of sitting, it seems the pike are not hungry as they are completely ignoring our worms.

"It doesn't matter," says Beretzkoy. "It is being here together that counts."

We shuffle back to the cabin, our layers of clothes making our progress slow. In the cabin the stove kicks out a wonderful penetrating heat and it is heavenly to shelter within the confines of the rustic wooden walls. We sit around conferring for an hour or so before we settle down for the night, each on a wooden bunk.

"Oh, what the hell," says Beretzkoy from his bunk. "We'll admit failure as fishermen and in the morning we'll go to the cave."

I am too sleepy to ask what cave this is and Morne is already snoring lightly.

-0-

The cave is called Malenky Kosty[54].

Long ago, long before I came to Zernoye Selo, small bones were found in the cave along with some small, bright stones. I know about this because there were speculation some of the bones were the remains of Tsar Nicholas' family who must have hidden in the cave in 1917 from the Bolsheviks and who were shot dead on discovery. The small bright stones were said to be diamonds. What happened to the bones and the stones we were never told.

"You will need food!" the *babyshka* calls out as she sees us walk in the direction of the cave. She runs after us and brings us a smoked sausage, three hard-boiled eggs, a milky watery goat's cheese, a loaf of black bread and a bottle of red wine. She has packed all into a small cardboard box.

"Pay me later," she says.

We crawl on all fours into the cave. Morne, who has been carrying the box of food, hauls it awkwardly along behind him.

"Watch out Tanya!" Beretzkoy calls out.

He speaks too late. I have put my hand down on a dead bat, its body slimy in decomposition.

We reach a large open space filled with white, pink and purple stalactites and stalagmites.

We sit down in front of a purple stalagmite.

"Aren't they majestic," murmurs Morne.

"Indeed," agrees Beretzkoy.

I feel sleepy after all the exertion and I drop my head on to my drawn-up knees. The air is warm. Warm and damp.

"Beretzkoy," I hear Morne say. "My dear friend, I did not come to Zernoye Selo for this reason, but I've been thinking. I think you should be published in the West."

---

[54] **The Cave of Small Bones.**

I straighten up, my eyes glaring at Morne.

"My dear friend, had you come for this, I would have to ask you to leave the moment we get back to Ob Street," replies Beretzkoy.

An uncomfortable silence descends over us.

"I am not really hungry," I say for the sake of saying something.

"Beretzkoy, is it so impossible for you to understand my thinking? I mean ...," says Morne.

"Shall we after all have something to eat?" I ask my voice unnaturally cheerful.

"Is it?" prompts Morne, tapping Beretzkoy on a knee. "Come on, tell me, is it such an outrageous idea?"

"For me to be published in the West is not possible," says Beretzkoy, firmly.

They are ignoring me.

"Beretzkoy, there are ways in which it can become possible," says Morne, shooting me a glance which begs support.

The box with food stands between Beretzkoy and me. He lifts it up and puts it down in front of me.

"What am I to do with it?" I ask him, ignoring Morne.

"What do you think?" he asks, angrily. "Either we eat the food now or we carry it all the way back to the cabin. You choose, Tanya. Or perhaps our learned friend would like to decide our fate?"

I look at Morne and I shake my head to let him know this is the moment to end what he had so regrettably begun.

Beretzkoy stands up.

"Let's get back to the lake," he says. No, he had issued a command.

"No!" says Morne. "Let us speak of this now."

I am shaking my head furiously at Morne: he had lifted his voice and his words were echoing through the cave.

"Morne, who among us writers does not desire to be published in the West? You don't understand. It is an impossible dream for us."

Beretzkoy stands up and so does Morne.

"Are we going?" I ask from the ground.

"Beretzkoy, I can help you!" continues Morne, "I can try and make the dream a reality. Your work should be shared!"

I watch Beretzkoy shaking his head. He looks at Morne despondently.

"In Russia we dream as compensation for our despair. You have no idea what you are talking about. Now, enough of this! Let's go!"

"But would you like to be published in the West?" asks Morne.

"It is not a question of what I want! What we want in this country is irrelevant."

"Beretzkoy, what if Stalin dies? He could die tomorrow, the day after, next year, in two years' time. Could we not prepare a book now? Get it ready at least?"

"Stalin will never die. His kind never dies," replies Beretezkoy.

His voice is hollow, his eyes fixed.

"We all die, Beretzkoy! And so will you and if you are not careful, you will be gone before you have been able to make your voice heard!"

Saying those words Morne's eyes have filled with tears.

"Please," I say to Beretzkoy. "He is crying. Please, no more of this."

"My friend, my friend," says Beretzkoy, suddenly tender. He puts a hand on Morne's shoulder. "My voice ... my voice is only words on paper. But words have the power to cut through a soul here in Russia. Have you ever seen a man whose soul has been cut to pieces? I have. I saw Vladimir Mayakovsky. In 1917 he wrote *This is my revolution*, but hardly were those words dry on his sheet of paper than he wrote *I think of this more and more often: why not place a full-stop of a bullet at the end of my life?* Morne, as you, the scholar, will know, this is exactly what he did. My friend, do not speak to me of publishing my poems in the West! No more, please. I beg you, no more!"

Morne shakes his head.

"Beretzkoy, my dear unhappy friend, poets never die."

"Blok died. Gumilev died. Yesenin died," argues Beretzkoy.

"But their words live, Beretzkoy!"

"Are we talking of men here or of words?"

"Of both. Of poets and of words. A poet is his words."

"But I am only a man," begs Beretzkoy in a voice hardly above a whisper.

He bends down and picks up the box of food and starts walking away from us and out of the cave. Quickly, I jump up and run after him. Outside the cave, the lake is again visible far below. Without warning, Beretzkoy hurls the box into the air. It hits the branches of an ice-laden tree which halts its descent and sends it back down to the ground with a muffled thud. We hear the shattering of glass and the *babyshka's* wine flows in rivulets from the box and turns the snow blood-red. It reminds me of how Vasily's blood flowed from his head that day the Chekists had come for him.

"Now look what you have done," I mouth silently to Morne.

"What a fitting name you've given me," he mutters. "*Morne!*"

I walk towards Beretzkoy and gently I take his hand. He does not acknowledge my touch.

The remainder of the day and night passes in silence.

-0-

The bus to Zernoye Selo leaves at eight. I ask the driver to drive slowly. I want to look back at the lake. He tells me he works to a tight schedule. Despite the fact we have not spoken to each other since we left the cave, Beretzkoy, Morne and I sit together on the bus. After a while, we turn onto the highway and Morne says he is going to sit behind the driver: he likes to see the road ahead unfold. We watch him walk away.

"Is he still angry?" asks Beretzkoy.

"I do not think he is."

"I am going to give him some poems, Tanya."

I stroke his beautiful face.

"What made you change your mind?"

"I didn't," he says. "I said no but all the time I was thinking yes."

-0-

Morne prepares to leave. I help him pack into his bag the few belongings he came with. We are in the bedroom.

Beretzkoy walks in. He is carrying sheets of paper.

"Take these. See what you can do with them," he tells Morne.

"Beretzkoy...? You ..?" begins Morne.

"Tanya, help Morne to hide these somewhere," Beretzkoy interrupts him.

"I will not betray your trust," pledges Morne.

"You will not publish the poems until you hear from me that you are allowed to do so. Prepare them now for publication by all means but you wait for word from me. From me or Tanya. Do you hear? Do you understand? Me or Tanya. No one else."

I help Morne with hiding the folder. We stitch page after page into the lining of his sheepskin jacket.

"Are you sure you're not a smuggler, Tanya?" Morne asks me, playfully.

-0-

We say all the usual things people say on parting. *It was so good of you allowing me to stay. Do come again. I will, I will, I will. Make it soon. I will miss you. We will miss you.*

We walk Morne to the gate. We bear hug. We watch him as he disappears down Ob Street.

The dog next door starts to bark.

"Shut up!" shouts Alisa from somewhere inside their *dacha*.

-0-

Morne writes from Moscow. He writes his friend, the fertilizer manufacturer, has found a way we can correspond. We are to send our letters to a *kolkhoz* near the town of Nizhni Novgorod. We should address the letters to the chairman of the *kolkhoz* and we are to misspell the man's name by changing the second 'O' of three 'Os' in his surname to an 'A'. We must always underline Nizhni Novgorod. Morne's letters to us will also come via the *kolkhoz's* chairman.

Nizhni Novgorod is far from Zernoye Selo, not to speak of how far it is from Paris, and this means that weeks, perhaps even months, will go by before a letter reaches its destination.

This is what is called freedom here in my country.

-0-

153

CHAPTER SIX

Some nights I have been feeling like breaking my promise not to read the novel. Some nights I have even gone to get the folder but always I decided that this I could not do to Beretzkoy, and always I returned the folder, unopened, to its shelf. Not even this summer do I read it and this despite that I am angry with him because he is taking Nadezdha Konstantinovna and the boys to Leningrad. He wants to show his boys Peter the Great's city.

He comes to say goodbye.

"I am looking forward to sharing this with the boys," he says.

"I understand," I lie.

"Children grow up so quickly these days. Before I know, they will be men and fathers."

I hear him opening and closing the drawers of the cupboard on the veranda.

"Tanya!"

He has dropped some folders on to the floor. I help pick them up.

"Keep that one," he says.

It is the green folder. The *Doctor Rudi Zinn* one.

"But you said ..."

"That was then and this is now."

He kisses me tenderly and I savour every second of this goodbye.

-0-

He has already written 390 pages.

The novel starts with the death of the mother of *Doctor Rudi Zinn*. Those pages I have read, but eagerly I read them again.

Rudi is ten years old and witnessing his mother's slow and agonizing death from cancer. The child is standing beside his mother's bed - his father who is a physician has been called away to bring a baby into the world - and on the other side of the bed stands a priest, who is holding a pure-gold crucifix encrusted with rubies and emeralds that glitter when they catch the light, in one hand, and a heavy leather-bound Bible in the other.

As Rudi has been reading his father's medical journals - he wishes to become a doctor - he is aware his mother's body is shutting down. She has lost consciousness and her body is emitting the sounds of death: liquid gurgles in her abdomen and her final breaths rattle in her throat. He wants to shout to the priest to work a miracle with his crucifix and his holy book and heal his mother. He wants to threaten him with the whip, even with a bullet to the temple, if he does not work such a miracle, immediately. However, Rudi says nothing because

155

he knows scientifically it is impossible to reverse the dying process. That to hope a chunk of gold, some rubies and emeralds, and a book, even if bound in leather, would draw his mother's sickness from her body, is sheer folly.

The woman dies. There is a last gasp for breath, a last sigh, a last tremble and her life has gone.

Still, Rudi remains silent. He realises faith is useless: there is no God. There is only science to come to mankind's assistance. Man and science.

Rudi, as he planned, becomes a physician.

In 1905, working at a St Petersburg hospital, he falls in love with a nurse, Yelena, whom he marries.

In 1917, the father of two sons, he is on the Russian Front fighting the Kaiser's soldiers, and in 1919 he is in the Urals with the Bolsheviks, fighting Kolchak's[55] White Army. On the Front he meets another nurse - Lili - whom he falls in love with and by whom he has a son although he does not leave Yelena. He loves Lili and he loves Yelena. *Zinn knows that his love for Lili can only grow and his love for Yelena will therefore one day cease to be. He knows that it is inevitable.*

This is as far as Beretzkoy has come.

I want to read on.

I am crying.

-0-

Beretzkoy sends me a note to let me know he is returning. Nadezdha Konstantinova and the boys are to remain in Leningrad for another week. I will go to the railway station. I know this is something I should not do, but I will do so all the same. I want to tell him I love his book. And I love him.

-0-

The train is late. I stand halfway along the platform. I am wearing a white frock and a wide-brimmed white straw hat. Both are new. The train steams in. Its doors fling open even before the train comes to a halt. Passengers jump off. Those who are making a first visit to Zernoye Selo look this way and that and then they disappear through the turnstile.

I see Beretzkoy. He is wearing white cotton trousers and a white *rybashka* and brown sandals. It is a hot day; it is mid-day and the sun is right above our heads.

"Beretzkoy!"

He sees me. Waves.

Next, he is at my side.

"What's wrong, Tanya?"

---

[55] **Alexandre Kolchak led the anti-Bolshevik White Army during Russia's Civil War.**

"I couldn't wait until tomorrow," I tell him. "I had to see you."

He is carrying a small suitcase. He puts it down.

"What is up?"

"I've read all of it! The novel! It is wonderful!"

He kisses me, but it is a peck on my forehead, the greeting of a father for a child who is first in her class: there are prying eyes around us.

"Tanya, Tanya. What would I do without you?" he asks. "What did I do when I didn't have you? I love you. I love you. Girl, how I love you!"

We wait for the train to pull out. The last of the passengers run into us trying to get to the turnpike as if, like the train, it will disappear any second. Their suitcases are large and heavy: there is more to buy in Moscow than here in the village. The train steams off. A young boy leans from a window. He waves to us. Hands from inside pull him back in.

Outside on the street Beretzkoy and I purposely walk off in different directions.

-0-

It doesn't take him long to come to Ob Street.

"Here," he says. "Open it."

He is holding a small black velvet box out towards me. I open it. He has bought me a gold pin in the shape of a Lily of the Valley. There is a card with the pin.

To Lili - my Lily of the Valley.

I wondered about Lili. He wrote so lovingly of her in his novel.

-0-

I ask Beretzkoy whether Nadezdha has read the 390 pages. He says she has. She told him to burn them. *Not that I do not respect talent. You know very well that I do, but this kind of thing I have no respect for.* This was what she told him, flicking the pages to the floor. Silently, he picked them up.

"She had more to say," he tells me.

"What was it?"

"Do not forget who we are. That was what she said to me."

"And what did you reply?"

"Tanya, my reply was: I know who we are. We are the wretched of this earth. "

Oh yes. We are the wretched of this earth.

-0-

CHAPTER SEVEN

Kolya rushes in. He brushes watery snow from his face.

"Tanya, who would want Comrade Kirov[56] dead?"

I have no idea what he is talking about.

He explains, speaking fast. Yesterday - it was the first day of December - a shot rang out in a room in Leningrad, in the Smolny, and Comrade Kirov fell down dead.

Stalin speaks to us from the front pages of *Pravda* and *Izvestiya*. He tells us counter-revolutionaries have murdered our beloved Kirov and he promises they will not go unpunished. *On my head I promise you.* He will be a guard of honour at Kirov's state funeral. It will be held in Moscow. Stalin says his heart is broken. He wants us - no, he orders us - to attend the funeral. We must show the slain hero how much we love him.

Kirov is buried.

I do not know anyone who has gone to the funeral.

-0-

Today is the fifth of December.

Kolya brings more news.

Pravda has run a new decree on its front page. It is the Decree of December 1, 1934. It consists of three articles. (1) No mercy will be shown to terrorists; (2) They will receive the most severe punishment, and (3) The punishment will be carried out immediately after pronouncement.

We know what is meant by the most severe punishment.

Kolya hands me *Pravda*.

"Look."

Ten *terrorists* have already been apprehended and were given this most severe punishment: a bullet to the head.

Pravda names them.

Beretzkoy walks in. He knows about Kirov and the ten *terrorists*.

Together the three of us search through *Pravda* for names we recognise.

---

[56]**Sergei Mironovich Kirov(1886-1934) was the governor-general of Leningrad.**

Brodov, Beretzkoy, Rozanov, Olminsky. In every home on Ob Street, on Lena Street, in Zernoye Selo, and I presume in every other place in our country, similar searches must be going on.

The Great Terror has begun.

Immediately, we call it the *Chistka*[57].

This word *chistka* has always aroused fear in us, even in the most brave among us for it is also the name we have given to a foul folk remedy made from goat's milk and rotten eggs which we all have had to drink as children to cure a stomach upset. It always had the desired outcome: the purging of the cause of the sickness and the expulsion of the germs.

Now, Russia is to be purged of political impurities.

Now, there is another *Chistka* in our lives.

Stalin's *Chistka*.

The Man of Steel is to purge our land.

-0-

We hear of arrests.

"My sister's husband has been taken," says the Widow Natalya.

The man was seventy-nine. He was ill. His doctor gave him no more than two months to live. His wife begged the Chekists not to take him. She told them he was going to die anyway. They carried him to the *black raven*.

A friend of Kolya's is taken.

He was twenty-four years old: a painter. He painted a portrait of Stalin and it was hung in a museum in Moscow. Stalin went to the museum, saw the painting and did not like it because he said the artist had made him look old. The painting was taken down. The young man's wife writes to Kolya she thinks the Chekists took her husband because of that painting. *Damned be the day he picked up a brush for the first time*, she writes.

Galina writes of friends and colleagues who have disappeared. My mother too writes of friends who have disappeared. My father writes just one word. *Voltaire.*

We decide to lie low.

"We will withdraw into our shells like tortoises," says Beretzkoy.

We will not draw attention to ourselves. We will not speak to anyone we cannot describe as a true friend. We will not even catch the eye of someone we pass on the street. We decide we will also no longer write to Morne. We will not even write to tell him we will no longer write to him. We will fall silent as the grave with the hope he will understand our silence.

"We will call our way of living tortoisesation," says Beretzkoy.

I write to my parents, to Dan and Yelena, to Galina: *live our way please*.

---

[57] **Cleansing in Russian.**

160

Not bloody likely, replies Galina. *I need to communicate.*

She starts working on a play entitled *Citizen Children*. She shows a first draft to Gozuzdom. The editors call it wonderful - a masterpiece. It is destined for one of Leningrad's top theatres.

Yelena sends a letter. *Dan has been taken.* The Chekists came for him early one morning. She was not at home. She went to Leningrad to attend a conference on decadent imperialist literature and when she arrived back home the front door to their apartment was wide open and Dan was nowhere to be found.

She starts to look for Dan the way I looked for Vasily. She calls in on anyone whom she thinks may be prepared to intervene with the NKVD on her behalf. She finds no one. Even her neighbours do not want to help her. *I was reluctant to involve them, poor things, but I had to find out if they had seen or heard anything unusual in the building during the time I was away.* They tell her no, they have not seen or heard anything unusual. Some invite her into their little rooms while others ask her from behind a closed door what she wants and when she tells them, they tell her to go away. A day later one of her neighbours, an old woman, stops her on the street. *I was not truthful. I heard and I saw,* she tells Yelena. Three men had come for Dan and they escorted him from the building. *He was in handcuffs. His nose and forehead were bleeding,* writes Yelena.

Yelena is dismissed from the university. She refuses to ask Gozuzdom for translation work. *I do not beg,* she writes us in a next letter. She starts to tutor the children of her neighbours. She is paid in potatoes and rice.

Galina has no choice but to adopt our tortoisesation. She has no choice because Gozuzdom, after having been so enthusiastic about her play, rejects it. She tears up the play and asks a former lover, the director of a Leningrad theatre, for work. Any work. The work she is offered is as supervisor of the man's theatre. With the work comes a tiny loft. The theatre is too inconsequential for her. She writes in a letter, *Here I am living on a back street in the outskirts of Leningrad. Fifty-five damned steps between me and the rest of the world. The steps are full of splinters and covered in rat shit. I am ashamed of ending up here. Life stinks! Oh how life stinks.*

"Yes life stinks but if we are able to smell it, it means we are still in the land of the living!" says Beretzkoy to Kolya and me.

Tanya this is not what we fought for, this is not what Lenin said it was going to be like when Nicholas was gone. Did Lenin deceive us or is Stalin deceiving Lenin? my mother asks in a letter.

It is not Vladymir Ilyich anymore. Now, it is Lenin.

-0-

CHAPTER EIGHT

Beretzkoy shows me a letter he has received. It is from a woman named Zinaida Zell. He has spoken about her often. She is a writer, the widow of Anatoly Mikhaylovich Vannikov, who was once one of tsarist Russia's most impassioned religious writers. In 1917 he had renounced his faith with the hope that doing so would save his life. The Bolsheviks executed him all the same. They hanged him.

Zinaida no longer writes. She now lives the life of a *starets*[58].

Her letter bears an Alma-Ata postmark. She is about to set off from there, from a monastery to make her way to Leningrad. She will be passing through Zernoye Selo. She needs a place to stay when she gets to the village. *For a night or two.*

"Nadezhda won't have her," says Beretzkoy.

"She can gladly come here," I tell him.

"You will like her," he promises.

I hope he is right.

-0-

I see a woman standing outside the dead poet's *dacha*.

I walk over to her.

"Are you looking for someone?"

"Who are you?" she asks, curtly.

"I live across the street."

"Are you Tanya?"

"I am, and you are?"

"Zinaida Yakovlevna Vannikovskaya, but Zell is the name I use. I loved my husband with all my heart, and I still do, but I never used his name. It was always his. I am Zinaida Zell."

It was only two days ago we received her letter, but here she already is. I take her indoors into the living room.

Beretzkoy comes in from the veranda.

"Zinaida! Zinaida! How good to see you!"

They hug.

"You old rascal! You did not tell me she's so young and so *very* pretty. What

---

[58] **A holy man (not necessarily a priest) who wandered across Russia preaching while living off alms.**

are you up to - you cradle snatcher!" she cries, giving him a powerful slap on his back.

Zinaida is tall and thin and she is dressed in a long brown hooded dress which I recognise as a monk's cassock. She has spilled something down the front of the dress and its hem is caked with mud. She smells of cigarette smoke and sweat. A bundle is tied to her back.

"How did you get here from Alma-Ata?" asks Beretzkoy.

"I hitched a ride on a truck."

She is wearing heavy wooden clogs on her pale dirt-smattered feet.

"I would love a bath," she says and looks at me.

"I'll wash your ... uh ... dress," I tell her.

I give her a skirt and a blouse to wear.

"She will have to sleep on the sofa here in the living room," I tell Beretzkoy when we are alone.

Zinaida reappears.

"You will have to sleep here on the sofa," I tell her too.

"Not tonight. I've been on the road for a week. Tonight I will sleep in the bedroom and in your bed."

"But I sleep in my bed."

Her hair is wet and she smells pleasantly of soap.

"Don't worry. I am not into sleeping with women. So, I will have your bed and you can have the sofa you so kindly offered me."

I start frying fish for supper.

"You do not want me here, do you Tanya," she says pulling a chair away from the table in the kitchen to sit down on.

She now smells of my *eau de cologne*.

I put the largest portion of fish down on the plate in front of her.

"I'm not hungry," she says.

"Are you saying you are not hungry because you think I do not want you to stay here with me?" I ask.

She is staring at me with small blue eyes.

"Well, do you want me here, Tanya?"

"I would not have asked you to stay if I had not wanted you here."

"I still do not want to eat," she says, adamantly.

"Are you fasting or something?"

"Why would I be doing that?"

"Aren't religious people supposed to fast ever so often?"

She laughs. It is a roar of a laugh which seems to come from every part of her.

"My dear, the religious stuff themselves. Jesus himself multiplied the fishes didn't he so no one need be hungry? And if I may say so, when he only had water to give his guests, he turned that water into wine."

"Do you drink?" I ask astonished.

"Why wouldn't I?"

"I thought ... you being religious ... and all that."

"Wine would be nice," she states.

I open the only bottle of wine I have in the *dacha*.

"I'm going to bed," she says.

She takes a mug and the bottle with her.

I did not have a chance to pour a glass for myself.

-0-

The sofa is surprisingly uncomfortable. Morne never told me. I lie this way and that. A metal spring digs into my back. I sit up, light a smoker and I start to read. The wall-clock in the kitchen chimes twice. I hear a voice. It is Zinaida speaking to someone. I tiptoe to the bedroom, shielding the smoker with my free hand. I put my head around the bedroom door. Not surprisingly, there is no one in the room with Zinaida. She is beside the bed and she is on her knees. She has one of my blankets wrapped around her naked body. She rests her body weight on her elbows and the palms of her ringless hands are pressed together against her forehead. Her fingers are long and slim, her nails broad and flat. I hear her mumbling repetitions of names, phrases; incantations. She is talking to God - her God - as if he is standing right beside her. She is begging him to take care of Vannikov. She lists Vannikov's kind deeds and asks her God to bear them in mind. I crane my neck to listen to her. I try not to move. Now, she is asking her God to make sure to look after someone named Semyon.

"He is my only child and he has a weak constitution. He was so tiny at birth Vannikov could hold him in one hand. Please, Heavenly Father, return him to me. What do you want me to do for you in return? What do you want of me, Lord? Tell me!"

She falls silent. Did I breathe too loudly and she has heard me? She opens her eyes and drops her hands to her sides and turns and looks at me.

"I was praying."

She scrambles back onto the bed and pulls the blanket up to her chin baring her pale legs and feet.

"I heard," I say.

"Have you ever prayed?"

"It is something I do not know much about."

"So you are a heathen like the rest of them?"

"I suppose I must be."

"There are times one has to pray."

"And do you get what you ask for?"

"Not always. One even has to plead at times."

"God's heart must be hard if one has to plead."

"We do not always understand his ways."

"Perhaps he just does not listen," I tell her.

-0-

165

Zell is not Zinaida's family name. She was born Zinaida Zelavsky.

"It was a burden, the name. So I rejected it!" she tells me.

Jewish, she was born in a *shtetl*[59] on the *Pale of Settlement*[60], on the eighth night of Hanukkah.

"What is Hanukkah?" I ask.

"It's a Jewish festival. A festival of lights. It lasts for eight days and nights. We light a candle on the first night and add a candle on each of the remaining nights and on the final night we eat nice things."

She was born on the festival's final night just as her father was lighting the final candle.

Not only did she reject the family name, but she also rejected the family's religion.

"I needed fire to heat my soul and Judaism is cold, it is as cold as the ice on the river that ran through the *shtetl* where I was born. I found the warmth I needed in the Christian faith."

At the age of fifteen, on holiday with an aunt in St Petersburg, she wandered into a Christian church.

"The door was open and I was curious to know what the inside of a church looked like, so I walked in," she says.

A service was under way and she thought she had never seen such beauty.

"I was mesmerised by what I heard and saw. I could not take my eyes off the brightly-painted icons ... the glistening chandeliers ... the jewel-encrusted crucifixes and the candelabra which were taller than the bearded old priests in their brocaded robes so long that they trailed behind their old bent bodies. So, like a young girl wants to know what it feels like for the young man she loves to take her, I wanted to know what the devotion I was seeing in the old priests would feel like."

She did not return to the *shtetl* or to her aunt's house.

"I sought shelter on a Kulak's farm and I milked their cows and I learnt how to wring the necks of chickens and pluck the birds for the pies the old woman baked. And each night I sat writing by candlelight. I wrote down the folk tales my mother used to tell me, and on the day a St. Petersburg publisher published my first book I met Vannikov. I loved him straightaway but I thought someone as famous and wealthy as him would take no notice of me, but no, he also fell in love with me. And he helped me to become a Christian."

They had three children - twin daughters and a son - and the five of them frequently travelled abroad, taking the train to Paris or Baden-Baden or Venice.

---

[59] **A shtetl was a small village in Central or Eastern Europe entirely inhabited by Jews.**

[60] **An area of Imperial (Holy) Russia created by Catherine the Great in 1791 where Jews were obliged to live by law.**

On one such holiday the Great War broke out and Nicholas II abdicated and against their better judgment they returned to Russia.

"But they would not allow my Vannikov to live," she says, bitterly.

They: the Bolsheviks.

The twin girls died of tuberculosis soon after their father's death and one day the Bolsheviks took her son from her.

"Semyon is his name," she tells me.

The name of her prayers.

She does not know where he is. She tried to find him. She knocked on all the small side doors as I had done and as Yelena too had done.

It was at that time she met Beretzkoy. She appealed to Profpro to intervene with the OGPU on her behalf to find Semyon and although it refused, one of the members - Beretzkoy - wrote to her offering his sympathy.

"They told me I was a crazy old witch and even if they knew where the boy was, they would not tell me. They told me: *He can't even remember what the word mother means, so you do the same, forget what the word son means.* Only your Beretzkoy listened to me. He told me, 'Zinaida, do not forget what the word son means, do not forget your Semyon'."

And she is refusing to forget. I tell her she is right.

-0-

CHAPTER NINE

Zinaida does not want to leave.

"I'm going to get a job," she tells me.

Now, she works at our House of Endeavour. She helps in the kitchen.

"I wring a neck just as neatly as before," she says proudly.

Maksim likes her. So does the Widow Natalya and the two of them pray together. *Our Father who art in heaven ...*

The days pass.

April starts. It is spring.

My garden is overrun with high grass and wild berries. Alisa comes to pick the berries and makes jam.

Gozuzdom publishes the second tome of the encyclopaedia and reissues a volume of Beretzkoy's poems, and Pierre commissions me to convert the Russian translation of Emil Zola's *Germinal* into simplified Russian for our schools. Gozuzdom sends Beretzkoy an advance on his royalties and Pierre sends me one for *Germinal*.

"God's smiling on the two of you," states Zinaida.

She makes the sign of the cross over me.

I buy a bicycle. I also buy an electrical ceiling fan for the living room. This is a folly, but I have had my eyes on such a fan, which is also a light, since the first time I walked into the dining room of the House of Endeavour and looked up at the ceiling and saw one hanging there. The fan, of brass and cane and oak wood with long blades, is German-made. Its manufacturer's name is Hiedler. Soon, we all call the fan Hitler's Fan because when we say Hiedler it sounds as if we are saying Hitler.

Gozuzdom asks Beretzkoy, who is popular in Moscow right now because the encyclopaedia is considered a great success, to come to the city to discuss publication of the next tome. He tells me that Nadezdha Konstantinova and the boys are to accompany him. She will even attend a Gozuzdom dinner with him.

"I do not know how you accept your situation," murmurs Zinaida, holding a hand over her mouth.

"These are the terms under which I came to live in Zernoye Selo."

"Have you ever asked him to leave her?"

"No!"

"Then ask," she orders.

Beretzkoy comes to say goodbye. He tells me to come to the bedroom. We sit down on the bed.

"You are the one I want to take with me to Moscow, Tanya."

169

"I would like to come."
"You are making me feel bad."
"So, feel bad," I snap.
He gathers together some files and sets off.
"I'll never ask him to leave her," I say to Zinaida.
"Well, you're making a mistake."
"He belongs to me already."
"A man never belongs to a woman."
I remember Yelena already told me this.

-0-

CHAPTER TEN

"God gives and he takes," says Zinaida.

Stalin does too. Despite the *Chistka* he does not halt the reforms of our New Era. Consequently, we are all a little better off materially.

I decide to redecorate the *dacha*. Zinaida offers to help so we start by painting the walls. We stand on chairs - there are no ladders to be found in the village - the tubs of paint between our feet. We paint the living room salmon pink, the bedroom, yellow. The kitchen, malachite green. All the doors, grey. Because we cannot reach to the ceilings they remain as they are. I buy a small cherry-wood table in the shape of a leaf for the living room. I put a large Chinese vase on it. On the vase, exotic painted birds swing from perches. I also buy an oak console for the living room. Kolya brings me a two-tier sculpted pink alabaster bowl to go with it. Maksim says he has just the thing I need to compliment the bowl. He gives me a green and beige Afghan carpet. The carpet is stained.

"Ink," he says.

I will wash it I tell him.

"No!" he cries.

Washing the carpet might destroy it and it comes from Stalin's Kremlin office. I should consider the ink stain a momentum of Stalin. Zinaida makes the sign of the cross over the carpet and next over us.

"Just in case the demons in the *Vozdh's* heart try to invade ours," she explains.

Beretzkoy, back from Moscow, brings a nineteenth century Italian dressing table over to Ob Street. It belonged to his mother but Nadezdha does not like it and is threatening to throw it away. He suggests I put the dressing table in the bedroom and despite the fact I think it far too pretty to put it where my neighbours will not be able to see it, it is into the bedroom it goes. He promises he will bring me something to put on the dressing table. He brings me an icon. It too had belonged to his mother. A golden-haired Jesus in a long white robe tied around his waist with a gilded sash, stares at me with melancholy in his eyes. No wonder Jesus looks so sad: a crown of thorns is pressed against his skull and a red line of blood runs from his hairline down across his face.

"He's weeping," says Zinaida, planting a finger kiss on Jesus's lips.

Weeping for our lost souls.

What to say?

-0-

CHAPTER ELEVEN

Encouraged by his popularity in Moscow, Beretzkoy decides the time has come to speak to our friends of his novel.

He writes to Yelena. *My dearest Yelena Fyodorovna, I have lent your name to a woman, the wife of a friend. I have not yet spoken of him to you - I met him in the winter of '34 - and in a moment you will read why. He does not exist. Or, he exists, but up here in my head. His name is Rudi Zinn and despite such a foreign name - you will know that zinn is German for tin and I saw the name on a crate at a building site in Moscow on one of those Thursday visits to Tanya - I can assure you he is indeed Russian. I know. I invented him. Yes, I am writing a novel - Dan always said I should. "Or I will," he used to say. You remember? I can hear him say it! I am taking the liberty of sending you what I have so far put down on paper. Tanya thinks that Tolstoy has been reincarnated, but then, she would because she is blinkered like a racehorse where I am concerned. So please can you cast your literary eye over these pages for me and give me your opinion? Thank you in advance. A word about your namesake. She is not you - of course! But she is a strong lady like you. You will know who this other Yelena is in real life and I hope that you will find a place for her in your heart. With Lili you will have no problem because I know you and our dear Daniel Mironovich love her as I do. As always. Beretzkoy.*

He writes to Galina next and his letter to her is different. *My Galya, had you ever met Doctor Rudi Zinn, I would have had no chance! But who is this man, I hear you ask? I've been working on a novel. Its title is Doctor Rudi Zinn. (Rodolphe is his full name). Tanya was concerned that the Vozdh would not care for such foreignness, but Rudi is a Russian - born and bred! You will like him. You will even fall in love with him because you fall in love so easily. You will also recognise Yelena and Lili, the two women in his life. They are very different, the one from the other, yet he loves both. He loves them differently. But I know you are going to say Rudi stopped loving Yelena when he started to love Lili and he should have sent Yelena to hell. I also know you are going to say Rudi's story is my story. Please do not, because I'm telling you now nobody's story is solely his own. As I've said to you before when you and I talked of impossible love, we only have to walk ten steps either right or left and there will be a man or a woman who, when you hear their story, you find you are listening to your own. I used to say and still believe this is a good thing, because it is our shared experiences which make us tolerant of one another. Let me know what you think of this effort of mine; your honesty is appreciated. Flattery, on the contrary, will be angrily rejected! Yes, I've thought of the possibility of punishment for the boldness of Rudi. And yes, my neck is ready for the stretch of the hangman's noose! Tanya sends you her love. So do I, but do I really have to tell you so? Your friend forever, Beretzkoy.*

-0-

It is June.

We - Beretzkoy, Zinaida and I - are sitting at the kitchen table drinking wine and reading *Pravda*.

The paper is running an outline for a new constitution. Stalin has invited us to write to him and to share our thoughts on it with him. Muscovites can drop their letters in a box set up in the Kremlin. The rest of us can just write 'Comrade Stalin' on our envelope and our letters will reach him. The new constitution - we are already speaking of it as Stalin's Constitution - guarantees us universal suffrage, a secret ballot, freedom of the press, freedom of speech, freedom to assemble and freedom to demonstrate our discontent on the streets. Such wonderful promises! And even more wondrous they are because for years now we have been told that we do have these things.

"So now, Beretzkoy, you can hand that novel of yours over to Gozuzdom," says Zinaida.

She is not supposed to know about the book.

Beretzkoy frowns and looks at me.

"Tanya?"

"I didn't tell her!" I say quickly.

"How do you know about the book, Zinaida?" he asks.

"Am I not a writer myself? Do I not recognise the urge to write when it overpowers one?"

He tells her about Rudi Zinn.

"A foreigner! Oh, he will be trouble! Mark my words," she warns.

"Rudi is Russian!" I intervene.

She shakes her head and looks at Beretzkoy.

"You will go Vannikov's way, as true as God is my Saviour!"

She does not want to read what he has so far written.

"Spare me," she begs. "When I find Semyon, then I will read it. They can kill me once I've seen my son again. And, Beretzkoy, they will kill all those who know about your Doctor Rudi Zinn!"

She hammers her fist down on the table in frustration and Beretzkoy lifts it up and kisses it.

"Don't worry, I understand," he says.

-0-

Zinaida waits for night to fall. She walks into the living room. I am lying on the sofa.

"Where is it? Beretzkoy's manuscript? Come and give it to me."

"Just take it, Zinaida!" I snap.

I am angry with her because I know Beretzkoy really needs our support right now.

"No," she snaps back, "you give it to me!"

"What has made you change your mind about reading it?"

"The look which came over his face."

"He was indeed disappointed you did not want to read it."

"Better disappointed than dead!"

I get up and I fetch the green folder and I hand it to her.

"I won't say thank you," she says. "I will say I wish he's not doing this."

-0-

Zinaida says she is leaving. She puts on her brown cassock and wooden clogs. We ask her what is going on. Where will she go? She says it is time for her to move on. She has said not a word about *Doctor Rudi Zinn*. Beretzkoy does not even know she has read it because I did not tell him she asked me to give her the manuscript.

"Zinaida, you can't leave," says Beretzkoy.

"Have you forgotten our policy of tortoisesation?" I ask her.

"I haven't, Tanya, but I am going all the same."

"Where will you go?" asks Beretzkoy.

"I'll go back to Alma-Ata."

"To the monastery?" I ask.

"What monastery?"

"Where you were staying before you came here to us," I tell her.

"I wasn't in a monastery. I was in a home. There aren't so many monasteries now, you know, so sometimes I have to go into a home."

"Whose home?" asks Beretzkoy.

"A home," she says. "An asylum. A house for lunatics."

"You were in an asylum?" I ask her, incredulously.

"Can you think of a better place to hide than a place where one is already under lock and key?" she asks.

She lowers her gaze to the floor.

"But you are not mad!" cries Beretzkoy.

She laughs hollowly.

"But I can pretend to be. So can you. So can Tanya. So can anyone."

She tells us the idea to seek refuge in a lunatic asylum came to her soon after Semyon was taken away from her. One day, on a Moscow tram, she overheard a conversation between two women. The older of the two was telling the other her husband was in an asylum. *How dreadfully sad*, the younger one said. *It's not sad at all. He's hiding there. Shackled and locked up, the Chekists can't get to him*, the older one replied. *But who'd want this for themselves? Who would choose to descend into madness?* questioned the younger one. *Who said anything about him being mad? He is pretending to be and, then, when he is no longer on the Chekists' list, then he will no longer be mad and he will leave the asylum*, said the older one.

"So I pretend as well," says Zinaida. "Pretend to be mad."

I can hear my mother say: *Pretend? Does not need to pretend. She's nuts!*

We do not want Zinaida to leave. We tell her she is playing a dangerous game and tempting fate by walking around in a monk's cassock.

"A nurse or a doctor will denounce you. Or a patient," I tell her.

"Have you heard of the Hippocratic Oath?" she asks.

As for a patient denouncing her, she tells us the insane do not bear malice.

"Malice is a monopoly of the sane. This I have witnessed time and again during my life," she states.

-0-

She gets ready to set off. Beretzkoy and I walk her to the gate.

"Come back if ever you find you want to," I tell her.

"Come and join me if ever you find you want to," she replies.

I tell her I will walk with her to the station.

"To the end of Ob Street only, Tanya. That will do."

"You didn't say anything about Doctor Rudi Zinn," I say to her at the end of the street.

"No, I didn't because I would have said Beretzkoy must continue writing."

"I will pass your words on to him."

She slaps the hand which is not holding her little suitcase against her forehead.

"Tanya, for the love of our dear good Lord, please don't!"

She does not want Beretzkoy's death, his murder by the Chekists, on her conscience.

-0-

We hear Maksim Gorky[61] has died in Moscow on June 18th.

We knew he had entered a hospital. He was admitted at the end of May. We heard he was poisoned, but both Profpro and Gozuzdom sent out circular letters saying he was suffering from some baffling intestinal illness. They also reminded us Stalin considered Gorky along with Chekov as the two greatest writers our motherland has ever produced.

Now, Gorky lies dead.

The House of Endeavour sends word it is hosting a remembrance gathering.

"I will go with Nadezdha Konstantinovna," says Beretzkoy.

So, I stay at home.

Kolya also does not attend. He arrives at my gate with a bottle of champagne.

"We will drink to tortoisesation because we are going to survive the *Chistka* thanks to it. We are just tiny tortoises, Tanya my girl, and Stalin is not interested

---

[61] **Maksim Gorky (real name Aleksey Maksimovich Peshkov) was a Soviet author and political activist.**

in us. He is going for the big turtles."

Gorky was a big turtle and he was poisoned.

Kolya and I drink to tiny tortoises.

We finish off the bottle.

-0-

In August, Kolya's words come true.

Two of our country's biggest heroes, men who fought for *the cause* alongside Lenin and who shared power with Stalin during the Triumvirate period - Lev Borisovich Kamenev and Grigory Yevseevich Zinoviev - are executed.

Branded as enemies of our people, they are shot at two-thirty one hot morning in a basement room of the Lubyanka. Stalin is on holiday in Sochi.

-0-

February 2004: Moscow (Gerald Lombard/Biographer)

Back in Moscow for further research, I ask those who agreed to speak to me on my previous visits about the *Chistka*.

They say they would indeed like to tell me about it.

They tell me of the spring of 1935.

They tell me Stalin made a speech and said *Life is better and gayer now*, and that so it was. They say perhaps life was not gayer but they want to know from me where in Europe was life gay those years with Hitler's shadow darkening the horizon?

"But you had no freedom," I argue.

"Can one eat freedom?" they ask. "Can one put freedom on your children's feet? Will freedom warm your home?"

I have to admit that, no, freedom cannot do such things.

"So why speak of freedom? Our stomachs were full, our children had shoes to wear and our homes were warm.

"We had a car industry, an aircraft industry and a heavy weapons industry. We were manufacturing tanks, cruise ships, warships and even submarines.

"Our roads were being asphalted. Steel bridges were replacing the old wooden ones. Dilapidated buildings were being demolished and modern residential blocks replaced them, and everywhere land was being cleared and new towns were being laid out.

"Schools, specialised colleges and universities were opening nation-wide. So were hospitals and clinics and scientific institutions.

"Railways, dams and canals were being constructed in the remotest of regions and we were even working on a scheme to turn the flow of our rivers so that water could flow from the sea instead of towards it in order to irrigate our deserts.

"We were producing millions of tons of timber, steel and coal, and billions of kilowatts of electricity.

"We were better dressed and in better health than we had ever been. We were painting the façades of our *dachas*. We were hanging new drapes and throwing out our old worn carpets and buying new ones in bright colours.

"We were buying furniture, fridges, electrical stoves, washing machines and electrical irons. Some of us even bought cars - Russian-manufactured cars at that! Few of us did, it was true, but who would have thought in those years of the Second Great Famine that one day there would be privately-owned cars in our country.

"The poet - the one they called Dushenka Koba - bought a car. He went to

179

Moscow and returned behind the wheel of a sleek black sedan. "Mine," he told us when we stopped to admire the car. He took us for rides and when we swept around Lenin's statue on Marx Square he allowed us to sound the horn.

"That … *that* was the *Chistka*."

I am reminded of what was going on in Europe while Russia was basking in such prosperity. Hitler had marched into the Rhineland and signed a non-intervention treaty with Austria making it a German state.

"Ask us about Hitler," they say almost angrily.

I ask them.

"When Hitler marched into the Rhineland your king and your prime minister did not lift a finger to stop him. Neither did the French president and neither did the American president. No, you were all too busy preparing for the Olympic Games which were to be held in Berlin that August."

They want to know whether I can remember what a disgusting spectacle the Games had been and I say I was only born in the Fifties.

"So, we will tell you," they say.

I should have seen Europe's politicians and crowned heads along with the rich and the famous kowtowing to Adolf Hitler.

"In the great opening parade, the French athletes even gave the Nazi salute although they afterwards claimed that it had been the Olympic salute, and what a laugh that was!"

They give me a demonstration of the two which are practically the same. Stiff old arms fling up in the air and heels click clumsily and I am told I should go and ask the Germans about Hitler instead of asking Soviet citizens about the *Chistka*.

"Do you know about that black runner - what's his name?" they ask me.

"Jesse Owens?"

"Oh, you know about him!"

"I know."

"Hitler refused to shake his hand. Stalin never refused to shake anybody's hand. Whatever you can say about Stalin, Stalin never would have done that. Refused to shake a man's hand because his skin was black."

They still have to speak about Spain, they tell me.

"Franco was in Morocco and unable to get his men and equipment into Spain and Hitler sent ships and planes to help him. So did Mussolini. And who came to the aid of the Spanish people? Stalin. Only Stalin."

Oh yes, the *Chistka* did happen. They will not deny that it did.

"So tell me about it?" I ask.

At the time, they say, there had been talk that hundreds of thousands, even millions, had been taken away in *black ravens*. To camps. To GULAG. Yes, there were camps and yes there were those who had been taken away.

The *black ravens* always used to come at night. Unexpectedly, and yes, at times, for no reason at all. They had begun to pack essentials into small cases which they kept at hand in case the *black ravens* came for them. Things like warm

180

clothing had gone into the cases. And dried bread and dried meat. A packet of dried biscuits, a sheet of paper and a pencil so that they could write home. Photographs of a loved one went into the suitcases too. Sometimes a book as well. Like Osip Mandelstam, the poet, who put a pocket edition of Dante's *Divine Comedy* into his case and just as well he did because a *black raven* had indeed come for him.

As for the villagers. Gosha, the baker, was taken. It was said he had stolen flour. Slava, the pianist at the Red Tavern, was taken. No one was sad to see him go as he was just a good-for-nothing drunk. Sveta, the telephone operator, was taken. She was spreading anti-Soviet propaganda over the telephone lines. This was what was said at the time although they all had believed her to have been innocent. Shura was taken too. She was the post woman. No one knew why she had been taken. And a *black raven* had come for Sas one night. It was because a disease had broken out among the pigs on the *kolkhoz* and because a similar disease had broken out in the past - it had been among the horses during the Second Great Famine - he was accused of sabotaging state property. He was a good man, was Sas. He was missed.

"So yes, the *Chistka* existed, but look at what was going on in Germany," they say.

I am asked who had been the greater evil.

"Was it Stalin or Hitler?"

I admit I cannot answer their question.

-0-

PART FIVE

CHAPTER ONE

It is winter and Stalin is coming to Zernoye Selo. He is to have treatment at our dental clinic.

Maksim, when he told us, put a finger over his lips: it was a secret.

It is Friday.

Stalin is due to arrive on Sunday.

There is mayhem at the dental clinic because it must be spick and span for the great man. Each member of the staff, regardless of rank and position, is given something to do. Nurses are scrubbing floors and dentists are helping the technicians with the washing of bed linen and towels, and the washing, darning and starching of tunics. Furniture is being polished until it gleams. Windows are being cleaned, and instruments scrubbed and disinfected, and there is a man banging around on the roof because it leaks and he is desperately trying to repair it. Even the clinic's security men are sent to the *kolkhoz* to see what produce the new chairman - Andrey Borisovich Afonov is his name - can provide for Stalin's meals.

All this activity is taking place in the greatest of secrecy because no one outside the clinic is to know the *Vozdh* has toothache.

"Does he?" asks Beretzkoy.

"He has," confirms Maksim.

We quell the urge to jump up and down, clap our hands and shout, *Good! I hope it hurts like hell!*

"Stalin suffers from malocclusion," explains Maksim.

"What's that?" I ask.

"It's the medical term used when one's final set of teeth grows out unevenly so that there is no contact between the top and bottom jaws. It makes teeth difficult to clean which accelerates the formation of tartar, and tartar, as you will know, rots teeth and rotten teeth, as you will also know, means one's mouth is full of bacteria and bacteria causes inflammation and infection which we call gingivitis. And gingivitis is painful and Stalin's is particularly severe."

Stalin comes to the clinic often and always in the greatest of secrecy. He insists on the same dentist treating him and the same nurse tending to him, and if a tooth needs to be extracted and replaced, it is the same technician who has to make the new tooth.

"I am the technician who makes Stalin's teeth," says Maksim.

He winks and promises to keep us informed.

-0-

On Sunday at noon fourteen black cars with white-painted hubcaps, black curtains over the windows, and our Soviet flag, peculiarly painted on bark, flapping stiffly in the wind from the windscreen, turn off Moscow Street in the direction of Land Development Street. They pull up outside the clinic. Before the chauffeurs cut the engines, the rear door of one of the cars - a Rolls Royce - flings open. Out jumps Stalin. A huge brown leather cape hangs from his shoulders and he holds a copy of *Pravda* over his head: it has been snowing all morning. The door of the clinic opens and half a dozen staff members, the acrid smell of moth balls clinging to their clothes, their heads bare despite the intense cold, rush over to our great leader. He greets them with bear hugs, holds them to him as if he were never going to let go of them. He dropped the *Pravda* and it lies on the ground and the feet of his admirers are trampling one of his speeches into the snow. He does not seem to notice. With his good arm he beckons to a hulk of a man standing with him - no doubt a bodyguard - to open the umbrella he is holding: Stalin does not want to get wet. He starts to run towards the clinic. The others run after him, arms waiving in unison for a nurse standing at the door to open it. The chauffeurs remain beside their cars and, when the clinic's front door is again closed, they waste no time to jump back in behind the steering wheels, blowing on their ungloved hands. The car engines growl into life, black fumes rise from the exhausts. The clinic's door flings open again and someone comes running and tells the chauffeurs they are to come indoors and get something hot into them but first they have to park their sleek autos - Stalin's Rolls Royce, three American Lincoln V12s and ten of our very own GAZ M-1s. Pravda told us that the GAZ M-1 looks like the 1933 model of the Americans' Ford V-9s but that our car is so much better than the Americans'. Who are we to argue?

Once the cars are parked and the chauffeurs are no doubt getting something hot into them in the clinic's kitchen, a guard in a brown uniform and carrying a rifle ambles up to the cars and sits down on the bonnet of one of the Lincolns. Clasping the rifle under an armpit, he lights a cigarette. He appears oblivious to the falling snow.

Stalin is to stay at the clinic for seven days.

Maksim keeps his promise and keeps us informed.

-0-

Stalin is in great pain. He must have two teeth - two upper premolars - extracted. One of his bodyguards - he has brought four with him as well as a male secretary, a doctor, a cook and a chambermaid - is driving back to Moscow for extra supplies of chloroform and morphine. Stalin never uses the clinic's chloroform and morphine, but always has his own supply.

The teeth are extracted.

Stalin's doctor stands by, holding a kidney-shaped enamel dish - one never knows but the great leader may just feel a little nauseous - and demands the dentist hands over the two extracted decayed teeth. He will dispose of them once back in the Kremlin, he says.

Five days pass and the dentist declares Stalin's mouth healed. Maksim is called to make an imprint of the illustrious patient's mouth. It takes over an hour for him to do so because the illustrious patient will not keep still. His body jerks as if in an epileptic spasm each time Maksim tries to insert into his mouth the arched metal plate filled with the ice-cold viscous pink liquid wax to make a perfect replica of the gums. Yet again Stalin's doctor is at hand with his kidney-shaped enamel dish and again he has a request, or rather an order: after the new teeth have been moulded Maksim will have to hand the wax imprints over to him.

Twenty-four hours pass. The new teeth are ready to be tried out. Stalin opens his mouth wide. Maksim finds Stalin's gums rather swollen, but he does not say so. Gently he pushes the two new premolars into the gaps in our great leader's mouth. Stalin groans. Maksim secures the two new teeth with a gold wire he fits around an adjoining tooth. He hands Stalin a mirror.

"Comrade Stalin, please say *nyet*?" he requests.

Saying the word *nyet* exposes the upper teeth.

Stalin says *nyet* more than once. Obviously, the word comes easily to him. He shakes Maksim's hand. He says Russia has the world's best dental technicians.

-0-

With his ordeal finally over, Stalin tells his secretary to organise a dinner party. The village's dignitaries are to be invited. The secretary sends out six invitations. Two of these are hand delivered to *dachas* on Lena Street. One to the Beretzkoys' *dacha*, and the other to that of the Dushenka Kobas'.

Maksim does not get invited.

"I would have liked to have gone. Even if only to see whether the teeth I made for him are sharp enough."

He giggles, obviously proud of himself.

Or rather proud of his handiwork.

-0-

Dushenka Koba, at his office in Moscow, rushes back to the village. Alexandra Alexandrovna telephoned him to say Stalin has invited him for dinner.

"I will tell him how much we appreciate him," says Dushenka Koba to Beretzkoy. Neither he nor Beretzkoy has as yet had the honour of being in Stalin's company.

Both Nadezdha Konstantinovna and Alexandra Alexandrovna think their husbands should wear their medals to the dinner. Beretzkoy has two: the Meritorious Medal for Musical Achievement awarded him when he was an eight-year-old schoolboy, and the Merited Poetic Endeavour Medal which he received in the year before I met him. Dushenka Koba has half a dozen, and no one, not even he himself, can remember why he received them. Kolya thinks he might have bought the medals. It is possible do so because a medal fetches quite a sum of money on the black market. Finally, it is Comrade Afonov, who will also be a dinner guest representing the *kolkhoz*, who decides medals must be worn.

Stalin's guests have to be at the dental clinic at 10.30 p.m. Stalin always dines late.

-0-

CHAPTER TWO

Beretzkoy and Dushenka Koba set off. They are on foot, Lena Street being near to the clinic. Cascading shards of snow slash at their faces.

At the clinic, in a ground floor reception room, a short plump man in an ill-fitting brown suit - he says his name is Valentin Sergeyevich and he is one of Stalin's secretaries and will be joining them for dinner - offers each a glass of tea. The other guests have already arrived: Vitya and his deputy, Afonov and his deputy and the chairman of the clinic - his name is Ivan Ivanovich Prutkov - and his deputy. All wear suits and, like Beretzkoy and Dushenka Koba, their medals. Prutkov slurps his tea and his many gold teeth gleam like jewels in a tsar's sceptre. His deputy has only one gold tooth, a large incisor.

For half an hour the guests make banal small talk, next, Valentin Sergeyevich says they should go upstairs. He leads the way up a flight of narrow green-tiled stairs and down a green-tiled hallway and into a green-tiled vestibule. A man with the build of a mountain gorilla is waiting outside; he is practically bursting out of his brown suit. He introduces himself as Igor Sergeyevich and says he is one of Stalin's bodyguards and he will also be joining them for dinner.

"But first I will have to frisk you lot!"

A third man joins them. He is tall and thin and he says his name is Oleg Sergeyevich. He too is wearing a brown suit. Perhaps the Kremlin has received a bargain consignment of brown suits from somewhere.

"We are the three Sergeyvichs," he says.

He does not say what his role in Stalin's entourage is or whether he will also be joining them for dinner.

-0-

Stalin is waiting in a small salon. He sits on a red Louis XV sofa. He is alone in the room. He rises when his guests walk in. He wears a white buttoned *rybashka* and a pair of badly-creased beige gabardine trousers. On his feet are embroidered peasant boots of which the heels seem higher than the heels of men's boots and shoes normally are. He walks to the middle of the room putting each booted foot down heavily like a man walking on slippery snow and trying not to fall. His hair, thick and black, is swept away from his pockmarked face. His eyebrows, also black, slant devilishly upwards and so does his bushy black moustache. Strands of wiry, grey-speckled hair grow from the lobes of his ears. He lifts an arm in greeting. It is his right arm, his good arm. The left, lame, hangs limply at his side as if he wants to have nothing to do with it. He has a skin-coloured mole to the left of his left eye.

189

"Glad to meet you at last, Boris Petrovich," he says to Beretzkoy.

Our Great Leader is smiling broadly.

It is a full-face smile, the smile of a circus clown whose only wish in life is to please the little children whose mothers have gone without food for several days to be able to put aside the few kopeks they had needed so that they could buy their little darlings an ice cream at the circus.

Smiling, dimples form at the corners of Stalin's mouth and the skin-coloured mole which, a moment before, looked like a malevolent third eye, disappears within a multitude of fine lines.

One cannot be indifferent to such a smile and all Stalin's guests, including Beretzkoy, involuntarily smile too.

-0-

Valentin Sergeyevich, with a nod of his head, indicates to the guests they ought to sit down.

"Over here, Boris Petrovich! I would like you over here with me," Stalin calls out.

The little finger of his bad hand ineptly points to the red sofa.

"Sit wherever you wish," Valentin Sergeyevich tells the others.

Dushenka Koba dashes across the floor towards the red sofa but waits until Stalin and Beretzkoy are seated in order to sit down on an armchair next to Stalin's side of the sofa.

"Let's wet our throats, shall we? Vodka for all?" asks Stalin.

Valentin and Oleg work in tandem filling small crystal tumblers.

Prutkov proposes a toast. His gold teeth are still gleaming.

"To our Great Leader!"

The vodka is strong. It burns Beretzkoy's tongue. The *kolkhoz's* moonshine? There is no label on the bottle.

Another toast follows. It is to the clinic. Stalin proposes it. He is smiling, the smile spreading to the corners of his mouth, baring his two new teeth. These have not been moulded in gold or silver but, as Maksim told us, in the finest Chinese porcelain. They are not white-white but have a bluish tint. They make his other teeth look like coffee beans.

"Good work you're doing here!" says Stalin to Prutkov.

Good work, good work, good work echoes through the room; the tumblers are held high.

"Speaking of good work," continues Stalin and turns to Beretzkoy. "I enjoy yours."

"Thank you, Comrade Stalin." replies Beretzkoy.

Previously, Valentin Sergeyevich told Stalin's guests they must address their host as 'Comrade Stalin'.

"Yours also," says Stalin.

He is looking away from Beretzkoy and towards Dushenka Koba who appears to be sitting on one buttock only as if preparing to fall to his knees at any moment in submission.

"Thank you, Comrade Stalin. Thank you. You are so kind!" he says in a half-whisper.

There is another toast. Vitya proposes it, and his hand, the one that holds the tumbler, is trembling.

"To Zernoye Selo!"

The tumblers are emptied in one gulp and Igor helps the other two Sergeyevichs to refill them once again. Playfully, Stalin slaps his hand. All think Stalin's playfulness is hilarious. They laugh in unison. They roar with laughter.

Stalin starts laughing too.

He turns to Beretzkoy and slaps him on the knee.

"What do you say, poet man? Do you think our people are producing great work?"

"I certainly do, Comrade Stalin," replies Beretzkoy.

Stalin nods, gratified by his line of questioning.

"I thought you did a splendid job with the encyclopaedia. I understand there will be four tomes. I love such decisiveness. I always say, *don't hesitate, don't falter, don't change your mind, don't go back on your word and don't back down.* My five commandments and the only ones we need. Forget the others. Who needs ten when five will do?"

Some of Stalin's guests look puzzled. They obviously do not know what he is talking about, yet they nod and murmur their concurrence none the less.

-0-

After an hour of drinking and inane conversation, Stalin announces, because he is hungry, they will eat. The dining room leads from one end of the salon. In the middle of the room stands a round table with twelve long-backed upholstered chairs arranged around it. A stiffly-starched white damask cloth covers the table. The cutlery is of sterling silver, the crockery of heavy porcelain, and the glasses - there are six for each setting - are of crystal like the vodka tumblers.

Valentin Sergeyevich waits until Stalin chooses a chair and then directs the guests to their chairs with flicks of his head and hand gestures. Prutkov gets the first chair on Stalin's right and Afonov the first on his left. Dushenka Koba gets the chair on Afonov's left. Beretzkoy is directed to a chair facing Stalin. Around the table stand three waiters in grey trousers and white short-sleeved shirts. One of the waiters has the face of a girl tattooed above his wrist.

The meal begins with caviar. It is served in a large crystal bowl. The bowl rests on an even larger crystal bowl filled with ice so finely crushed that it looks like snow. Next follows a selection of cold meats and after the meat some marinated smoked salmon. The waiters move smoothly around the guests like dancers doing a *pas à deux*. They hold the dishes high as if they were trophies.

They start serving egg soup.

"*Ghkhtma*. Georgian. Mother's milk ... as good as," explains Stalin.

He fills his spoon to the brim and the soup runs down his chin.

Dushenka Koba tries to draw Stalin's attention with a gesture of his hand to the soup which has started to drip onto his *rybashka*.

"Comra ... Comrade Stalin ... your ... uh ... chin ..," he tries.

Prutkov silences him with a single glance.

After the soup, an entire suckling pig, roasted to a crispy brown, fat dripping from its snout, is carried in. Two of the waiters are sharing the load. The third waiter carries in a plate of grilled quail, the tiny little birds lying on a bed of small green grapes. The three deftly dismember the little birds working fast like crazed killers – an incision here and another there and the little carcasses are without wings and legs and heads. Now, it is the pig's turn to go under the knife. From it escapes a belch of air and bloody juice as one of the waiters plunges a black-handled carving knife into its large shiny belly.

Stalin and his guests eat baked potatoes covered in *smetana*[62] with the pig and quail.

Dessert is a compote of fresh fruit, mint-flavoured ice cream, nuts and sweetmeats.

As the empty bottles on the table prove, they finished off a dozen and a half bottles of wine, red and white, dry or sweet.

-0-

The eating lasted two hours and now Stalin and his guests are back in the salon.

"Smoke, please smoke," encourages Valentin Sergeyevich.

"Yes," says Stalin. "Smoke! This is a pleasure my doctors have forbidden me."

Only Dushenka Koba appears to prepare to light up. He takes a pipe, a pouch of tobacco and a small box of matches from one of the pockets of his jacket. He cradles the pipe in his left hand and allows tobacco to trickle into the bowl of the pipe. When it is full, or looking full to those watching - this includes Stalin who is contemplatively stroking his lips with his good hand as if wondering whether to pounce on the pipe - he stamps the tobacco down gently and allows more tobacco to trickle into the bowl. He repeats the process one more time. No one says a word which makes the ticking of a clock drifting from somewhere behind the walls sound suddenly very loud, like a hammer hitting a metal object.

Dushenka Koba strikes a match. A quivering yellow flame shoots up in the air but dies almost immediately. He strikes three more matches - Valentin Sergeyevich had stepped forward with an ashtray - before a flame lasts long enough to light the tobacco. He allows the flame to only singe the tobacco when

---

[62] **Double cream.**

he extinguishes it with an audible exhalation of air, and restarts the process right from the start. Finally, he is gripping the stem between two fingers and inhaling lightly, filling his already chubby cheeks with the tobacco's aromatic vapour.

"Edgeworth," he says after having exhaled blue-grey smoke into the air. He holds up the pipe.

"And that's a Dunhill pipe?" states Stalin rhetorically.

All in the room know Stalin, before his doctors forbade him to smoke, only ever smoked a pipe and that pipe was a Dunhill and the tobacco he smoked was Edgeworth.

Tea is served. Stalin rises and so do his guests. They form a wide circle around a mahogany trolley with gilded legs. Little silver bowls of shiny caramelised nuts and sweetmeats are on the trolley too. Stalin pops a lump of sugar into his mouth, balances it on his tongue and fills his mouth with the boiling-hot tea. He ignores the caramelised nuts and sweetmeats because his dentist had advised him to avoid eating nuts and sweetmeats until his new teeth have *settled in*.

"Exercise. More doctors' orders," he says and starts to pace the floor. His right hand is pushed in between the third and fourth buttons of his *rybashka*. The withered left arm hangs limply by his side.

He halts in front of Dushenka Koba.

"Ooi! I like your boots! Leather?"

Beretzkoy knows that Dushenka Koba has bought the boots especially for the dinner before he set off from Moscow.

"Reindeer skin, Comrade Stalin," replies Dushenka Koba.

"Looks like horse leather."

Dushenka Koba shakes his head.

"I love horses, Comrade Stalin."

"Wouldn't kill a horse in order to have boots? So what about the reindeer? Did you walk up to him and ask him to give you the skin off his rump?"

"I do not ... well ... I do not love reindeers as much as I love horses, Comrade Stalin. Man can relate to the horse."

"What rubbish you are speaking!" snorts Stalin.

"I mean ..."

Stalin walks on.

"I love birds," he mutters to no one in particular.

He stops in front of Vitya's deputy.

"Birds fly!" he says.

He mimes a bird in flight. He bends his knees, lifts his arms - yes, even his bad arm - and sways left and right.

"So they do, Comrade Stalin," replies Vitya's deputy.

"I would like to give all Russians wings so we can all fly like birds," continues Stalin.

He walks on. He circles the room twice and halts in front of Vitya's deputy again.

"Where will you fly to with your wings, huh?"

"Comrade Stalin, any gift from you will be a gift to cherish."

"But come on tell me, where will you fly to? America? I hear you all want to go live in America and become rich by exploiting your fellow man."

"Comrade Stalin, before you stands a Soviet patriot," says Vitya's deputy, his upper lip twitching nervously.

"A good Russian, hey!"

Stalin taps the man on the shoulder.

"I strive to be, Comrade Stalin."

"Bah! Let us sit," says Stalin.

Seated, he again taps Beretzkoy on the knee.

"I've heard your style is being compared to that of our dear departed Alexsey Maksymovich[63]."

"I have not heard this, Comrade Stalin."

"Your style too," says Stalin, turning his gaze to Dushenka Koba.

"As Comrade Beretzkoy has just said, I too have not heard this," Dushenka Koba hesitantly replies.

"*Ooi*, these bashful poets! Let us drink a toast to bashful poets."

The three Sergeyevichs fill a clean set of crystal tumblers with vodka.

Stalin, his face red because of the alcohol, taps his chest with his good hand. As he is holding his tumbler with that hand, vodka spills on to his *rybashka*. He seems unaware of it.

"I ... I always say a leader's might is his word, but a nation's might, is its written word," he bellows.

"Hear! Hear!" shouts Afonov.

"Hear! Hear!" shouts Dushenka Koba.

Hear! Hear! Hear! Hear!

The clock's ticking can no longer be heard.

Dushenka Koba rises, turns to Stalin, gives a little bow and begins to clap his hands. At first, slowly, then faster and louder, and the two chairmen look to the three Sergeyevichs for guidance and the three nod in unison, and all of Stalin's guests rise and begin to clap their hands. They are applauding our Great Leader. He does not rise, no, he remains seated and smiles a feline smile; his acceptance of his guests adoration.

"Pushkin. Let us drink to Pushkin!" he hollers over the din.

They do.

Next, they drink to the purity of Pushkin's work, and then to the purity of our people and then to the purity of our forests, our mountains, our rivers, our lakes, our revolutionary past, our future and our present.

-0-

---

[63] **Maksim Gorky.**

The dinner is over. Stalin and the three Sergeyevichs accompany the guests out onto Land Development Street. The guests are back in their overcoats but Stalin is still in his *rybashka*. The three Sergeyevichs, before stepping out, asked Stalin to put on something warm, but he refused. They therefore removed their own jackets and are now, like him in shirtsleeves, and braving the blankets of swirling snow. Bravely, they try not to shiver. They put their arms behind their backs and keep on bending and straightening their knees as athletes do in warming up. But our Great Leader stands stock-still. Even when his *rybashka* is soaking wet and clings to his body.

He turns to Beretzkoy.

"Boris Petrovich, I want to talk to you some more about literature."

"I would like that, Comrade Stalin," replies Beretzkoy, his teeth clattering.

"You must come to Moscow. You will join me in Moscow for dinner. Then we will talk. Valentin Sergeyevich will be in touch with you."

He puts his arms around Beretzkoy. It is a bizarre lopsided embrace.

The guests begin to walk away. At the end of Land Development Street Beretzkoy and Dushenka Koba turn round and they see Stalin and the three Sergeyevichs are still standing outside the clinic. A *dvornik* is with them. Stalin is saying something to the old woman. She is leaning on her broom. Stalin turns to Valentin Sergeyevich and says something to him and Valentin takes something from his trouser pocket and hands whatever it is to the old woman. She drops her broom and grabs Valentin's hands and kisses them. Next, she falls to her knees in the snow and she is kissing Stalin's embroidered boots. He bends forward and pulls her to her feet. He takes her face in his hands and kisses her briskly full on her mouth. Twice.

"Look at that! What a wonderful man! That's a leader!" gushes Dushenka Koba.

"The tobacco, the Edgeworth where did you get it? And the reindeer boots?" asks Beretzkoy.

"The First Secretary at the British Embassy gave me the tobacco. Of course I do always smoke it but I'd run out."

"And the boots?"

"They were a gift from the chairman of one of our reindeer breeding *kolkhozs* up in the North. He wrote a manual on breeding reindeer and he appealed to me for membership of Profpro. It was a brilliant manual. We sent it down to Kamchatka and I understand the production of reindeer skin products there has already increased. I can assure you his membership to our union was a mere formality because his brilliant manual earned him his membership. I did not want to accept the boots, of course."

"But he insisted, did he?" asks Beretzkoy, sarcastically.

Dushenka Koba nods and his *shapka* drops down over his eyes.

"I know what you are thinking, but he would not allow me to refuse his gift. So, what was I to do?"

He pushes his hat back. He is wearing fur-lined leather gloves.

CHAPTER THREE

We still feel it necessary to keep our heads down like tiny tortoises but we feel more confident knowing Stalin suffers from malocclusion. It has made him ... well ... human. Yes, a human being with fallibility and frailties like the rest of us.

We decide to risk writing a letter to Morne. We tell him we feel we will make it through the *Chistka* but the time is not yet right for the publication in Paris of Beretzkoy's poems.

Two months pass.

Morne's reply arrives.

How glad I am to hear from you. Oh, how I missed your letters and how I miss you both.

He writes about the past year's events in Europe. Events we have heard snippets of, but know little detail.

Hitler marched into the Rhineland on March 7 1936. France's ambassadors at a meeting of French ambassadors in Paris to discuss the Nazi problem called him a pirate. And a civil war has broken out in Spain.

He also writes about Trotsky who is now living in Norway.

Trotsky's new book is with his publisher in Paris. This is not generally known but I can confirm that it is because a young editor from the publishing house has allowed me to read a few pages. Trotsky is not well. He collapsed when he heard of the Kamenev-Zinoviev trial and execution. Trotsky heard that Stalin had both men brought to the Kremlin and offered them their freedom if they owed up to planning a counter-revolution with Trotsky. They refused to denounce him which it seems sealed their fate. Trotsky, by the way, is looking for another country which will have him. Some say that Paraguay is willing to do so. Mexico is also a possibility. He is apparently, understandably, in a highly nervous state.

He continues there are rumours there is a woman in Hitler's life.

It is said that she is very pretty. She has shapely legs apparently and she makes Hitler laugh because she is good at imitating his ministers. Her name is Eva.

What excites us most about Morne's letter is he is trying to obtain a visitor's visa for the Soviet Union.

I may just turn up on your doorstep one day although I do not know as who or what. My friend – the fertilizer manufacturer – thinks he may again be able to include me in a forthcoming visit to Moscow.

He does not mention Beretzkoy's poems and we feel somewhat relieved. Just as well because Stalin has dismissed Yagoda as head of the NKVD and the new man, the one who will now direct the *Chistka* is Nikolai Ivanovich Yezhov. Yezhov we know of. Know more of than we would like to know. He comes to the NKVD from the Central Control Committee of the Party. He is very close to Stalin. Being short and with a round rosy face and chubby cheeks - we

197

wonder whether he ever has to shave - we nickname him *The Bloody Dwarf.*

-0-

CHAPTER FOUR

How strange life is. The *Chistka* is raging yet Dan has returned home. Yelena telephoned Beretzkoy to tell him. "Dan's here! Dan's back!" she shouted. He was tired and thin but he was back and fighting back too as he had immediately started to write.

She tells us Dan has been in GULAG, in a camp in Siberia, one hundred and twelve kilometres from Sverdlovsk, where, in 1917, when the town was still called Ekaterinburg, Nicholas II and his family were executed.

The NKVD first held Dan in an isolation cell in the Lubyanka and then, after a mock trial, during which Dan's state-appointed defender pleaded for clemency, he was sentenced to eight years of hard labour in a camp in Siberia. His crime was not stipulated. With forty *zeks*[64] he made the journey to Siberia in the last wagon of a freight train that carried heavy farm machinery, a gift from Canada, to Siberian *kolkhozs*. The journey took eighteen days.

Why Dan was released after having served just two years they do not know.

One day Dan was told he was being transferred to another camp and a koshevy[65] was waiting for him and it took him and three others, men who also had not served their full punishment, to the Sverdlovsk station. From there he had to make his way back to Moscow himself and he had done so either by hitching rides from train drivers or on foot; on foot in the valenkys he had worn throughout his internment. The valenkys had finally disintegrated on the muddy streets of Moscow and he had arrived here at home, barefoot, writes Yelena.

-0-

Dan and Yelena come to Zernoye Selo. They are staying at the House of Endeavour. Beretzkoy arranges for the man with the horse-drawn buggy to pick them up and bring them here to the *dacha*.

Dan is first to descend from the buggy.

"Tanya, my dear girl, today I am asking you to do something which my father told me never to do. To allow a convict into your home. My convict number is 208060812 and I graduated *with honours* in thievery from GULAG University."

"I'll take my chances, Dan," I tell him.

Two deep furrows which were not there before span his forehead.

---

[64] **The inmates.**

[65] **An open cart usually pulled by horse or mule.**

I want to say something that will make him know how glad I am he has returned and I love him, but the words will not come.

We do not hug or kiss. I know I should throw my arms around him, but all I am capable of is to stare at him.

His blue eyes are filled with tears.

"Come on in," says Beretzkoy.

"No," says Dan, trying to smile. "First, you have to know I have no scruples and I have no shame and I won't hesitate to pilfer whatever takes my fancy. This *zek* will even snatch your last morsel of bread from your mouth."

"Dan's angry," apologises Yelena.

"Dan's bloody angry," he corrects her. "Bloody furious!"

He is wearing his long black overcoat, a black woollen bonnet and his black furred boots. On the day the Chekists had come for him he was still in his pyjamas and as this was how they took him off, his overcoat, bonnet and boots were spared destruction in GULAG.

Yelena is not in her favourite red dress and red cape. She is wearing a white frock and open-toed sandals.

We sit down in the kitchen. I have already laid the table. A beam of sunlight falls across Dan's face. His skin is the colour of cement and the few strands of hair creeping from under his hat look as if they will be as brittle to the touch as pine needles.

Beretzkoy gets up to uncork a bottle of *Dom Perignon* which he put on ice on his arrival in the morning. We bought the champagne from Maksim. Later we will drink Cognac. The dark round-bellied bottle stands on the table. Beretzkoy has had the Cognac for a long time. He has been telling me he is keeping it for a very special occasion.

The cork flies from the champagne bottle and hits the ceiling with a crack. The Kravchinskys' dog starts to bark from the garden next door.

"*Le voilà!*" says Yelena. "Your canine neighbour heard the cork pop and wants to join us for a drink."

I see her face has changed. A criss-cross of lines surrounds her eyes, and her lips are white-grey.

Beretzkoy holds the bottle with both hands and waits for the initial cloud of smoky-vapour to fade away and when it does he fills the flutes we are holding eagerly out towards him.

"We will drink to the death of that malformed, pock-featured Ossetian. May he rot in hell," says Dan.

We eat like gluttons. We start with *botvinia*[66]. Alisa cooked it. I watched her chopping up whatever vegetables I could get hold of - a cucumber, an onion, a few spinach leaves and some horseradish - and into the pot went some carp and a whole crab, some vodka and kvass. The kvass we bought from Leonid. He brews it from black bread in their loft.

---

[66] **Cold vegetable soup.**

Next, we have *bitochky*[67] with red cabbage and sautéed potatoes.

Our dessert is a square almond cake. It is covered in honeyed icing. Alisa has baked this for me too.

When the meal is over, we show Dan and Yelena the *dacha*.

"Nice, nice," says Yelena. She smacks her lips. At the table she had done so too.

Dan lies down on the bed.

"You will excuse me but I find a soft bed is now something irresistible," he says.

The name of the camp Dan was in was Metelovsk. The camp of blizzards. He arrived there in a blizzard, and a blizzard raged on the day he left.

"It was Dan's nose that saved him," says Yelena.

"His nose?" I ask.

"Yes. His Podol."

She pinches Dan's nose and he playfully slaps her hand away.

She explains in the Podol district of Kiev where they hail from, the Jews believe God puts his mark on the most pure amongst them by giving them a long sharp nose like Dan's - a Podol. This is so they will be easily recognisable on the day of the resurrection of the dead when the pure are to assist the Messiah in the creation of a new, better world.

"So Daniel Olminsky with his huge hooter has thus been singled out," says Dan with a wink.

"But you do not believe in the existence of a God," I say.

Yelena taps me on the arm.

"Tanya, my dear, one day the Messiah will come ..."

Then God will exist.

-0-

---

[67] **Beef meatballs.**

CHAPTER FIVE

Morne is to return. We receive a letter from him. It comes via Gorky as Nizhni Novgorod is now named.

On June 14th I will be on the noon train.

He is returning as an agronomist named Jean Thomas. His visa is valid for two weeks. Now that collectivisation has ended agronomists are most welcome in the Soviet Union.

Two and a half years have passed since we have last seen our French friend and Beretzkoy meets him at the railway station.

The two take the buggy to Ob Street.

"How long has it been, Tanya?" asks Morne.

"It has been a long time, Morne. Too long."

I hand him a sprig of lily of the valley from my garden. On the table, in the kitchen, stands a bowl filled with salt and another holding a loaf of bread. We are welcoming him in the Russian way.

He takes the flowers from me.

"Pretty."

"They are from my garden."

He smiles.

"I am not speaking of the flowers."

He has brought us gifts. Beretzkoy receives a leather-bound first edition of Jules Verne's *Michel Strogoff* as well as a pocket knife. He found the book in an antique shop in Paris' Latin Quarter and the knife he bought on a safari to the Cape of Good Hope. The knife's handle is of ivory and beautifully carved into the form of a bare-breasted woman. My gift is a lacquered music box and inside is secreted a ring with a small blue stone. I lift the music box's lid and a yellow-haired boy-doll dressed in a blue and gold uniform begins to beat a drum. I slip the ring on the middle finger of my left hand. I hold my hand up for the two men to admire. My right hand, the hand conspicuously lacking a wedding band, I drop to my side.

-0-

I introduce our agronomist friend to our neighbours. The Widow Alexandra grabs him by the elbow.

"The Russian people will be grateful for what you will do for our country."

Maksim also meets Morne.

"Have you met Hemingway? I know he lives in Paris, so perhaps you have met him," Maksim asks before Morne can even shake his hand.

"I'm afraid I haven't met him, no," replies Morne.

The Widow Alexandra invites all the neighbours for lunch. Kolya too is invited. She serves grilled carp. Maksim smiles at me from across the table and I am reminded of the night I vomited over him. She has baked a *pashka*[68] for dessert. It is not Easter, of course, and not that Easter means anything to us anyway, but she says the cake, because it is pyramid-shaped makes a good centrepiece. Centrepiece? She has obviously lived a high life in the past. She has covered the cake in dark-yellow icing. Kolya has brought his sketch pad and he asks the Widow Alexandra not to cut the cake yet because he wants to draw us sitting around the table.

"For posterity," he says.

"Wait!" says Morne.

He runs back to my *dacha* and returns with a camera. It is a *Box Brownie* he tells us. It indeed looks like a small black leather box, but he points it at me and a shutter at the front of the box opens and almost immediately closes again with a loud click.

Alisa throws her hands up in the air.

"My! My! What will they think of next!"

Morne says we must go outside because he wants to take a group photograph of us and he needs natural light.

"Dan and Yelena should have been here today," I whisper to Beretzkoy.

They have returned to Moscow.

-0-

Beretzkoy decides he and Morne will go back to Lake Legyshka for some summer fishing. I would like to accompany them, but I do not say so.

The two will be away for three days. They will take the bus we took before and they are to camp in the forest, sleep in sleeping bags under the stars and cook over a twig fire. I pack a picnic hamper for them of a smoked sausage, a dozen hard-boiled eggs, two loaves of black bread, two bottles of red wine and a bottle of vodka.

I hope the three days will pass quickly. This is selfish of me, I know, yet I do.

-0-

They return.

Beretzkoy tells me he missed me.

Morne hands me a large bundle of wild flowers he picked in the forest.

"How was it?" I ask them.

---

[68] **A cake eaten in Russia at Easter.**

"We explored the Malenky Kosty thoroughly this time," replies Beretzkoy.

"... and the forest too. And we fished much more successfully," adds Morne.

I say it sounds great. I heat the samovar. If they do not want to tell me about the three days at the lake, so be it.

-0-

Morne and I spend the day in the garden. He throws a ball across the fence and the Kravshinsky's dog runs to retrieve it and returns it to him.

Beretzkoy is on the veranda, working.

"Walk with me to the gate," he says at the end of the day.

At the gate, he takes my hand.

"I did really miss you," I tell him.

"I told Morne about the book," he says. "About *Doctor Rudi Zinn.*"

"I see."

"I read it to him."

I did not know Beretzkoy had taken a copy of the manuscript with him to the lake.

"And?" I ask.

"I will have to ask you to type a copy for him. He's going to take it to Paris."

"*Khorosho*[69]." I say.

This is a neutral word lacking in conviction. We say it when we say 'yes' and mean 'no'. We say it when we would rather be saying *I do not know,* or *I would rather not tell you what I really think.* It is a word to hide behind.

"You are not pleased?" asks Beretzkoy.

I tell him I want what is best for him and if he thinks this is the best course of action, then, I am pleased.

Yet, this is not how I feel at all. If only I had known he was taking the manuscript to the lake. I would have talked him out of it.

-0-

"He told you," says Morne.

He stands at the kitchen table watching me.

I nod.

"Yes, he told me."

"And you are not pleased?"

"I am scared, Morne."

"I will not do anything to harm him, you know that don't you?"

"No .... Yes ... I mean I know you love him as I do but I will all the same warn you I won't let anyone harm him."

"I won't harm him, Tanya. He is like a brother to me. And yes, I love him."

---

[69] **Good.**

"Beretzkoy is my life. I cannot lose him," I tell Morne.

-0-

I begin to type a copy of the manuscript. While I am typing the voices of the two men drift from the veranda.

"Wait until I tell you that you can go ahead with its translation," says Beretzkoy.

We hide the manuscript in Morne's sheepskin jacket, just as we had done previously with the poems.

The day of departure is here.

We walk Morne to the gate.

He has to be satisfied with only a nod from me because a lump in my throat makes it impossible for me to say goodbye.

-0-

CHAPTER SIX

This is a summer of warmth and of bright light.

Every day my neighbours tell me my garden looks beautiful. In the spring I planted sweet pea seeds and now maroon, purple, pink and white flowers cling to furry, green stems taller than I am, filling the air with their sweet hypnotic scent.

Kolya sits on the steps leading to my front door and draws lines with a child's measurement ruler in a sketchpad. He calls what he is doing groundwork for a painting. Alisa comes to stand beside him to see what he is doing and he quickly closes the sketchpad.

"It's all still raw," he says, dramatically.

Beyond the confines of my beautiful garden the *Chistka* continues. We hear the Chekists have now started to kill by quota. Each week each Chekist unit is issued with an order to kill a certain number of people, and if it fails to meet the quota, its own agents are executed. To save their own lives, the agents are picking people off the streets, quite at random, or they burst into rest homes and take the first old folk they can lay their hands on. They even march into hospitals and order the ill from their beds, and those who are too ill to walk to the shooting ranges, are carried.

While we digest such news we hear nine members of the Red Army High Command have been arrested and were shot for high treason. One of the nine was the immensely popular Marshal Mikhayl Nikolayevich Tukhachevsky, a decorated hero of not only the First World War, but also of the Civil War, the 1920 Russo-Polish War and the 1921 Kronstadt anti-revolutionary uprising. The Marshal, we hear, was plotting to storm the Kremlin with troops and assassinate Stalin.

The Marshal's death is followed by a clean sweep through the Red Army with thousands arrested and executed.

Next, it is the Chekists' turn to be cleansed. They too are executed in their hundreds, branded as enemies of our nation.

For them, we do not cry.

-0-

I am lying in bed. It is deep in the night. I cannot fall asleep. I hear the rumbling of an engine, first faintly, then louder. A car is coming down Ob Street. I sit bolt upright. Cars hardly ever come our way, and if they do it is certainly never at night. I know, I just know, the Chekists have come for someone. The engine dies. The night falls silent again, but not in the way it should, not in a peaceful way. I slither out of my bed and crawl across the wooden floorboards to the wardrobe. I keep a small suitcase in there. We all have such small suitcases which we keep packed for a night like this.

The cupboard door creaks. I want to tell it to shut up because the Chekists will hear. In the dark I feel for the suitcase. I touch it, grabbing hold of the handle, making sure it is there. I have some warm clothing, a pair of fur-lined boots and a cloth-bound edition of Beretzkoy's poems packed in it.

With a deep growl, the car's engine starts up again. I crawl to my living room, to the window, for a better view of the street. I peer through a tiny hole in the curtain. On Kolya's urging I cut this little hole in the curtain to be able to look outside without being seen from the garden or the street. The vehicle is a black foreign-made four-door sedan. It has pulled up in front of my *dacha*, but it drives off again towards the wasteland. It will have to make a U-turn and sure enough I see its headlights illuminating the rutted surface of Ob Street as it drives back towards me. I grab hold of the curtain like a child grabbing hold of its mother's skirt. I can hear gravel from the road-surface pinging against the car's bumpers. It has rained so little this summer and the earth is bone-dry.

I wonder whether the Chekists will give me time to put on warm clothing before they drag me off. No, I know they will not; we have heard that the bodies of their victims are being burnt every day in the fields and forests around our cities and often the bodies are clad in pyjamas or nightgowns. The car approaches. It passes my gate. I close my eyes tightly and a mantra circles round and round in my brain, *go away go away go away*. The engine dies yet again. I open my eyes and see the car has stopped in front of the Kravschinskys' *dacha*. The couple's dog always barks at the slightest movement at their gate but this night he does not bark at all, even when his master's gate is being kicked open. I wonder how Alisa and Leonid are keeping him quiet.

The dog's name is Nilats – Stalin spelt backwards. I have learnt his name only recently because everyone always calls him just 'the Kravschinskys' dog' or occasionally other more unsavoury names.

The hedge between our gardens makes it impossible for me to see what is going on next door, but I can hear raised voices and next the visitors start banging on my neighbour's front door.

I hear the door opening.

I hear Alisa's voice.

"No, there is a misunderstanding. It is not this Leonid you want. This is my husband. His name is Leonid Pavlovich Kravschinsky. You must be looking for a Leonid Petrovich Kravschinsky or something. Yes, I am sure that you have made a mistake."

Silence follows.

The clock in my kitchen ticks the seconds away.

I hear footsteps again. My neighbours' gate groans on its hinges. Alisa appears into full view. I grab the curtain and press my face against it. She is in a lemon-yellow nightdress and her grey hair is down and hangs to her waist. I am not aware her hair is so long because she always wears it tied in a bun in the nape of her neck. She looks, somehow, younger this way. Leonid is beside her. He is wearing an overcoat but looking at his legs I can see he is wearing pyjamas underneath it. His hands are handcuffed behind his back. There are two men with them, dressed in black leather. Of course, they are Chekists! They must have known they were coming for an old man who would not be able to offer resistance or there would have been more of them. Alisa tries to pull Leonid free. One of the men is carrying a small brown suitcase. It must be Leonid's, the one he has kept packed and waiting in a cupboard. The Chekist hurls the suitcase into the boot of the car and they shove poor Leonid onto the rear seat. Alisa is standing helplessly beside the car, one hand groping at the open door. One of the men hits her hard on the knuckles with his gloved fist and she instantly recoils, stumbling backwards against her own gatepost. The car's doors slam shut and rapidly the car pulls away, throwing up dust and grit in its wake.

From somewhere within the Kravschinskys' dacha, Nilats begins barking wildly.

-0-

As soon as all is silent once more and my courage returns, I creep next door with a bottle of vodka. I find Alisa hunched behind her front door, her knees pulled up under her nightgown. She is smoothing down the yellow fabric over and over. I can see a dark swelling forming on the knuckles of her right hand.

"You've heard?" she whispers.

"I saw."

I kneel beside her.

"He was a good teacher. Tanya, he was a good teacher. He believed education is our saviour. He believed an educated man cannot be a savage. And yet - we are savages."

-0-

CHAPTER SEVEN

"Tanya, what will you say, if I say, I am going to come and live here with you?"

We are on the veranda. Beretzkoy sits at his desk, sheets of paper and many sharpened pencils are laid out in a row in front of him. He is ready to start a new day of work. I am standing in the doorway.

"I would say, yes do," I reply flippantly.

He must be joking, trying to cheer me up because of what has happened to Leonid.

"Great. Then it is done," he says.

He explains. His boys are leaving for a holiday at Lake Baikal and Nadezdha Konstantinova has decided to accompany them. They will be away until September. Or rather she will be, but the boys will not be returning to the village. After their holiday they will enter a Moscow gymnasium.

"I will be able to stay here on Ob Street with you until September when I will be going up to Moscow to be with my sons, with them and their mother, for their first day at the new school. I will be away for no longer than forty-eight hours," he tells me.

"So you will have the summer together. That's nice," says Alisa.

I smile dutifully and make noises of approval. I can feel a knot in my stomach. He is only staying for the summer. When he told me he was coming to stay, I thought he was going to tell me he has left his wife. I hoped he was going to tell me he finally left her.

-0-

CHAPTER EIGHT

Beretzkoy brings his belongings to Ob Street in a wheelbarrow. The wheelbarrow is packed high with cardboard boxes, newspaper-wrapped packages, an old leather bag, a typewriter and strangest of all, a cat. The cat perches regally on the typewriter. I have heard of both the typewriter and the cat. The typewriter is a Cyrillic-keyboard like those at *Pravda* and it was a gift from Galina during their love affair. Beretzkoy wanted to bring it over to Ob Street for some time but, as Nadezdha Konstantinovna, unaware of its history, uses it for her personal correspondence, it stayed at Lena Street.

The cat is Sekret and Beretzkoy loves him very much. He is six years old: a black-and-white tomcat. Someone gave him, then only a couple of months old, to the Dushenka Koba children, but Alexandra Alexandrovna refused to have a cat in her house. Beretzkoy took him in, but as Nadezhda Konstantinovna shared her friend's dislike of cats, its existence remained a secret for a while. Thus, he was named Sekret. Sekret, I was told by Kolya, is not a loveable cat. He scratches. He scratches people's ankles. Beretzkoy denies this. Or at least, he admits that Sekret scratches ankles, but only of those he takes a dislike to.

I look at Sekret and he looks at me: yellow eyes, wide and questioning. I also do not like cats but I have been expecting this one was going to come with his master to stay at Ob Street.

"It will be strange to have a cat in the *dacha*," I tell Kolya. "Strange to have a man here too all day long and ... nights too."

A man who will be here in the morning when I wake up and at night when I fall asleep. A man who will be here in the middle of the night when a sudden storm starts up and someone has to get up to close the windows.

A man who will be here because he loves me and I love him.

-0-

213

August 2005: Moscow (Gerald Lombard/Biographer)

My editor wants to know about Daniel Petrovich Olminsky, so getting back to Moscow for further research, I ask those who have been so helpful before about him.

They knew him.

"He was the one with the Podol," they say. "Yes, we knew him. He used to come to the House of Endeavour with his wife. Her name was Yelena. He was sent to Siberia. He squeezed credits from the forests."[70]

"Two-thirds of the world's forestland was here," they tell me.

Statistics beaten into one's head stay there forever.

"So, tell me about Dan and how he squeezed credits from the forests?" I ask.

-0-

Metelovsk was the name of the camp to which Dan was sent. It was one of GULAG's smaller camps. It had five or six barracks. Each was fifteen metres wide and twenty metres long and housed about sixty *zeks*. That gave each *zek* a space about the size of a grave.

"For many it indeed was a grave," they tell me.

Forests encircled Metelovsk. Once, the forests had pretty names - Big Bear, Tall Top, Clear Water - but hard-nosed Soviet bureaucracy wanted everything to be numbered. A number was neat. A number was professional. Authoritarian. So the camps were numbered. As were the barracks. The *zeks* as well. Dan's number was 208060812. The camp's number was 9003599. It was Dan who gave the camp the name Metelovsk. *The place of blizzards.*

Dan's life as a lumberjack was in Forest Seven. It was in the month of May that he arrived there. It was still snowing in Siberia. The *zeks* of Metelovsk, dressed in prison garb - trousers, *rybashkas, fufaikas*[71] and *galoshes*[72] - were trucked into the forests at four each morning. On arrival at Forest Seven, Dan and his

---

[70] **The expression *squeezing credits from the forests* was coined by Trotsky who realised there was wealth in Russia's forestlands in the form of exportable timber.**

[71] **A padded jacket.**

[72] **An overboot.**

fellow *zeks* had to line up for the tools which they would be using on that day. Each was handed either an axe or a saw depending on what lay on top of the pile when the front of the line was reached. On Dan's first day he was handed an axe. Never having had to handle an axe, its weight astonished him, but he took hold of it as if it weighed less than a pencil because he did not want to appear weak. A foreman - not a *zek* but a free Sverdlovsk man - told him to chop, and so Dan chopped. The next day he was handed a saw and he was told to saw and so, he sawed.

There were rules which had to be obeyed in the forests and each day as if the *zeks'* memories were unreliable, the rules were read out using megaphones. There were days when this was done repeatedly. After a few days, Dan knew the rules by heart. One: you are not to stop work to talk, or stop to rest, but you can stop working to relieve yourself, but only if you have succeeded in drawing the attention of a guard. Two: at noon a siren will announce the start of your meal break. The break will last for eleven minutes. You are not allowed to talk or relieve yourself during the meal break. Three: you must start work the moment you have received a tool from the overseer. Four: four sirens will sound at 4 p.m. which will signal the end of the day's work. When you hear the first siren you must stop work instantly and all tools must be returned to the overseer by the sounding of the third siren. At siren four you must be seated in the trucks. Five: you are not allowed to relieve yourself on your way back to the trucks. Six: you are not to remove anything from the forests. Seven: you are not to bring any object into the forest. Eight: you are to report any disregard of these rules when witnessed by you. Failure to do so will be judged a grave error. The Commissariat of Forestry will not tolerate such a grave error. You will draw a guard's attention in the following manner: put your hands on your head and shout out your number. You will keep your hands on your head and you will continue to shout out your number until you have drawn the attention of a guard.

The meal handed out never changed. It consisted of a chunk of salted meat and a chunk of black bread. The *zeks* were never able to agree on what kind of meat they were given. One thought, on first seeing it, it was a rat. "I should know," he said almost with bravado. "I cut them up by the thousands during the famine." He had been a butcher by profession.

As for relieving themselves, there were no latrines in the forests therefore when a *zek* received a call from nature, he did what he had to do right there where he stood.

"This was not as awful as it sounds because whatever hit the ground froze instantly," they assure me.

The *zeks* worked in the forests from the beginning of the month of March to the end of the month of November, the months when the temperature was most moderate. But from December to February when the temperature plunged to twenty or more degrees below freezing, and their earth and all on it turned into ice, they were trucked into Sverdlovsk, to the town's sawmill. State Sawmill

Number 12.

They could never decide which was worse: working in the forests, or working at the mill. Just as they had been unable to make up their minds about which was the worst season: summer or winter?

"There was one thing they did know and this was that they never wanted to be where they were. When they were at the mill, they wanted the winter to end so they could return to the forests and no sooner had they returned to the forests than they wanted the summer to end so they could return to the mill. They spent their days wishing. Always wishing to return to the place they had a moment ago wished to leave," I am told.

Dan spent two summers and three winters at Metelovsk; he counted his time in seasons.

The first season which he had to cope with was summer. It came without warning. One day the sky was grey and a cool wind blew through the truck which took him back to the barracks at the end of his day's work and he clung to the *zek* sitting beside him, the two emaciated bodies sharing the little warmth there was in their blood. In the morning, a sunbeam broke through the clouds and where it hit the ground the ice began to glisten and soon he was dancing on a glittering carpet. Summer had come. His euphoria lasted though only until the following morning because that night's thaw turned the glittering carpet into a swamp of putrid black mud. The foreman told him to take his *galoshes* and his trousers off; they were not to become soiled. "You will work barefoot and bare-arsed. We're all men here. You have nothing the others haven't seen before," the man told him. Dan, all the same, tried to hide his nakedness by tying his trousers around his waist. His effort provided a moment of comedy. Those *zeks* who had been working the forests for years were unable to stop laughing at such modesty.

Dan soon noticed that working the forests in the summer, barefoot and with one's body exposed, did terrible things to a human being. The body rot. One morning he saw that the toes of some of the *zeks* had turned black during the night. Again, there was a moment of hilarity. "Hey look!" one of them called out. "I've grown some nigger's dick on my foot! My wife's going to love this when she sees it!" The *zeks*, who had seen many seasons in the forest come and go, said not a word. They knew what was awaiting the men with black toes. The black began to spread, first across the men's feet, then around their ankles, then, up into their thighs and within hours, tiny yellow worms started to wriggle in their pubic hair. "Oh sweet Jesus, Son of God, you bastards have got the black rot!" an old *zek*, who had once been a nurse, called out. The guards came running." Oh shit, black rot!" one groaned and added, "Go on! Down with those stinking trousers, you lot, and let's look at the filth you've got hidden in there!" A lamentation rose in the air because at least thirty *zeks* were infected. A truck drove up. They were to be taken for treatment. As soon as the stricken men marched from the barrack, some of the remaining *zeks* threw themselves onto the clothes and the belongings which were left behind. They knew once the black rot had started to eat a *zek*, that the poor man's days were numbered: he would not return to claim his property.

"That was what summer was like in the forests," I am told.

Autumn was no more bearable because that was the season when vermin invaded the barracks. It began with fleas. They were everywhere and so fast that no *zek* could have said he has seen one. They knew only they had been bitten when they began to itch. After the fleas came lice. At least those could be seen. Not that seeing them served any purpose, because no sooner was one squashed than another replaced it. Next, arrived the ticks and the *zeks* learnt what tick fever did to a man. The fever began with a crick in a man's neck as if he had slept in an awkward position during the night. The next stage was numbness in the legs. One night one of the novice-zeks began to scream he could not feel his legs. A long-standing *zek* on the bunk beside his lit a candle to see what was going on and, then, he too, began to shout. The novice-*zek's* legs were swollen to three times the size of an adult man's legs. The commotion which followed in the barrack drew the attention of the guards who, furious at having been awakened, started to lash out with their whips at the *zeks*. The barracks' overseer, a bald fat man from Sverdlovsk, ordered all zeks with swollen and painful legs or joints to put their hands on their heads because they had tick fever. Hands shot up. Again a truck pulled up. The tick fever victims were told they would be driven to a sick bay and there they would be given treatment and painkillers. It was with loud moaning and groaning that the stricken *zeks* shuffled from the barrack and on to the truck. As had happened with the *zeks* who had caught the black rot, the tick fever victims never returned.

Soon afterwards, Dan learnt what winter was like.

His first began officially one morning towards the end of November when at four in the morning the trucks, instead of driving into the forests, turned onto a tarmac road and headed for State Sawmill No. 12. The trucks drew up at the town of Sverdlovsk's southern periphery and from there the *zeks* were marched to the sawmill which was on the town's northern periphery. It was a long march. On descending from the trucks they were handed balaclavas so that the town's folk would not be able to see their faces. "Keep your ugly convict mugs covered!" they were told.

The mill was tsarist-built. It was inaugurated in 1909 by one of Nicholas II's uncles. Which uncle no one was able to remember. It was a sprawling single-floored stone building with two tall chimneys.

On that late November morning when Dan arrived at the mill for the first time, he heard the superintendent ask if any of the *zeks* spoke the German tongue, and for those who did, to step forward. Four stepped forward. Dan was one of them. Without offering an explanation, the superintendent told them to follow him. He walked them down a steep flight of wooden steps to a large basement room. In the basement, guarded by several armed men, stood the explanation. It was a very old steam boiler. It looked like a huge iron teapot, but a teapot with not one spout, but several. The boiler was the mill's source of power; its only source of power.

"This, here, you will have to look after," the superintendent told Dan and the other three *zeks*. He handed them a maintenance manual. It was in German. It had been printed in Cologne in 1900. Thirty-seven years had passed since then and twenty-eight years since Nicholas 11 had bought the boiler from the Kaiser, his cousin, yet, no one in those years thought of having the manual translated into Russian.

Once the four newcomers joined the *zeks* already looking after the boiler, there were in total twenty on the maintenance team; eight of them overseers and free Sverdlovsk men. Those eight overseers worked shifts because there always had to be someone watching over the boiler. It was never to break down or shut down because it was a great commotion to get it working again.

The maintenance team *zeks* wore blue dungarees, knee-high sheepskin boots similar to those the Zernoye Selo gravediggers wore, and for protection they had to wrap cloths around their heads. Three times each day each of them received a bowl of soup and a thick chunk of black bread. Apart from the soup and the bread, they also had a supply of tea and sugar so they could brew their own on a samovar connected to the boiler. The other *zeks* called them pampered, yet did not envy them because maintaining the boiler was the most strenuous, and, as Dan learnt, the most dangerous work at the sawmill. Dangerous, because the Chekists believed that knowledge of a foreign language was evidence of a man's interest in the people whose native language it was, and, to them, such interest meant one thing and one thing only: they were spies. That was the reason why armed guards stood watch over the boiler. The *zeks* were not to be trusted. It was believed they would sabotage the boiler at the first opportunity.

Dan was not long on the maintenance team before he discovered the depth of the mistrust.

It happened on a morning which began pleasantly enough. That day's head overseer was a man with whom the maintenance team had established a friendly relationship. He never raised his voice to them or insulted them and at slow times of the day he allowed them to sit down. Then, when they were sitting down, warming their hands against the hot tin of their tea mugs, he told them about himself and about his family. He was thirty-eight years old, married and the father of four sons.

On that morning, the overseer had just told the maintenance *zeks* that the eldest of his sons was going to study chemistry at Moscow University when the usual gentle hum of the boiler turned into ear-splitting whines which could be heard throughout the sawmill. Rapidly, the overseer explained to Dan and the other three new arrivals that the boiler was overheating and it would have to be shut down or it would explode. Hardly had he spoken than the sawmill's superintendent came running down the stairs shouting that no one should touch the boiler and that saboteurs would be punished. The overseer calmly but firmly explained it was not possible to shut down the boiler without touching it, and, if it were not shut down, it would explode. By then the guards had stepped up and cocked their rifles ready to shoot. Rapidly they realised that the superintendent did not have the authority to shut down the boiler. Only the Commissariat of Labour based in the Kremlin in Moscow had such authority, and only the Commissariat of Forestry, also based in the Kremlin in Moscow, had the authority to request the Commissariat of Labour to authorise such a shut down. Furthermore, only the chairman of the Sverdlovsk District Soviet had the authority to approach the Commissariat of Forestry to ask it to ask the Commissariat of Labour to grant permission to shut down the boiler. The process was to take at least two days, a time during which the sawmill would be at a standstill. The *zeks* - all but those on the maintenance team - were told to put on their balaclavas and they were marched to the trucks and driven back to Metelovsk. The maintenance *zeks* were told they would stay with the boiler and no food would be given them. It did not take two days but five days for word to arrive from the District Soviet that the Commissariat of Labour had authorised the Commissariat of Forestry to shut the boiler down. By then the maintenance *zeks* were half-dead with hunger because not only had they been deprived of their daily soup and bread, but, with the boiler out of order, also of their tea.

Seventy-two hours it took the maintenance *zeks* to find what had caused the boiler to overheat - a washer somewhere had perished - and to get it running smoothly again. There was not a hint of congratulation but instead the superintendants immediately set about routing out the culprits responsible for the 'sabotage'. As a result, three men on the team were chosen at random and marched off at gunpoint. Like the *zeks* who had caught the black rot and tick fever, they, too, did not return to the barracks.

Dan was released on a grey April day. Early in the morning of the third day of the month when the *zeks* were preparing to set off into the forests, a guard stomped into his barracks and called out, "Olminsky! Over here! Quick!"

"Dan almost did not step forward because, having not heard his name being spoken for a long time, it was as if he'd forgotten he was Daniel Olminsky," they tell me.

Taken to the camp's supply depot he was told he was to be released. He was handed an old tatty suit, a red *rybashka*, which had been starched and darned, and a thin cloth overcoat for his journey back home to Moscow. It was twenty degrees below freezing and snowing hard. He was also told to find some footwear from a pile of worn boots and shoes. Having been unable to find a pair which fitted him, but recalling Yelena's shoe size, he helped himself to a pair of boots for her. Once dressed, he was handed a brown envelope and told to open it to check its contents. In it he found a release order issued by the Commissariat of Interior, a work permit issued by the Commissariat of Labour - without such a permit no one in the Soviet Union could work - a *miagky* rail ticket to the town of Perm, as well as some rouble coins. "Count the money," the guard barked at him. "I don't want you coming back here with a nonsense story that I stole your money. There should be twenty-four one-rouble coins in there. A rouble a month. Twenty-four months. Twenty-four roubles. Your wages for working the forests. And there must be three copies of the release order and two of the work permit, and you sign all of them and hand them back to me." Dan did as he was told, and the guard handed the originals back to him." These are for you," he said, "and you're going to need them, because don't think the outside world is going to welcome scum like you with their arms wide open." Dan thanked the man. "What for?" he wanted to know. "I would much rather not be talking to scum like you."

From Perm, Dan had to make his own way back to Moscow.

"He did not want to spend his twenty-four roubles so he hitched rides on trucks and when there were no trucks on the road or the drivers did not want to stop for him, he walked," they tell me.

They recite Dan's poem *Metelovsk*, or rather, the few lines of it that they can remember.

As breath makes the man
A name breaks the soul
As moon makes the night
Metelovsk breaks the might

"But Dan Olminsky's might, Metelovsk did not break," I am told.

-0-

PART SIX

CHAPTER ONE

Zinaida has found Semyon, the child she lost so many years ago. We receive a letter from her written in Moscow. *Semyon - my Semyon - I've got him back! Praise the Lord!*

Semyon has been living under our noses, but we did not know the man named Semyon Alexandrovich Zukhov, a novelist of four highly-acclaimed historical sagas, and Gozuzdom editor, was Zinaida's lost son. He also did not know who his parents were, and that one of them, his mother, was alive, and that she had been searching for him from the day they had taken him away from her.

He is married and awaiting the birth of his first child, her letter continues. *His wife's name is Anna, but he calls her Malyutka and so do I. They call me Mamoshka[73], which I cannot become accustomed to as so many years have passed since I have been a mother. He looks like his father. At least I think he does. Malyutka says he looks like me. I told her that even I do not look like me. I told her that she should have seen me when I was her age and she smiled at me sympathetically as if she understood what I meant. How can she? Her father loves Stalin. Her husband loves Stalin. Oh, it pains me that a child of Vannikov is sustaining Stalin's tyranny, but that is how it is. So how can Malyutka know what I have been through?*

It was Semyon who found Zinaida.

He told me that although he remembered that he once had parents and siblings, he could not remember anything about us and accepted the story he had grown up with. This was that his parents and siblings were dead. That was what they had told him at the orphanage in the Urals where he had been placed after they had taken him away from me. He had become curious about his family background when his wife told him that he was going to become a father and he asked Gozuzdom if they could not help him find out who his real parents were. It did not take Gozuzdom long to do so - for me they could not do this, remember? All they had to do was to contact the orphanage in the Urals which passed their enquiry on to the childcare authorities and a month later they were told that he was the child of Vannikov. My name was not mentioned. Gozuzdom then first obtained Semyon's birth certificate before they told him whose son he was. Inexplicable as such things are, he was at the time reading one of Vannikov's books! He did not tell me which one, but he had found it lying somewhere in the Gozuzdom building, yellow with age and flecked with fly-shit. Well, knowing that he was Vannikov's son, it took him only forty-eight hours to find out that I was still alive. And do you know what? He was given the addresses of all the monasteries I have been in these past years, even the address of the asylum in Alma-Ata. Explain that to me! I'd just arrived back

---

[73] **Mama.**

here in Moscow - I'm staying with Vannikov's sister Anastasya on Baku Square - but he was given this address as well.

So, he came to Baku Square. He knocked and when I opened the door he said, "I am Semyon".

I asked this young man whether I was supposed to jump up and down, because he is telling me his name? His reply was, "I hoped that you would, Mother". He pushed his identity passport into my hands and I saw the name Zukhov and I laughed and said that my son Semyon's surname must be Vannikov and he said that had been his surname, at birth, and he then shoved his birth certificate into my hands. We did not fall into each other's arms. I can't speak for him, but as far as I am concerned, at that moment, the child I had lost was still lost and the man who stood in front of me was just that - a man. I had loved and yearned for a child and it was that child that I wanted back. Not a grown man with a wife and soon to have a child of his own. But I have started to accept that the child will never come back because now he lives in the body of the man. A man I must still get used to as he is still a stranger to me. He eats things his father and I would never have given him to eat; he reads things his father and I would never have allowed him to read; he says things his father and I would have forbidden him to say; he believes things his father and I would never have allowed him to even hear and he knows nothing of our Lord God the Almighty. I asked him if he could still remember Our Lord's Prayer and his reply was, "I didn't know he had one". This from the man who as a child used to recite Our Lord's Prayer so movingly that he brought tears to our eyes. I ask myself whether I will be heartbroken if he comes to tell me that a terrible mistake has been made and that he is not Semyon after all. No, right now, I will not be heartbroken. I will be upset, certainly, to think that I would no longer be able to walk in the park with my new friends, but my heart won't break, because it is still broken.

But Zinaida is working on this. One way of doing so is, she is joining her son and his wife, this summer, on a visit to Zernoye Selo.

The *dacha* Gozuzdom is allowing Semyon to use for his holiday is the vacant one on Ob Street: the dead poet's *dacha*.

-0-

CHAPTER TWO

I hear a car kicking up the stones lying on Ob Street. I am in my front garden. Remembering the night the Chekists came for Leonid, I start to shake. The car pulls up in front of the dead poet's *dacha*. I peep through a bush anxious not to be spotted. The Zukhovs and Zinaida have arrived. The car is a GAZ M-1. Nothing foreign for a Gozuzdom man.

Semyon is out of the car first. He wears a beige cotton suit and black sandals. A moment of vivid recollection tells me I have seen this man before. Gozuzdom! My trip to Moscow during the famine to beg Gozuzdom for translation work! This is the man who refused to give me translation work. He has lost a lot of his hair since the day I sat opposite him in his office. As if he knows someone is watching him, he runs a palm over the bald patch. He walks around the car opening the passenger doors. Zinaida and Malyutka step out. Zinaida looks elegant, almost unrecognisable without her brown cassock and clogged feet. She is wearing a white summer frock and a blue floral turban is wrapped around her hair. On her feet are flamboyant red sandals with a little heel. Probably unaccustomed to heels, she walks clumsily to the gate of the *dacha*. Malyutka, as I can see, is plain-faced and dowdy. I suspected she, the wife of an *apparatchik*[74], would be. She puts a white-socked sandaled foot onto the road and slowly the rest of her emerges. She has long, brown hair which hangs limply down to her waist. She wears a brown woollen skirt and yellow blouse the cotton fabric of which pulls tightly over her heavily pregnant stomach.

I watch until they disappear into the *dacha*.

"You should see Zinaida!" I say to Beretzkoy.

"What does she look like?"

"Different. Elegant. Happy."

"Well, she's a mother again," he says.

I go and stand in front of the cracked wardrobe mirror in the bedroom and I smooth my dress over an imaginary stomach bulge. I see myself staring steadily back. My face is strangely unfamiliar, almost frozen. I tell myself I must accept I will never be a mother. That this is how it must be.

-0-

They come to greet us. They are dressed as they were on their arrival, but

---

[74] **A member of the Soviet bureaucracy.**

Semyon has added a brown fedora to his outfit.

We go into the kitchen.

"I stayed here with Tanya," says Zinaida to Malyutka.

"So you've said, Mamoshka."

The young woman gives me a wan smile: it says, poor thing, she's not so young anymore and easily forgets.

"Drink anyone?" asks Beretzkoy.

"What's the strongest thing you have here?" asks Semyon.

"Vodka," I say coolly.

"That would be most welcome."

He is smiling at me passively. I wonder if he remembers that morning in his office.

"I am happy to see the two of you again," says Zinaida.

"Same here," I say. "It's lovely to see you again."

"You look well, Zinaida," says Beretzkoy.

Zinaida leans over the table and strokes my arm.

"My dear, do tell me what *well* means in our world?"

There is no answer for Zinaida. Not from me, nor from anyone else around the table. I do not know about the others, but I have no idea what is meant by *well* in our country.

Semyon and Malyutka begin to tell us of the dead poet's *dacha*. It is a lovely old place they say, but it needs airing and a lick of paint.

"Unfortunately, it smells of cabbage!" states Semyon.

We laugh but quickly we realise Semyon is not.

"I can't bear the smell. I grew up in an orphanage as my mother," - he tilts his head towards Zinaida - "would have told you. So you could say I cut my first tooth on a cabbage leaf."

I touch Zinaida's hand under the table.

"Soon now I will be a grandmother, Tanya," she says, melancholically.

"So, I see, Zinaida," I tell her.

-0-

CHAPTER THREE

Galina too has news for us. She writes in a letter she is no longer living in the loft at the theatre. Not that she has returned to her chessboard flat. The Moscow Housing Committee seized it during her absence and confiscated and sold what she left in the apartment. No, she has a new home now. She also has a new lover. She has a new home, because she has a new lover. His name is Mikhayl and she is living with him. More she does not tell us, but she gives us a telephone number where we can reach her. I walk to the post office to call her. I ask Filya - he has replaced Sveta who was recently taken away by the Chekists - in whose name the number is registered so I may learn the surname of Galina's new lover, but he tells me if I do not know it is because I should not know. Sveta would have told me.

Galina tells me we will soon meet Mikhayl as the two of them are coming to the House of Endeavour for a holiday.

The Olminskys are also coming to Zernoye Selo for the summer.

"For the first time we will all be together," I say to Beretzkoy.

-0-

Another car drives down Ob Street. This one is foreign, a brand new Ford belonging to Mikhayl. He sounds the horn and we run outside to tell him to stop. It is mid-afternoon and my neighbours will be starting to lie down for their afternoon rest.

Galina looks beautiful and glamorous. She is wearing an ankle-length black skirt and a white taffeta blouse. The skirt is pleated and so are the sleeves of the blouse. Between the pleats run thin gold-coloured threads. She turns to see where Mikhayl is and the skirt lifts slightly in the breeze, revealing her slender legs. They are adorned with black stockings with a *fleur de lis* in red on the outside of each ankle. I look closely at her shoes. They are transparent with sky-high heels as thin as spikes.

Mikhayl gets out of the car and walks – no, glides - towards us, the toes of his shiny patent leather shoes pointing outwards. The walk of a dancer. His name is Mikhayl Petrovich Moyseyev.

"Call me Misha," he tells us.

Misha is a slightly-built man with a pencil-thin black moustache and long black hair parted in the middle and tied in a tiny pony tail at the nape of his neck. He is a choreographer, which explains his walk. In the kitchen he takes off his pristine white jacket and hangs it over the back of a chair. His hips are

229

narrow and his black trousers seem to cling to his legs. He is wearing a red tie with a gold tie clip to hold it in place. On the clip is engraved a tiny violin. Beretzkoy asks him whether he plays the instrument and he says he likes his music a bit louder.

Alisa has baked a cake for me, and Misha insists on cutting it. I cannot help observing as he picks up the knife that his hands are uniformly smooth and pale, his fingers long with neatly clipped nails. My mother would say this is a man who has regular bowel movement. He wears a gold band on the ring finger of his left hand. Galina wears a matching ring, but on the middle finger of her right hand.

-0-

"He's my dresser," says Galina.

She and I are in the bedroom.

"Your dresser?" I ask.

I still find it awkward when Beretzkoy as much as undoes a button for me.

I tell Galina this: she hoots with laughter.

"Oh, you silly girl! He advises me on what to wear. He does not *dress* me!"

She is enjoying my naivety.

"But why would anyone in this country need advice on what to wear as there is nothing to wear here in the first place?" I ask her.

Again, she explodes in fits of laughter and throws herself onto the bed, her skirt up around her thighs. A pink suspender belt holds up her stockings.

"I shop abroad," she says. "Diplomatic bag. Misha knows diplomats at all the missions and you will be surprised how willing they are to run errands for a couple of tsarist gold roubles."

"Tsarist gold roubles!" I screech.

I tell Galina, in that case, I will never shop by diplomatic bag as Beretzkoy and I find it difficult to accumulate a couple of roubles never mind a couple of tsarist gold roubles!

Galina's blouse and skirt come from Paris. She says they are *couture*. She does not pronounce the word correctly, but as she is the one wearing it, I quell the desire to correct her.

She does not tell me how she met Misha and she does not speak of a future with him. She says she has learnt love is like life. Here today and gone tomorrow. She is satisfied with living with him. They live in a *dacha* belonging to him on the outskirts of Moscow.

-0-

The Olminskys arrive and Beretzkoy and I decide to have everyone over to Ob Street for a party. It is not wise, financially or otherwise to hold a party, but it is summer, and as Beretzkoy once said to me, in the summer no one is wise.

230

We give Maksim a list of what we will need in the line of food and drink. He is invited to the party too of course. He asks if he can bring a girl from the *kolkhoz*.

"See," I say to Kolya, "He has a girl. He's not interested in me."

We tell everyone to come at six.

-0-

CHAPTER FOUR

The Olminskys come at four. They walk over from the guest house. They look healthier and have definitely put on weight. Yelena's cheeks have filled out and Dan has a slight double chin.

"Are we too early?" asks Dan.

"The others are late," replies Beretzkoy, diplomatically.

In the kitchen, Yelena helps me set out the food. She hangs her red cape - she and Dan arrived dressed in their trademark clothing - behind the kitchen door. She sees I have a plate of herring fillets and she asks if she can make us a herring salad. I watch her chop up the fish, the knife flying over the fillets. She also slices a hard-boiled egg and mixes it in with the herring. She adds lemon juice, *smetana* and sugar. Esther, her mother, used to make such a herring salad. Her mother lost her life during a pogrom[75] The tsars, she once told me, where cruel, perhaps even more so than Stalin. Remembering this, I tell her we will have to be careful what we say in front of Semyon.

The others come at six.

Semyon is wearing his hat again. He takes it off and hangs it behind the kitchen door with Yelena's cape. Malyutka's lips are painted and she has a yellow bow in her hair. Zinaida is wearing a blue dress and it clashes with her shoes as she is again in the red heels. I watch as Yelena and Zinaida - Beretzkoy told me the two women did not always hit it off - take stock of one another.

"We haven't seen each other for a long time," says Zinaida to Yelena.

"Yes," says Yelena, "I hear you have been all over the place."

"So I hear has Dan," retorts Zinaida.

"So I have, but I had no choice," says Dan from the other side of the kitchen.

"Neither had I," Zinaida tells him.

The rest of the conversation is talk of hardships, spoken in guarded snippets so Semyon should not hear.

-0-

We have many things for us to eat. There is the herring salad, and cold cucumber soup; fish paste on *blinis;* sweet and sour beef balls and cold rice. There is also more drink flowing than there should be and soon we find

---

[75] **A violent attack on Jews, sometimes by a mob, but mostly by tsarist troops.**

everything highly amusing. The night is hot even with the windows open and Hitler's Fan is whirring full-blast above our heads and messing up our hair. Malyutka says she wants a fan like that. We light smokers and set them up in the *ogorod*[76]. Moths fly into the flames emitting a pungent smell from their charred wings. Black bats dive down from the roof and appear to want to join in the feasting. The men start a chess game in which they do not play against each other, but play together against an invisible foe. While this is going on, we women go to the bedroom and Galina shows us the correct way to pluck our eyebrows and paint our nails. She applies our lipstick as well which I think she does because of the clumsy way Malyutka had applied hers. Zinaida says she wants to have nothing to do with such devilry and looks angrily at Malyutka.

Misha calls from the living room.

"Come on, we are going to dance!"

He fetches a large wooden box from his car. On top of the box is balanced another, smaller, box.

"Walnut-wood," says Galina, pointing to the two boxes. "Very expensive."

Dan admires the wood. He touches it, strokes it, smells it.

"I know all about wood," he says. "I squeezed credits from our forests for two years."

Misha puts the two boxes down on the floor to open them. In the larger box is a gramophone and in the other several brown envelopes. The gramophone is an Edison: he tells us this. We crowd around him in a circle like children trying to get a better look. The Edison has a large bronze horn. Misha notices a fingerprint on it and he brushes it away with his elbow. He is in shirtsleeves tonight. The brown envelopes hold round plates. We are told they are not for eating on but for making music: they are vinyl records. He also tells us they are not in envelopes, but in sleeves. On each sleeve is the word Decca. Galina is already humming and tapping a foot. She is wearing her transparent shoes again, but she is bare-legged and I can see her well-tended toenails are painted the same scarlet shade as her finger nails.

Misha says he will explain how his gramophone works. He takes a pair of white gloves from the smaller box, pulls them over his hands and chooses a record from one of the sleeves and fits it onto the gramophone's turntable. Next, he pulls a lever down over the turntable and shows us there is a tiny needle at its tip. He fits the needle into the record's outer groove and the music begins. A man's voice rings out in a rich baritone. Beretzkoy and I rush to close the windows saying the music is loud and we do not want to keep the neighbours awake. But really, as most of the neighbours are with us, our real fear is that this kind of music - foreign music, foreign dance music - is banned in Russia.

Misha takes Galina in his arms and asks us to move the carpets out of the

---

[76] **A garden at the back of a house, usually for growing vegetables.**

way. He begins to steer her across the uncovered wooden floor.

"Slow waltz," Galina mouths over Misha's shoulder.

Galina's small feet in their transparent high-heeled shoes trace broad circles over the floor as they strive to keep up with Misha's larger feet in their shiny patent leather shoes.

The furniture should also be moved out of the way, this is clear, and Beretzkoy and Kolya do so.

Maksim and the *kolkhoz* girl - her name is Oksana - also start dancing. Oksana is dressed in trousers and a *rybashka* and her blonde hair is cut short like a young boy's. She has striking features, especially her eyes, but she is not what you will think of as pretty because her figure is that of a young boy, straight up and down. I think it a little odd that Maksim is attracted to her. He himself is neatly dressed in a black suit, white shirt and red tie.

Dan and Yelena begin tentatively to dance. It is clear from how Dan is accidentally steering poor Yelena into the others and the way she keeps stepping on his feet, dancing is a new experience for them.

I turn to Beretzkoy.

"Shall we?"

"No," he says.

I read in his face dancing is not something he feels he can do.

"But you studied music!" I say, surprised.

"Not this kind of music!" he snaps.

It is strange I learn only now Beretzkoy cannot dance. Also, for the first time, in some time, I think of Vasily. Of how he and I used to go dancing.

"Would you like to dance Tanya?" Semyon asks.

Malyutka is sitting on the sofa with Kolya and he is telling her his dancing days are over, but once his *mazurka*[77] left many a girl breathless.

"Don't tell me you dance!" Zinaida calls out to her son with disgust in her voice.

He winks at me.

"Just watch, Mamoshka!"

He takes me by the hand. A waltz floats from the gramophone now. He waits until there is a gap between the three dancing couples on the floor and then he begins to sway. He moves naturally, smoothly, steering me left and right between the others, but soon beads of sweat form on his forehead and start to run down over his cheeks, dripping onto the front of my dress. My dress is new, the prettiest pale pink dress I have ever owned, with a little white frill around the hem and the neck. I look at the splashes on the fabric and it makes me feel anxious. He smiles his apology but he pulls me closer to him all the same, and I am sure now he has no recollection of the day I had begged him for work.

From Misha's box of tricks come more waltzes, fox trots, quicksteps,

---

[77] **A folk dance which originated in Poland which is danced very fast.**

rumbas, sambas, tangos and something he calls boogie-woogie.

We dance until all Misha's needles are blunt. The needles, as he tells us, rancour in his voice, have come all the way from New York.

"He often visits New York," brags Galina.

She tells us what he paid in American dollars for the needles.

"That is a sum that could keep a family of four in comfort for a month," mutters Zinaida disapprovingly although I am sure, she like us, have no idea of the value of the amount Galina mentioned.

"I think we should apologise to Misha for having danced his needles blunt," I say.

"The day has yet to come that I would apologise to an exploiting capitalist," Oksana whispers to me.

She urges Misha to put something else on.

"I need to practise my boogie-woogie!"

She is a little drunk I think, but then we all are. A little.

-0-

CHAPTER FIVE

On a hot, humid afternoon, Beretzkoy and I lie entwined on a blanket in the back garden. Beretzkoy wears black swimming trunks, and I, a bathing dress, which has no sleeves, and leaves my legs bare below the knees. We splash water over each other and Nilats, when he hears our laughter, crawls through the fence so we can splash water over him. He runs around in a circle trying to bite his own tail and leaves wet-dog prints on our blanket. He runs home when he hears Alisa calling and next we hear her angry voice: he has left muddy paw marks on her kitchen floor.

Beretzkoy points towards my *dacha*.

"Look!"

A tree is throwing a shadow against the *dacha's* back wall. The shadow is undeniably man-shaped. I can clearly see the man's legs, torso; his head. The torso is stocky. The head, large, and the hair that frames it, bushy, and the tips of a moustache are sticking out from each side of the lower part of the head.

I know who the shadow reminds me of.

"*Vodzh*," I say.

"You think so too?" asks Beretzkoy. "It is not my imagination?"

"It is not your imagination."

"Oh well!" he sighs and closes his eyes.

"I don't like this," I say. "It is an omen. A bad omen."

"Don't be silly," says Beretzkoy.

Ants are scurrying up and down the wall in two quivering black rows. A cockroach, large, black, its back shining in the sun, crawls from a crevice in the wall. Almost immediately, the ants converge on it and attack. It tries to escape, haltingly crawling up the wall and into another crevice, the ants eagerly following. The crevice is about where Stalin's nose would be, had Stalin actually been standing there, leaning against the wall. Getting to my feet, I shudder at this grotesque spectacle.

"It's just a shadow, my love," says Beretzkoy.

"It's Stalin's shadow. It is Stalin!"

"It's a shadow, Tanya!"

"Yes, it is, but it is Stalin's shadow!" I insist.

"You're being silly," he says.

"It's a bad omen," I say. "Let's go in."

I insist we go indoors, out of reach.

"We've had enough sun for one day, anyway," I tell him.

"You go. I'll stay here a little longer," he says.

I go inside. I keep watch over Beretzkoy from the kitchen window. He has rolled over on to his stomach and fallen asleep.

Soon, the sun sets behind the *dacha* and Beretzkoy walks sleepily into the kitchen.

"Stalin's gone," he says with a half-yawn.

-0-

We tell the Olminskys about Stalin's image on my back wall and they nod their heads supportively. They are in agreement with me. It is a bad omen.

"Don't encourage Tanya," reprimands Beretzkoy.

He is angry.

-0-

CHAPTER SIX

Nadezdha Konstantinovna is not due back for another two weeks and Beretzkoy says we are going to be daring and slip away for a few days, go somewhere together. My better judgment tells me we should not take such a risk, but I want to go and I agree. But where to go?

I remember a group of wonderful old men from a nearby valley who used to come to Zernoye Selo during the famine, selling us potatoes. They told us about their valley and said we should one day visit them. In my bedroom I find a telephone number one of them had written on a scrap of paper. I suggest to Beretzkoy we should go to the old men's valley.

I walk to the post office and call the number. We are welcome to come to the *dolena*[78] says the woman who takes the call. The number is that of a railway junction. The woman I speak to is the wife of the master of the junction. Her husband will take us down into the valley in his pony trap and we can stay with her aunt. We would not have to pay her husband or her aunt. A gift, small, would be in order.

"... a bottle of something ... perhaps some *rykovka*[79] for my husband and some *papirosi* for my aunt," she says.

I tell the woman we have a cat and she says he is most welcome too.

We take the Moscow-Kiev night freight train. It has a *zhestky* carriage and all night the train crawls south stopping at every station, junction and siding to load and unload goods. At noon we reach the junction in the valley. The junction master is waiting for us with his pony trap. It will take twenty minutes to our hostess' *izba*.

"Her name is Valentina Grigoryevna Pavolovna. My name is Igor and my wife is Valentina like her aunt," he says.

Valentina Grigoryevna Pavolovna is well into her eighties. She cannot remember the exact date of her birth, but she knows at the time Russia still had serfs, not that she was born a serf. This she wants us to understand. She was born free.

"Of the gentry," she says, her lined face grimacing at the obvious lie she is

---

[78] **The valley.**

[79] **Popular name for vodka derived from the name Alexei Ivanovich Rykov, Chairman of the Council of People's Commissars from 1924-1929, who ended prohibition so that vodka could be sold again.**

telling.

Valentina's *izba* looks like a large stack of logs. I wonder what we have let ourselves in for, but Beretzkoy whispers to me it reminds him of a place where he used to go as a child with his grandfather. The *izba* stands a distance away from the others of which there are about twenty in this valley which Valentina simply calls *Dolena*. The steep sides of the valley are covered in majestic swathes of trees in full leaf. At the bottom runs a thin silvery ribbon: a river. The river, like the valley, has no name other than *Reka*[80]. It is not really a river, just a trickle of water and looking down from the *izba* it lies across the valley like a discarded ribbon.

"I live alone," says Valentina. "My husband is dead."

The words hang heavily in the air.

She takes us into her living room. To the left of it, we can see a small bedroom, and to the right, a kitchen.

"It's cosy here," says Beretzkoy.

"My husband built this place with his own hands," she says. "And without assistance."

On their wedding day he carried her over the threshold and straight into the kitchen to cook him a meal.

"Life was different then. People were happy. There was no Stalin then. No collectivisation, and now it is just a matter of time before Stalin's bullies are going to arrive with their bulldozers because the valley is to be turned into a *kolkhoz* too," she tells us.

The bedroom is to be ours. She will sleep in the kitchen.

"Oh no," I say. "The bedroom is yours."

She shakes her head firmly, the sagging skin of her neck and face quivering from side to side.

"I will sleep in the kitchen. It is where I always sleep. I have not slept in the bedroom since my husband's death."

Valentina's husband died, she tells us, in the same year as Lenin. Her eyes fill with tears as though it happened yesterday. She seems equally saddened by Lenin's demise as that of her husband. The tears run over her wrinkled face and she does not wipe them away.

In the kitchen stand a wood-burning stove, a scrubbed wooden table and four chairs, a rickety camp bed and a large corner-cupboard.

The camp bed stands on wooden blocks which have nails protruding from them. This means there are mice, or perhaps rats in the *izba*, the nails having been banged into the blocks to dissuade the rodents from climbing up. Glad I am we have brought Sekret, an accomplished rodent killer, along. He is sitting by the door, his pink-tipped nose sniffing at the unfamiliar smell coming from three large copper pots standing on the stove.

---

[80] **Russian for river.**

"Chicken stew," says Valentina, lifting the lid of one of the pots to stir its boiling contents with a wooden ladle.

Sekret purrs as if he understood what she said: he loves chicken.

Valentina licks the ladle and next she dips a finger into the stew and offers me her finger to lick.

I lick the finger.

She has potatoes boiling in a second pot and in the third, the largest of the three, she has water boiling for us to be able to wash our faces in hot water before we go to bed because the *izbas* do not have running hot water.

"We accept nothing from that devil in the Kremlin," says Valentina. "What we wish to eat, we grow. I wrung this chicken's neck myself and the vegetables come from my nephew's *ogorod*."

A copper samovar stands on the stove and begins to emit gurgling sounds. Valentina offers us tea. We sit down at the table and she puts a plate of walnut-encrusted biscuits down in front of us.

"Eat," she says. "You are both thin. You need some good food into your bellies."

It is Stalin's fault we are so thin, she laments.

-0-

All of Dolena's inhabitants are aged, it seems. They come to greet us and they are in their best clothes. The men are in white - *rybashkas* and flared pantaloons tied with ribbons around the ankles - and the women are in black dresses which cover them from chin to ankle. Valentina, who is also dressed in black, introduces us as Boris Petrovich Beretzkoy and Tatyana Nikolayevna Beretzkaya. We do not correct her. We are asked to promise we will call in on each of them and politely we promise we will. Our week in the valley is to be a busy one if we are to get to visit everyone.

-0-

Late afternoon we tell Valentina we need to rest after our journey and we go to the bedroom. She nods at us understandingly. There is an acrid smell in the bedroom, the smell of over-ripe apples. We think Valentina may have stored apples in the wardrobe. I open the window to let in some air and beneath us in the garden stand two tall apple trees. The trees are covered in tiny red apples. I realise I have never seen an apple on a tree before.

Beretzkoy comes to stand behind me and wraps his arms firmly around my waist. I feel a pulse of excitement travel through me as his lips touch my neck. I feel his hands moving down to lift my skirt, pressing between my thighs. We do not come out of our room again until Valentina calls out that we ought to come and eat the stew or it will get cold.

In the morning, a sparrow wakes us. It is perched on one of the branches of one of the apple trees, pecking away at an apple so ripe it has begun to turn speckled-brown.

Our breakfast is a feast of fish and fried eggs on fried bread. A neighbour who has four cows brings over a bowl of warm milk with oily yellow cream floating on top. Valentina scrapes off the cream, puts it in a small bowl and says it is for me. Its taste is bland like *smetana* which has stood out in the sun. I really do not like the taste, but I tell Valentina I have never eaten anything as delicious.

Beretzkoy and I go for a walk along the river. Its water is clear and we can see pebbles lying scattered on the bottom. We lie down on our stomachs on the bank and drink from the river. The water is deliciously cold.

We cross the river, jumping from one large slippery stone to another. On the facing bank, we flop down. I rest my head on Beretzkoy's shoulder.

"This is what I call happiness," he says.

I agree.

-0-

We cannot avoid having to call in on the valley's inhabitants whose *izbas* we pass because they call out to us. The *izbas* are neat and they smell of food because at any time of the day, here in the valley, there is cooking going on. The people want us to taste what they are cooking and hand us little offerings, all of which taste wonderful. On the walls of the *izbas* hang faded photographs of laughing young men and women and of small children who have since grown up and live in Moscow or Leningrad and do not come to visit often enough. This, the old people tell us. One couple's son lives in Alaska. He is spoken of as if he is still a child. We ask how old he is. They say they have forgotten.

"What's age after all?" they tell us.

-0-

I want to stay in Dolena forever. I am lying on the bed, a blanket pulled up to my chin. Beretzkoy is sitting on the windowsill. Sekret lies on the sill beside him, asleep.

"Beretzkoy, I want to ask you something," I tell him.

"Go ahead."

"Can't we stay here forever?" I ask.

"That would be wonderful," he says, dreamily.

This is the encouragement I need.

"So let's do it," I say, hastily, getting out from the covers.

He gets up and comes to sit on the bed. Sekret, too, jumps off the sill and onto the bed.

"Are you serious, Tanya?"

"I'm serious," I say.

"There is no electricity here, my love."

A smoker stands on a bedside table.

"Valentina lives without electricity. In Zernoye Selo, we do too, sometimes. Even in Moscow the people often have to live without electricity," I argue.

He puts his hands over my eyes.

"It will be dark," he says. "Dark like this."

"I like the dark."

"Tolstoy wrote," he says, "to think you can change your life by changing its outward conditions is just like thinking that by sitting on a stick and taking hold of it at both ends you could lift yourself up."

I know what he is trying to tell me.

-0-

Valentina comes in the pony trap with us to the railway junction.

"Come and visit again, please," she says.

"We will," says Beretzkoy, kissing her on the cheek.

"If we write to you, will you write back?" I ask.

"No," she says, smiling. "I cannot read and I cannot write."

I suggest she asks someone in Dolena to read our letters to her and she could dictate her reply.

"No," she laughs. "There is no one in the valley who reads and writes. We do not need that kind of thing. We've got all we need. God has given us all we need."

-0-

For days Number One Ob Street smells of apples because Valentina insisted we bring some back with us.

I write her a thank you note despite knowing she will not be able to read it.

Thank you for everything. If God finds it in his heart, we will see you again soon.

I have not ever felt a need for God - a god - in my life, but I, here, writing this thank you note, mentioned God. That is, the God Valentina worships. Why did I do it? I do not know. Perhaps it is because I wish to return to her valley to escape the bitter reality my lover has a wife and two sons.

-0-

CHAPTER SEVEN

The time comes for Beretzkoy to return to Lena Street. He asks whether he can leave Sekret with me.

"Won't he be missed at Lena Street?" I ask.

"The boys would miss him, but the boys won't be there."

"Will you be missed if you were not to return?"

He nods slowly.

"The boys would miss me."

"But the boys won't be there."

"But I must be there for the boys," he says.

I do not feel I can argue.

Beretzkoy leaves as he had arrived. He pushes the wheelbarrow stacked high with his belongings. I walk with him to the wasteland carrying Sekret. I want to see whether the cat will run after his master. He does not. Kolya tells me cats are solitary creatures. I tell Kolya I know how they feel.

Beretzkoy goes to Moscow to see his sons to their new school and to escort Nadezdha Konstantinovna back to Zernoye Selo. He will be away for two weeks and not just for twenty-four hours as he initially planned. He wants to make sure his sons settle down well.

My *dacha* is suddenly very quiet. An emptiness fills its walls. I walk from room to room. I try to read, but I cannot concentrate. Maksim comes over. He asks me to have supper with him at the Red Banner. I do not accept his invitation. Kolya asks me to the Red Banner too and because I do not want to hurt Maksim's feelings, I turn Kolya's invitation down as well. On top of everything, our friends come and tell me they are returning to Moscow.

First to leave are Zinaida and the Zhukovs. They come to say goodbye. Semyon offers me a hand to shake. Malyutka kisses me on both cheeks. Zinaida kisses me in the Russian fashion, on the mouth. She hugs me tightly and tells me she plans to spend the autumn and winter in a monastery near Alma-Ata. They drive off and the two women lean out and wave but the car lurches forward and quickly disappears around the corner at the end of the street. Semyon must have put his foot down hard on the accelerator.

Galina and Misha leave next. Galina says I should have gone with Beretzkoy to Moscow and Misha says when I do come to Moscow I must look them up.

"Come over to the theatre," he says.

"He'll give you the best seat in the house," adds Galina.

I see the Olminskys off at the station.

"When will we see you again?" asks Dan.

245

"Soon I hope," adds Yelena.

"So do I," I say, knots forming in my throat.

"You should have gone to Moscow with Beretzkoy," says Yelena.

"Women!" groans Dan.

I hand them their luggage through the window and I jump onto the train to give them another hug. They are returning to Moscow as *miagky* passengers. Dan says he wants to spoil Yelena. That she merits spoiling.

"Tanya, don't stay here alone," says Yelena.

I tell her I will try to come up to Moscow before the year ends.

"Don't wait too long," says Dan, his eyes smiling.

Yelena begins to cry and I struggle to hold myself together.

"We love you," says Dan.

The train whistle starts up.

"You're off," I say, realising tears are falling freely from my eyes.

I am still standing at their bunk and the other passengers give me worried glances.

"There's no hurry," says Dan. "They sound three warnings to let you know your time is up."

"What if they do not do so this time?"

"No," says Dan. He takes my hand, "No, we've got two more warning whistles before the good old Soviet train will take us off. Not even God shows such courtesy to mankind before he takes us."

I jump down on the platform and wave. I continue waving even when the train has disappeared from sight.

-0-

I begin to clean the *dacha* hoping the time will pass quicker if I am busy. I clean until there is not a speck of dust to be seen.

I decide to cook jam. Alisa shows me how. I buy whatever fruit I can find, put it in a big pot, add water and sugar, and let the ingredients boil. I fill several big jars.

"You behave like a woman who does not know what to do with herself," says Maksim.

In the evenings, on his way from the clinic to his loft, he looks in on me. I wish he does not do so because I fear I will become accustomed to his presence. Yet, I am happy to see him each evening.

"I'm at a loose end," I tell him.

"What about dinner then?"

"Yes, that will be nice. Thank you," I reply.

I swear I spoke without thinking.

"Tomorrow evening," he says.

I tell Kolya I will be at the Red Tavern with Maksim and I ask him to come over to join us for a drink.

-0-

Maksim arrives. He looks at me askance. I have taken care not to look good, wearing an old dress, no jewellery, no make-up. He did, however, make sure to look good. He is in a white jacket, black trousers and shiny shoes. The top three buttons of his white shit is unbuttoned. His chest is smooth.

The Red Tavern's food is simple: soup, fish and boiled potatoes. Maksim talks without even seeming to stop to swallow. He is talking about his work, Stalin, Hemingway. I listen. And I look at him. He has tiny beads of sweat above his upper lip and above his eyebrows. I decide he is a very attractive man.

Kolya walks in and pulls a chair over and joins us. Rodya comes to ask what he would like to drink. He asks for a beer. Maksim makes no effort to pay for it, so Kolya pays for it himself.

"That was clever of you," says Maksim walking me home.

"Kolya is lonely."

"Tanya, I was worried about your loneliness, not his," he says quietly.

He bids me goodnight at the gate.

I lie awake most of the night. Beretzkoy must come home now! I am lonely!

-0-

Maksim comes to ask me to go dancing with him. A dance is going to be held at the *kolkhoz*. I say I cannot go.

"I know you like to dance, Tanya, so why do you say no?" he asks.

"What about Oksana? She also likes to dance."

"Oksana now lives in Leningrad."

I shake my head as if to commiserate.

"Well, I think you should take a pretty girl to the dance."

"That is what I am trying to do," he says, grinning.

I tell him I do not think it is a good idea for us to go dancing.

Then, I say I will go.

I decide to dress up this time yet I do not know why. I do not want to flirt with Maksim. Perhaps I am going with him, because my self-esteem is low because after the summer my lover returned to his wife.

I put on a long red skirt, a white sweater and high-heeled white shoes. I comb my hair back into a roll and I secure the style with a pretty pin of red beads. I bought this pin so many years ago, before I married Vasily even. I have even forgotten its existence until I came across it during my cleaning frenzy. I pluck my eyebrows the way Galina showed us to do on the night of our party and I put red varnish on my fingernails. On my toenails as well. My shoes are open-toed and I want Maksim to see I am a sophisticated young woman.

He comes to fetch me in a small white van. The van belongs to the clinic.

"You drive!" I say, astonished.

He is wearing a dark blue suit. It fits him well. It is not baggy like a Russian-made one.

"It's Italian," he tells me.

His red and white striped shirt is also Italian. It is of silk.

"Feel the silk," he says. He opens his jacket for me to do so.

I shake my head. I think I ought not to touch him.

"My hands are dirty."

He is not wearing a tie, because, as I know, at the *kolkhoz* it would be considered bourgeois.

His two-toned shoes, black and white, are also Italian.

He looks gorgeous.

"You look … really handsome tonight," I say.

"I was going to say the same to you, but you beat me to it," he replies.

The dance is held in the *kolkhoz* school. First, we listen to Comrade Afonov thank the *kolkhozniks* for the work they put into the year. He goes on and on. Zernoye Selo is now the leading corn-growing region in the world, he says. The applause is long and loud. An award ceremony follows. Six *kolkhozniks* are given medals. Comrade Afonov has a problem pinning the medals onto their *rybashkas*. He keeps on pricking his fingers. One finger begins to bleed. He licks the finger. He says he has talked enough and we should go and get ourselves something to eat. Food and drink are set out on a table which stands against a wall. Quickly only bones and dirty plates are left on the table. The dirty things having been removed, the table is folded up and musicians step forward. Russian music and not the music of Misha's gramophone. This pleases me because to Russian music one has to jump, clap one's hands and slap one's thighs and one hardly touches one's dancing partner.

Maksim wants to dance only with me.

-0-

CHAPTER EIGHT

The evening ends. We wander outside and climb with weary limbs back into the van. The seats might have been comfortable when the van was new, but the springs have cut through the leather upholstery. One spring sticks into my spine.

"Have you ever been inside the clinic?" asks Maksim.

"My parents gave me good teeth. So no, I haven't."

It is after midnight and the streets are deserted.

"Would you like to see what the clinic looks like inside?"

"No, not really."

"I'll show you where Stalin slept."

"Really?"

Maksim does not drive straight to the clinic, but turns down towards the south-eastern triangle and the streets named after rivers. He talks non-stop. Again about Hemingway. He has just finished rereading *Death in the Afternoon* in English. He read it out loud to practise his pronunciation.

"My English is excellent now. The Americans will be able to understand me well," he says proudly.

"In that case, I take it you still plan to leave us?" I ask.

"Yes, Tanya. I still plan to leave and it will be soon, unless …"

He does not finish his sentence.

"Unless what?"

"Unless. Just unless."

We change the subject and speak of the weather. He says he wonders whether it will be sunny in the morning and I tell him it is already morning.

He pulls up in front of the clinic which is black inside. I do not wait for him to walk around the car to open the door for me. He leads the way to a side door for which he has a key. We go up a steep cement staircase and up and down several corridors of which the walls as well as the floors are covered in brown tiles. He keeps on switching lights on and off as we go along. A heavy odour of ether hangs over the place. It intensifies as we go down another corridor. He pushes open a door.

"This is it," he says.

He steps into a room, switches on another light and beckons for me to follow him. The room is small and has one curtainless window.

"Surprised?" he asks.

"Is this Stalin's room?" I ask, indeed surprised.

He nods.

"It is so plain."

"Stalin is a man of simple tastes. You may think I'm crazy saying this, but it is true. He is a simple man. Not a simpleton, hear. A simple man. Relatively undemanding. Even, dare I say, likeable."

"*Mon dieu*," I reply, making Maksim laugh.

The walls of the room are covered in brown cloth and the floor in green linoleum. On one wall hangs a print of a bouquet of flowers. The flowers have turned brown with dust. Stalin's bed is the traditional high and narrow hospital bed. The bed is unmade. The mattress is stained. A pillow lies on the bed. On one side of the bed stands a metal table, and on the other, an upright wicker chair. Over the back of the chair hangs a straw bath mat, and on the metal table stands an enamel bedpan. Above the bed's headrest is an instrument panel with numerous plugs, switches, hooks, and a fitting for a light. There is no bulb in the fitting and the plug and the switch are broken. This room is only used by Stalin.

I shake my head.

"So this is where the devil sleeps?" I whisper.

"You hate him, I can tell."

I nod.

"I must say I do not dislike him," says Maksim.

"But do you like him?"

"If you cornered me, I would have to say that I do not hate him."

"So why do you want to leave Russia?"

"Because Stalin's policies are, unlike him, unlikeable."

"If you are leaving for Hemingway, bear in mind he may well one day come to Russia and Beretzkoy could, through Profpro or Gozuzdom, be able to arrange a meeting for you."

"I cannot wait."

"Some people do wait for what they want, you know."

"Are you talking of yourself?"

"No. We are talking about you."

He shakes his head.

"Are you sure?"

He moves towards me and I feel my nerves begin to jangle.

"I am only trying to understand why you think you cannot stay in Russia. Especially now that I know you find Stalin *likeable*."

I spat out the word *likeable* as if I have swallowed a fly.

"Are you asking me to stay, Tanya?"

He has stepped closer to me.

"I have no right to do so, Maksim."

"If I give you the right?"

"Then I will use it to ask you what you will do if you do not like America, because you know you will not be able to come back here?"

"I will like it."

"If you are lonely …"

"You can do something to prevent such an eventuality."

He is looking at me with a calm, firm gaze. His expression lays his plan out in full view.

"This has nothing to do with me, Maksim," I say rapidly.

"If I ask you to be part of it?"

"I can't be part of anything."

"Can I still ask?"

"No."

"Because you prefer to wait for what you want?"

"Yes."

"Like I said, I don't want to wait."

"I know and you are going to go to America because Hemingway most probably does not think Stalin is a likeable man and therefore will not come to Russia. And you have to meet Hemingway. Absolutely have to!" I say.

-0-

He says he wants to show me something else. His workroom. It is on the ground floor. We retrace our steps and again he switches lights on and off. I follow him silently. His workroom looks out over an inner courtyard. The window is open. It has started to rain and there are flashes of lightning over the horizon.

"Winter will be here soon," I say casually.

"I won't be here this winter."

He closes the window.

There is a dentist's chair in the room and a stool and a steel cupboard on which lie several sets of false teeth and solidified imprints of people's mouths. The imprints look as if they are screaming with laughter. He offers me the dentist's chair and he moves the stool up to the chair and sits down himself.

"I won't be here this winter," he repeats.

"We will miss you, Maksim."

"Don't you want to ask when I'm going to go?"

"When?"

He says he is going to attend a conference in Budapest from where he will go by boat to Vienna and from there by train to Paris and from there by train to Le Havre and from there by boat to Quebec and from there he will make his way to New York.

"I do not know half of these places," I admit.

"Budapest is in Hungary," he says.

"Where is Quebec?"

"Canada."

"I've never heard of it."

"They speak French there."

"Then I've heard of it. Wasn't it French once?"

"So was your father."

"Not anymore."

I tell him not to stay too long in Vienna, because there is going to be a war in Austria.

"There is going to be a war everywhere, Tanya," he corrects me.

I ask him what he will do in America in a war.

"What will you do in Russia in a war?" he asks in turn.

"I am Russian. I'll cope," I say cheerfully.

"I am Russian too - remember? So, I will cope too," he tells me.

The chair I am sitting on is of brown leather. It is quite comfortable, but I have to lean back as over it hangs a metal arm.

"So when will you be leaving, Maksim?" I ask.

He pushes the metal arm out of the way. His face is much closer to mine now the metal arm is out of the way. I can smell the soap he has used on his skin.

"Soon," he replies.

"Will you come to tell us before you go?"

"You will know when I leave for the conference, yes, but I will not say I will not return, but you will know."

"What about Beretzkoy? You say I will know, but will you tell him. Don't you want him to know?"

"I'm not going to tell him."

"Don't you want me to tell him either?"

"I don't want you to tell him about tonight, Tanya."

"Why?"

"Because I am going to keep you here for a while still."

"Against my will?"

"Will it be?"

I tell him it will not be.

-0-

There are rooms at the back of the building where those who accompany overnight patients, sleep. To one of these we go, holding hands, not speaking. I do not know why I am going. I think Maksim is beautiful, but he does not captivate me as Beretzkoy always has. Perhaps it is the loneliness, or the need to be admired, perhaps it is the need to feel someone close against my skin which is the reason why I am walking beside him.

The room is small and utilitarian; a narrow bed, metal bedside table, a wardrobe with a long central mirror which has a jagged crack. No pictures hang on the walls. No mat on the wooden floor. No sheet or blankets on the bed.

I stand at the door. The door is closed but there is no keyhole so we will not be able to lock the door. What if someone should walk in?

"This is quite private," says Maksim as if he is reading my thoughts.

"I think I should go ... after all. This is not right, Maksim. I'm so sorry," I say almost pleadingly.

He is standing close to me and for a moment it looks as if he is going to reach for the doorknob behind me to open the door and let me go, but instead he steps right up to me and bending his knees slightly so our faces are at the same height, he kisses me lightly on my forehead and then on my tip of my nose, and then he bends down a little more and touches my lips with his.

"Wait," he whispers, pulling away from me.

He begins to undress and I stand stock-still, my back pressed against the cold door, but I cannot prevent myself watching him. He lets the dark blue jacket drop to the floor. He undoes the buttons of his shirt and pulls it free. He has an exquisite body; lean, with sculptural definition and hairless. An intense sensation of heat spreads over my skin. I dig my fingernails into my palms. He pulls off the rest of his clothes and moves toward me. He is fully aroused and I am amazed I do not find this ungainly. Instead, I want nothing more than to touch him.

"Let me undress you," he says.

His movements are swift and confident and my skirt and sweater fall to the floor. I reach behind my back to undo my bra myself. I step out of my heels. I run my hands over Maksim's torso; his skin is hot, smooth and scented. I try to put a name to the musty scent: patchouli maybe. We move across the room and lie on the bed side by side. It creaks and groans under our weight. Maksim runs a finger along my hairline; he cups my face in both palms and kisses me deeply. I am unaware of where I am. I have no ability to stop what is going to happen; my body is aching for him. He moves over me, his hair dripping salty drops onto my breasts and he kisses them away. He is more muscular, more passionate than I am used to. Our bodies curve and entwine, exploring and convulsing. He enters me and a sound escapes him. "Tanya!"

I hold him tightly, my head buried in his chest. I feel I am part of him and I want to fall in love with him.

-0-

Back in the van, driving to Ob Street, we exchange very few words. On the horizon the sky is pink. Day has come.

We draw up at my *dacha*. He leans over to open the door for me. I turn to look at him. Our lips meet briefly. It is the kiss of a brother to his sister. Of a mother to her child.

"This is not the way to end this, Tanya," he says.

I am stricken with a fear which shakes me to the core. I walk towards the *dacha*. I do not look back at him.

What have I done?

-0-

Does adultery show? Was this adultery? This, I ask myself standing at the gate waiting for Beretzkoy to arrive. He wears a new black pullover. He had his hair cut in Moscow and now there is a lot of grey showing at his temples. I wonder whether the grey was there before and I just had not noticed it.

"You look great," he says.

"I missed you. If only you knew how much!"

"I hoped you would," he says, smiling.

I take Beretzkoy's hands and I kiss them, my eyes just cannot seem to meet his.

I love these hands, this face; this living soul.

I realise what happened with Maksim is something I will never allow to happen again. Not with Maksim. Not with any other man. I know this. I belong in my entirety to Beretzkoy.

-0-

CHAPTER NINE

Beretzkoy and I are very close this autumn. All through the day he makes excuses to seek me out. He rushes to where I am and says, *Tanya, come and sit down as I'd forgotten to tell you something,* or *Tanya, don't do that now because I want you to listen to this.* He also calls from the veranda. *Tanya, where are you!* I run to him thinking something terrible has happened, but he only wants me to sit down with him for a while.

Because of Beretzkoy's need for closeness, he helps me for the first time to prepare the *dacha* for winter.

We close down the garden, raking up leaves, trimming the trees, cutting the grass and lifting the fragile plants to transfer them to the loft. We check and replenish my supply of logs and with Kolya's help we put up a lean-to of planks and corrugated iron in the *ogorod* in which to store them. We take the curtains down, wash and iron them and hang them back up again. We wash the blankets. Again with Kolya's help we install a *fortochka* [81] in the kitchen door because this winter there will be a cat in the house. We unpack the cupboards to see what we have and what we would have to buy to get through the winter. We decide we would have to do without most things and it does not matter as we have each other.

The fountain on Marx Square freezes on the first day of October. Maksim is the one who discovers this. He has started to come over much less frequently and when I do see him, we do not know what to say to one another.

With the colder weather our problems return. Or rather, they never left us. We had left them. Briefly.

News of Hitler comes in a letter from Morne. *Do you know that Mussolini has been to see Hitler? Mussolini, the man-of-the-people, naturally took a train to Germany although it was not zhestky that he travelled. There were four days of receptions and parades, the likes of which Europe may never see again. And the uniforms of both Le Petit Corporal et le Gros Duce and their respective entourages were pure opera.*

We know Mussolini has been to Germany - in September - and that the visit began in Munich where Hitler was waiting, and that it ended in Berlin. We also know there were, not only receptions and parades and fancy uniforms, but also military manoeuvres and a rally in Berlin's Olympic Stadium attended by almost a million people. These things were reported in our papers. We tried to imagine

---

[81] **A small window which is left open in winter to allow air into a room, but it is also a flap in a door for a cat.**

a million people in one place.

Morne writes on. *Mussolini was even taken to the tomb of Frederick the Great and spent a few happy hours with Goering, the two playing with the Reichminister's miniature electric railway. It is said here that Mussolini's biggest supporter in Germany is Goering. The two met back in '33 when Hitler sent him and Von Papen (he is the Vice-Chancellor) to Rome. Goering, Mussolini and the head of the Italian Air Force lived it up so much that Goering collapsed on the flight back to Munich! Later Goering said that the collapse was due to bad weather, low altitude (for safety reasons they had to fly at 20,000 feet) and shortage of oxygen. Diplomats here say that Mussolini was not at all that impressed with either the troops or the equipment he'd seen in Hilter's military manoeuvres. He was heard to say to his Chief-of-Staff, Marshall Badoglio, that whatever the Germans can do, the Italians can do better and that the German weaponry did not look all that lethal to him. The Italians were going around saying that Mussolini was right when he said the English - and the French, I must add - lacked brains and some even, after a Schnapps or two too many, said that Hitler lacked grey matter and that it will therefore be Mussolini's task to save the world. What an arrogant pig! Another thing I hear is that Hitler was doing impersonations of Mussolini's oratory at the Berlin rally. He pushes his stomach out - sometimes even stuffs a cushion under his tunic - and standing with his legs apart and his toes pointing outwards, he pounds the lectern with his left hand while his right remains fixed in the Fascist salute.*

Our papers had written that the Italian newspapers reported it was just a matter of time before a formal alliance would be signed between Italy and Germany. Grim news, we thought. News which scared us.

The news coming from Moscow scares us too. The Yezhovschina's[82] thirst for blood is intensifying. It is now targeting foreigners. These people, all Communists who have left their own countries and loved ones to come to Russia to help us build the world's first communist state, are being pulled from their beds in the middle of the night to be driven to the nearest wood where firing squads are waiting to mow them down.

They are taking them all, Dan writes. *What an awakening for these poor idiots after having dreamt the big dream, the dream of all dreams.*

Even foreigners who have sought sanctuary with us from the German, Italian and Spanish Fascists and whom we received with banners and fanfare, are being taken into our woods.

My mother writes of her concern for my father because a French-born friend has been taken. *They came for Old Man Leo Petrovich last week. He asked them why and one six-foot brute knocked him down. "That's why, spy!" he shouted. Dear Leo is 86 and a diabetic. Dare your father go and speak up for him? Being foreign-born himself! I have asked someone about you, by the way, and I was told that as you were born of a Russian woman, you are Russian. Does your father dare go to the NKVD? If he should tell them that Leo was with Lenin in Zurich, would it mean anything to these people? They will most probably think*

---

[82] **A term used to describe The Great Purge (1936-1939). The word derives from the name Yezhov, Head of the NKVD from 1936 to the end of 1937.**

that Zurich is the name of a local Turkish bath as I hear that they are connoisseurs as far as those are concerned; that is where they go to soak out the stress. Sometimes we wonder whether Stalin can really be this cruel, then we hope that he does not know what is going on and that he will find out and stop it. But this soon passes ….

From one of Galina's letters, we learn Stalin is really this cruel. *Someone in the know told us that Yezhov does nothing without checking with Stalin. He sends execution demand lists to Stalin for his approval and Stalin, with his blue ink - he uses only blue ink - jots down comments like, "agreed"; "swine (death to him!)"; "dog (death without doubt!)" and "pig (shoot shoot!)", beside the names. Sometimes he writes only the two words "first degree". This means death by shooting. There is a list being circulated here in Moscow which gives the names and locations of all our labour camps. You won't believe it when I tell you that there are now thirty-five clusters of such camps, each with about 200 camps? Most are in the Arctic – 20 degrees below freezing on a warmish day! We asked how many would be held in these camps and the answer was five maybe six, maybe seven million depending on whether you are a pessimist or an optimist. Men and women. Is that what they meant when they promised us equality of the sexes?*

Yes. This is what they meant, is Beretzkoy's reply to Galina.

This autumn it also becomes illegal to appeal a court sentence, or to petition for clemency, or to seek publicity for a loved one's arrest. None of these things, of course, were ever permitted.

Oh yes, how well I remember all the appeals I put in the post to the NKVD when they took Dan, writes Yelena, sarcastically. *Oh yes, how well I remember the days I stood in front of Lenin's mausoleum with a placard begging for clemency and the interview I gave to all the foreign correspondents who asked me about Metelovsk.*

This autumn too we hear Stalin has ordered the history of our October Revolution to be rewritten. He is to make himself the hero alongside Lenin. Dushenka Koba is put on the project.

Laugh, laugh, laugh my dear friend because we shan't,
I don't even have to tell you why
Each morning in the first light,
We think that we still might.
But each night we know that we can't,
I don't even have to tell you why.

This, Beretzkoy writes to Morne.

It is his way of telling him it is not yet time to publish the poems in Paris.

But there are still some who laugh - Dushenka Koba who is going to rewrite our people's history; Semyon and Malyutka because their child, a boy, is born. They name him Iosef.

-0-

CHAPTER TEN

"Tanya, he's dead!"

I do not know of whom Beretzkoy is talking, and the colour drains from my face.

"He's dead," he repeats. "I killed him. Last night, I killed him!"

I realise he is speaking of *Doctor Rudi Zinn*. Last night, at his home, he finished writing the novel. He wants me to come to the veranda, immediately, as he wants to read me the end of the book. We sit down and he begins to read.

It was not a gentle death, the death of Doctor Rudi Zinn, but it was not nearly as violent as he knew death could be, or as he remembered the death of his mother had been.

I listen to Beretzkoy's voice. Normally never intense, it sounds today as if his words are coming from deep within him.

Doctor Rudi Zinn is sitting on a tram. He is an old man. His overcoat is too large for him. He tells himself that this is because the cloth has stretched from long years of use. He does not want to face the fact that he has shrunk with age. He is reading *Pravda*. He looks up from the paper and sees sitting at a tram stop on the opposite side of the street, a young girl in a purple coat. She reminds him of Lili from whom he had parted during the famine to return to his wife and children, and whom he had not seen since. His aged mind decides that the girl is indeed Lili. He shouts at the driver of his tram to stop so that he can disembark, but the driver shouts back that he has a schedule to follow. Rudi, determined not to lose Lili again, jumps off the tram. He slips in the snow and falls under the wheels of a tram coming the other way. Lying crushed and dying in the snow, he sees the girl's tram pull up and, she, unaware of the accident, gets on. He tries to call out to her - as happens in dreams he thinks he is calling to her - but the tram passes and she does not even look at him. She is talking to another passenger, a man, smiling sweetly at him. The man is young, handsome. Rudi thinks that oddly the young man resembled him in his younger days.

Doctor Rudi Zinn sighs and life abandons him.

"I want to read the last paragraph, for myself, please," I tell Beretzkoy.

He hands me the last page and I read it aloud.

And so the life of Doctor Rudi Zinn ended. Those who came to see what was going on, to gasp and wonder who the old man was, saw that when the end came, he was smiling. They would never know that the old man had died a happy man because he had seen the girl smile and he knew, like all men know, that an unhappy girl does not smile. He had not therefore broken her heart when he had left her. That was what he had feared.

259

I look at Beretzkoy. He is weeping.

I also start to cry.

-0

In the afternoon Beretzkoy asks me to type the manuscript. There are 690 of his handwritten pages. There is writing on both sides on some of the pages. Those are the pages he wrote during the famine when our country had run out of paper. He asks for four copies. One for us and he wants to send one to the Olminskys, one to Galina and one to Morne in Paris.

I set the typewriter up on the kitchen table and I start to type. He walks into the kitchen and asks me to let him have five copies instead of four as he wants to send Semyon one too.

"I would like this novel to be published here in our own land. Doctor Rudi Zinn's voice should be heard because a nation who cannot free itself from the crimes of its past, cannot live in peace and harmony with its present and, thus, has no future," he says.

-0-

Maksim brings me typing paper, carbon paper and typewriter ribbons, and he wants to know what I am typing. I tell him Beretzkoy has written a book.

"Is it fiction?" he asks.

"It is about Russia," I say.

"Then it is not fiction," he says.

"No," I say. "It is about life."

I type every spare moment I have and deep into the night.

"You do type fast!" says Ivan.

The Gromyko *dacha* is across the street. I did not know sound reached so far on Ob Street.

"The noise is rather intrusive," he says.

"What is it you are typing?" asks Anna.

I cannot tell her as we have not told my neighbours about the novel.

"The encyclopaedia," I lie.

Comrade Stalin is in a hurry for it to be published I tell them and Anna's eyes open wide.

"Well, then you should type, my dear girl!"

They will, they tell me, play some records should the noise become too intrusive. Their daughter who lives in Moscow has sent them a gramophone and a few records.

"But we're going to run out of needles," says Ivan.

"I need gramophone needles urgently," I say to Maksim.

I am waiting for him on the street at the hour I know he will be passing on his way from work.

"Are you going to start giving dancing lessons?" he asks, smiling only a little.

"I want to give them to the Gromykos as my typing is annoying them."

He brings me six packets of gramophone needles manufactured in America.

There is not another complaint from the Gromykos, but I do hear their music, wonderful Russian music.

I type the 690 pages in a week. Typing in the kitchen during the day and at night on the veranda. My brain is full of the clackety-clack noise of the keystrokes, and the pads of my fingers are blackened with ink, and are quite numb.

"We make a good team," says Beretzkoy.

"You're a good employer," I quip.

"I would have liked to have been a good husband too. A good husband to you."

I tell him he is.

-0-

CHAPTER ELEVEN

It is deep into the night. The telephone fastened to the wall in the lobby of the Beretzkoy *dacha* rings out loudly. Beretzkoy runs to answer.

"Did I wake you?" a voice asks at the other end of the line.

It is Dushenka Koba.

"Not only me, but all of Lena Street," murmurs Beretzkoy.

"I thought you were not going to pick up," says Dushenka Koba.

"Well, here I am!"

"Have you heard the news? Olminsky has been arrested?"

"Dan?"

"Do you know another?"

"Of course," says Beretzkoy. "Yelena."

"No, it's him. As for her. She came to Profpro for help. That's how I know of the arrest."

A dishevelled Yelena rushed into the Profpro building demanding to speak to our union's chairman.

Beretzkoy wants to know when this happened.

"This morning. She came to the office this morning."

Dushenka Koba does not know when Dan was arrested.

"Where is he being held? Do you know?"

Dushenka Koba also does not know this.

"She was insulting, that Olminska woman!"

"Did you help her?"

"Who am I to be of help?"

"Profpro," says Beretzkoy. "You. Whoever. Anyone at Profpro."

No, no one at Profpro even agreed to listen her out.

"He was a rabble-rouser," says Dushenka Koba, firmly.

"Do you know where Yelena is now?"

"Am I her keeper?"

"That's from the Bible," says Beretzkoy. "Shall I denounce you as a secret Denizen of Heaven?'

"Now you are talking rubbish!"

Beretzkoy hears footsteps coming down the stairs and Nadezdh Konstantinovna appears behind him. She is barefoot and wrapping her dressing-gown tightly around her.

"What is all this about?"

"Daniel Mironovich Olminsky has been arrested."

"And who is it on the phone?"

Beretzkoy tells her.

"And he calls you at this time of the night for trash like Olminsky? Has he lost his mind?"

"No," says Beretzkoy to his wife, "we have all lost our minds."

She turns and walks back up the stairs, muttering to herself.

Dushenka Koba, who must have heard the conversation between Beretzkoy and Nadezdha Konstantinovna, explains he would have waited until morning to call, but he wanted to make sure only Dan was arrested.

"What do you mean? Only Dan?"

Dushenka Koba coughs.

"My dear friend. I feared you, too, were taken. With the company you keep, these days, it won't surprise me if you should be."

"Sorry to disappoint you, my friend," replies Beretzkoy.

-0-

CHAPTER TWELVE

We sit in the kitchen. Kolya is with us. We can talk of nothing but Dan and Yelena. Maksim joins us. Earlier, a patient who had just driven down from Moscow told him of the arrest.

Beretzkoy and I decide one of us would have to go to Moscow to be with Yelena. I say I will. I know Beretzkoy and I have already spent too much money this summer, but we must give Yelena our support. Maksim says I could economise by not taking the train to Moscow.

"Take our bus."

The dental clinic has a bus now which runs between the village and Moscow. It is for its patients only, but Maksim says he will arrange with the driver to allow me on.

"That's a great idea," says Beretzkoy.

Not wanting to be indebted to Maksim, I was going to decline his offer, but not wanting to make a fuss, or arouse Beretzkoy's suspicion, I go along with the plan.

I go and pack.

Maksim having returned to his loft, Beretzkoy joins me in the bedroom and stands watching as I carelessly shove clothes into a suitcase.

"Why does Maksim always have to interfere?" I snap.

"Interfere? What a strange word to use as far as Maksim is concerned."

"All the same, it's not really his business."

"I think he's trying to help, Tanya, and you are being very unreasonable."

He is annoyed.

"It's just ... just that I do not want to be a nuisance ..."

"Not a nuisance, Tanya. But silly!"

-0-

"Your boyfriend won't be long," says the driver of the bus.

"My what?" I ask apprehensively.

"Comrade Maksim Mikhaylovich of course."

The bus is parked outside the clinic and we are waiting for patients who have finished their treatment and are returning to Moscow. The driver has shown me to the rear seat. He is friendly. He sits down on the seat in front of mine, rests his arms on the back of the seat and starts to tell me about himself. He is a retired Red Army sergeant. He lives in the village now. He lost his wife two years ago. He is grateful for the driving job as it is giving him an opportunity to meet people.

"Like your boyfriend," he says.

"He is not my boyfriend," I say matter-of-factly.

"What a pity," he says, "Such a fine young fellow."

I tell the man I am a married woman: to me, this is what I am.

Maksim, carrying a suitcase and a small wooden box, walks up with the other passengers. He puts the suitcase and the box with mine on the rack above our heads and sits down beside me.

"This was not planned," he says, quickly.

"I'm the one who should not be here."

We drive off. The passengers wave to a nurse who is leaning from a window. Maksim waves to her as well and I feel compelled to do so.

The waving over, Maksim turns to me and to draw my attention he taps on my shoulder.

"Tanya, I want to say, seeing this is the first opportunity I have to do so because neither Beretzkoy nor his spy, Kolya, is with us, that I apologise for that night this last summer. I do not regret it, that I cannot say, but I regret that you regret it."

I bite my lip.

"Forget it," I say rudely.

I scan the scenery behind the window for some sort of distraction. We pass Lenin's statue on Marx Square. The fountain behind it is frozen.

Maksim puts a hand on my arm.

"Oh Tanya, come on!"

He sounds like a school boy trying to persuade a chum to join him in stealing some apples from a neighbour's apple tree.

I look away from the fountain.

"I regret that night, yes."

"I know you do. I knew that night you would."

"Then you will understand I feel guilty, guilty and ..."

The hand on my arm trembles slightly.

"You don't have to say anymore, please."

The retired Red Army sergeant drives slowly as the Moscow-Minsk highway is covered in ice and he pulls off the road frequently to inspect the tyres by knocking against them the way a doctor knocks on the chest of a child who has a cold. He calls from his seat we can disembark if we want to stretch our legs, or relieve ourselves when he pulls up again. We will have to do the relieving behind a tree.

In Moscow, I hand Maksim my parents' telephone number.

"Why?" he asks.

"If you have a free moment, you could visit."

"Thank you. I take it that the invitation is a conciliatory gesture?"

I do not reply and he slips the paper swiftly into a pocket.

My mother comes to the door and as I am again turning up without prior warning, she turns pale as she did on the previous occasion.

"Mother, it's not what you think!" I say quickly.

I tell my mother about Dan.

"You should not get involved," she warns, sternly.

I ask her how she can say such a thing.

"Voltaire!" she says, sounding like my father.

My father is not at home. He has gone to play chess with a friend at a nearby Park of Culture and Rest.

"Life is getting back to normal here in Moscow. The *Chistka* is not over yet of course, but we feel a little less worried now and your father has been playing chess quite often," my mother explains.

Speak for yourself, mother! my inner voice screams.

I leave for the Olminsky apartment immediately.

-0-

Yelena does not come to open the door. I knock and I knock again and again.

"Yelena, are you alright?" I ask through the closed door.

I press my forehead against the door.

"Yelena, please, open up!"

"Looking for someone?" a voice asks behind me.

I turn round and see a young man in pyjamas.

"Yes. I've come to visit Yelena Fyodorovna Olminska."

"Her door's not locked. Turn the knob," he tells me.

The knob turns in my hand and I push the door open stepping into the living room. The room, which on the most tranquil of days was untidy, is today in total disarray. The upholstery of the sofa and armchairs have been ripped; the bookcases have been turned over; the books have been torn in half; a mattress blocks the doorway to the bedroom; in the kitchen some floorboards have been removed and on the table stands a pot of rotting *kasha*. It stinks.

"Do you know what has happened here?" I ask the young man; he has followed me into the apartment.

"No."

"Do you know of anyone who would know?"

"No."

"These people are my friends and I want to know what happened to them. If you know, please, please tell me."

"I don't know, but I know someone who might."

He takes me down the hallway to a communal kitchen. A woman stands ironing a damp sheet.

"She knows," says the young man.

Before I can thank him, he has gone. He had almost run from the kitchen.

"My name is Tatyana and ..."

"I'm not interested in who you are. I mind my own business," she interrupts me.

"Please. I want to know about Yelena Fyodorovna Olminska. She is my friend."

"Not mine!" snaps the woman, leaning forward to push extra pressure on a deep crease in the sheet on the table in front of her.

"Fuck you!" I snarl.

I turn to leave.

"Listen! Wait! Don't go!"

I turn back to the woman. She has put the iron down on a metal stand. Steam rises from the sheet.

"You're despicable," I tell her.

"Someone told me she's left," says the woman quickly.

"When? When did she leave?"

"Not this morning."

"Yesterday?"

"Not yesterday. The day before."

"Was she alone when she left?"

"They came for her. That's all I know."

"I am her friend. I want to help her."

"You won't be able to help her."

"It won't stop me trying."

"Well, I can't help *you*!"

"You have already. Thank you."

The woman squints her black, pitiless eyes at me.

"I mind my own business. I just mind my own business, and so should you," she whispers.

-0-

I take the tram back to my parents' apartment. My father is back from his chess game. My mother told him about Dan and that I have gone off to see Yelena. My father is in the kitchen, sitting at the table, drinking tea and reading *Pravda*.

"*J'imagine qu'elle n'etais pas la.*"[83]

"Papa, please," I say.

I know he is upset because he spoke in French, but I do not think I can stomach his condemnation right now.

"Well, she wasn't, was she? At home?"

"No," I say, "she wasn't there, because they have taken her too."

My father pulls out a chair for me and motions for me to sit down.

"Tanoshka, there is nothing you can do for her."

My mother walks into the kitchen.

"Vasily," she says, harshly. "*Remember?* There is nothing one can do, Tanya!"

---

[83]**I imagine she was not there.**

"But are we then nothings, of no value in this country?" I ask her.

"We are nothing," confirms my father, determinately.

"Well, damnation to Russia!" I shout.

I bang my fist against the table and the teapot flies off the samovar, spilling tea all over my father's *Pravda*. He calmly picks up the teapot and puts it back onto the samovar and my mother hands him a cloth with which to mop up the spilled tea.

"I'm sorry. I don't know what to do," I apologise.

My father sighs.

"My dear Tanoshka, you are *so* wrong. You must not send Russia into damnation for the madness of a few individuals. Russia is suffering too. Our poor beloved country is suffering too. Suffering just as we are. But we will not suffer forever and neither will our beloved country. One day ... one day it will come right for us and for Russia too. So, don't let me hear you curse Russia again. Do you understand me?"

I decide my only course of action is to seek help from Profpro. As Yelena had done. She was unsuccessful, but I may succeed. I will go directly to Dushenka Koba. He is not a friend of mine, and I am not a friend of his. In fact, I know he dislikes me, just as I dislike him. I met him for the first time at a Profpro meeting. I had just joined *Pravda* at that time and he was already an important personality within our union. In a conversation, I had corrected him when he called Versailles the capital of France. "It was just a slip of the tongue," he had told me, brusquely and angrily. I know he and his wife are friends of the Beretzkoys and although I have not laid eyes on the couple since I moved to the village, I know he - and his wife too - must hate me for what I am.

I call him from a post office near my parents' apartment.

"My name is Tatyana Nikolayevna Brodovskaya. I would very much like to come and see you."

"At three," he says. "Five minutes."

I did not tell him why I wanted to see him.

His secretary offers me an uncomfortable stool to sit on. She tells me to wait. She is not a young woman, wearing glasses which perch on the tip of her nose. Her teeth are uneven and yellow. She is typing with some difficulty as the typewriter's space bar is missing and she must turn the little wheel at the side to move from line to line. At three, precisely, she gets up and asks me to follow her. Dushenka Koba is sitting behind his desk. His shiny bald head is bent over a ledger. He takes no notice of the two of us walking in. The secretary looks at me and pouts her lips and she turns and walks out. I stay where I am. I start to count in my head and I count to one hundred and twenty before Dushenka Koba looks up and at me. He does not greet me, but points to a chair.

"Thank you for seeing me," I say, sitting down.

"I said ten minutes and ten minutes it will be."

I am tempted to ask whether I could add two for the time I have spent waiting for him to notice me. Instead, I tell him I will be brief.

There are two piles of paperclips on his desk. One on his right; one on his left. He picks up a clip from the pile on his right and starts to straighten it. In less than half a minute, I tell him Yelena has disappeared and she was most probably arrested and I hope he will be able to do something for her.

"Like what?" he asks.

The paper clip has been straightened and now lies on top of the pile on his left. He glares at me.

"I really would like you to tell me what you think I can do for her? Wave a magic wand and here she is?" he continues.

"I don't mean you personally, but our union."

He reaches for another clip.

"I am not aware you are still a member of our union."

Quickly, the clip is straightened out and he is reaching for the next one.

"I am still a member, but it is irrelevant as I am not here to speak of myself."

"It's relevant as you are the one who is here and appealing to our union for help."

"But not for myself. For Yelena."

"Let me stop you instantly. There is nothing we can do for that woman."

"You could try. There must be something."

I am almost begging him.

"There is nothing more to say."

"I do not know anyone else I can go to. Please?"

I am indeed begging him.

"So, you think, you can come to me, because you know me? I was not aware we are acquainted."

He looks at me with disgust oozing out of every one of his pores.

"You know me," I say.

He laughs.

"You're right, I have heard of you. I know all too well who Tatyana Nikolayevna Brodovskaya is!"

"This is not about me," I cry, my voice cracking.

"Get out of here!" he yells.

He slams his palms down onto his desk and both piles of paperclips collapse.

The door opens and the secretary walks in. She must have been listening at the door; her face is flushed and she is trembling.

"Show this woman out! See her to the street, there were she belongs!" he shouts at her.

The secretary says nothing, but beckons for me to follow her.

"You are lucky I do not have you arrested for demanding clemency for terrorists!" Dushenka Koba shouts after me.

The secretary and I do not speak, but on the pavement, she turns to me and tells me she has three children and she is bringing them up on her own.

"Why do you tell me this?" I ask.

"I am telling you so you should understand why I did not tell that bastard to go fuck himself," she replies.

-0-

Maksim is at my parents' apartment. He called my mother who asked him over and she is frying onions for him because he told her he loves fried onions. I can see Maksim is not the only one who likes something here. So do my parents. They obviously like Maksim.

-0-

Supper is over and I walk with Maksim down to the street.

"Tanya. On my way over, I passed a tavern. It looked like a nice place. Let's go and have a drink," he offers.

"No, Maksim," I say. "Thank you, but no."

He says he expected me to turn his invitation down, but he hoped I might say yes.

I do not tell him that, these past few years, I have learnt it is hopeless to hope.

-0-

On the bus back to Zernoye Selo, I tell Maksim about my visit to Dushenka Koba. The retired Red Army sergeant is behind the wheel once more. Today, he drives even slower because the windscreen wiper does not work and he has to lean out of the window to see the road.

I ask Maksim not to tell Beretzkoy of my visit to Dushenka Koba.

"We seem to collect secrets," he smiles.

He will tell me another.

"I came to Moscow to finalise my defection plan."

He is leaving in a fortnight.

-0-

CHAPTER THIRTEEN

The telephone rings in the Beretzkoy *dacha*. It is again late into the night.

Beretzkoy has not yet gone to bed and he is working at his desk. A woman's voice comes over the clearest connection he has ever heard. Comrade Stalin wishes to speak to him.

"Hold on please," says the woman.

Beretzkoy thinks someone is pulling his leg.

"Good evening, I hear the weather down your way is no kinder than ours here in Moscow," a man's voice says.

It is indeed Stalin. Beretzkoy recognises his nasal Georgian-accented voice.

"Good evening."

Beretzkoy has forgotten to add the *Comrade*.

"You must have thought I'd forgotten we agreed to get together to speak of poetry. But no, no, no. I have not forgotten. It is only that they are keeping me busy here in Moscow."

Stalin sounds jovial.

"I understand, Comrade Stalin."

This time Beretzkoy did not forget to add the *comrade*.

"You remember we planned to meet here in Moscow, now do you?"

"Yes, Comrade Stalin, I remember."

"Then your memory is better than those of the cretins I am surrounded with here, because believe me, they even forget to get up in the morning!"

Stalin laughs. It is a roar of a laugh.

Beretzkoy wonders whether he should also laugh.

"In any case, it is poetry I want to talk about now. Or about those who write it. Or should write it, but instead prefer to belittle others."

"Do you mean other poets, Comrade Stalin?"

Beretzkoy looks at his watch. It is twenty-five minutes after midnight.

"No, no, no! I mean politicians. Leaders. People who are doing their best to put food into every mouth and a warm overcoat on every back."

"Oh. I see, Comrade Stalin."

"Tell me? What is being said down your way about Olminsky?"

"Olminsky, Comrade Stalin?"

"O-l-m-i-n-s-k-y," spells Stalin.

"We ... him and I ... are both poets, Comrade Stalin ..."

"And friends?" interrupts Stalin.

"And friends, yes, Comrade Stalin."

"But you have your differences? Is this what you want to say to me?"

"No, Comrade Stalin. This is not what I am saying. What I am saying is ... is ... I try never to insult a fellow human being."

"Well, good for you!"

Again, Stalin wants to know what is being said in Zernoye Selo about Dan's arrest and Beretzkoy tells him he has not spoken to anyone who is aware Dan has been arrested.

"What are you saying! Don't tell me the people of Zernoye Selo still cannot read! It's been in *Pravda* and *Izvestiya* and after all the money I've spent building schools, the people should be able to read! Don't tell me I will have to come down to see what is happening in those schools?"

"The schools are fine, Comrade Stalin."

"They better be. So, the people will know about Olminsky. What are they saying?"

"I do not know, Comrade Stalin."

"They must be saying Olminsky did a vile thing with that poem."

What poem does Stalin mean?

Beretzkoy asks him.

"That filthy one about me!"

"I am not aware of such a poem, Comrade Stalin," Beretzkoy tells Stalin, honestly.

"I can see you do not want to defend him."

"On the contrary."

Stalin grunts.

"In fact, Comrade Stalin, I would like to speak to you about Olminsky and not only about him, but also about all of us."

"Come up to Moscow and you can do your talking, but right now I want to know about Olminsky only."

"We can talk about Olminsky, yes, Comrade Stalin, but I would like to talk about life."

"Life? Hm? Not a bad idea."

"And death, Comrade Stalin. I would like us to talk about life and death."

"Life and death. These are just big words for small events. You are born and you die. Life! Death! Ooi!"

There is a sound on the line as if someone is tapping against the mouthpiece with a sharp object. Silence follows.

"Comrade Stalin? Comrade Stalin?" asks Beretzkoy.

There is no reply.

Stalin has hung up.

There is a noise behind Beretzkoy.

"Did you say Comrade Stalin? You called that person Comrade Stalin!"

Nadezdha Konstantinovna stands in the doorway as she did on the night Dushenka Koba had called about Dan.

"That is how he is to be addressed," a bemused Berezkoy tells her.

She brushes her hair from her face. She is ashen.

274

"You were speaking to Comrade Stalin?"

"Yes."

She claps her hands in glee.

"The boys won't believe this!"

She runs back up the stairs and Beretzkoy calls after her she should tell her sons Comrade Stalin did not say goodnight.

That Comrade Stalin has no manners.

-0-

There is another call. It is morning and Beretzkoy and Nadezdha Konstantinovna are having breakfast. She jumps up to answer. It is Semyon on the line. He explains who he is and she says she is delighted to be speaking to him. She runs back to the kitchen to tell Beretzkoy to get to the hallway to take the call.

"I like it!" says Semyon immediately.

"Like what, Semyon?" asks Beretzkoy.

"Your doctor!"

"The novel?"

"The novel. We all liked it."

"All?"

"Gozuzdom."

His secretary typed copies of the manuscript and these he handed out to all Gozuzdom's editors. They want to publish the novel.

They would though like to make a few changes.

"I emphasise the word *few*," he says and adds, "It's splendid, your novel, just splendid. Congratulations!"

He will be writing a letter to Beretzkoy about it.

-0-

CHAPTER FOURTEEN

We have had three days of heavy snow and I shuffle out into the garden to see what damage has been done to my trees and winter vegetables. My gate is open: Maksim walks into the garden.

"Tanya? What are you doing out in weather like this?"

He pulls the sheepskin collar of his leather jacket over his ears and joins me. The jacket must be new because I have not seen him in it before.

"Have you a moment?" he asks.

I gaze over my shoulder at Beretzkoy who is working on the encyclopaedia on the veranda and visible through its glass panels.

"Certainly," I say. "Let's go inside."

"No, not inside. Out here. What I want to say won't take long. I'm leaving tomorrow."

"America?"

He nods.

"It's sad," he says. "Now I am going, I find it sad."

"Perhaps it will be possible for you to come back one day. If not for good. Then just for a visit."

I want to tell him he does not have to go but these are not the sentiments which come out.

He swallows several times. There must be a knot in his throat.

"No, it will never be possible to return. I have no illusions about that. There will be no return."

He tells me he has been walking around the village looking at everything, touching everything, and saying to himself, it is for the last time he is doing so. That he will never come this way again.

"It hurts."

He turns away from me so I cannot see his face.

"Tanya, it hurts like hell and I didn't expect it would be as hard as this to leave. I've been trying to find reasons to stay, to forget the whole thing."

"But you haven't ... found a reason?"

"I thought I had."

He still does not turn to face me and I am glad he does not. I long to touch him and comfort him, but my arms remain at my side, stubbornly refusing to obey my head.

"I do not want Beretzkoy to know," he says.

"Maksim ... look at me," I tell him.

He does. His eyes are filled with tears.

277

"I ... you ... I will only say ... tell everyone … this includes Beretzkoy, I am leaving for a dental conference in Budapest."

"If this is how you wish it to be, of course, Maksim."

"I wanted to ask whether I can come and say goodbye to you later."

"Later?"

"In the evening."

I turn as I hear footsteps crunching through the deep snow. Beretzkoy is coming towards us with his hand outstretched in greeting.

"That's some jacket Maksim!" he says, clapping him on the shoulder.

"It is American," says Maksim.

"As you will be one day," says Beretzkoy.

How true.

Maksim tells Beretzkoy he is setting off for a conference in Budapest. He will be away for five days.

"I've heard people say Budapest is the most beautiful place in the world," Beretzkoy tells him.

"They say the same of Leningrad," replies Maksim. "And of Venice."

"And Paris," I add.

"She dreams of seeing Paris one day," explains Beretzkoy, grinning.

"Women are dreamers," says Maksim.

He dreams too he says.

"I know," I say. "Of America."

"And other things, Tanya."

The eyes of both men are digging into mine.

If only I can read thoughts.

It is cold outside and Beretzkoy says if we want to talk more, we should go inside, but Maksim quickly holds a hand out to him.

"No, I'll be off. I'll say goodbye now as we probably won't see each other again before I set off for Budapest, and I want to keep this short as I am no good at saying goodbye."

"It's only for a few days," says Beretzkoy.

"Yes, a few days," I add.

"In that case, we will not say goodbye," replies Maksim.

The two men shake hands and Maksim shakes my hand too.

-0-

I am waiting for Maksim. Night has fallen. It is snowing heavy flakes. Sekret lies asleep over my feet. Maksim walks in. He is carrying two boxes. One is big; the other, very small. The big box he puts down on the floor beside the sofa where I am sitting. Sekret wakes up and runs from the room.

"This, Tanya. This, is for you."

Maksim hands me the small box.

"You should not have, Maksim!"

My throat tightens.

"Open it later, after I've gone. And oh yes, the big box is for Beretzkoy."

I tap the sofa and he sits down. Sekret has walked back in and is sitting on the box.

"Maksim, how will we know you have made it to America?" I ask.

"You will know, because I will tell you now, I will make it to America."

"You are confident, which is good, but here is another question. How will we know you have made it in America?"

He wants to know whether I have heard of the American magazine called *Time*? I have, I tell him.

"I will be in *Time*."

"How can you possibly be so certain of this?"

He says he can be because *Time* writes only of wealthy people and he is going to become wealthy, very wealthy.

"But Maksim, what if, just say, you are very poor in America. What then?"

"There are no poor people in America."

"But Maksim, what if you are unhappy in America?"

"I will be happy. Oh Tanya, I will be very happy, because I will be in America. But ... but I will also be very sad, because I will not be in Russia. Happy to be there and sad not to be here."

"I have given up on dreams, Maksim," I tell him.

"I know, Tanya. I know. But as for me ... I now have only my dreams. These are what I have to live for from now on. My dreams."

-0-

Maksim does not want me to walk with him to the gate.

"You will catch cold."

On a chair lies a rug. I pick it up and slip it over my shoulders.

"I'll come to the gate."

"Don't stay out here. Go on! Get back in!" he says at the gate.

"If I catch cold, I will have vodka."

"Have a tumbler or two in any case. Drink to America."

I tell him I will.

He asks if he can kiss me.

I nod slowly.

He leans over the gate; his kiss is long and tender, but he touches me only with his lips as his arms are folded behind his back. I also do not touch him. I am the one to break the kiss.

He strokes my face.

"Tanya, may I ask how you will remember me?"

"I will remember you as a good friend. Someone who cared for me. Someone I cared for."

"That's good enough for me."

"Maksim, I met Beretzkoy first."

"If you had not, would I have had a chance?"

"Yes, Maksim, you would have had a chance."

"And that, Tanya, that's good enough for me too. To know that."

I tell him he will meet a wonderful girl in America. I tell him he will marry her and just as in Hollywood films they will live happily ever after. His eyes start to smile, yet they are also brimming with tears.

He begins to walk away.

He walks away with his back hunched against the snow and he does not look back.

"See you some time, Tanya," he says without turning round.

-0-

I put the big box on my bedside table and I open the little box. Maksim has given me a heart-shaped locket on a thin gold chain. In the locket is a picture of Beretzkoy. It has been cut from one of the photographs Morne took of us on the day we all lunched at the Widow Alexandra's *dacha*. Morne sent us copies of the photographs and I had given some to Maksim. I find a letter in the box too. The letter is folded into a small square and pushed into the lid of the box. *Dear Tanya Nikolayevna, I will never forget you and your poet. If I ever take to praying, I will pray that we meet again. I ask you to stay as you are. Do I have to tell you I love you?'* The letter is signed Maksim Mikhaylovich Zorin.

I am glad I was not entirely truthful with Maksim.

He would have had a chance with me, yes, had I met him before I met Beretzkoy. His chance would only have lasted until I set eyes on Beretzkoy.

-0-

CHAPTER FIFTEEN

It is two weeks since Maksim left and the Widow Alexandra stands in front of her *dacha* calling me. She has been clearing the snow from the street in front of her *dacha*, and I am doing so in front of mine. I have been avoiding her because I do not want to discuss Maksim. He told her his delegation would be in Budapest for ten days. He should have returned four days ago.

I ignore the Widow Alexandra's shouting but Beretzkoy appears at the gate and tells me I should go and see what she wants.

"Maksim Mikhaylovich," she whispers, her face very close to mine. "He has not returned."

Beretzkoy has gone back into my *dacha* and the Widow Alexandra and I are the only human beings standing out on the frozen street, but she is whispering conspiratorially.

"Surely not. He must be held up in Moscow," I whisper in reply.

"They came yesterday to look for him."

"Someone from the clinic?"

She shakes her head.

"The Chekists."

Two men came. She at first thought they were from the clinic so she invited them in. They asked her whether she was related to Maksim and she told them he has no relatives because he was a *bezprizornik*.

She begins to cry. Tears are running over her cheeks.

"This is so strange. What would they want with Maksim? Do you think he will come back?" I ask.

I know I am blushing because I know I am lying because I know he will not ever ever ever return.

"I don't think he will. The Chekists went up into my loft and carried all his things away. They told me to get another lodger," says the Widow Alexandra.

She wipes the tears away with the collar of her coat.

"Come now, don't cry," I mumble, putting my arm around her, trying to console her.

"He was like a son to me. I am going to miss him so very much," she says.

-0-

Beretzkoy waits for me in the living room.

"Maksim's gone," I say.

He nods.

"I know. I had a feeling he was not going to come back from Budapest."

He says he did not tell me as he did not want to upset me. I tell him I knew Maksim would not be returning. I fetch the big box from the bedroom and the little box too. I show Beretzkoy the locket and he opens it and smiles on seeing his picture. I tell him the big box is for him and he opens it and takes from it a leather jacket with a sheepskin collar, similar to the one Maksim had worn.

"We did not say goodbye," says Beretzkoy, a look of deep sorrow crossing his face.

I do not tell him I did say goodbye and I keep the letter Maksim wrote me a secret too. Like Maksim said, we – he and I - were good at sharing secrets.

-0-

CHAPTER SIXTEEN

Dushenka Koba is given a week's rest from rewriting the history of our October Revolution and he comes home from Moscow. His success in his new role has made it possible for him to buy a car. Slowly, he drives through the village and waves to everyone, acquaintance and stranger, he passes. He turns into Lena Street and slams a hand against the horn. He wants his wife and children to know he has arrived. His children come running out. Beretzkoy watches from Number Fourteen's living room window. The car, a GAZ M-1 like Semyon's, is packed with boxes. The children jump up and down and want to know what he has bought them. Alexandra Alexandrovna, out on the street too, tells them to behave. There is also a box tied to the roof which Dushenka Koba cannot get down. Beretzkoy goes out to help him.

"Nice car," he says.

"I have news for you," says Dushenka Koba. "She has been released."

"Who?"

He is speaking of Yelena.

The two get the box down from the roof and the children want their father to open it immediately. Dushenka Koba obliges. It is a doll's house in the box. It has pink wooden walls and a yellow roof. It looks like a giant marzipan cake.

"I have good children," says Dushenka Koba to Beretzkoy. "This is to thank them for their goodness."

"What about Yelena?" asks Beretzkoy.

"She's been released," says Dushenka Koba tetchily.

"Is she alright?"

"How would I know!" he yells, walking quickly away.

-0-

The sun is shining and I am standing at the window of my living room. Kolya is with Beretzkoy on the veranda. I hear a loud bang on the gate. Kolya calls out he will go and see who it is, but the gate swings open and there stands Yelena. She is clutching a small suitcase and a bundle wrapped in newspapers. She is not wearing her red cape, but a brown coat. Her head is bare. On her feet are bedroom slippers. I run out.

"Is this Tanya's place?" she asks.

"Yelena!"

She gives a little laugh.

"Oh, it is you, Tanya."

283

Beretzkoy and Kolya come running out. Kolya takes the suitcase and the bundle from Yelena, and Beretzkoy puts an arm around her.

"I had an umbrella," she says to Kolya. "I appear to have lost it."

Kolya tells her not worry, the sun is shining and she does not need an umbrella.

We take Yelena into the living room and she sinks down onto the sofa.

"They let me go, but they've still got Dan."

Her face shows no emotion as though the words are meaningless. But her hands are shaking violently. I sit next to her and take her hands in mine to try and stop the shaking.

Beretzkoy brings Yelena a tumbler of vodka. She drinks it down, fast.

"I was in the Lubyanka. Good God! I was in the Lubyanka!" she sobs.

She holds the empty glass to her mouth and Beretzkoy takes it from her and refills it. She empties it quickly again. He suggests she should lie down for a while; rest and we can talk later. We help her to her feet and into the bedroom. She is wearing a summer frock under her overcoat and her skin is icy to the touch. I pull the blankets out of the way. She falls on to the bed and turns her face to the wall. Beretzkoy and Kolya stand at the foot of the bed, staring. I cover Yelena and tucking her in I tell her to sleep. She sleeps until after midnight and on waking she calls out for me to come to the bedroom. She apologises for having barged in on us; she looks tiny in the bed, the blankets seem to swamp her. I tell her she has nothing to apologise for. I go to the kitchen and make her a sandwich and a glass of tea.

"I lost my cape," she says, standing at the window, a blanket wrapped around her.

"I noticed you were not wearing it."

"And … Tanya, I am going to lose Danny as well."

-0-

I tuck her back into bed with pillows around her and I put the tray with the glass of tea and sandwich on the bed beside her.

"I have to tell you about when the Chekists came," she says.

I sit down on the other side of the bed.

Dan and Yelena were awakened from a deep sleep by a loud bang on their front door. She switched on the light and saw it was three in the morning and she knew the Chekists had come. She went to open the door. Dan began to dress.

She tells me there were six men and a woman standing in the hallway. The woman was in her twenties, small and thin, with bad skin and foul breath. The men were middle-aged and wore long grey overcoats. One wore pince-nez glasses and another had a handlebar moustache." Where's Olminsky?" the latter asked and she told him Dan was in bed, where a good husband should be at that time of the night. Handlebar - this is what Yelena calls him – emitted a grunt and the woman sneered.

Dan appeared behind Yelena. He was in his long black overcoat, his woollen bonnet on his head. Handlebar handed him an arrest warrant. Yezhov, as Dan saw and pointed out to Yelena, had personally signed the warrant. "I am glad to see I have given him something to do," Dan told Handlebar.

Dan and Yelena were ordered to sit down and the Chekists began to search the apartment. Handlebar did not participate in the search, but sat staring at Dan and Yelena. Until dawn the three of them sat in the living room while the others slowly destroyed the apartment. They overturned the bed and plunged knives into the mattress and the pillows and they cut holes in the carpeting on the living room floor and ripped up the floorboards in the kitchen and in the bedroom. They emptied the contents of all drawers, tins and boxes out onto the floor and swept all the books from the bookcases and they scraped the still smouldering coals from the stove onto the floor to see if something had not hastily been burnt. The coals started a small fire in the kitchen which they put out by emptying a bag of flour over the flames. The apartment wrecked, they proceeded to smash the pictures - family photographs – hanging on the walls. They smashed them using Dan and Yelena's menorah, and then they smashed the menorah against the stove. Next, they strolled into the living room to tell Handlebar they found nothing incriminating.

The Chekist woman spoke for the first time. She asked Yelena to go with her into the bedroom. Yelena refused. "Up to you," she said, "but take your clothes off." Reluctantly, Yelena followed her into the bedroom where she had to lie down on the ripped mattress and spread her legs. The woman proceeded to inspect her internally. "Just relax," she told Yelena. "Pretend I am a gorgeous man." In the living room Dan underwent a similar search. He refused to take off his overcoat. He unbuttoned his belt and when his trousers lay on the floor, he bent forward, but he would not stand naked in front of the Chekists.

Yelena asked the Chekists to arrest her too. They refused even when she begged. "Your turn will come," Handlebar told her. "Therefore, save yourself the trouble of having to come back for me. Take me now!" she argued.

They pushed Dan from the room.

Yelena ran after them and out into the hallway. There she continued to plead they should arrest her as well. "My husband is ill," she told them. "He's dying. His heart keeps on stopping." "In that case, why wasn't he sitting in front of the fire like an invalid, instead of plotting terrorist acts?" they jibed.

The woman told Yelena to go back to bed. "Go," Dan agreed. "Go back and sleep some more." He told her he would be alright, would be back by lunchtime. *They've got nothing on me*, was what he told her. *This is just show. I'll be right back.* "If you're not, I'll come fetch you," Yelena told him. "Promise me, Danny, promise me you will come back," she begged. He nodded, forcing a smile to his lips. He asked Handlebar to allow him to kiss Yelena goodbye. Handlebar thought that funny. "Whatever for, aren't you coming right back?" he mocked.

"The Chekists pushed Dan down the stairs and the one with the pince-nez pushed me back into the apartment. I ran to the window. A *black raven* was parked outside. Handlebar got into the rear with Dan. I watched ... I was crying. The car drove off. The foul-breathed Chekist woman was driving," says Yelena.

The Chekists came for Yelena a week later. She had not yet restored order to the apartment, had not even tried to put the books back onto the bookcases. Two men came for her, both hardly out of their teens. They were remarkably polite which surprised her. They asked her whether she had prepared herself for arrest and when she said she had been prepared for arrest from the day of her birth, they told her that she ought not be such a pessimist. "You will be back home soon."

Yelena was taken to the Lubyanka. To a cell on one of the building's upper floors. There were two bunks in the cell and a girl of about twenty lay whimpering on one. Yelena lay down on the other. The young girl tried to start a conversation, but Yelena pretended to have fallen asleep. After a few hours the door to the cell opened and a man's voice asked the girl, "So? What has the old bitch got to say for herself?" The girl replied, "The old bitch fell asleep instantly."

The girl left with the man.

Yelena was held for six days. Twice on each day she was taken to a cavernous room where she was interrogated by a team of young men. Always the same young men. One called her *Babyshka*. She was never tortured, not even maltreated. The young men had begun their questioning always with, *Come on now, do tell us*, or, *now wouldn't you like to be on the next tram going back to your nice little warm home?* Some of their questions were ridiculous; some deeply insulting, and some treacherous. Such tenuous lines of enquiry like, *Your mother's brother, the one called Jacob, but whom your family called Joe, had he ever been arrested for stealing a neighbour's sow?* Her reply was that she doubted her Uncle Joe would have stolen a sow, because as an Orthodox Jew, he would not even have wanted to lay his eyes on a pig, never mind, touch one.

"My reply was interpreted as my admission my uncle had been a thief though not a pig thief. Next, they wanted to know whether I had accompanied him when he had gone stealing. I pointed out to them that my uncle had died over thirty-five years ago and the last time I'd seen him was when I was about ten years old. And what did they say? They said, *Men die, but their sins live on after them.* I did not even have to try not to incriminate myself because it was all a foregone conclusion," she tells me.

Finally, Yelena had confessed to having been her uncle's thieving accomplice and she was given a sheet of paper and a pen and ordered to write down the names of her uncle's other accomplices. *Let's just get this over and done with because we like clean slates, and then, you can go home.* She filled the page with invented names and she signed her name at the bottom.

"Then they let me go," she says.

She says she wants to show me something and reaches for her coat. She hands me the coat and tells me to put my hand in its pocket and read what I will find there. It is a small sheet of paper. On it is scribbled a poem.

Easier said than done, boy
Said the mother to her son
When Nicholas came for your father, your Pa
Said I will be back soon,
When Lenin came for your brother he said, Ma
I will be back before noon,
I said I know the tune,
When the bell tolled for your Pa
The priest said, Dear Russian Mother
Our land still needs your son's brother,
I said one son is enough
But the priest said one is none,
I said easier said than done
And in the end son,
Stalin would not let you run.

-0-

Dan wrote the poem on the day of his arrest. The Chekists had not found it. Or perhaps they did but were unable to read.

-0-

CHAPTER SEVENTEEN

We decide Yelena should stay at Number One Ob Street for a while. We need to keep an eye on her. We borrow a bed from Alisa, which we put beside mine in the bedroom. At night, I hear her cry.

Beretzkoy tells Kolya although his heart bleeds for Yelena, he finds her presence disturbing. Kolya comes to tell me and says he thinks Beretzkoy looks tired. I have to admit to Kolya I think he is right. I too think Beretzkoy looks tired.

"How are you feeling, Beretzkoy?" I ask.

We are on the veranda. I close the door because I do not want Yelena to overhear our conversation.

"A little down," he replies.

"Why don't you take a week off?"

"I can't relax at Number Fourteen, and frankly, I need you near me to be happy," he tells me.

"So, come here to Ob, but don't do any writing. Just relax. Sit around. Read."

Slowly, he hooks his arms around my body and buries his face into my stomach. I lean down and kiss the greying hair on this weary head.

"Do you want Yelena to go back to Moscow?" I ask him.

"Oh no! I know I am a selfish brute at times, but not that selfish. She needs support and we must give it to her."

"You are a good man, Beretzkoy," I tell him.

-0-

The year of 1937 promised to be a good year and so it was in the summer, but now it is ending and it is doing so in such an awful way. Not only for Beretzkoy and me and our small circles of family, friends and neighbours, but for everyone. By everyone I mean the people of the world.

The word *continuation* is cropping up everywhere.

In Germany, Hitler is continuing his rearmament and continuing to speak of *Lebensraum*. Morne writes this means the formation of a German-Austrian Union is imminent and this new Great German Reich will march into Czechoslovakia and Poland to seize the areas in those countries which have an ethnic German population.

France and England continue to speak of peace - appeasement some say - and Prime Minister Neville Chamberlain sends his Foreign Secretary, Lord Halifax, to Hitler's mountain retreat at Berchtesgaden for some friendly small talk.

In Spain, the civil war continues and Russians are among its victims. This is not written of in our newspapers. We know because of Morne's letters.

In the Far East, the war between Japan and China continues with Hitler and Mussolini signing a tripartite pact with the Japanese Emperor, and Stalin falls in behind China, signing a non-aggression pact with Chiang Kai-shek, the Kuomintang leader.

As for Russia: our *Chistka* or *Yezhovschina* or *Stalinschina* as some call it, plainly blaming Stalin for the purges, continues and our armed forces are totally ravaged. So is our social and industrial infrastructure.

The strain takes its toll on us all. Therefore, who can, in times of such turmoil, wonder why Beretzkoy is looking tired?

-0-

I try once again to get him to take a break.

"Beretzkoy," I say, "why do you not go to one of Profpro's guest houses for a few days' rest?"

He tells me he may do so, but he wants to welcome the New Year in with me.

"We still have many other years to see in together," I argue.

He decides to go to Yalta. The boys are home for the end-of-year school holiday and they will accompany him. Both the boys wanted to become surgeons, but they have changed their minds and now they want to join the Red Army. He is going to try to talk them out of it.

-0-

CHAPTER EIGHTEEN

It is the last day of the year and Beretzkoy is away in Yalta.

"What happens in Zernoye Selo at New Year?" asks Yelena.

"If possible we have nice things to eat. Otherwise we just try to be happy."

She says the only thing which would make her happy is for Dan to walk in.

I lay the table prettily and we drink a sparkling Armenian wine. The wine looks pink in the bottle, but it is purple in our glasses. We finish off the bottle and for the first time since Yelena has come to stay, she is laughing. She laughs at everything.

I open a second bottle. We take the bottle and our glasses into the bedroom and fully clothed we crawl into our beds.

We begin to tell jokes. Some of Yelena's jokes I do not find funny, but I scream with laughter. I know not all my jokes are funny to her either, but, she screams with laughter too.

I have a third bottle in the kitchen cupboard and fetch it. I trip walking back to the bedroom and the wine spills over Sekret. He arches his back and hisses and for a moment I think he is finally going to scratch my ankles, but he does not.

In the bedroom, I find Yelena asleep, curled up like a child with the blankets up to her chin.

I sit down on my bed and I drink messily straight from the bottle. After a few mouthfuls I leave the bottle on the floorboards next to the bed and I draw up my legs under the covers.

On waking I look at the time on my bedside table clock. It is five in the morning.

The year 1938 is with us.

-0-

On the first day of this new year the sky is dark grey and threatening us with snow. A film is going to be shown at Stalin Hall in the afternoon and Yelena and I will be going to watch it. Kolya said he would meet us at the hall. The film is about a boy of seven who runs away from home to join a *kolkhoz*. They are making our heroes younger and younger these days. Every time the boy appears on the screen the audience cheers, but when his parents are shown, there are jeers and whistling. Kolya, to amuse himself, cheers and jeers and whistles loudest of all and he encourages Yelena and me to join him. After the film, our voices hoarse, the three of us walk to the Red Banner. We walk through the

Wood of Somnambulism where, despite the cold, young people are dancing to the music of a balalaika. Yelena suddenly falls quiet. I wonder what memories there must be for her in the music of a balalaika.

Marx Square is decorated. It is decorated for the Orthodox Christmas celebration which is to start in a week. Paper flowers and glittering streamers and pom-poms hang from the buildings. Even from the NKVD building. A fir has been placed on the frozen fountain, and from around Lenin's waist hangs a banner which reads *C Novim Godom!*[84] As Vitya is allowing street vending and street entertainment there are stalls on the square. We buy grilled sausages from a *babyshka*. Outside the Red Banner a juggler is throwing tin plates into the air and a young boy is pulling faces at a monkey pulling faces back at him. The Red Banner is packed but when Rodya and Roma see us, they quickly clear a table. Roma says the beer is strong today. He brings each of us a tankard full of it. The beer is frothy, warm and bitter, but when Roma looks our way again we ask him for refills.

At midnight, Yelena and I bid Kolya goodnight and we set off for Ob Street. The *babyshka* is still selling sausages and we stop to buy some more. We eat them on our way home. We take the long way home because we do not want to traverse the wasteland in case a coffin might fall from one of its trees. A feral dog with matted fur starts to follow us. We reach Number One and quickly slam the gate behind us so the dog cannot follow us in. Yelena says I should throw a piece of sausage over the fence and he will go away. So I do, but the poor animal just starts barking incessantly for more. I go out once more to throw another piece of meat over the fence, leaving the front door open. A ribbon of light stretches from the living room across the garden. I turn back to go in and I see a man silhouetted in the light. He is standing perfectly still in the doorway. He is not looking at me, but towards the *dacha* as if undecided whether to go in. He is dressed in a long overcoat which reaches almost to the ground. On his head is a woollen bonnet. *It is Dan.* I walk towards him my arms stretched out and I open my mouth to call out to Yelena to come and see who is outside, but the front door slams shut and the garden is plunged into darkness.

Dan is gone.

I am completely alone.

Out on the street, the dog falls silent.

I do not tell Yelena what happened outside. I have, after all, had quite a few beers to drink at the Red Banner.

Stalin's image on my back wall. Dan here now in my front garden.

What does this new year hold for us?

I close the front door behind me, leaving Dan - Dan's wandering spirit - somewhere out in the bitter night air.

-0-

---

[84] **Happy New Year.**

Yelena decides to go back to Moscow before Beretzkoy returns from Yalta. I try and convince her to stay with me a while longer but she is adamant. I walk with her into town to see her off at the railway station.

"I feel there is news from Dan at home," she says, wringing her hands.

"I hope so," I say. "I hope there is news of Dan."

"From. News *from* Dan," she corrects me.

I am sure she expects to find Dan sitting in his chair when she opens their front door.

The train steams noisily into the station and I help Yelena on to it with her things, getting on with her. The first whistle goes. I remember what Dan had said. We have two more to go.

"Danny was right, God does not give us three warnings. Stalin does not give us three warnings either...," says Yelena.

The second whistle drains her voice.

I jump from the train not waiting for a third.

-0-

CHAPTER NINETEEN

Beretzkoy and I decide we will make a trip to Moscow. I want to make sure Yelena is alright and Beretzkoy wants to see Semyon because he needs his support.

Gozuzdom has launched a literary magazine, *Slova*, and there is an excerpt from *Doctor Rudi Zinn* in the first issue. Galina sent us a copy. *Let me warn you that you will not recognise your work. The magazine has turned Rudi into a mealy-mouthed apologist for Bolshevism's excesses, and Lili into a drunken whore, whereas the Stalin-loving Yelena has become a warm and loving wife and mother. They have massacred your novel,* she wrote to Beretzkoy.

I doubt Semyon will be on Beretzkoy's side, but I do not say so.

-0-

In Moscow everything seems bleak. The weather and the buildings. Even the people. I stand at the window of my parents' living room - I am staying with them and Beretzkoy is in a Profpro guest house - and I tell myself I am fortunate to be living in Zernoye Selo. I never want to live in Moscow again. Through the window I see people in rags lining up at the tram stop across the street. I see a young woman, a mother, holding her little daughter's hand. The child has outgrown her coat. It does not quite reach her knees, and the buttons she can no longer fasten, and the sleeves leave her wrists uncovered. She is not wearing gloves and I can clearly see her hands are blue with cold. I see a woman leaning against a tree. She is trying to interest another woman in something she has in a bag. It is a bottle of vodka. A tram pulls up. It was snowing during the night, but it has now started to rain and the snow on the road is turning into slush. The mother and her child run for the tram and the child slips. No one, not even her mother, helps her up. The conductor calls out to the child to hurry. She scrambles to her feet and jumps onto the tram as it starts to pull away. The woman with the bag is still leaning against the tree. The bag she is holding up to her mouth, taking long swigs. I do not blame her.

My parents are glad to have me with them.

This time, my unexpected appearance on their doorstep did not scare them: one becomes accustomed to anything and everything in this country of mine. I plan to ask them to come and spend a few days with me on Ob Street as my father has not yet seen my *dacha*. Not that I have not invited them, I have, but my mother always found an excuse not to come.

I know how she feels about me and Beretzkoy - the married man - and this is why she keeps her distance.

-0-

I buy a sprig of thyme from an old woman at a stall and the herb's fragrance rubs off on my fingers.

The thyme, a symbol of courage, is for Yelena.

I hold it out to her.

"You've heard," she says, quietly.

She stands in her doorway. She is in a torn, stained petticoat from which her arms dangle like those of a ragdoll. Her hair is matted and wildly unkempt. Her eyes are shot with red. The sprig of thyme she has dropped to the floor.

"Heard? No Yelena. What?"

"He froze to death!"

She almost screamed the words, her body shuddering and swaying.

"What? What happened, Yelena?"

I try unsuccessfully to push the half-naked Yelena into the apartment.

"They let Dan freeze and starve to death!"

A woman steps from a door at the other end of the hallway and pulls the forefinger of her right hand across her throat. With a smile, she flicks imaginary blood onto the floor.

Manoeuvring Yelena by the shoulders, I manage to shut the door behind us only to find it is utterly freezing inside the apartment. Yelena's skin is the same, like touching the limbs of a corpse. She has cleared up the mess the Chekists had made of the place. She has returned all the books back onto the shelves. The menorah which the Chekists smashed has been repaired with rope and adhesive tape.

"Yelena, tell me slowly what has happened to Dan?" I ask.

"They told me he is dead."

She falls down on the sofa. I notice the windows are wide open, the curtains floating into the room on the wind. I close them tightly and cross the room to sit down beside her.

"Profpro told me," she says. "They sent someone to come and fetch me. Dan was taken to Kolyma.[85]"

"Are you sure of this, Yelena? This isn't just a story Profpro got hold of?"

"How can I know? I don't know what is true and not true anymore."

She tells me the story of Dan according to Profpro.

Dan left Moscow on October 10 of last year and arrived at Vladivostok about two months later, around the end of December. He made the journey on the Trans-Siberian Express train, escorted by two men carrying pistols although they were not in uniform. There were several overnight halts when he and his

---

[85] **A region in north-east Russia which was part of Stalin's GULAG.**

escorts slept in one of the local *izbas*. Such nocturnal comfort is not the normal procedure when transporting prisoners to GULAG, but inexplicably this was how Dan was taken to Siberia. In Vladivostok, Dan was taken by *koshevy* to a transit camp some seventy miles inland. Dan, they said, was being incredibly argumentative, asking too many questions, so the camp commander decided it was necessary to put him in a punishment cell. Five days later he collapsed, his heart unable to cope. The camp's medic did his best to save his life, but it was not possible. He died on New Year's Eve.

New Year's Eve. When I saw Dan in my front garden.

"So he did not die of cold, Yelena. His heart gave in," I tell her in an effort to comfort her.

"No!" she snaps at me. "He died of cold. When he returned from Metelovsk he told me about GULAG's punishment cells."

She tells me they are tiny hovels in the earth so narrow it is impossible to lie down in them, and the *Zeks* are naked when they are thrown in and they are not given anything to eat.

"Not even a piece of dried bread," she says. "So Tanya, my Danny died of hunger and cold!"

-0-

I persuade Yelena to have a bath and to get dressed. I see her into the bath and I go out to see what food I can buy. I find potatoes, leeks and a marrow bone. I light the stove and put all into a pot of water for soup. I retrieve the sprig of thyme from the floor where Yelena had dropped it and I put that into the pot of water too.

After a while Yelena walks into the kitchen with her hair wet, tied in a bun in the nape of her neck. She smells of coconut. Because of an absence of soap in our country, we use coconut milk as shampoo.

"I do not want to eat," she says.

"You really should. It's soup."

"All the same. I do not want to eat."

She has put powder on her face. It emphasises the lines which cross-cross her brow and obscure her eyes.

"Fine. You can eat the soup later, Yelena. Later when you are hungry."

"I won't get hungry and the soup will rot."

"Then offer it to one of your neighbours, but do not waste it. It will also stink should you leave it to rot."

"Like our lives here in this country of ours," she says. "Left to rot and stink."

"Galina once said the same and do you know what Beretzkoy's reply was to her? He reminded her that if we can smell it, it is because we are still alive," I say, gently.

"Oh Tanya, I do not want to live anymore!"

What to say to that?

Is there something one can say to that?

-0-

I tell Yelena I will be in Moscow for a few days still and I will come to see her every day and I would like her to come back to Ob Street with me.

She shakes her head.

"I must stay here."

"Just for a few days, Yelena."

"No!" she says, angrily. "No, Tatyana Nikolayevna, I am staying here!"

"Come to stay with me in a few weeks then," I say.

"No, I am going to stay here. I must stay here. Dan may come back."

I again do not know what to say to her.

I move the pot of soup from the stove. I put it down in front of Yelena, to remind her it is there.

"Do you want me to come over tomorrow, Yelena?" I ask.

"No!"

"Yelena, you do not have to be alone."

"I am alone, Tanya. I am alone now."

-0-

Beretzkoy is at my parents' apartment. Semyon has agreed to see him. He wants me to accompany him. As his assistant. Of course.

-0-

CHAPTER TWENTY

Beretzkoy's appointment is at four. I can tell he is nervous: his hands are shaking. I try to reassure him everything will turn out just fine. I doubt it will.

The Gozuzdom receptionist tells Beretzkoy she is happy to see him again and she will take him upstairs immediately.

He turns to me.

"Come."

The receptionist shakes her head.

"She waits here."

She is scowling at me.

I do as I am told.

The lobby reminds me of a public library. The walls are painted dark green and green linoleum covers the floor. The linoleum is worn almost to transparency in a line which runs from the front door to the staircase. Along one wall is a counter on which lie several piles of newspapers and magazines, all Russian. From a picture railing behind the counter hang three portraits. One is of Marx, one of Lenin and the other of Stalin. The portrait of Stalin hangs on the left and it is slightly bigger than the other two. *I am reminded of Pravda.* In front of the wall facing the counter stand a writing desk and two brown leather armchairs. A mousetrap, set with a piece of orange-coloured cheese, is pushed underneath the writing desk. *Cheese for a mouse when we, the Russian people, have even forgotten what cheese looks like.*

The receptionist behind the counter informs me I may go upstairs. I must go to the last door to the right on the first floor.

"You don't have to knock."

In the room, a red-haired woman calling herself Olga, is waiting for me. She is Semyon's secretary. She calls Semyon *Comrade Zukhov.* I go with her to a small auditorium with rows of upright wooden chairs facing a stage. On the stage stands a table with chairs pushed up around it. Behind the table hangs a red velvet ceiling-to-floor wall-to-wall curtain onto which numerous notes are pinned. A chandelier of copper balls and candle-shaped bulbs hang overhead. Olga and I sit down at a small table at the foot of the stage. She opens her notebook and arranges her pencils in a half-circle in front of her. She sets white sheets of paper and several sharpened pencils out in front of me.

She winks at me, but before I can wink back, the door opens and in walks Beretzkoy and Semyon. Behind them follow Dushenka Koba and five others - three men and two women. I do not know any of the five. Only Dushenka Koba looks at me. Only briefly. There is recognition on his face and he pulls up his nose as if he smells something very bad.

"Hmmm yes," mutters Semyon, stroking the little hair he has left.

They sit down around the table. Semyon and Beretzkoy sit facing me. Beretzkoy is wearing his dark suit. Semyon is in shirtsleeves.

"We were going to speak of how the freedom of the press is realised in practice in our country, but as you know, I hope, we are going to talk about something else too today," begins Semyon.

He is smiling. He looks over to where Olga and I are sitting, sees me and stops smiling.

"We are going to talk about Comrade Beretzkoy," says one of the women.

She is grey-haired and wears a grey suit and a red blouse with white buttons. She sits to Beretzkoy's right. She gets up, pushes her chair back, pulls it towards her again and sits down yet again.

"Shall we start, Comrade?" Semyon asks the woman, irritatingly.

She says she hopes everyone will agree with her Comrade Beretzkoy is a talented poet. The others nod.

"This is our dear Comrade Stalin's verdict also," she says.

"Aha but …," the other woman cuts in. "Comrade Beretzkoy is not satisfied with the extract *Slova* published of his novel, *Doctor Rudi Zinn.*"

The woman, the one who spoke first, picks a briefcase up from the floor and takes a copy of the magazine from it. She slams it down onto the table as if it is burning her hands.

"Boris Petrovich, can you tell us what exactly is your complaint?" she asks.

Beretzkoy looks at the woman.

"My complaint *exactly* is that what was printed in *Slova* under my name, I did not write."

"We only corrected your grammar, Comrade! All writers need their grammar checked. Even Dostoyevsky and Tolstoy needed their grammar checked. Even Comrade Semyon's grammar has to be checked because his short adjectives and his declensions of inanimate masculine nouns are appalling."

"It was more than grammar checking," replies Beretzkoy, softly.

"Dear man, we had to clean up your story. We had to trim down your doctor's anti-revolutionary gibbering."

This came from a man sitting beside Dushenka Koba. Like the latter, he too is totally bald. Both are sweating heavily. Rivulets of perspiration run down from their shiny bald heads.

Olga begins to scribble into her notebook. Thinking I should do so as well, I begin to draw circles and crosses on the sheets of paper she had given me.

Beretzkoy starts to defend *Doctor Rudi Zinn.*

He speaks of Rudi's childhood, youth and adulthood. Of how he had endured with dignity, honour and intrepidity the imperfections and excesses of tsarism just as he had borne, in his old age, the immoderation of those in whom he had once seen only fair play and integrity.

"What is anti-revolutionary in this?" he asks.

No one replies.

"Do you know the meaning of the world *zinn?*" one of the men asks Beretzkoy.

"Your question is insulting, Comrade," replies Beretzkoy.

Around the table they look at one another and smile.

"It means tin," says the man nonetheless. "Your Doctor Rudi Zinn is made of tin. You have therefore chosen a suitable name for your pathetic doctor. He is made of tin!"

Now, all are laughing.

Semyon bangs lightly on the table and the laughter stops.

"I'm afraid, *Gozuzdom* stands by *Slova,*" he says to Beretzkoy.

"And I'm afraid I've been wasting your time," replies Beretzkoy.

-0-

With this the meeting ends. Chairs are pushed back. The men and women start walking from the room. Beretzkoy looks at me and smiles. Olga takes me to an adjoining room. She points to a desk with a typewriter on it.

"The ribbon needs to be replaced," she says.

She gives me a ribbon and says she hopes I know how to remove the old ribbon and fit the new one. She also tells me should I have a problem reading back my notes, I could always ask to read hers. She has a wicked glint in her eyes: I am sure she knows I have been scribbling instead of taking notes.

For an hour I type the alphabet.

-0-

Beretzkoy says he is going to take me out for dinner. He fetches me. We walk to a restaurant. It is raining through a low mist and we share an umbrella.

The restaurant has red-chequered tablecloths, pewter goblets and the only light comes from black candles in old wine bottles covered with straw. The restaurant is called *Susasin* after Mikhayl Ivanovich Glinka's opera *Ivan Susasin.* The waitress wears a red caftan and hands me a red paper rose. Only two tables are taken: two couples, *apparatchiks* as their elegant clothes and glittering jewels reveal, sit with their heads down. They are cutting into roasted ducks. They take no notice of us. The waitress tells us, as they do not expect a full house, we can sit where we want. We choose a table at a window.

"This way we will see the *Chekists* coming," says Beretzkoy.

I can see on his face he is not joking.

We ask the waitress what we should order and she suggests we leave it to the chef. She brings us a bottle of red wine. The bottle looks like the one holding the candle.

"*Chianti.* Italian," explains Beretzkoy.

The chef sends us our first course. It is a boar-liver terrine on triangular canapés. The main course is grilled turbot with boiled potatoes and a hot cucumber sauce. The dessert is strawberry-flavoured ice cream. Overcome with guilt and shame at such a feast, we walk back to my parents' apartment.

"I am going to withdraw the novel from publication," says Beretzkoy suddenly.

"Because of today?"

"Not only. But yes. Today is one of the reasons."

"I do not want you to."

"My mind's made up and please do not try to change it."

"Cold feet?" I ask, cautiously.

"Cold feet. Yes, Tanya, my love, I have cold feet again."

He does not come up to my parents' apartment.

I watch Beretzkoy walk away. He stumbles slightly and looking back he laughs calling out the Moscow pavements are in poor condition. Someone should telephone Stalin to tell him so. I do not laugh with him as my attention is taken by watching him walk. He has a stoop, and a curve to his back and shoulders, which I have not noticed before.

In the morning I will go back to Zernoye Selo and he will follow in a few days' time. He first wants to call in on his boys at their school.

-0-

CHAPTER TWENTY-ONE

Valentin Sergeyevich, the secretary who accompanied Stalin to Zernoye Selo, calls Beretzkoy at the guest house. Stalin has heard Beretzkoy is in Moscow and wants to see him. He is invited to dinner.

"Will this evening be convenient?" asks Valentin Sergeyevich.

"Yes. Perfectly convenient," replies Beretzkoy.

A car calls for him at just after eight. The driver is a young man in a cheap overcoat. The car is a black Ford. On the rear seat sits a man.

"Rivers. I am in charge of keeping our rivers clean," says the man.

He is on the Moscow City Committee; he is one of Stalin's dinner guests.

The car reaches Red Square in just a few minutes. The driver turns right into a side street and next left towards the Kremlin wall, coming to a halt at a rusting metal gate. He sounds the car horn twice, the sound echoing against the old stone wall. The gates swing open and a sentry in a blue-grey uniform steps out. He holds a rifle in one hand and a glowing paraffin lamp dangles from the other. He recognises the car and steps aside to let it through.

It is Beretzkoy's first visit to this both revered and feared fortress.

The driver puts the car into its lowest gear and dims the headlights and for another five minutes they weave through a labyrinth of short narrow lanes and dark bare courtyards. Eventually, they pull up at the entrance of a long low building. No sooner has the driver cut the engine than another uniformed sentry appears.

"Stick around and be sure you don't get drunk!" the sentry barks at the driver.

He asks Beretzkoy and the City Committee man to follow him. He takes them to a vestibule and he frisks them. He takes a packet of *papirosa* from the City Committee man.

"You won't need these," he says and slips the packet into his trouser pocket.

He takes them up to the second floor in an elegant elevator with wooden panels, and next down a long wide corridor lined with gilded statues, to a door behind which leads yet more corridors and passageways. Finally, he knocks on a door.

Valentin Sergeyevich opens the door, drawing Beretzkoy into a bear hug.

"Delighted to see you, Comrade!"

"Same here," says Beretzkoy.

"Comrade Stalin will also be happy to see you again."

Valentin Sergeyevich and another man have been playing a card game as cards are set out on a table. Both are wearing *rybashkas* and grey flannel trousers.

303

Beretzkoy and the City Committee man are in suits but are not wearing bourgeois ties.

The second man introduces himself.

"Innokentiy."

He is from Tblisi in Georgia. He is the editor of an engineering magazine and has known Stalin since their school days.

The City Committee man looks impressed.

Valentin Sergeyevich offers drinks but before these can be poured a door pushes open and Stalin walks in. His good right hand is ready to be shaken. He is dressed as on the night of the dinner in Zernoye Selo. His pipe is in his mouth. It is lit and his moustached mouth grins.

"Boris Petrovich! At last you are here!"

He pulls Beretzkoy against him. A moment later it is the City Committee man's turn to be hugged.

The aroma of a field of ripe tobacco clings to Stalin and a cloud of smoke hangs in the air. So, yes, he has indeed started smoking again.

Valentin Sergeyevich motions for everyone to be seated. He, himself, walks over to a table on which bottles and glasses are set out.

"Big ones, Valya!" Stalin calls out.

At the Zernoye Selo dinner, Stalin was more formal and addressed his secretary by his first name and patronymic.

Valentin Sergeyevich fills tumblers with vodka and hands these out. The guests propose toasts to their host, next, to the Soviet Union, then, to all of the country's poets, and then, to all of its engineers. Quickly, the tumblers emptied, and were refilled.

The evening is to begin with a film.

Stalin and his guests take a yellow-carpeted staircase down to a projection room. The room is dimly lit and chairs are arranged in a half-moon between a screen and a projector. A reel of film is already in the projector. Stalin sits down in a chair directly in front of the screen. Valentin Sergeyevich will be their operator. He switches off the lights and for a few moments the room is in total darkness and the ripe smell of Stalin's pipe-tobacco becomes oppressively heavy. White stripes flash across the screen and suddenly the room is filled with violin music. The words *Anna Karenina* appear on the screen followed by more white stripes.

"It will come. It will come!" choruses Stalin like an excited child.

Names begin to flash onto the screen. Greta Garbo, Fredric March, Basil Rathbone. The violin music stops and on the screen two men walk into a room. They are speaking to one another in English. Valentin Sergeyevich begins to give a simultaneously Russian translation. A few minutes into the film, more flashing white stripes appear on the screen. Stalin explains the reel has come to an end and a second will be fitted into the projector. While Valentin Sergeyevich does so Stalin chats to Innokentiy whom he calls Kesha. The second reel starts and the audience returns their attention to the screen.

304

"Stupid Americans! Can't they put the entire thing on one reel? We do!" moans Stalin.

The second reel runs for about fifteen minutes and then the flashing lines reappear. Angry, Stalin jumps up. He walks from the room to an adjoining room. From there he calls Beretzkoy to join him. Beretzkoy looks at Valentin Sergeyevich for guidance.

"I'll call you and Comrade Stalin when the third reel is in place," says he, nodding encouragingly.

Stalin is sitting on a brocaded blue chaise longue. He has taken off his leather boots. One boot lies crumpled on the floor and the other on the chaise longue. The room is small and stiflingly hot from the heat pumping out of a tiny electric heater.

"Sit," says Stalin. "I want to talk to you."

Stalin points with his pipe to a leather armchair facing the chaise longue.

Beretzkoy sits down as told.

"I wondered what I would have to do to get you to Moscow, but let's not bother ourselves with that now because here you are! I wanted to ask you what you have to say about your friend writing those deceitful poems about me?"

"This is what we talked about when you telephoned me, Comrade Stalin," replies Beretzkoy.

Stalin bites on the stem of his pipe. His teeth are darker than Beretzkoy could remember them and his moustache is darker as well. Dyed?

"So we did," agrees Stalin. He strokes his moustache.

"He's dead now, Comrade Stalin," says Beretzkoy.

"Yes, he is dead now. He died of pneumonia."

"I heard he had died of heart failure, Comrade Stalin."

"Pneumonia," says Stalin, firmly. "He died of pneumonia."

He wants to know whether Beretzkoy has ever had pneumonia and Beretzkoy tells him he was once very ill with influenza and it might have been pneumonia.

"Awful thing. Pneumonia," says Stalin, looking almost moved.

Something will have to be done to stop pneumonia killing our people, he says.

"Indeed," murmurs Beretzkoy.

"It is such a waste of human life," murmurs Stalin.

"Indeed," repeats Beretzkoy.

"But tell me," continues Stalin, holding his pipe in his good hand. "Have you read this poem we are talking about?"

"Which poem would that be, Comrade Stalin?"

"The Nose and the Noose."

"The Nose and the Noose? Dan wrote a poem called the Nose and the Noose?"

"Do you not read what your fellow poets are writing?"

"I've read most of Olminsky's poems, but this one I do not know, Comrade

Stalin."

"It's a load of rubbish!"

"I would have to read it before I could comment, Comrade Stalin,"

Stalin smiles, his teeth clenching his pipe in a crooked leer.

"So you will, Boris Petrovich. Valya will give you a copy. Then, after you have read the poem, you can tell me what you think of it."

Beretzkoy says he will.

"I can see you are a loyal friend, Beretzkoy, Comrade Poet. I like that. I like loyalty ... it is everything. There is not enough of it around these days. But I want to speak of something else. I've read your manuscript. How shall I put it? It has left a bitter taste in my mouth. Like vomit. Yes, vomit on my tongue."

Voices and laughter come from the projection room.

"Do you want to defend your novel?" asks Stalin.

"It is no longer a novel, Comrade Stalin. I have already decided when I get back home to Zernoye Selo, I will burn the manuscript."

Stalin looks surprised.

"I have a copy. Do I burn mine too?"

"It is for you to decide, Comrade Stalin."

"I was going to ask Gozuzdom to see to it that your novel is published, because as you know, I am not one for censorship."

Beretzkoy says nothing.

"What do you think?" urges Stalin.

"It is for you to decide, Comrade Stalin. As I said, it is your decision."

"But what do you think?" insists Stalin, his voice like a growl.

There is a sudden silence in the projection room as if the men there are eavesdropping on this conversation.

"The novel," says Beretzkoy, "the novel, I now consider as something of the past, Comrade Stalin. Something which no longer exists."

Stalin shakes his head.

"No," he says, "this is not satisfactory. I want you to tell me what you think of what you have written."

Stalin is red in the face and he is kneading his good fist into the boot that lies beside him.

Again, Beretzkoy has no reply.

Stalin's eyes do not leave Beretzkoy's face for a second.

Valentin Sergeyevich appears in the doorway.

He coughs.

"The third reel is in place. Would you like something to drink, Comrade Stalin, or shall we watch the rest of *Anna Karenina* immediately?"

"Might as well watch the rest of the American rubbish," replies Stalin, his eyes yet resolutely fixed on Beretzkoy.

Without another word, Stalin stands up, sweeps up his boots - not putting them on - and walks from the room. There is a hole on the heel of one of his socks.

Valentin Sergeyevich takes Beretzkoy by the arm.

"We call this room the grill room. It is to this room Comrade Stalin brings those he wants to … well … grill," he whispers.

"I was indeed being grilled, so thank you for rescuing me," Beretzkoy whispers back.

-0-

The meal begins with smoked herring. They are in a dining room, sitting around an oval-shaped table covered in a red cloth embroidered with white flowers. Innokentiy is on Stalin's left and Beretzkoy on his right. Valentin Sergeyevich and the City Committee man face the three. The cutlery is of heavy silver, the glasses of sparkling crystal, the crockery of porcelain so fine that when a knife or fork touches a plate, it does so almost soundlessly.

Several bottles of wine and vodka stand in a circle on a side table.

Two servers push a trolley into the room. Both are of slovenly appearance: they have not shaved for days or have had a haircut for weeks. Could they really be professional waiters, or are they bodyguards?

On the trolley are small plates of herring. Clumsily the two hand out the plates. On each lie half a dozen herrings. Each little fish has been disembowelled and flattened. The heads have remained intact. When there is a plate in front of each man, one of the men begins to open a bottle of white wine. He had pushed the corkscrew too deeply into the cork, and the cork was crumbling. He looks towards Valentin Sergeyevich for assistance.

"Push the cork right down into the bottle. It's only cork. Can't harm us," advises Stalin.

The wine is Georgian.

"Drink, drink! It is supremely good," orders Stalin.

He clatters his pipe down in an ashtray. There is an ashtray as well as a small silver basket, holding cigars and cigarettes, at each table setting. He pushes his chair back noisily, as if in a lowly tavern, lifts his glass above his head and proposes they drink a toast to Socialism.

The men all get to their feet and do as their host commands.

They sit down again and Stalin points to the plate of herring in front of him.

"My favourite."

Grabbing a fistful of salt from a silver salver with his bad hand, Stalin, ignoring his knife and fork, and using his good hand, picks up the biggest herring on his plate, and, throwing his head back and baring his discoloured teeth, he bites off the fish's head. Slowly, he chews it, spitting out a small bone and not caring where it falls - fortunately for his guests, it falls onto his plate - and next he swallows, in one go, the rest of the fish, as well as the salt, left on the plate in front of him.

The guests stare guilelessly at their own plates knowing they must replicate their host's technique.

Stalin grins at the worried faces around the table.

"That was how, in my childhood in Georgia, we ate herring! Now eat!"

"Herring is also my favourite, Comrade Stalin," says the City Committee man, probably trying to delay the moment he has to swallow a fish covered in salt.

"Ah, but I am sure you've never eaten it as one should eat it!" taunts Stalin.

All in the room - guests and waiters - watch the City Committee man choose the smallest herring on his plate. They watch him bite off the fish's head.

"Good?" asks Stalin.

"Good," confirms the City Committee man, his mouth full of fish head.

He swallows the head without chewing it.

Stalin is grinning.

"Now, have the rest of the fish. But salt it! And salt it like a real man would and not like a weak little grandfather will do!"

The City Committee man pulls the silver salver over and looks around for a spoon he can use but Stalin scoops up a fistful of salt and throws it over the man's plate.

"Now! Eat!" he orders.

The City Committee man flinches, but he picks up the herring his teeth have a moment before beheaded, now white with salt, and bites into it. Slowly he chews it. Water starts to run from his eyes. He chews with his mouth open as if to make sure Stalin sees he is eating the herring. His teeth crunch the fish into a grey ball. He swallows. Once. Twice. Again. His Adam's apple jerks and more water runs from his eyes.

Stalin chuckles.

"Well? How was that?"

"Delicious. Really quite quite extraordinarily delicious, Comrade Stalin!"

The City Committee man is red in the face.

"I knew you would like it," grins Stalin.

He slaps his good fist down onto the table. The glasses, filled to the rim, quiver, and wine spills onto the beautiful tablecloth.

Next on the menu is pork. It is served in large tender cubes over which a thick sweet sauce has been poured.

"Refresh my memory," says Stalin, turning to Innokentiy. "This isn't Georgian, is it?"

"I wouldn't know, Soso," replies Innokentiy. "You know I am an engineer and not a cook."

Stalin says so he is indeed.

"And an excellent one too," he adds.

"Oh, Soso!" gushes Innokentiy. "You are such a wonderful friend!"

"We're far ahead of the Americans in engineering," states Stalin.

An example of Soviet expertise is Moscow's Metropolitan. He praises Nikita Sergeyevich Khrushchev, the man in charge of its construction. Another example of Soviet expertise is the Moscow-Volga canal. The City Committee man was on the project before he was transferred.

A dessert of carrot cake is put on the table. The two waiters fill glasses with *shamspanska*[86] and Stalin wants to know who they should toast. Valentin Sergeyevich suggests they drink to the Moscow Metropolitan.

"As we're talking about it."

They raise their glasses.

"Stop!" Stalin calls out. "We have a poet here, so we shall drink to poets."

He points silently to Beretzkoy and all at the table turn their heads.

The glasses are raised.

"To Boris Petrovich," says Valentin Sergeyevich.

"Boris Petrovich," echoes Stalin, leaning heavily over the table, "tell my guests about your book."

"It is not a book, Comrade Stalin."

"What is the title of your book?" asks Innokentiy.

"*Doctor Rudi Zinn*," replies Stalin.

"A strange name," says Innokentiy. "This fellow *Zinn* sounds like a foreigner."

"He wasn't a foreigner," says Beretzkoy quietly to Innokentiy, showing no wish to enhance his explanation.

"What do you mean *wasn't*?" asks Innokentiy.

"He has destroyed his manuscript. Or, is going to," explains Stalin. "This Dr Zinn is a thing of the past."

"You will destroy your work?" asks Valentin Sergeyevich, surprised.

"Yes, I plan to burn the manuscript on my return to Zernoye Selo," Beretzkoy tells Valentin Sergeyevich.

The faces at the table look on in cautious silence.

"But the main character dies at the end of the book and that is also why he used the past tense," explains Stalin to Innokentiy.

"Does he?" asks Valentin Sergeyevich of Beretzkoy. "Do you kill him off?"

"He dies, yes."

"Sad," says Innokentiy flatly. "Sounds a sad story."

He prefers books with happy endings, he explains.

"That's idiotic!" snaps Stalin. "What are you? A rosy-cheeked school girl?"

It is idiotic, he continues, because at life's end, we all die.

"So we do, Soso," agrees Innokentiy, meekly lowering his gaze.

"Tell me, Boris Petrovich, you who are the poet, tell me, is death the end?" asks Stalin.

Beretzkoy nods.

"Death is the end, Comrade Stalin. I believe that, yes, death is the end."

"Explain what you mean, if you will. You know some say death is a beginning, a doorway to a new life, but what does the poet in you think of such

---

[86] **Russian-made sparkling wine.**

a concept?"

"Death is not a beginning in my view, Comrade Stalin," replies Beretzkoy, candidly.

"Not?"

"No. After death there is nothing, and death itself, the departure of life from the body, is but a moment of nothingness, and this moment of nothingness is followed by the after-death."

"After-death?" asks Stalin, stroking his moustache.

"This is what I believe, Comrade Stalin."

"What do you mean by the after-death, man? Come on explain!"

"What follows the last breath. The eternal nothingness which follows the last breath."

"So, death is a moment of nothingness, which is followed by the after-death, which is an eternal nothingness. A non-existence?" asks Stalin.

He rests his elbows on the table beside his plate.

"This is what I believe, Comrade Stalin."

"So there is no life after death?"

He turns his head to face Beretzkoy, awaiting his reply.

"I do not know whether this is so, I am only presuming this is so, Comrade Stalin."

"I like that," says Stalin. "The after-death is an eternal nothingness. It seems right!"

Valentin Sergeyevich is nodding.

"This is how I understand death. And life," confirms Beretzkoy to Valentin Sergeyevich.

"So we have only one life?" he asks.

"Yes," replies Stalin in the place of Beretzkoy, rising to his feet. "This is what I've been saying all along. We have one life, just this one life and therefore we have to make the best of it. Respect one another; help one another; be kind. That's what I've been saying all along. Forget about what comes after death. Concern yourself only with the life you have now."

All rise and drink to life.

Stalin sits down again, motioning for all to do the same. He is still looking at Beretzkoy.

"It hurt when I read your book. After having read only a few pages, I wanted to throw it into the wastepaper basket. But I read on. Now, I am glad I did, because I am going to ask you to write me another book. I will do so politely because I am a polite man. I will say please and thank you to you. I want you to write of our shortcomings and our suffering, just as you did in *Doctor Rudi Zinn*, but I want you to make it clear in your new book that we are no longer suffering and that we are working on our shortcomings. But no lies, please, no exaggerations. I never lie and therefore I cannot tolerate lying. You told so many lies in *Doctor Rudi Zinn*. So, you write me a book filled with the truth. I will call you once a week to hear how the book is coming along. The first call will be in a week's time. I'll give you a year to write me this book. That's twelve months from this moment."

He slaps his good hand against the table. Again, wine spills from the glasses on to the beautiful tablecloth.

-0-

Abruptly, the dinner begins to end. Stalin gets up, stands at the table, sombrely shaking hands with his guests. He does not say a word. There is no return to the salon, or to the projection room, and neither coffee nor a final drink is offered.

At three in the morning, Beretzkoy and the City Committee man climb back into the black Ford. Innokentiy is staying overnight at the Kremlin. The driver smells of stale wine.

"Despite what Comrade Stalin said about your book, I have a feeling he likes you, but dislikes me," says the City Committee man to Beretzkoy.

"Should I celebrate?" asks Beretzkoy.

The driver tilts his head, slightly. Obviously, he wants to follow the conversation.

"This is not the question you should be asking," says the City Committee man.

"What is the question I should be asking?"

"The question you ought to be asking me is, 'Comrade, what are you going to do now?' And I will tell you I wonder whether I should, later this morning, tie one of Stalin's prefabricated concrete slabs around my body and jump into the Moskva?"

"Would this not be a bit drastic?"

"I do not think so. I've been thinking for a while it is only a matter of time before I will not be cleaning our rivers but my remains will be polluting them. And now, knowing Comrade Stalin dislikes me, now I know my premonition is justified."

"Perhaps my body will join yours," says Beretzkoy.

The driver nods and laughs insincerely.

"So will mine, Comrades."

-0-

In the morning, a poem - The Nose and the Noose - is delivered to the guest house. It is a long narrative poem. It has a subtitle: One day a cockroach crawled into the nose of one Iosef Vissaryonovich Dhughasvily, this vilest of vermin, which we all detest. Beretzkoy does not doubt it is Dan's creation, Dan having sought inspiration for his poem in the image of Stalin which had appeared on the back wall of my dacha.

The vilest of vermin, not being the cockroach, but Stalin.

After reading it through, Beretzkoy shreds the pages and burns these in the wastepaper basket in his room.

-0-

CHAPTER TWENTY-TWO

I expect Beretzkoy back at noon. It is Kolya who comes. He has a bicycle now and he has decorated it with streamers, and when he goes fast, the streamers rustle in the wind. He rides around the *dacha*, throws the bicycle down and bursts into the kitchen.

"What's going on?" I ask, immediately concerned.

"Beretzkoy!"

Kolya stands in the doorway. Beads of perspiration cling to his brow, and he is out of breath.

"You must be careful. Don't go so fast on that bike of yours. You can fall. And Beretzkoy isn't back yet, but he should be..."

I stop.

"Beretzkoy didn't come back last night," blurts out Kolya.

"Didn't ...?"

"He had to stay in Moscow. That's what I've come to tell you. He's in hospital. He had dinner with Semyon and he didn't feel well. But ... it isn't serious. He just fainted."

"Fainted?"

"Semyon took him to his home first - he lives in Arbat[87] - and then he took him to Kremlin Hospital. Semyon called Nadezdha Konstantinovna to tell her."

There is something wrong with Beretzkoy's stomach. The doctors do not know what, but they are carrying out tests. He is in pain, but the doctors are controlling the pain with medication. *Morphine.* My heart beats faster. I know morphine is used for intense pain only.

I am shaking.

"I will go to Moscow."

Kolya says I cannot.

"How can you say that! You can't forbid me to go! Who do you think you are!" I shout.

"Of course, it is not for me to tell you what to do, but you really do not have to rush to Moscow. You have misunderstood me. Beretzkoy is not dying. He is not even seriously ill. He is exhausted which is why he fainted. Fatigue can hit one in all sorts of ways. One way is to upset the stomach. This was what has happened to Beretzkoy in Moscow. Don't worry, Tanya!"

He assures me I will know every minute of the day how Beretzkoy is getting

---

[87] **A street in Moscow where most residents were apparatchiks.**

on as he will keep on asking Nadezdha Konstantinovna and he will keep on coming to tell me what she says.

Kolya tells me that when Beretzkoy collapsed, Semyon was discussing *Doctor Rudi Zinn* with him, trying to persuade him not to destroy the manuscript but to make a few changes. Suddenly, Beretzkoy closed his eyes and, in the moments which followed, he slid to the floor in a faint.

"But Tanya, Beretzkoy is not dying!"

Kolya is adamant I understand this.

-0-

My neighbours bring me things to eat. The Gromykos bring me a small basket of wild strawberries. It is March and there is a first burst of berries in the Wood of Somnambulism. Alisa brings me a loaf of rye bread which she has baked herself, and she tells me she will keep Nilats quiet. I tell her to let him bark. I do not tell her a dog's barking is preferable to the voices arguing in my head. One tells me I must go to Moscow and the other says I should not. Both voices are mine of course.

A telegram comes from Galina. *Seen him. He sends love. He's fine. Will write.*

Who it is who will write, she does not say.

"I hate telegrams," I say to Kolya. "They say nothing."

Kolya rides between Ob Street and Lena Street several times a day because both Semyon and Dushenka Koba are keeping in touch with Nadezdha Konstantinovna by telephone, and he comes to tell me what they are reporting. Beretzkoy is feeling stronger every day, I hear. The doctors initially thought he had a stomach ulcer, but this is not the case. It must have been something he ate. Something poisonous and not just rotten.

"He will be home soon," says Kolya.

-0-

Within a week Beretzkoy returns to the village.

He comes to the *dacha*.

"Do not speak of what has happened," he says, firmly.

He holds a small black velvet box out to me.

I waited for him at the gate. I watched him walk the length of the street to get to me. I take his case from him and we walk slowly to the living room.

"What happened?"

I cannot stop the tears from filling my eyes.

"Do you not want to open your gift?" he asks.

He has lost weight. His clothes hang loose on him. His hair is greyer than how I remember it. I tell myself I am imagining it.

His eyes fix on me and his face breaks into a smile.

"I'll open the gift," I say. "Of course I will."

314

The box holds two small star-shaped earrings.

"See whether they fit."

I laugh for the first time in what seems like an age.

"Earrings always fit," I tell him.

"Go and have a look in the mirror."

I go into the bedroom to look at myself. Beretzkoy comes to stand behind me.

"You are beautiful, Tanya. I do not know what I've done to deserve the happiness you bring me."

I turn to look at him.

"Strange," I say, "I've been wondering the same."

I do not tell him I would so much rather have wanted a ring from him. A wedding band.

-0-

CHAPTER TWENTY-THREE

It is the first day of April and Beretzkoy finds a large envelope in my post box. It is addressed to him. He tears it open. It is a copy of the second issue of *Slova*. Galina sent it. A note is clipped to the magazine. She wrote: *What need I say?* Beretzkoy holds the magazine up so I can see its cover. He is pale - he is these days and my neighbours are asking me whether he is ill - and the hand which holds the magazine shakes. I read the words *Olovoy Chelevek*[88]. The words are printed in large letters. The cover is yellow; the lettering black. The magazine is devoted to *Doctor Rudi Zinn*.

"Come," he says.

We must go to the bedroom. We sit down on the bed.

Slova is divided into three sections. The first is a reprint of the extract which appeared in the previous issue, and the second is a long synopsis of the novel. Beretzkoy reads the synopsis to me. *Slova* edited out all of the novel's events and incidents which show our country, people and leaders in a favourable light. The third section is an analysis of the novel and of the kind of mind capable of writing such a book about our motherland. In this third section there is also an open letter to Beretzkoy. The open letter bears eleven signatures. Two of the signatures we cannot decipher and three we cannot put a face to, but the other six signatories we know. Dushenka Koba is one. Another is Semyon.

We read the letter. It begins with the word *shame*. Shame is in italics. In each paragraph that follows there is a word in italics and there are eight paragraphs. The nine words in italics form the sentence *Shame On You As Your Country Certainly Loves You*. It is not only an inventive way of warning Beretzkoy, but it is also a line from *Doctor Rudi Zinn*; it was said by Yelena Zinn to Rudi. The magazine does not point this out. The letter ends, *As for the author of this book: he has in the past written wonderful patriotic verse which moved the hearts of all who read him and which gives us hope that the malice which drips from this book has not come from his quill but from the evil force which surrounds him. We beg him to remove this evil force from his life and that he will apologise to his motherland for spitting in her face. He must burn this book!*

It is not easy to understand whether the magazine speaks of the fictional *Doctor Rudi Zinn* or of Beretzkoy. Either the one or the other is described as a dolt, a thug, a coward and politically immature.

I lie down on the bed and I put my hands over my eyes and I hear Beretzkoy laugh. Surprised, I open my eyes and look at him.

---

[88] **Tin man.**

"I have to laugh or I will cry."

I start to cry for him. It is too much for me, this life of ours. To always be living in fear.

"No Tanya," he says. "Please don't."

He drops the magazine onto the floor and lies down beside me.

"The evil force," I say. "That's supposed to be me, isn't it?"

"I am in this alone."

"No. I am in this with you, and they know it."

He tells me to forget about *Slova* for a while. We pull the covers over our heads and we hide in the darkness, his lips covering mine.

-0-

It is night.

Semyon calls Beretzkoy to apologise for having signed the letter. He wants Beretzkoy to understand he had no choice but to sign. Malyutka is expecting another child; she needs him. Iosef, their son, needs him. Beretzkoy tells him he understands.

The phone rings yet again in the Beretzkoys' *dacha*. It is Dushenka Koba on the line. He wants Beretzkoy to know he had no choice but to sign. Beretzkoy tells him he understands.

"Thank you," simpers Dushenka Koba.

He lingers on the line trying to make polite conversation. Beretzkoy holds the phone to his ear and listens impassively, his face blank.

"Beretzkoy, my old friend, I want to give you advice. If I may," says Dushenka Koba.

"You are not the only one," says Beretzkoy. "So, go right ahead."

"Brodovskaya. Brodovskaya is no good for you. She is poisoning your mind, that woman. All this misfortune is her doing. Think of your wife and your sons. They need you. You should send her packing, if you know what's good for you." he grunts.

Beretzkoy replaces the receiver, cutting him dead.

-0-

Beretzkoy starts receiving insulting letters. The letters are sent either to Lena Street or to me. He brings Lena Street's over to Ob Street unopened as Nadezdha Konstantinovna says she wants to have nothing to do with them, or with *Doctor Rudi Zinn*. I read all the letters. I read them at night when I am alone so Beretzkoy will not be tempted to ask me to read them to him because I think it is better he should not know what is being said about him. The letters come from all over the country and some do not bear a signature. Quite a few do not bear a postmark, which means they have been dropped into our post boxes by villagers.

As my neighbours now know of the novel and what is going on, Alisa wants to know what I do with the letters after I have read them and I tell her I tear them up into tiny pieces which I throw away with the rubbish. She tells me this is a waste of good firewood. I should use the letters to light the stove. I ask her whether she would like to share the letters with me and she says she would be delighted to.

"Firewood is so expensive," she moans.

The Gromykos come to ask whether they can read the novel and why did we not tell them Beretzkoy was writing one? They speak in whispers as if they have come to see a new baby and fear their voices will wake it.

"Do you really want to read the novel?" I ask.

"We wouldn't ask if we do not want to," says Igor.

"No," I say, "I'm sorry, but it is better you do not read it, better to have no knowledge of it."

They say perhaps I am right.

It seems I am right, because more *Chistka* news arrives. Stalin has had three members of Lenin's Old Guard, men with whom my father fought *the cause*, executed. Nikolay Ivanovich Bukharin, Aleksey Ivanovich Rykov and Nikolay Nikolayevich Krestinsky. The three stood in the dock with eighteen other accused. One of those eighteen was Yagoda: *Yagodka, the little berry*, Yezhov's predecessor. One of the charges he faced was that he ordered the murder, by poisoning, of Gorky. All twenty-two pleaded guilty to the charges against them although Krestinsky, at first, angrily protested his innocence. All but three were sentenced to death. The sentences were carried out within minutes of being passed. The accused were shot. Stalin had the court equipped with hidden microphones so he could listen to the proceedings from his private Kremlin apartment, and when Bukharin's sentence was pronounced, he twirled his moustache gleefully, and said, *Good, let death come to the old dog swiftly!*

For only one of the twenty-one, we have no sympathy: *the little berry*.

There is also news of Hitler. It comes in a letter from Morne. On March 12 Hitler's Eighth Army entered Austria. Hitler, personally, went to Austria. He went straight to the Linz suburb of Leonding to lay a wreath at his parents' grave. He wept at the grave and the Austrian people wept with him. Later that day he spoke of Austria as a province of the German Reich.

Beretzkoy reminds me of what Morne wrote in a previous letter. He wrote Hitler planned to annex all the European countries which have ethnic-German populations: countries like Austria, Czechoslovakia and Poland.

And now, what country will be invaded and annexed after Austria? Czechoslovakia? Poland? Is this the war Morne spoke of? Will this war free us of the *Vozdh*? Perhaps we do not need a war to do this. Perhaps the Russian people will do so themselves.

Beretzkoy does not burn his novel. We wrap it in a thin cloth and place it beneath the floorboards of the veranda.

Stalin does not call to ask about the novel he ordered Beretzkoy to write.

-0-

CHAPTER TWENTY-FOUR

I set off in bright spring sunshine for the railway station. My parents are coming to stay with me. I am wearing a yellow dress, white sandals and socks, and a white straw hat. I am the only one waiting on the platform and my parents are the only passengers descending. My mother touches my face, my father takes my hands and they tell me they look forward to seeing how I live.

We take the buggy to Ob Street. As this is my father's first visit to Zernoye Selo, I ask the driver to take the longest way. My father looks around and I point buildings out to him. I point to the NKVD building on Marx Square and the driver turns round and tells my father there is not a better place to stay in the village. "There are no shortages in there," he says. "Even of death, there is an abundance."

Beretzkoy is waiting.

"Welcome. You should have come before now."

This was what my parents once said to him.

"Yes … well," says my father.

My mother is already looking around and telling me she can see I have put a lot of work into the place.

"It wasn't all this comfortable when Tanya moved here, now was it Beretzkoy?" she says, accusingly.

"Tanya has always been happy here," he replies, firmly.

-0-

"He does not look well," says my mother.

Beretzkoy has left for Lena Street. My parents and I are sitting in the garden, at the table where we had lunched. The sun, which shone bright and warm all day, is now low and the table has fallen into shade. My father fetches a sweater for my mother and a jacket for himself. Sekret sits beside the table and is pleading with his eyes for something to eat. I drop a piece of left-over meat onto the ground and he gobbles it up hungrily. My mother gives him a stern look. She dislikes cats. She looks at me and the expression on her face does not change.

"Yes, I think Beretzkoy does not look well. His skin is sallow and he eats very little," my father says, giving her his support.

"Please don't tell him so," I ask.

"Why, Tanoshka? Isn't he well?"

I tell the story of Beretzkoy's Moscow trip, how he was taken ill. I explain about the book, that Beretzkoy receives insulting letters every day. I speak of his fear I may be arrested and my fear, he will be.

"But does Beretzkoy have a health problem?" insists my mother.

"He's fine. That incident in Moscow, it was something he ate."

"Has he seen a doctor since?" asks my father.

"Not since."

"I think he should."

My mother agrees with a vigorous nodding.

-0-

Gozuzdom summons Beretzkoy for another meeting.

"Can I come too?" I ask.

"Not this time," he says.

I want to accompany Beretzkoy because our neighbours are all agreeing with my parents he does not look well. Alisa speaks of the pallor of his skin, and the Widow Alexandra says he has lost weight. Kolya, who sometimes walks with him from Lena Street to Ob, tells me Beretzkoy becomes short of breath easily.

Beretzkoy will leave for Moscow on the same train as my parents.

"We're going to try to persuade him to consult a doctor while in Moscow," promises my mother.

I decide that while he is away, I will paint the back wall of the *dacha*.

"I will help," says Kolya.

I want to paint the wall yellow because I think yellow is such a cheerful colour. It will also help me forget how, that summer's day, Stalin's image had appeared on the wall.

I want to obliterate Stalin from our lives forever.

-0-

CHAPTER TWENTY-FIVE

I am waiting for Kolya to come over so we can start with the painting of the wall. I hear a vehicle turn into Ob Street. I am in the back garden and I run through the *dacha* to the front garden to peep through a crack in the hedge. I have to see who on the street is getting visitors. A *black raven* is driving up the street. I start to shake. I close my eyes because I cannot bear the sight of it. I hear it come closer. The engine cuts out. I do not have to open my eyes to know the car has stopped in front of my gate. I hear its doors open. Nilats starts barking. There is a loud bang on my gate. I open my eyes, my body numb, and yet it is moving towards the source of the noise; I do not know who is controlling my legs.

"Tatyana Nikolayevna Brodovskaya?"

Three men stand between the *black raven* and the gate. One wears a grey fedora.

"Yes?"

"May we have a word?"

I step aside.

The man in the fedora is short and fat. He does not look unkind, not like a Chekist, but neither did those who had come for Vasily.

"What's this about?" I mumble.

The man takes off his fedora. Across his forehead, from ear to ear, runs a fleshy scar.

"Who are you?" I ask him.

"Inside," he orders.

I am escorted into my own living room. Again I wonder how my limbs are managing it.

"Can we talk here?" asks the man with the fedora.

"What do you want to talk about?"

"We're here to clear up a point or a couple of points."

"What is it? How can I help?"

I try to sound jovial.

"I'll speak plainly," says the man. "Comrade Brodovskaya, you have been ignoring our trade laws. You've been marketeering."

An involuntary laugh bursts from my lips.

"I have!"

"You know someone called Zorin?"

"Maksim Mikhaylovich Zorin?"

"That's the one. Do you know where he is?"

"I thought he was in Moscow. He's left the village."

"We know he has left the village."

"So what do you want from me?"

"We think you know where he is."

"Why would I know?"

"You've been doing business with him."

"How do you mean?"

"The two of you are partners."

"Is this about Comrade Zorin?"

"It is about you and him. The two of you have been marketeering."

"Comrade Zorin worked at the dental clinic and now he is at a clinic in Moscow. I am Comrade Beretzkoy's assistant. Comrade Beretzkoy is compiling an encyclopaedia on Russian literature. Comrade Stalin is most eager for the project to be completed and I've been typing virtually night and day so I certainly have not been marketeering. I am not a marketeer. Call me a secretary. A typist if you wish, bu ..."

"You will have to come with us," I am interrupted.

"Why?"

"You will have to make a statement."

"I can do so here."

My eyes begin darting around the room. There is no one here to defend me. The man shakes his head.

"There are others who want to have a word with you."

"They can come here."

I begin to lose my nerve, my knees are buckling under me.

"No, Comrade Brodovskaya, you are going to come with us. You must collect your things."

The man comes with me into the bedroom. I take the suitcase from the cupboard. He looks at it and smiles broadly.

Sekret follows us out to the street and wants to get into the *black raven* with me, but the man with the fedora picks him up and throws him back over the wall.

-0-

It is suffocatingly hot in the back of the *black raven*. I am sitting on its floor. There is only one chair, a steel one chained to the side of the vehicle, and the man with the fedora sits on it. He holds a truncheon. He is tapping the truncheon against the metal floor. The noise is deafening. I think the truncheon is made of wood. Its handle is grooved and his thin fingers fit neatly into the grooves. His grip on the truncheon must be firm as his knuckles slowly turn blue.

We are on our way to Marx Square. I know as I am keeping track in my head of the turns we make. We are going to NKVD headquarters. I relax a little as I feared they were going to drive me to Moscow, to the Lubyanka. We pull up. Someone opens the door from the outside. The man with the fedora jumps out and motions for me to follow him. I slide from the van on my behind as the ceiling is too low for me to stand up. My dress catches on a nail and rips. We have pulled up in a courtyard - I did not know there was a courtyard inside the NKVD building. I wonder whether this is where the Chekists brought Leonid. The courtyard is cobblestoned and the heels of my shoes slip between the cobbles, making me stumble. *Why did I not change into flat shoes?* My suitcase is heavy as though I have packed for a long stay. We go into a small vestibule and I have to put my suitcase down on a table. A woman steps from behind a bamboo curtain and opens the suitcase and with a couple of swift movements she sweeps its contents onto the table. One of the three who came to fetch me picks up the book of Beretzkoy's poems I have packed.

"Ah hah!" says the woman.

She has dreadful acne and I am reminded of Vladymir from *Pravda*, how he dabbed at his oozing pimples on the night he accused me of bourgeois behaviour. It seems a lifetime ago.

"Come with me," the woman orders.

We go down a long corridor, up a metal staircase and down another long corridor lined with metal doors. The woman unlocks one of the metal doors and behind it is a cell.

"Inside!" she barks.

Four steps and I am standing in the middle of the cell. On my left is a dilapidated wooden bunk, on my right a wash basin. Brown water drips into the basin from a rusty tap. Underneath the wash basin stands a bucket. The stench that comes from it explains its purpose. On the wooden bunk lies an army-issue blanket. I think of what Dan told us about Metelovsk.

The woman leaves and I sit down on the bed. Soon, I have no idea of time because the cell is in semi-darkness. It can be night, or it can already be a new day. A light comes on in the cell. I look up. A single bulb dangles from the ceiling. It is protected with barbed wire. Ah-ha, I could cut my wrists with the nails should my life in this cell no longer be worth living. But no, the ceiling is high. Too high for me to reach. And I would not be able to push the bed over to it because the bed is chained to the floor.

-0-

Unexpectedly, the door flings open. Two men walk in.

"Come!" yells one of them.

They are dressed in grey uniforms and black boots. They walk me to a small room at the other end of the corridor. There are two upright wooden chairs in the room and a table. A man gets up from one of the chairs; he is young and wears glasses with thick lenses. The lenses magnify his black eyes. He looks like a bullfrog and I stifle a laugh.

"My name is Gorbalev," he tells me.

"I am Tatyana Nikolayevna Brodovskaya."

He smiles.

"Yes, Comrade Brodovskaya, I know who you are."

He also knows I have been profiteering, he says.

The two who fetched me from the cell, stand at the back of the room.

"This is not true! I am not a marketeer," I protest.

"I'll tell you something, I might be wishing I was doing something else right now, so let's not waste time with you answering me back. You will listen and I will speak," says Gorbalev.

"I am also wishing I was doing something else right now so …"

He silences me by picking up his chair, using only one hand, and hurling it across the room.

"Shut up, woman!" he shouts.

I am told they have evidence I have run a *nalevo* business with Maksim.

"We do not have time to waste, especially on women like you, so I am going to give you a confession to sign and then you can go home. We want to know where Maksim Mikhaylovich Zorin is. As for you, we do not care two shits about you," he tells me, grinning ghoulishly.

I hold up a hand like a child at school.

"May I say something?"

"May I say something, Commandant Gorbalev."

"May I say something, Commandant Gorbalev?"

"Make it brief!"

"I do not know where Comrade Zorin is and I never ran a *nalevo* business with him."

"You're a stupid cunt, woman!" he shouts, his face purple with anger.

-0-

People say there is no such thing as night and day in a hospital. Now, I know there is also no night and day in the NKVD building.

I spend long hours lying on the bunk, looking up at the ceiling and wondering how I am going to get to the nails. Apart from my interrogator and the two who come to fetch me for each interrogation in the room at the end of the corridor, the only person I see is a wardress who asks me to call her Natasha. She says she knows I was Maksim's lover and would I, at least, admit to this.

"Yes, sure. Maksim and I were lovers," I say, exasperated.

"You were in love?"

"We slept together - once. I wouldn't describe it as being in love."

"Neither would I," she said. "I would call it whoring. You're a whore!"

"Whore is as good a word as any other, but don't call me a marketeer." I tell her.

"He was one, and when you lie down with dogs, you get up with fleas," she sneers, slamming the door of the cell.

-0-

She returns.

"You are to go," she says.

"Go?" I ask. "Go where?"

"Where do you think, you stupid bitch? You are going home."

I have lost count of the days I have been held here.

The woman, who booked me in, joins us. This is the first time I see her since that day.

"I feel I've seen you somewhere before," she says.

I nod.

"You were here on the day I arrived."

"No," she says. "I mean I've seen you in the village. Now I hear you live with the poet. I love his poetry."

She tells me to get my suitcase and to follow her. Back in her office, she gives me a form to sign and I sign it without reading it.

"You should always read everything you are given to sign," she kindly advises me.

"What do I care!" I tell her.

"You should care," she advises.

-0-

It is night outside and I am grateful for the dark. My clothes are filthy and I stink and I know I must look dreadful.

The front door at Number One is not locked. I walk through the *dacha* straight to the kitchen and I start to boil water for a bath. I fill the bath and I climb into it fully clothed.

I sit in the bath until the water is cold, yet I still feel dirty. Filthy!

-0-

I have no idea what day it is.

I climb from the bath, pull the wet clothes off, and run, naked, to the bedroom. Sekret lies asleep on the bed. I stroke his head and he wakes up. He crawls under the blankets with me.

The clock on the bedside table shows it is half an hour past four o'clock.

-0-

CHAPTER TWENTY-SIX

Kolya stands beside my bed.

"Tanya, when did you get back?"

The clock on the bedside table shows it is eleven o'clock. It is light behind the window.

"Where's Beretzkoy?" I ask in a groggy voice. "Is he still in Moscow?"

I am naked so I cannot sit up. Kolya perches on the end of the bed.

"Where's Beretzkoy?" I repeat.

"When did you get back?"

"In the night. They let me go. But where's Beretzkoy? What day is it?"

"Thursday."

"Thursday of what week?"

"They took you away last Wednesday. You've been away eight days."

"How's Beretzkoy? Why isn't he here?"

"Beretzkoy won't be coming over today," says Kolya. He looks away. "He's not well."

I forget I am naked and jump up in the bed. For a moment my breasts hang exposed. Quickly, I pull the blanket up to my chin.

"Where is he?"

"He's back from Moscow. He did not feel so well there. Then, three days ago, he collapsed again."

Kolya walks over to my side of the bed. He sits down. He puts his arms around my shoulder. He says it was a haemorrhage, a bleed in Beretzkoy's stomach. Nadezdha Konstantinovna heard him vomiting in the bathroom. She went to see what was going on and found him on the floor, unconscious. She ran to the Dushenka Kobas for assistance and luckily Dushenka Koba was home. He went to the Beretzkoy's *dacha* while his wife sent one of their children to the dispensary to fetch the doctor. The doctor said it was an ulcer. They carried Beretzkoy to his bedroom and helped him into bed. The doctor gave him a brown liquid to drink.

"He is taking belladonna and valerian. The belladonna for the pain and the valerian is to calm him down. Both are taking effect and Beretzkoy is feeling better," says Kolya.

"I cannot go there, can I? To Lena Street?"

"Tanya, you know the answer."

"This is stupid!" I cry out.

-0-

I walk from room to room, in and out of the *dacha*. I sit down but cannot stay sitting down. I lie down and the bedroom walls start to close in on me. I run outside and stand by the gate hoping this is a bad dream and soon now, any moment now, Beretzkoy is going to come walking down the street from the wasteland. *If only I can go to Lena Street because I want to see him, hold him.* Surely Nadezdha Konstantinovna would not refuse to allow me into her house?

"Yes, she would," says Anna Gromyko.

She knows what she is talking about, she tells me. Once she was a married man's lover.

"It was long ago, before I met Ivan. My lover had fallen ill and his wife refused to allow me to see him. This is how it is. How it is always. There is the wife, and there is the other woman. The wife has the upper hand."

"What happened to him?"

"Oh, he recovered, we lost touch and I met Ivan. I would do the same now to any woman who should get her claws into Ivan. Now, I understand why that wife had refused to allow me into her house."

What to say?

-0-

Pierre sends me a parcel and a letter. He writes he is sending me several articles to translate. I will find them in the parcel.

There are no articles to be translated in the parcel, but a slim book of Beretzkoy's poems.

The book was published in Paris. Twelve pages, roughly bound. Beretzkoy did not tell me he had given Morne permission to publish the poems. Pierre does not explain how he had obtained the book.

It makes clear on the book's front cover the copyright is not held by Beretzkoy but by Morne. On the back cover is a warning the book is not to be distributed in the Soviet Union.

Will the copyright notice and the warning protect Beretzkoy?

I do not think so.

-0-

CHAPTER TWENTY-SEVEN

It is the first day of June and there is not a cloud in the sky. Kolya comes to tell me Beretzkoy is feeling better and he is going to come over.

He walks in just before noon.

I hear the gate open and close. I hear his footsteps approaching the front door. I do not rush to him. I remain sitting behind his desk on the veranda. The glass door which separates the living room from the veranda is open. Sekret lies on the grass patch, outside, one leg up in the air, his little pink tongue washing his stomach.

"Taken over, have you?" Beretzkoy asks, jokingly.

He is standing in the doorway.

"Someone has to work," I joke back.

He has lost so much weight I cannot bare to look at him. His cheeks have hollowed and his eyes seem to have sunken back into their sockets. Yet, the face remains the face I love: the man remains the man I love.

"I am back," he says, unnecessarily.

It may be my imagination, but his voice sounds different too. It is deeper, lower, and his breathing comes in slight irregular gasps.

"You fainted again," I say, getting up from behind the desk.

"I have a small problem with my lungs. And I have an ulcer too now."

"Kolya told me."

"The ulcer had begun to bleed, but it has healed now. And my lung problem too is something of the past."

"Do you feel well?"

"Never felt better in my life!"

"Your poems have been published in Paris," I say. "I've got the book. Pierre sent it to me. The book looks great."

"*Khorosho*," he says.

The neutral word.

"Do you want to work?"

"Not immediately," he says. "Later."

He asks whether I have milk in the *dacha*, I say I do, and he asks whether I could warm a glass of it for him.

In the kitchen, he sits down at the table and says I must tell him about my arrest. I tell him I would much rather speak about his illness and his book.

"The illness is behind me now, so let us speak about the book."

"I didn't know you gave Morne permission to publish the poems in Paris," I say.

331

"I wanted it to be a surprise."

"I'll go and fetch the book."

"No," he says. "Sit down with me. Drink your tea first."

I pull a chair over. I want to sit close to him. He takes one of my hands and kisses it.

"Are you in pain?" I ask.

"No talk of pain or illness, please Tanya. Here with you," he says, "everything is going to be alright again now."

-0-

It is late afternoon. Beretzkoy and I are still sitting in the kitchen. He asks whether I will mind if he did some work for a couple of hours, and I, delighted he wants to work because an ill man would not want to work, say I do not mind.

"But take it easy. Do not overdo it," I warn.

I set off for the Wood of Somnambulism.

In the wood, the sun shines through the trees. A woman is digging in the soil. She has taken her apron off and it is spread out on the ground. She has planted potatoes in the wood, which is, of course, illegal and now she is harvesting them. She offers me a potato and I take it. She is buying my silence and I sell it to her.

The sun is warm on my skin. It is going to be a hot summer. I decide I will ask Beretzkoy if we can go away again in the summer, go back to the valley. I will call Valentina's niece at the railway junction and tell her we are coming.

-0-

Back in the *dacha*, Beretzkoy calls me to the veranda.

"I've got something for you."

He holds a sheet of paper out to me.

"What is it?"

"Don't get alarmed," he warns.

He hands me a *To Whom It May Concern* letter.

He is giving me the copyright to *Doctor Rudi Zinn*. The letter bears this day's date and is effective from today.

"Why are you doing this?" I ask him.

"No reason other than I think you deserve to hold the copyright. Nadezdha Konstantinovna has shown no interest in the novel and in any case, the novel is as much yours as it is mine."

"Is the copyright not yours?"

"It is, but now I am giving it to you."

"What about your boys?"

"They have their own plans."

"I do not want the copyright. Thank you. But I do not want it."

I hand the letter back to him.

He shakes his head.

"It is not a copyright, Tanya. Not in the true sense of the word. It is just a piece of paper. It is just a …"

"This is not necessary. You are here and we do not have to talk of copyrights."

"We do have to."

"No, we do not!"

I am getting angry and hot tears sting my eyes. "Tanya, it's done!"

"Beretzkoy, this is a testament, a - bequest," I protest.

"No," he says. "It's a copyright."

"Are you hiding something from me?"

"No," he says. "Of course not."

"Beretzkoy, if you are ill and you're not telling me," I almost threaten him.

"I'm not! No one needs to know about this Tanya. It concerns only the two of us. We will put it away somewhere. We need never speak of it again. Come, let us put it away."

He slips the letter into a red folder and he pushes it underneath other red folders in the bottom drawer of his desk.

"Testaments are final, they always have the last word," I protest.

He closes the drawer.

"This is not a testament, this is just something important to me."

"It looks like one to me."

"Well, not everything is as it looks - and Tanya, I am the one who will always have the last word."

He is laughing.

I cannot laugh with him.

-0-

He says he will have to start walking back to Lena Street. He asks me to walk with him to the wasteland.

"Don't you want to see your book first?" I ask.

"Tomorrow," he says.

"No," I say. "Now!"

I fetch the book from the bedroom where I had left it. I hand it to him. He flips through it without interest.

"Take it with you," I say.

He puts the book down on his desk.

"Tomorrow, Tanya, tomorrow."

We walk slowly to the wasteland. Beretzkoy walks like an old man struggling through wet sand on a beach. He rests on each foot.

"Let's sit for a moment," he suggests.

The sun has set and it is cool. We sit down under a tree and he leans his head back against the trunk. A sheen of sweat illuminates his features, and his hair is pasted to his forehead.

"About that letter, Tanya."

I shake my head.

"Not now. Let's just sit here for a while."

"Now," he says, "and please don't interrupt me."

I force a laugh.

"Two minutes," I say.

This time he is the one not laughing. He does not even smile.

"These past days I've started work on a play. Its title is *Deaf to Beauty*. Work is perhaps a big word as I've only taken some notes. It is set in the nineteenth century. The main character is a wealthy but liberal landowner who, when Alexander frees the serfs, decides to, not only let his serfs go, but also to hand his estate over to them. A poor man as a result of this act, he sets off for Lake Baikal to become a fisherman, but on his way to the lake he is rounded up and forced into Alexander's army. The title of the play describes Alexander's two-facedness. He frees the serfs, but forces free men into his army. He is like a man who claims to love all things beautiful, but is, in fact ... deaf to beauty. As I said, I've only jotted down a few lines, but tomorrow I will give you another letter as I want you to have the copyright of this play as well. This is, of course, if I ever get down to writing it."

He is also going to give me a letter for Morne. He has not written it yet.

"I'll write it tonight. I want him to know you hold the copyright to the novel and you should be consulted on any future plans he has for it. We will also send him *Deaf to Beauty*."

I shake my head.

"I'll just ask you what you want to do."

"I am speaking of a time when you won't be able to ask me."

"Why wouldn't I be able to ask you?" I cry.

He strokes my face and his fingers rest on my lips.

"Keep these closed," he says, "and listen to me."

He tells me no one lives forever and here in our country a man's expectation for a long life is even more of a dream than anywhere else.

"So, Tanya, one day, not this very day, nor tomorrow, nor the day after, but one day, you may have to make a decision about *Doctor Rudi Zinn*, or about the play, and the letter I gave you today and the one I will give you tomorrow, are for such a day. Whatever you decide to do with the novel and the poem - burn them if you want - will be alright as far as I am concerned."

"So, it's just a precaution really?" I ask.

"Exactly."

I ask him to speak to me of his health.

He turns to me. He takes my face in his hands. I notice how the thickness of his hands and arms has diminished.

"I am well," he says. "Don't you worry your pretty little head over my health. Yes, I am feeling good, much better, but I have felt better. This, I must admit. I am not saying I am ill, no, oh don't think that! I am only saying I've had better health and would like to have better health once more."

He will not be able to come to Ob every day anymore, he tells me. The walk is too strenuous and he needs his energy for the restoration of his health. I need have no fears. He will get better. He will recover.

"Promise me, please," I beg.

"I promise you, Tanya, I'll be fine, just fine. Soon."

He pulls me to him and I press my face against his body.

"I love you," he says. "The best thing that has happened to me was meeting you."

I have no reply. I know if I speak, I am going to cry and if I cry I will tell him to walk back with me to Ob Street and I will go to Lena Street and I will tell Nadezdha Konstantinovna Beretzkoy is not coming home. That she should not expect him home. Not this night. Not any night. Not ever again. That he is living with me. That he is mine now.

-0-

He says he must go. I walk with him to the other end of the wasteland.

"What do you plan for tomorrow?" he asks.

"Nothing," I say.

"No," he says, "we must do something even if it is only sitting out in the sun."

"So we will sit out in the sun."

"Now, I must really go," he says. "Time's up."

I watch him walk up Lena Street. At Number Fourteen he turns and lifts an arm and waves.

I allow my tears at last to fall.

-0-

335

FOR THE LOVE OF A POET

CHAPTER TWENTY-EIGHT

I am sweeping the street. I see Kolya racing up Ob Street. The streamers on his bicycle fly in the air. He reaches me and jumps off the bike.

"What?" I ask.

"Beretzkoy has had another bleeding."

Kolya's lower lip is trembling like that of a child bravely trying not to cry.

"No. Oh no!" I groan.

"It happened during the night."

He is still holding the bike. A breeze blows a streamer into my face.

Alisa suddenly appears.

"What?" she asks.

"It's Beretzkoy ... he's ...," I stutter.

"Calm ... calm ...," she says.

She points to my *dacha* for us to go indoors. Meekly, like little lambs, we follow her, Kolya pushing his bike to the front door and letting it fall to the ground.

"Beretzkoy had a bleeding during the night," Kolya explains to her.

He and I sit down at the table.

"Ulcers bleed," she says. "They have to. You know. Get rid of the bad stuff inside them. He will be alright."

Alisa starts opening and closing drawers, tins and packets. She wants to make tea. She does not know where I keep the tea things.

"Don't Alisa," I say. "We don't want tea. We can't drink tea now."

"I'll make it all the same," she says.

Kolya begins to tell me what happened in the Beretzkoys' *dacha* but a buzzing in my head prevents me hearing all the words. I can make out Beretzkoy started vomiting in the night, but he would not allow Nadezdha Konstantinovna to call the doctor. First thing in the morning she asked Alexandra Alexandrovna whether one of her children could fetch the doctor. The doctor does not want Beretzkoy to continue with the belladonna. He thinks Beretzkoy may have taken too much of it accidentally. He would like Beretzkoy to go to Kremlin Hospital for further tests, but not immediately. First, he should recover from this latest haemorrhage. His lung problem has also flared up: he has difficulty breathing and he has vomited a little blood.

Alisa pours the tea. She drops three lumps of sugar into the glass which she puts down in front of me.

"Sugar calms the nerves," she says.

Nina's words on the day during the influenza pandemic when I heard

Beretzkoy was ill with influenza.

If only this can be just influenza.

-0-

It is night. I am lighting a smoker in the living room. I am waiting for Kolya to return with more news about what is going on at Number Fourteen Lena Street.

I hear the tinkle of the bell of Kolya's bicycle. I run outside.

He is ashen white.

"What ... what ... what?" I stutter.

"They've started to speak of the end."

They've started to speak of the end!

"Tanya, did you hear me?" he asks.

Heard him!

"They've started to speak of the end," he repeats.

"I heard you," I snap.

How could this have happened? We were happy. We were planning, or I was, to return to the valley in the summer. Now, *Beretzkoy is dying!*

"I must go to him," I say.

"Tanya, dear Tanya, you know you cannot."

"I have to! I must tell that wife of his he is not dying!"

"The doctor told her to prepare herself."

"The doctor speaks rubbish!" I snap again.

Kolya does not reply.

"Do you not know the ill look to those around them for encouragement to fight their illness?" I scream at him.

"We are encouraging him," he says, quietly. Gently.

"By speaking of death?"

"We are not the ones who are speaking of death. Not in front of him, we do not."

"Should I thank you all for that?" I ask.

I am furious.

Sekret wanders up to us. He is meowing. He wants something to eat. I had completely forgotten to feed the little creature.

"I'll feed him," says Kolya. "Just tell me what I have to give him."

While Kolya feeds Sekret, I pace the garden in the darkness.

Beretzkoy has been in my life for six years and can six years just end like this? No goodbye. No farewell.

Yes, I suppose it can.

It can when one is the other woman.

Again, Alisa appears as if from nowhere.

"I saw Kolya arrive. How is Beretzkoy?"

"They say he is dying."

I sink down to the ground. She sits down beside me.

338

Kolya comes to say he has fed Sekret and he ought to get back to Lena Street in case he is needed there. He is holding Sekret. He puts him down on my lap. Sekret licks my hands. His little tongue is rough, dry. I wonder if he knows his master is ill.

Ill! I do not dare think of Beretzkoy as dying.

-0-

It is a week later.

Kolya has been coming to Ob Street several times a day to tell me what the situation is with Beretzkoy.

He has been telling me Beretzkoy slips in and out of consciousness. The periods of unconsciousness are though becoming shorter and the doctor says it is a good sign. The doctor is even speaking of transferring him to Kremlin Hospital for treatment. Dushenka Koba has offered to fetch him - him and Nadezdha Konstantinovna because she will go along. She has accepted the offer.

"What about Beretzkoy. What is he saying?" I ask Kolya.

As for what Beretzkoy himself is thinking; he is manifesting reluctance to go to Moscow by shaking his head when it is mentioned at his bedside. Shortness of breath makes it impossible for him to speak.

My parents and our friends send me telegrams. They tell me not to give up hope. They will come to Zernoye Selo if I should need them. They also want to visit Beretzkoy. They were going to come for another holiday this summer in any case, they say. Of course, is it not summer?

I sit at the window in the living room for hours, staring at the gate. I want it to open and I want to see Beretzkoy come walking towards me. Even at night I sit at the window. Sekret lies on my feet; he stays close to me now. A bottle of vodka stands on the floor beside the chair. After the third or fourth tumbler, I hear the gate open, but I look and it is still closed. Alisa tells me she did the same after the Chekists had taken Leonid.

"Then I gave up hope," she says.

I will not give up hope.

-0-

CHAPTER TWENTY-NINE

Dushenka Koba telephones Nadezdha Konstantinovna from Moscow; Beretzkoy has been expelled from Profpro. The expulsion was decided democratically: by secret ballot.

"I voted against," he announces.

"Would you have voted this way, had it not been secret?" she asks.

"I have a wife and children. I must consider them. Their safety," he replies frankly.

Next, Semyon calls her.

"Gozuzdom has cancelled the encyclopaedia project. It was decided by vote. I voted against of course."

"Was it a secret ballot?"

"Yes."

"Would you have voted against had it not been a secret ballot?"

"I have a wife and a son and another child on the way. I have to think of them."

"I understand," she replies.

Pravda wastes no time reporting both the expulsion from Profpro and the cancellation of the encyclopaedia project. One must belong writes *Pravda*. Be it to a family, a factory, a town, a village or a labour union. Beretzkoy did not want to belong and not to belong is individualism and individualism is counter-revolutionary and this is against our law. Beretzkoy is guilty of individualism. It is an ugly crime, a particularly abominable crime.

Nadezdha Konstantinovna writes a letter to *Pravda*.

I would like to point out my husband loves Comrade Stalin and his country, as do our sons and I. I want to point out my husband has instilled in our sons a deep love of our country and our leaders. I therefore say with honesty our sons love their father and their mother, but most of all they love Comrade Stalin and our country.

Pravda runs the letter. I read it aloud to Kolya. I find I cannot stop myself weeping.

"Nadezdha Konstantinovna is trying to save what there is to save," he explains on her behalf.

-0-

A letter arrives by special delivery at the Village Soviet. Vitya takes it to Lena Street. He puts it into Nadezdha Konstantinovna's hands.

"This is *so* important," he says. "It is from Comrade Stalin."

341

"The boys will be pleased," she says.

Stalin writes, *Dear Boris Petrovich, I hear you are not well. Might you be in need of anything? I have asked Valentin Sergeyevich to visit you and you can then speak to him about your needs and he will do his best to help you. The weather at Sochi this time of the year is lovely - perhaps it is Sochi's best season - so if you would like to go down there, just tell VS and he will arrange it. I wish you a speedy recovery and excellent health for the future. My best wishes go to you with these words.*

The letter is handwritten. It is signed *Iosef Vissaryonovich Stalin.*

Nadezdha Konstantinovna reads the letter to Beretzkoy and then she puts it on the mantelpiece in the lobby.

"Such a letter should not be hidden. Such a letter should be seen," she tells Kolya.

-0-

There is an improvement in Beretzkoy's condition. He no longer slips into unconsciousness and the doctor puts him back on belladonna and valerian. He is no longer in pain it seems. He is also breathing more easily and can therefore speak again, though only a few words at a time.

Kolya tells me Nadezdha Konstantinovna reads Stalin's letter to Beretzkoy every day. He listens, closes his eyes and does not comment. I tell Kolya the words must be like poison seeping into his body, polluting his soul.

Kolya says Beretzkoy has asked him to tell me that as soon as he can do so, he will write to me. I ask Kolya whether he will take a letter to Beretzkoy, but he says the time is not yet right.

"When it is, of course I will take him a letter."

-0-

CHAPTER THIRTY

June comes to a slow and monotonous end.

Galina and Misha arrive in Zernoye Selo. They drive straight to Lena Street. Nadezdha Konstantinovna says they cannot see Beretzkoy. She does not even allow them into the *dacha*.

"Beretzkoy! Beretzkoy!" Galina shouts from the street.

Beretzkoy hears her and calls out to his wife to allow them in.

They come to Ob Street.

"He looks much better than we expected," Galina assures me.

The two are, as always, elegantly dressed. She is in yellow trousers and a white belted jacket. I have never seen yellow trousers before.

"I was under the impression trousers come in three colours only: black, brown or grey," I tell her.

She hugs me. She has cut her hair and changed the colour to yellow too, almost the same yellow as her trousers. A curl falls over her eyes. She brushes it away. Her eyes are full of tears. Misha wears the same dark suit and shiny patent leather shoes he had worn on the night of our party. I find it painful to think of the party and impossible to believe it was only last summer that we danced joyfully to Misha's illegal foreign music.

I offer tea but Galina and Misha ask for something stronger. I put a bottle of vodka on the table and Misha fills three tumblers.

"Does Beretzkoy really look alright?" I want to know.

"Would we lie to you?" asks Galina.

"What did he say about his illness?"

"We didn't speak of it," says Misha.

"Did you speak of me?"

"We spoke of you," says Galina.

"And?"

"We should not have."

Beretzkoy had started to cry.

"We changed the subject," says Misha.

"I want to see him," I say, a painful ache stabbing at me inside my body.

Galina shakes her head.

"He is emotional. He could not even cope with us speaking of you, so to see you would be quite unbearable for him."

Misha takes my hand.

"When he's better, we will arrange for you to go and see him."

Yelena takes the train to Zernoye Selo. I am at the station to meet her. We take the buggy to Ob Street. Yelena is crying soundlessly. She does not wipe the tears away. The driver turns to look at us.

"That image on your wall, the shadow of Stalin ...," she murmurs.

"Beretzkoy wouldn't believe it was a bad omen," I say, linking my arm in hers.

"Dan did. Both he and I did."

She walks to Lena Street. I walk with her to the end of the wasteland and I watch until she reaches the Beretzkoy *dacha*.

Nadezdha Konstantinovna, although she has always disliked the Olminskys, has no objection to Yelena seeing Beretzkoy. She even invites her into the kitchen for a glass of tea.

"I did not accept the glass of tea," Yelena says on her return.

She, as Galina and Misha did, tells me Beretzkoy looks better than she had expected.

"Are you saying this to make me feel better?"

"I would not try to fool you. You're an adult, although you were still such a child at the beginning. Now you are a woman. Alas!"

A car pulls up in front of the *dacha*. Yelena looks through the living room window.

"It's Semyon and Zinaida," she tells me.

Zinaida is carrying a bunch of flowers.

"May the Maker of the Universe bring peace to this house," she says, pushing the flowers into my arms.

"This is no time for such talk, Zinaida," reprimands Yelena.

"This *is* the time for such talk!" she replies hotly and makes the sign of the cross into the air.

"We've seen Beretzkoy," says Semyon, intervening.

"We were with him for more than an hour," says Zinaida.

They do not agree with the others that Beretzkoy looks good. They say he looks very ill. The problem is no longer only the bleeding ulcer. He is also severely anaemic and his heartbeat is weak. And one lung has collapsed.

"What did Nadezdha Konstantinovna say about Beretzkoy?" I ask.

"She told us the doctor says it's like a chain reaction. One thing leads to another," replies Semyon.

Beretzkoy's sons are home from school because it is summer holiday time.

"Did the boys speak to you?" I ask.

"They are tearful, very tearful," says Semyon.

"Which does not surprise me because grief without faith is an inconsolable grief," states Zinaida.

Again, she makes the sign of the cross over us.

"Oh Zinaida!" groans Yelena.

-0-

Semyon asks me to go with him to the veranda so we may speak in private.

"I understand you have not seen Beretzkoy," he says.

We are standing at Beretzkoy's desk.

"No. I haven't."

"Do you want to?"

"Of course, I am desperate to see him. But how can I?"

"Do you understand the situation?"

"Yes, I understand the situation."

"I am speaking of the medical situation, not the domestic one."

"So am I!" I reply, irritably.

"If you want to go to Lena Street, tell me and I will arrange it."

"How Semyon? How will you be able to arrange it?"

"I will find a way Tanya. Trust me," he whispers.

-0-

The day has arrived for them all to return to Moscow.

Galina and Misha, the first to have arrived, are the first to leave. We are standing beside Misha's sleek, immaculate car: a small ballerina in a pink tutu hangs from a mirror above the dashboard. Misha opens the door on the driver's side and the ballerina turns round and round in the breeze. Galina is in pink too: dress, jacket, shoes, nails and lips. They tell me they will be coming back to Zernoye Selo soon.

"I love Beretzkoy too," Galina whispers into my ear.

Semyon and Zinaida drive up. He sounds the horn to summons me outside.

"If we come in, we will stay too long," he apologises.

He reminds me about the conversation we had on the veranda.

"I have not forgotten," I say.

"Good. I'll be in touch." he says.

I watch them drive off.

Zinaida waves and Semyon, unlike last summer, waves too, and at the end of the street, he even slaps against the side of his car.

-0-

I take Yelena back to the railway station in the buggy despite the driver is now charging a rouble for the ride.

"You were there for me, Tanya, so now I am here for you," she says.

I again board the train with her.

The first whistle blows.

"Missing someone is terrible," she says, her voice thick with emotion.

The second whistle blows, followed almost immediately by the third and I have to jump off the train before I have really said my goodbyes.

Yelena leans out of the window and waves.

Once again, I watch the train until it disappears into the distance.

Tears stream down my face all the way to Ob Street.

Alone, at home, the *dacha* is suddenly very quiet.

Yelena spoke of how terrible it is to miss someone.

I already know what she means.

-0-

A large parcel arrives from Pierre. I open it reluctantly. I have no interest anymore in doing translations for him. There are two smaller parcels in the large parcel, both wrapped in old *Pravdas*. I tear open one and a book falls from its wrappings. I see Beretzkoy's face on the book's back cover. It is a copy of *Doctor Rudi Zinn*, the title written in neat black lettering with Beretzkoy's name underneath it. The novel was published in Paris. It is beautifully bound with a dust jacket the colour of mustard. The picture of Beretzkoy on the back is a copy of the one Maksim slipped into the locket he had given me. A brief biography of Beretzkoy is printed underneath the photograph. *The author was born in Leningrad and lives with his wife and two sons in the poets' village of Zernoye Selo, south of Moscow.*

True, of course.

I tear open the second smaller parcel. I expect to find another copy of the novel, but I find French bank notes. Thousand-franc bank notes. A letter is pinned to one. *My dear Beretzkoy, Please accept these. They are not for Doctor Rudi Zinn, but the poems. Morne.*

I decide I should hide the money. I rewrap it in the old *Pravda* and I push the parcel into a hole in the kitchen wall. The hole has been here in the wall from the day I moved in. I have been planning to plaster it over, but I have not got round to doing so. I push an old cupboard in front of it.

I did not count the money.

I leave the letter with it.

-0-

CHAPTER THIRTY-ONE

Kolya brings me two sealed envelopes from Beretzkoy.

I take the two envelopes into the bedroom, but I ask Kolya not to leave.

"Can you put water on for tea?' I call over my shoulder.

Beretzkoy has numbered the envelopes '1' and '2'.

I open envelope '1'. It contains a two page letter. *Tatyana Nikolayevna Brodovskaya, I will not hold it against you if you ask who this man is who is writing to you. Taking a chance that you have not forgotten me, I will start by saying that I have been rather ill but that I am feeling better. The pain has gone. I must remember to ask the doctor when he comes later in the day what his explanation is for such sudden tranquillity. Whether it is good or bad.*

I will tell you about these past days in case you have been wondering about my condition. I have been sleeping much, always waking up thinking I am at Ob; I want to call out to you but before I can do so I slip back into non-existence. I am in a state of non-existence, a mental vacuum. A hole. A nothingness. There are no dreams in this vacuum, no nightmares. Perhaps this is what the nothingness is which is the nothingness of death. I do not know.

But enough of this now.

I love you. Have I told you this? Recently? Often enough? I miss you. I want to be with you at Ob. Not just for the hours of daylight, but for every moment of darkness too. We may not be able to go away this summer as I know you were planning, but we will do so when my strength returns. It will return. I know. I am already stronger. I think we could go to the mighty Volga. We will rent an izba and we will stay there all winter and I will look after you. My dear little girl, why have we been separated like this?

But I must write now of other things. I want you to continue to live as if I am with you. Don't forget this. If you are asked to make a decision concerning me, then make it. You know I think as you do. Now I must end this letter. I will always love you. I will love you even when the final great nothingness is upon me. Your Beretzkoy.

I open the envelope marked '2'. It holds three sheets of paper. One is a codicil to the testament Beretzkoy left with me. He is giving me, as he said he would, the copyright to *Deaf to Beauty*. The second sheet is a letter to Morne which he asks me to keep until I see Morne again. The third sheet of paper, is a poem.

The trees are whispering
of old men whimpering.
They no longer see in the night,
love's light glistening.
On the ground was snow: blisteringly white.

At the window your face, like the moon in shadow.
But as all old men come to die
so will I,
and then those trees will begin to cry
as our last breath, at last released,
in blissful solitude, I bid you goodbye.

-0-

"You can write to him," says Kolya.

"I will do better," I say.

I ask him not to leave yet. I jump on my bicycle and I cycle to Constitution Street. I will send Beretzkoy a gift. I curse my poverty as I have only one rouble to spend. I buy him a handkerchief.

"Five kopeks," says the flower seller.

"Do you have children?"

"One."

I give the woman my rouble.

"Keep the rest and buy something for your child."

"It's a boy. His name is Boris," she says.

The handkerchief is light blue. Dark blue geese, their wings spread, fly across it.

-0-

I write a letter to send with the gift.

My love, How could you think I have forgotten you? This man who has written to me such beautiful words is everything to me. I love him and I do so with every part of me. I want to see him, oh how I want to see him! I want to hold him. I cannot wait for that moment. Number One Ob is not the same without you. Zernoye Selo is not the same without you and I am not the same without you. Beretzkoy, get better and come back! Please get better. Get better, get better, get better. I beg you. I love you, Beretzkoy. You are my life. Tanya.

I give the handkerchief and the letter to Kolya to give to Beretzkoy.

"You've kept your letter cheerful did you?" he asks, sternly.

Beretzkoy's reply to me is another poem.

Dark is the night, yet we see geese in flight.
Where do they go?
Why can they fly?
Worse, is man's plight
we have no such right.
In the blackness of night

348

that blinds the eye, the day will come,
when we cower and die.

-0-

Morne lets me know excerpts from *Doctor Rudi Zinn* have been published in Italy and Germany. He no longer sends his letters to the *kolkhoz* chairman in Gorky, but in the diplomatic bag to Pierre. An American publisher is interested in American editions of not only the novel but all of Beretzkoy's works. The most exciting, and also the saddest news, is talk abroad of Beretzkoy meriting the Nobel Prize in Literature. Our newspapers do not report this, just as they do not tell their readers *Doctor Rudi Zinn* has been published abroad. Nadezdha Konstantinovna knows. Semyon called her on the telephone and told her. She decides Beretzkoy should not be told of the novel's publication or of the Nobel Prize.

"I'll tell him in a letter," I say to Kolya.

"No, you will not!"

"It will encourage him to fight his illness."

"He is fighting it."

I tell Kolya I will wait a week and if Nadezdha Konstantinovna has not told Beretzkoy about the publication of *Doctor Rudi Zinn* in Paris, or of the Nobel Prize, I will undoubtedly do so.

"Just you try to stop me!"

It is a threat.

-0-

CHAPTER THIRTY-TWO

I am cleaning the *dacha* because I see cobwebs and dust everywhere. I am in the veranda sweeping with a thickly-bristled broom. I look up and here stands Kolya: I did not hear him come. He is ashen and shaking.

"No!" I cry.

He does not have to speak. The look on his face is doing so.

"I'm sorry, Tanya ..."

He smells of onions and herrings and is dressed in an odd assortment of clothes: flowing trousers, an orange high-necked tunic underneath a blue pull-over, galoshes on his feet and a floppy brown hat.

"No!" I cry.

I know what he has come to tell me.

"Yes, Tanya," he says.

"Why are you lying to me?" I shout.

He does not reply.

I hear a cry; almost a scream. I know it has come from me, but it seems distant. I drop the broom. It clatters to the floor. My legs are giving way but Kolya catches me before I fall.

"It was better him going," whispers Kolya.

I grab him by the arm.

"Don't you say that!"

"He started bleeding again."

"I don't care! Never is death better than life!" I shout.

"I did not mean to be ... I meant he went quietly. This was what I meant. His death was quiet."

"Death is not quiet! Don't you tell me death is quiet! Death is never quiet, do you hear me? Death is the end. The end. He said so always. Now there is nothing left of him. Nothing! He said death is a nothingness. Now he is nothing!" I shriek.

Alisa walks in from the garden. She comes to stand beside me. My other neighbours appear in the doorway behind Kolya. Ivan Gromyko is shaking from head to toe and Anna's face is as grey as ash. The Widow Alexandra is crying and the Widow Natalya walks in and immediately out again and goes to sit on the grass patch outside the veranda.

"What happened?" I ask Kolya.

"Not now, Tanya. I will tell you later."

He has started to shake violently and Alisa fetches a glass of water for him and one for me. I pour the water over the desk; I do not know why I do so.

Kolya begins to cry; breathless raucous sobs. No one speaks. Alisa offers him a handkerchief to wipe his face. Deep furrows encircle his wet eyes. He looks old suddenly.

Beretzkoy will never be old. He has been saved this shipwreck which is old age.

The Widow Natalya walks back into the room.

"Life's pointless," she mumbles. "Death makes life entirely pointless. Why do we have to live at all?"

-0-

February 2007 : Moscow (Gerald Lombard/Biographer)

I have returned to Moscow to hear about the poet's death, but I hardly have to ask them to tell me about it, so eager are they to speak of it.

They say they were there at the funeral. They say many had gone to pay their respects, even from as far away as Leningrad. Foreigners too had come. Diplomats, foreign correspondents, writers, poets.

"He was going to be awarded the Nobel Prize in Literature, you know," they say.

-0-

He had a nurse in those final days. Her name was Sonya Konstantinovna Stroganova. She was in her sixties, a woman who never married. She was a good person. Everyone said so. Even Nadezhda Konstantinovna, who was not the gentlest person, said so. And he, the poet, he used to say to Sonya Konstantinovna she would have made a wonderful wife and mother; why had she not taken a husband? *It's good I didn't, Boris Petrovich, because now I've met you,* she replied.

He died on August 28.

The trees had started to lose their leaves. He wanted his bedroom window to be left open. He told them he was keeping an eye on one particular leaf on the old oak tree in his garden. He said that each day the leaf died a little more, and one day he said to Sonya Konstantinova, "I, too, am dying and perhaps I will go first", but she reprimanded him for his pessimism. "Boris Petrovich," she said to him, "such talk will get us nowhere!"

That night he died.

The previous morning when he still had not woken by noon, Sonya Konstantinova told Nadezhda Konstantinovna she was going to wake him. Nadezhda Konstantinova disagreed. "Let him rest," she told the nurse. "It's preferable for the ill not to sleep during the day as it makes their nights easier," Sonya argued with her. Reluctantly, Nadezhda Konstantinovna had agreed. Beretzkoy was glad Sonya had woken him. "I don't have time to waste on sleep," he told her.

It was about half an hour later that he started to complain of heaviness in his chest. He joked about it - "I wonder whose ghost is dancing on my chest?" he said - and when his sons walked into the room, he asked them to find a crossword puzzle for the three of them to do. There was one in a magazine Sonya Konstantinovna was reading. The boys sat down on their father's bed and amid laughter and joking, the three completed the crossword. In the afternoon

353

Beretzkoy had fallen asleep again and unlike the morning, Sonya allowed him to sleep. Night had already started to fall when she woke him and immediately he asked for the window to be opened: he wanted to see the leaf. He looked flushed so she wanted to know from him whether he was in pain again. He admitted only to a little shortness of breath. Nadezdha Konstantinovna decided to send for the doctor. The doctor arrived at eight and told her that her husband's pulse was slow but the night's dose of valerian would correct it. The doctor promised to return early the next morning.

The boys had gone to bed soon after the doctor had been, but first they had gone to bid their father goodnight. They told him they had found another crossword puzzle and he told them not to cheat by looking at it beforehand. They promised him they would not. "I'll keep the two of you to your word, because a promise is a promise," he told them.

At ten that night Nadezdha Konstantinovna walked into the room but by then her husband had fallen asleep. She asked Sonya Konstantinovna whether she thought he looked better than he had in the afternoon and the nurse confirmed he did, but she had all the same decided to stay with him throughout the night. "Good," Nadezdha Konstantinovna told her, "but do try to sleep." Because there was not a second bed in the room, she handed the nurse two blankets in order to sleep on the floor.

At four in the morning Sonya Konstantinovna had been awakened by Beretzkoy's coughing and she saw he had vomited. "I'm so sorry, but there was no time to call you," he apologised. Sonya assured him there was no need for him to apologise. "This is why I am here, Boris Petrovich," she told him. She helped him change into clean pyjamas and she changed the sheets on the bed and when she asked him whether he was feeling better after having vomited, he asked her to repeat her question as he had become a little hard of hearing. "I cannot see you so well either," he told her. "Since when has this been so?" she asked him. "Oh, only since I've woken up," had been his reply. She told him to lie down and close his eyes and to try to sleep. "Your eyes will clear." She pushed him gently back against the pillow. He closed his eyes and when it looked as if he had once again fallen asleep, she had gone to lie on the floor again, but she kept her eyes open and on him. After a few minutes she saw he had opened his eyes. "What is it Boris Petrovich?" she asked from the floor. "It's hot in this room," he replied. "Yes," she agreed, "it is." "Is the window still open?" he asked. "Yes, Boris Petrovich," she told him, "the window is still open. I won't close it without asking you." The window was indeed open and it was cool in the room. His body had then begun to tremble violently.

"Sonya Konstantinovna?" he called out, trying to sit up.

She jumped up from the floor.

"Boris Petrovich, I'm here!"

"I want you to remember about the window."

"Yes, Boris Petrovich, I will remember about the window."

"Tomorrow you must open the window."

"Don't worry about the window. It will be open. I will not close it, Boris Petrovich."

Beretzkoy's face was turned to the nurse who was standing beside his bed, but she knew he was not looking at her, could not see her. His sight had gone.

"The window must be open ... remember ... tomorrow ..."

"It will be, Boris Petrovich."

"Wide open. Remember ... wide open. Light. Through the window. Light. Life."

He sighed, slowly he closed his eyes and the nurse knew he had gone.

-0-

"The nurse stayed with the poet for what was left of the night. In the morning when she heard movement in Nadezdha Konstantinovna's bedroom, she went to tell her that her husband had died. Nadezdha Konstantinova wanted to know when that had happened and when the nurse told her, she said, 'And you did not call me. Did you not find it necessary to call me?' 'It was over quickly. It was very gentle,' the nurse told her. 'Should I be grateful for that?' she asked. 'It is the kind of going we should all hope for,' the nurse replied. 'In that case I will not reprimand you for not having called me,' said Nadezdha Konstantinovna."

This is what they tell me.

They continue:

"The poet's wife - the dead poet's wife, her eyes dry, had then gone to wake the two boys who burst into noisy tears on hearing their father had passed away. Kolya, the artist, helped the nurse dress the dead poet. Kolya quarrelled with Nadezdha Konstantinovna over whether the dead poet should wear a *rybashka*, or a shirt and tie with his dark suit. Kolya, and the nurse agreed with him, that as many would come to pay their respect to the dead poet, he should be dressed in a shirt and tie, but the widow had put a *rybashka* down on the bed. 'He was a poet, yes, but he was a proletarian poet and as such he will be honoured!' she told the two. Kolya and the nurse put rouge on the poet's cheeks, not much, only a dash, and they dabbed tinted powder on his forehead and chin to give his pale skin, colour, and then they laid him on the bed and covered his legs and feet with a green bedspread with gold tassels. But Kolya said, 'Wait!' and from his *izba* he fetched a red paper rose which he had made himself. He wanted to put the rose on the poet's chest, but the nurse pushed it into the poet's folded hands. While Kolya and the nurse were preparing him thus, Nadezdha Konstantinovna sat in the kitchen with Alexandra Alexandrovna telling her of the great love which existed between her and her husband. She spoke in the past tense and later Alexandra Alexandrovna said she wondered whether Nadezdha Konstantinovna's use of the past tense was because her husband had died, or, because her husband had strayed."

"The two boys spent the first day without their father pinning notices of his death to the village's trees," they tell me.

-0-

PART SEVEN

CHAPTER ONE

I am sitting in my back garden because I cannot stand the sight of the things - the furniture, our plates, knives and forks, our bed - in the *dacha*. Kolya arrives. He sits down on a sunny patch of grass. He scratches in the soil between us. He tells me Beretzkoy will be buried in the village cemetery in three days' time. He has been in touch with my parents and with our friends. They will all be coming to the village. He is unable to look me in the eye.

"I would like Yelena to stay with me," I say.

"Your parents will be staying with you, so Yelena will be staying with me in the *izba*," he tells me.

He collects my parents at the railway station in the buggy. They say little. When they do speak it is to ask me how I am. I shrug. They do not speak of Beretzkoy's death. They do not speak of Beretzkoy.

Our friends arrive. Yelena drove down to the village with Galina and Misha, and Semyon and Malyutka brought Zinaida with them. Zinaida does not stop speaking of heaven and hell; death not being the end but a beginning. Yelena shouts at her to shut up.

Finally, my father mentions Beretzkoy.

"Tanoshka, what will you do now Beretzkoy is not here?" he asks.

"He is still here," I reply.

I mean Beretzkoy is still in my heart and in my head.

My mother joins us.

"You have to decide what you are going to do. Can we talk about it?" she asks, gently.

"There is another little thing, Tanoshka?" says my father. "Will you be going to … you know … the funeral?"

I tell my parents I do not know. And the sad thing is: I really do not know.

-0-

CHAPTER TWO

My friends tell me what is happening at Number Fourteen Lena Street.

The villagers have started to pay their respects to Beretzkoy.

Nadezdha Konstantinovna stands in the lobby and hugs each villager and receives the offered condolences with a smile. She says she is not sad because poets never die. The boys - Paul Borisovich is sixteen and Grigory Borisovich is fifteen - stand beside their mother, clumsily shaking hands with those their mother has just hugged. Dushenka Koba, who is helping Nadezdha Konstantinovna with the funeral arrangements, stands with her. He is the one who takes the villagers up the stairs to Beretzkoy's bedroom. He does not enter the room but stands in the doorway.

"You go right in. I'll follow," he says.

He does not follow.

Beretzkoy's bedroom is small and impersonal, my friends tell me.

"It is as if no one has ever slept there in that bedroom, that it has been used only to die in. And it is so cold in there because the window is wide open," says Malyutka.

The full-length wardrobe mirror is hidden under a sheet. On one side of the wardrobe stands a chair of faded red upholstery. A man's dressing gown hangs over the chair. A small console table stands on the other side of the wardrobe. On the table lie the usual paraphernalia of a sickroom: a pot of salve; a half-empty bottle of pills; a water jug, empty; a glass, dry but water-stained; a brush and a comb, strands of grey hair entwined between the bristles; a small wooden spatula, the kind doctors use for pressing down the tongue of a patient to look into the throat; a kidney-shaped metal bowl for vomiting; a thick rubber band for tying a tourniquet. The bed faces the wardrobe, the window at its foot end. It is a single bed, the kind the French call a *lit de bateau*, the bed of a ship. It is the bed of a man who sleeps alone. Between the bed and the wall stands a bedside table. On the table stand two items: a candle in a saucer and a thin cloth-edition of Beretzkoy's poems. The book's pages flutter in the breeze which drifts through the open window.

Dushenka Koba does not allow anyone longer than five minutes in the room then he calls them out with a gentle cough. He stands aside until all have left the room and he follows them down the stairs.

When they reach the front door, he reminds them that on the day of the funeral the procession of coffin and mourners will leave the *dacha* at noon.

"We'll be walking to the cemetery," he says.

-0-

"Tanya, will you be walking with us?" asks Kolya.

"I do not know."

"Do you want to go to Lena Street before the funeral to … you know …?"

"I do not know."

"You have only one more day."

The two of us are on the veranda. Semyon joins us.

"I wanted to ask," says Semyon, "whether you have made a decision about going to the funeral?"

"We're talking about it right now," Kolya tells him.

"So, I've come at the right moment."

"Tanya has not yet made up her mind," says Kolya.

They are speaking as if I am not on the veranda with them.

"I told her I would arrange it with … his wife," says Semyon.

"I will not go into that *dacha!*" I shout, interrupting them.

They swing round and stare at me.

"You won't?" says Kolya, calmly.

"I won't … I can't … "

I decide I do not want to see Beretzkoy in his nothingness: cold and still. I will remember him as a living human being. I will remember him full of life. I will remember him as he was the last time I saw him, when I walked with him across the wasteland, when he turned and waved. I will remember him as he was when I first saw him that day at *Pravda*. I will remember him the way he was when he made love to me.

But I *will* accompany him on his final journey.

-0-

My mother and I will wear black. All I have in black is a skirt and a sweater, but it will have to do. My mother has brought a black dress with her. My father puts on a dark suit and a grey *rybashka*.

We walk to Lena Street. We traverse the wasteland, this wasteland which I was told was haunted, but which still has to show me its ghosts. Nearing Lena Street we hear a gentle murmur like water running over pebbles. My father says it is voices we hear. It is. It is the sound of very many voices: a small crowd has gathered all along the street. We make our way through the people to the other end, passing Number Fourteen, but not looking at it. It is half an hour after eleven. The pale sun is in the middle of the sky. It is the first day of September. Soon the fountain on Marx Square will freeze.

At ten minutes to noon the front door of Number Fourteen opens. Dushenka Koba, in a black suit, appears on the street. He cups his hands around his mouth and calls out the procession is about to leave. He asks the people to stand aside so the hearse can pass. The hearse turns into Lena Street from behind us. It is a flat-topped horse-drawn cart. It is covered in shiny black cloth and black cloths have been thrown over the backs of the four brown mares that pull it. The driver tips his top hat to me. He knows me and I know him. He is the driver of the buggy which runs from and to the railway station.

At noon sharp the hearse halts in front of the Beretzkoy *dacha* and the house's front door swings open. Six men in black appear. The coffin rests on their shoulders. I do not know any of them. The coffin is of dark wood and the wood catches the sun. The six grip the handles of the coffin so firmly their knuckles are turning white. Bloodless. Nadezdha Konstantinovna is respecting the old Russian tradition: one end, the head end, of the coffin is open. From where my parents and I are standing I can see the white silk lining of the coffin which is dazzling to the eye. I am too far away to be able to see Beretzkoy's face. Suddenly, I feel like laughing. The aperture in the coffin's lid reminds me of a *fortochka* and I tell myself this is just a play being performed here on Lena Street and any minute now Beretzkoy will sit up and step through the *fortochka*. He will give a little bow while awaiting our applause.

A woman walks immediately behind the coffin.

"His wife," my mother whispers to me.

For six years I have lived in Zernoye Selo and I see her for the first time.

I cannot see her face clearly, but I can see her hair is grey and she has a matronly figure. Beretzkoy, when he spoke of her on that night he came to Vasily's room for the first time, spoke of a tall, slim, elegant woman and that was how I pictured her. I could have asked our friends, especially Kolya, to describe her to me, but I never did. I never wanted to know. She is all in black. A black dress reaches to her ankles and she is wearing flat-heeled black shoes and black gloves. Behind her walk two young men. They must be the sons she brought into the world for Beretzkoy. They, too, are not as I imagined them. I always pictured them in my mind's eye as two small boys in shorts and embroidered *rybashkas*. Here now I see two adult men in dark trousers and plain white *rybashkas*. One carries a large black and white framed portrait of Beretzkoy, the other a green felt bag, the kind which holds a musical instrument. Nadezdha Konstantinovna is carrying a small bouquet of white flowers. Behind the boys follow Dushenka Koba, Alexandra Alexandrovna and their seven children, and behind them, our friends. Kolya is dressed in white as he was on the day he came to introduce himself; Yelena in black; Zinaida and Malyutka in black; Semyon in a grey suit, white shirt and black tie, and Galina and Misha are also in black. Misha, like Semyon, wears a black tie.

The coffin is lowered onto the hearse. I know the route the procession will take. It will traverse the wasteland, go up Ob Street, through the south-western triangle of the village, next, through the centre of the village past Marx Square and Lenin's statue, into and through the north-eastern triangle, past the railway station. The cemetery lies on a hill east of the station, the villagers' last abodes marked with flat white slabs of stone.

The procession sets off.

My parents and I walk right at the back, my neighbours just ahead of us. We turn into Ob Street. I lower my eyes but I count my steps to know when we are passing Number One. My mother feels for my hand. She presses it.

We walk for at least an hour before we reach the cemetery.

Beretzkoy's grave, I have been told, is halfway up a small hill. My parents and I have decided we will not go up the hill. We will stay at the bottom. While the six men in black lift the coffin from the hearse, I drop my eyes yet again. I keep them down.

"Child, open your eyes please," says my father. "You may later regret you closed them."

Not Tanoshka, but child.

White-painted stones mark Beretzkoy's grave. The stones, looking at them from where we stand, form an imperfect circle around the hole which has been dug almost on the highest peak of the low rolling hill. The coffin, still open, rests on braided rope. Nadezdha Konstantinovna's bouquet of white flowers lies on the coffin, the black and white portrait of Beretzkoy leans against the foot of it. One of the pallbearers steps forward.

No one should be untouched by the death of a poet!

His voice echoes around us.

"I know our dear Comrade Stalin is with us today. I know our dear Comrade Stalin weeps with this widow and these two orphans!"

He takes a piece of paper from the breast pocket of his jacket. He waves it in the air.

"My name is Valentin Sergeyevich and I am here to represent our dear Comrade Stalin. This here, this piece of paper, is a letter. I will not read it to you as it is a special letter which I have been asked to hand to the widow of Boris Petrovich Beretzkoy, the mother of Paul Borisovich and Grigory Borisovich and, this I do now. This is a special letter; it comes from a special person - our beloved leader Iosef Vasiryonovich Stalin - and it carries a message. I will hand it to Nadezdha Konstantinovna."

Nadezdha Konstantinovna theatrically takes the letter he offers her. She kisses it.

The mourners start to clap.

Dushenka Koba steps forward.

"We shall weep!" he calls out. "We shall weep with our dear Comrade Stalin!"

Nadezdha Konstantinovna and the boys step forward. After a brief discussion between them and Dushenka Koba, the three walk to the coffin, the boys bend over and kiss their father's face. Nadezdha Konstantinovna brushes a finger over the coffin.

The boys wipe their eyes.

The pallbearers and the driver of the hearse walk to the grave and begin to close the coffin. They struggle to fit its final panel. Dushenka Koba and Kolya step forward and with some pushing and pulling, the panel slips into place. The pallbearers pull on the rope and the coffin starts to slide into the hole in the ground. Not gently, but jerkily. Several times the pallbearers grab it in order to steady it.

One of Beretzkoy's sons, the one who was carrying the green felt bag, and who is still holding it, steps forward. He takes a flute from the bag. He lifts it to his lips simultaneously filling his lungs with air. He stands with his knees bent slightly. Notes high and low begin to fill the air and sweep over the hill, down to the village. I recognise the gentle pastoral melody of *Dance of the Blessed Spirits* of Gluck's *Orfeo ed Euridice*.

-0-

The mourners start walking down the hillside.

My father turns to me.

"They will be passing us, Tanoshka."

I know he is speaking of Nadezdha Konstantinovna and the boys.

"Shall we go?" asks my mother, hastily.

"We'll stay," I say.

Nadezdha Konstantinovna, her sons on each side of her, does not look at me. She looks straight ahead of her. The boys look at me. One does so for just a moment. His eyes are blue and icy like a frozen winter Siberian sky. The other, the musician, keeps his eyes on me for quite a while. His eyes too are blue, but they are the blue of the sky over a field of ripe corn. I see compassion in them; interest. The two are fair-haired, fair of skin as their mother was in her youth. I look at her. I see a woman who looks as if she has not had a single moment of happiness in her life. Her shoulders are stooped, her walk is that of an invalid and her mouth is drawn into a scowl. But strangely there is still beauty in her. Her skin is alabaster pale and her hair falls gently to her shoulders. I can see why Beretzkoy once loved her dearly.

-0-

My parents will stay with me for one more day but as soon as we get back to Ob Street our friends come to say goodbye.

"Dear Tanya, you will be alright, won't you?" asks Zinaida.

"Absolutely."

"I'll always be there for you."

"I know."

She tells me she needs to withdraw from the world once more and she has already made plans to return to a monastery near Alma-Ata, but she will return to Moscow in the spring.

"Not an asylum," she says and unsuccessfully tries to smile.

"Let me know when you are back in Moscow," I tell her.

"Come to Moscow then," she says.

"I'll see," I tell her.

"Why do you not come up to Moscow now? With your parents tomorrow?" Yelena wants to know.

"I can't decide right now."

"You can come and stay with me because now we are … well you know …"

"Both grieving?" I finish her sentence.

"He was a good man," says the heavily pregnant Malyutka.

"When is your baby due?" I ask her.

"In a month. Perhaps sooner. One can never tell."

"We plan to have one a year," Semyon tells me.

"Children are life," says Zinaida. "Through them, we continue to live."

They all scramble into the two cars parked outside and today, for whatever reason, no one waves goodbye.

-0-

My parents and I return to the kitchen. They try to persuade me to do as Yelena suggested: return to Moscow with them. I tell them that right now I want to stay where I am.

"Are you able to do so?" asks my father.

"What do you mean?"

"You are no longer working for …"

"Beretzkoy. For Beretzkoy. You can mention his name you know!" I snap.

"It is always best to be decisive," says my mother.

"I will wait until the Chekists get to me. With Beretzkoy gone, they are sure to do so," I tell them.

"And what will you do then?" asks my mother.

"Who knows? Whatever *they* decide, I suppose."

"Have you not yet learnt provocation does not pay?" asks my father.

-0-

My parents go to bed. I go and sit on the veranda. My head is spinning from the wine I drank with supper. I drank too much of it. Beretzkoy had still bought the wine from Maksim. It seems a lifetime ago.

Maksim.

I wonder where he is. Did he make it to America? Is he happy there in the land where no one is ever unhappy as he assured me?

I wonder whether Morne did not hear of Beretzkoy's death because there has not been a word from him since he sent Beretzkoy the francs. Surely he must know Beretzkoy has died. The foreign correspondents who attended the funeral must have reported his death.

A smoker stands on Beretzkoy's desk. It throws a slim beam of light across the veranda. The light penetrates the veranda's glass panels. Sekret lies in the front garden in the beam of light, sleeping. I wonder if he knows he will never see his master again? What will happen to the cat should I return to live in Moscow? Will he take to life in Moscow?

Will I take to life in Moscow?

-0-

The time comes for my parents to leave. Kolya comes along in the buggy to take them to the railway station.

"I will come down to help you move out," my mother tells me.

I tell her I am going nowhere.

"If you say so," she replies.

-0-

Dushenka Koba walks in. I no longer lock the gate or the front door and he has walked straight in.

"I won't stay long," he says, coolly, looking me up and down.

"I have time."

"Sadly, I cannot say the same."

"What brings you here?"

I offer him a seat. He looks around the room and chooses the sofa.

"You were lucky to have ended up here," he says.

He has come to tell me I am to collect together everything in the *dacha* which belongs to Beretzkoy.

"His wife and sons want his possessions to be returned. I can give you a day to do so. I will come over with my car to pick up the items. If you need cartons, say so, and I will bring them over later today."

"I don't need cartons."

"If you decide you do."

Cartons are hard to come by.

"I didn't know you were in marketeering," I say, sarcastically.

"That's your line, I believe," he snaps.

"I won't need cartons because I do not plan to part with anything. Everything in this *dacha* belongs to me," I tell him.

"I thought you were going to say this, yet, I hoped - foolishly as I now realise - you would be decent and not cause problems to Beretzkoy's grieving widow and their sons," he says, sounding angry.

"There is only one thing here which does not belong to me. It is the *dacha* itself," I tell him.

"That is not *my* department, but I have no doubt someone will be on to you about the *dacha* before long." He rounds on me with a look of steel in his eyes. "You have no right to keep his work. I'm thinking of papers. His writings."

"He always took everything to Lena Street."

"He was working on a play."

"I know nothing about a play."

"He mentioned a play to me."

"Not to me."

"Look for it. It must be here somewhere. I will be back."

He does not say when and I do not walk with him to the gate.

-0-

Strangers - foreigners - come to the *dacha* and pull sealed envelopes from their pockets. They tell me the contents will be mine if I would be so kind as to tell them about Beretzkoy.

"Have you ever heard of the Nobel Prize?" asks one.

The man's sing-song accent tells me he is English.

I tell him, incredible as it may appear, I have heard of the Nobel Prize.

"He would have been nominated," says the man. "He was a great poet and unlike here in the Soviet Union, in England we appreciate great poetry."

"Some here do too."

Someone else comes to the *dacha*. A young man: Russian. He stands in the doorway and nervously moves his weight from foot to foot.

"I'm from Profpro."

I tell him to come in. It is raining and his clothes stick to his body.

"Have you come to kick me out?"

"To evaluate the property."

His shoes are muddy. He takes them off and leaves them in the doorway.

"Evaluating the property is kicking me out," I say.

Sekret lies on the sofa and jumps up, running from the room and out into the front garden.

The young man sits down.

"I'm really not here to kick you out. I am here only to evaluate the property. We want to know how big the family can be who will move in here."

"I live here. I am a member of Profpro and I am therefore entitled to union accommodation," I say.

"That is not my department. I only evaluate."

A flash of lightning and a loud clap of thunder send Sekret running back into the living room. He is soaking wet.

"Where do we start to evaluate?" I ask the young man.

We walk through the *dacha* and he is taking notes. At the front door, he puts his muddy shoes back on.

"I apologise for the inconvenience I have caused. I am so sorry, but I have to do what I am told."

"Don't we all."

"I liked Boris Petrovich's poetry," he says.

"So did I," I say. "I still do."

He laughs.

"Of course," he says, "Poets never die."

The lightning and thunder have chased the rain away so I walk with the young man to the gate.

"Have you read his novel, the one everyone is talking about?" he asks.

"Not just once," I say. "Many times. I typed it too. Many times."

"I thought it was just a ruse that you typed for him."

"No," I say, "it was not a ruse. I typed for him."

"I would like to read the novel."

"You shouldn't. Read it I mean. It is an illegal act."

"Sometimes I do what I should not do."

I fetch him a copy of the manuscript.

"Now, I am the one, who is doing something I shouldn't," I say.

He takes the manuscript and jams it into his briefcase.

"You are kind. I'm sorry I trampled all over your place."

"Profpro's place," I correct him.

"I will see what I can do so you have time to find another place."

I thank him.

"The union is normally accommodating," he says.

I laugh hollowly.

"I used to be with *Pravda* and when I was dismissed, I was told they would be accommodating."

He laughs as well.

"And were they?"

"In their way, yes. In any case, it didn't matter, my dismissal, as I had Beretzkoy."

He says he understands what I mean and I need not fear I will find myself out on the street. He also will not let the manuscript fall into the wrong hands.

I receive a letter of eviction in the post. I have a fortnight to move out.

-0-

I telephone my parents from the post office and they say I can of course move back in with them.

"I will get used to the cat," says my mother.

"He's a good cat."

"We will adapt," says my father.

"Yes, we will get used to having a cat about the place," adds my mother.

-0-

CHAPTER THREE

I walk through the *dacha* in tears trying to decide what I will take with me. I will not be able to take the furniture. I am going to tell Kolya to take what he wants and to give away or sell what are left. I will take the gifts I have received these years in Zernoye Selo: the alabaster bowl; the Afghan carpet which once covered the floor of Stalin's Kremlin office; the Italian table, which belonged to Beretzkoy's mother, and the icon with the golden-haired weeping Christ. The books will go with me to Moscow. Hitler's Fan will stay. Kolya wants it and he will take it down once I have left. The kitchen things and the linen I am taking; my mother will be able to use it.

I do not know what to do with the money Morne sent to Beretzkoy. I do not want it.

My neighbours and Kolya bring me cartons, old bags and suitcases. I fill them fast. Having accepted the fact I have to leave, I want to get the leaving over with.

-0-

It is my last night at Ob Street. There is knock on the front door.

"Tanya!"

I recognise the voice.

I am sitting behind Beretzkoy's desk on the veranda; not even a pencil lies here now. I do not get up.

"Tanya!"

Morne appears in the doorway.

"He has died," I say.

"I know, Tanya, I know. I had to come."

"He's been buried," I say, the words drying out in my mouth.

"Your Embassy in Paris refused to grant me a visa."

A French government minister threatened the Kremlin with the cancellation of a contract if they did not give him a visa.

"It took time, but now I am here."

He walks to the desk, bends over and kisses me on the forehead.

"I'm leaving, Morne."

"I can see," he says. "You've been packing."

Boxes, cartons and suitcases are piled high in the living room.

"I leave tomorrow."

"I wanted to be here for … well, since I heard Beretzkoy has fallen ill, I've wanted to come."

"You are here now," I say.

I look down at my hands.

"I would have wanted to see him again."

Morne has aged. His hair has turned grey and deep lines circle his eyes and lips.

I suppose, I, too, am no longer the young girl I used to be when he first saw me.

I am probably just a shadow of that girl now.

-0-

Morne tells me thousands of copies of *Doctor Rudi Zinn* have been sold in France and the novel will soon be published in Berlin, Rome, London and New York. The poetry volume too is selling well.

"I have to talk to you about something," I tell him.

I get up and walk around the desk.

"Come."

I take Morne to the kitchen. I see he is looking around and I know that, the household things having been removed, the kitchen has become soulless.

"I still have this," I say.

I walk to the cupboard which hides the hole in the wall. I push it out of the way. I take the *Pravda*-wrapped parcel from the hole. I put it on the table.

"The money?" he asks.

"There was no time to give it to Beretzkoy. I was not even able to tell him about it."

"It's yours now."

"I do not want it. I do not even know how much you sent."

"It's yours," he repeats.

"It isn't mine, Morne!"

He tells me to wait a moment. He walks from the kitchen. On his return he hands me another *Pravda*-wrapped parcel.

"These should go with those."

He rips open the parcel. It contains more bank notes. What seems like hundreds of them.

"I really do not want the money!" I cry out.

He begins to protest but I will not hear of it.

"If you leave it here, I will burn it!" I tell him.

"For God's sake, Tanya, it is money, a lot of money! Did you and Beretzkoy never discuss the financial aspect of publication in the West? Do you not have testaments here in the Soviet Union? Did he not write a testament in which he named his heirs?"

"We do not do things like that here in the Soviet Union."

He wants to know whether I am sure Beretzkoy did not leave a testament with me and I convince him he did not.

"But I know what you can do with the money. Take it to her. Take it to his wife. She may need it. The boys, certainly, will," I tell him.

He shakes his head.

"It is yours, Tanya."

"No, it is *their* money. Not mine."

Reluctantly, Morne sets off for Lena Street.

One of Beretzkoy's sons opens the front door.

"My mother is lying down. My father's not here. My father's dead," says the boy.

Morne tells him it is important he should speak to his mother. The boy goes to wake Nadezdha Konstantinovna and returns to the living room with her. She is in her nightgown; her hair is flattened on one side of her head from lying down. Morne explains who he is.

"I've never heard of you," replies Nadezdha Konstantinova, icily.

Quickly, Morne tells her Beretzkoy earned royalties from the Paris publication of his novel and the volume of poetry.

"I know nothing of the last and I want to know nothing of the first," she replies.

He takes the two *Pravda*-wrapped parcels from his briefcase and puts them down on the floor in front of Beretzkoy's widow's feet.

"I've brought you the royalties."

She picks up one of the parcels, opens it, and, seeing the money, she inhales deeply, but says not a word.

Beretzkoy's son steps forward to see what has silenced his mother. He sees the money. He inhales deeply, but he also does not utter a word.

"No one has to know about the money," says Morne, breaking the silence.

"Is there any document I would have to sign?" asks Nadezdha Konstaninovna.

"There is no document to sign."

"My sons are going to study medicine. They will need the money."

"You must be proud of them."

"I am and so was their father. He loved them more than anything else on earth."

Morne tells Nadezdha Konstantinovna he knows Beretzkoy loved his sons. He also tells her there will be more money later; he will discreetly get it to her somehow.

"Thank you. It will go towards our sons' education," she says.

I do not tell Morne of the testament which Beretzkoy left with me. Neither do I give him the letter Beretzkoy had written him.

-0-

My neighbours come to say goodbye. They say I was a good neighbour and they hope the next tenant will be as quiet as I have been. Alisa fears the next tenant may not put up with Nilats's barking. Igor and Anna Gromyko fear the next tenant may not like them playing their gramophone. The Widow Alexandra fears the next tenant may commit suicide as the poet at Number Four had done; it had been such a mess. The Chekists questioned them all as if they had murdered him. The Widow Natalya fears the next tenant will be a Chekist.

I already no longer exist as far as they are concerned.

-0-

Morne is to spend the night at Alisa's *dacha*. He says he knows I want to be on my own this final night at Number One Ob Street.

It is not my wish to be alone this night. I want Beretzkoy to be here with me.

-0-

CHAPTER FOUR

A truck comes to take me back to Moscow. I demand of myself that I will not cry. I stay behind the driver and his mate as they walk from the *dacha* to the truck and back to the *dacha*, carrying out my belongings and demolishing the life I have shared here with Beretzkoy. Kolya and Morne stand beside the truck, talking. I think they can face neither me nor the fast-emptying rooms of the *dacha*. All the same, I am grateful they are with me. Morne will come to Moscow with me. We will have to sit in the back of the truck. Sekret too will be in the back with us.

The moment comes to leave.

"Shall we be off then?" asks the driver's mate, a man with a ruddy complexion and bulging muscles.

"Give me a moment, please."

The driver, overweight and out of breath, is already sitting behind the wheel.

I walk through the *dacha* one final time.

My footsteps are as noisy as a tap dancer's footfalls on the bare floorboards. I welcome the noise. I do not step onto the veranda, but I stand at the door. The desk, robbed of the pencils, the books, the dictionaries and the sheets of paper filled with Beretzkoy's small neat writing looks huge and out of place because the veranda has once again become a veranda.

I sit down on the rickety bed in the bedroom. My throat begins to contract and, unable to breathe, I jump up and I walk from the room. I do not look back.

In the kitchen, I stand in the doorway. I have pushed the cupboard back over the hole in the wall. I wonder what the next tenant will hide there.

In the living room I switch on Hitler's Fan and I stand underneath it. The whir of its turning blades seems louder than in the past.

I close my eyes against the blast of air.

I hear the music of a gramophone playing somewhere in my head.

I do not close the front door behind me.

-0-

Kolya kisses me on the forehead. He is holding Sekret and pushes him into my arms.

"Moscow is no place for a cat," he says.

"Sekret has no choice."

"Tanya, it was wonderful having you here. How will I endure this village now without you?"

375

"Kolya, it was wonderful being here, and ... you will survive."

His eyes fill with tears. Quickly, I get into the truck. The driver starts up the engine with a stuttering roar.

Morne bids Kolya goodbye.

"We may never see each other again so I will say now it was an honour knowing you," says Morne.

"Oh, we will meet again."

There is no conviction in Kolya's voice; tears stream over his face.

"Kolya!" I shout over the engine's din. "You must come up to Moscow. Stay with Yelena."

He nods.

"Let me hear from you often, Tanya."

"Of course, Kolya, of course."

The driver's mate steps forward and closes the truck's back door and Morne, Sekret and I are locked in.

"Yes," I say to myself, "let's go."

-0-

Morne and I sit on tip-up seats. The only light in the back of the truck comes from a small window near the ceiling. Morne holds Sekret tightly as he is squirming. The window is too high for us to be able to see through it, so I follow our progress through the village by keeping track of the turns the truck makes just the way I did the day the Chekists had come for me.

When there are no further left or right turns, I know we are on the highway.

"I thought I'd be there forever," I tell Morne.

He presses my hand.

"I know."

"I would have liked to have remained here in the village."

"I know."

"I really thought I, no, that we - Beretzkoy and I - will stay here forever."

"I know."

I tell Morne of the young man from Profpro who came to evaluate the *dacha*. I also tell him how Dushenka Koba came to collect Beretzkoy's papers. My throat contracts for the second time in two days and this time, as I heave in a life-giving breath, I cannot stop the tears from flowing.

"Tanya, time will dull the pain," says Morne.

He looks at me, but he does not touch me.

"No," I say, "nothing will dull the pain. The pain will always be with me. It will be my companion."

"Don't say that. You are starting off on a new phase of your life. A new life."

I shake my head.

"Tolstoy wrote," I say, "that to think you can change your life by changing its outward conditions is like thinking that by sitting on a stick and taking hold of it at both ends you will lift yourself up."

I am only changing the outward conditions of my life.

I will always be Tanya, the girl who is in love with a poet.

THE END

ALSO BY MARILYN Z. TOMLINS

BELLA ... A FRENCH LIFE

"AN EVOCATIVE FRENCH LOVE STORY"

Men leave, says Bella.

There is Jean-Louis - French, a successful Paris lawyer and wealthy, elegant and a good-looker, but arrogant, selfish and scornful of 'losers'. And he is married and the father of two daughters.
Colin - English, a writer, cultured, kind and protective - steps into Bella's life, but in his own words, "I always run. I always have to be elsewhere, in some other place."

Will Jean-Louis leave his wife? Will Colin stop running? Bella, alone this winter at her guest house on the beautiful Normandy coast of France, recalls words once said - pray that your loneliness will spur you into finding something to live for, something great enough to die for - and she hopes that this 'something' will be either Jean-Louis or Colin.

Romantic, intelligent and truly evocative of the sights, sounds and tastes of rural Normandy; Bella…A French Life will stay with you long after you have finished reading it.

If you have a smartphone, you can scan the barcode below to buy *Bella … A French Life*

Bella

... A FRENCH LIFE

THE COOKBOOK

MARILYN Z. TOMLINS

Photograph by Paula Rae Gibson

"YOU ASKED FOR IT…SO HERE IT IS"

Since the launch of Bella…A French Life in 2013, reviewers have loved the novel for the way it immerses the reader into rural France; helped in no small way by the descriptions of French cooking that Bella creates for the men in her life or while dining in restaurants.
The cooking is seamlessly woven into the text such that while evoking the sights, smells and tastes of Normandy, it isn't easy for the reader to replicate these themselves.

So by popular demand, here is Bella... A French Life - The Cookbook.
It details the recipes from the novel with complete ingredients lists, methods, how to serve and what wine to drink with. All this set against a narrative of events in the novel that inspired them.

The author hopes that you enjoy creating these as much as you enjoyed the novel. Bring the smells and tastes of rural France into your kitchen.

If you have a smartphone, you can scan the barcode below to buy *Bella … A French Life – The Cookbook* on Amazon Kindle

A spring night in Paris. The most beautiful city in the world is dark and silent. Uncertainty devils the air. As does normality: war time normality. The Nazis' Swastika flutters from the Eiffel Tower. The Parisians are huddled indoors.

Suddenly the night's stillness is shattered by sirens and excited voices.

For days foul smoke has been pouring from the chimney of an uninhabited house close to the Avenue des Champs-Elysées. Police and firefighters are racing to the house to break down the bolted door. They make a spine-chilling discovery. The remains of countless human beings are being incinerated in a furnace in the basement. In a pit in an outhouse quicklime consumes still more bodies.

Neighbours say they hear banging, pleading, sobbing and cries for help come from inside the house deep at night. They say a shabbily-dressed man on a green bicycle pulling a cart behind him comes to the house, always at dawn, or dusk.

The house belongs to Dr Marcel Petiot – a good-looking, charming, caring, family physician who lives elsewhere in the city with his wife and teenage son.

Is he the shabbily-dressed man on the green bicycle?

If so, what has he to say about the bodies?

Marilyn Z. Tomlins has crafted an enthralling and suspenseful page-turner about one of history's most fascinating and notorious serial killers. This grisly World War Two era thriller will have you teetering on a slippery edge from beginning to end.

Don Fulsom, veteran UPI and VOA White House correspondent, Washington, D.C. reporter, author of the bestseller Nixon's Darkest Secrets: The Inside Story of America's Most Troubled President, and a professor of government at American University in Washington.

With style, Marilyn Z. Tomlins' Die in Paris, tells the incredible story of France's most prolific murderer. Readers will discover a truly psychotic serial killer.

J. Patrick O'Connor, author of the bestsellers The Framing of Mumia Abu-Jamal and of Scapegoat: The Chino Hills Murder and the Framing of Kevin Cooper, and the creator and editor of www.crimemagazine.com

"Die in Paris" will give you new insights into the horrors of Occupied France.

If you have a smartphone, you can scan the barcode below to buy *Die in Paris:*

ABOUT THE AUTHOR

Marilyn lives and writes in Paris. She writes whatever takes her fancy: spoof news, book reviews, posts for her website, gossip about showbiz stars and royalty, short stories, poetry – and books. She also reports crime.

She was born in British Colonial Africa and is a British national. Eight years ago she became interested in the Second World War French serial killer, Dr Marcel Petiot, and she researched him for two years and then over the next two years she wrote her true-crime book DIE IN PARIS. Next, setting murder aside, she wrote the novel BELLA … A FRENCH LIFE, an emotive love story set in Paris and the beautiful Normandy coastal region of France.

Russia, a passion of hers, she has planned For the *Love of a Poet* for at least ten years.

CONTACT DETAILS

Visit Marilyn's website:
www.marilynztomlins.com

Follow Marilyn on Twitter:
www.twitter.com/MarilynZTomlins

Like or join Marilyn on Facebook: **www.facebook.com/marilyn.tomlins**

Cover designed by: Raven Crest Books

Published by: Raven Crest Books
www.ravencrestbooks.com

Follow us on Twitter:
www.twitter.com/lyons_dave

Like us on Facebook:
www.facebook.com/RavenCrestBooksClub